Sarah'

By Rhc

MW00768307

Author of *Elizabeth's Journey*

"The heart of a man plans his ways, but the Lord directs his steps."
Proverbs 16:9 (ESV)

"And we know that God causes all things to work together for good to those who love God, to those who are called according to His purpose."
Romans 8:28 (Ryrie NAS)

"He has made everything beautiful in its time. Also, he has put eternity into man's heart, yet so that he cannot find out what God has done from the beginning to the end."
Ecclesiastes 3:11 (ESV)

We were made in God's image for perfect harmony with Him and our hearts yearn for this because of our eternal nature.

ISBN 978-0-9988045-4-5

Dedication

With eternity set in our hearts by God our creator, we are creatures who struggle against death and the concept that this life is all we have, then nothing. We were not created for a lifetime but for eternity, and to believe anything less, is to believe a lie.

Our mortal flesh will age, grow ill, and perish, but it is only our temporal body, a tent to house us while we sojourn on earth. We beloved are more than our bodies. We are soul and spirit which is eternal. We beloved will either

—live eternally in a glorified body with God in heaven,

—or live eternally separated from God in hell.

This book is dedicated to those living in mortal bodies indwelled by the Holy Spirit, and all those who will come to know the saving power of Jesus Christ.

Chapter 1

Sarah was intently studying the painting, El Alba Rosa, unaware that she was being intently studied. Fillip saw her with the eye and the heart of an artist and the instincts of a man of romance. Her wedding finger had a small friendship ring on it, but nothing more, and she was clearly alone. She was not a classical beauty, but her bone structure was fine and delicate and her bearing elegant yet simple. Her honey-brown layered hair stirred about her shoulders as she tilted her head, and the light above the painting accented natural highlights. Fillip estimated she was five-foot-six, and guessed that, if he could see her eyes, he would be wading in pools of deep amber.

He moved closer toward her hoping to see if he could awaken her awareness of him without startling her. From his new vantage point, he could more clearly see hints of makeup which defined and accented her quiet beauty. Fillip also became aware of an aura that emanated directly from her. He was just trying to persuade himself that the aura was the reflection of the light from above the painting when she turned and look directly at him.

As their eyes met, he found that her eyes were pools of deep blue and he felt as if he was drowning in them. He smiled, as was his habit with women who interested him. Her face lit up as she returned his smile. The smile all too soon faded as the color in her cheeks rose into a blush, and she apologized, and turned to move away. "I'm sorry. I didn't mean to keep the painting to myself."

Fillip Castañola was an important businessman who was used to controlling his staff, his employees, and his women. He reached out a hand and gently stopped Sarah. Her dress, a simple jade green polyester, was common for a tourist coming to Toledo, Spain. The dress accentuated the curves of her petite but very womanly figure. "Please don't leave on my account. We can share it. Sí?" He responded in perfect English, but his Spanish accent and warm mellow masculine voice tantalized Sarah's ears. She turned and looked at him while he continued. "Tell me what you find so interesting in such a simple painting."

She turned her head away and sighed. "I don't think I can." Then in a half-whisper she added. "It's would be silly to tell you that it beckons to something deep inside of me."

Fillip didn't want to let her go so he drew her back to himself. "It's just a painting of a beautiful house yet you studied it for a long time." He moved closer to her and leaned down to whisper into her ear. "Tell me what you like about the painting and I will understand."

Sarah's senses were now sending alarm messages to her brain because of his gentle touch, his nearness, and his breath on her ear. He was a stranger, a man whose name she didn't even know, and he was causing feelings she had never felt. Fillip took in her perfume as Sarah took a step away from him.

"It isn't just a beautiful house, but a mansion, really. It is more house than I've ever known, yet, it makes me want to live there. I want to plant flowerbeds to naturalize the naked grounds. And, I want to see children and a dog romping on the pristine lawn without a care. The house beckons to me to come embrace it and grow old there cradled in its warmth. It's like seeing a house with a "For Sale" sign on its lawn and knowing you've found your forever home."

Sarah turned back to Fillip and smiled. "See how silly it sounds." She glanced down to the floor in embarrassment and turned back to the painting. His silenced forced her to say more to cover her awkwardness.

"This house is here in Spain, thousands of miles from my home, and yet it calls to something inside of me." She could feel his dark blue eyes on her back and she flushed to think of how she had just shared her innermost feeling with an attractive stranger.

"Perhaps," he said after thinking over what she had just shared with him, "it is like a ghost that haunts you, and if you see it the haunting will stop."

Sarah shook her head "no" then added to clarify her response, "I don't know where it is, and I certainly wouldn't disturb the owners."

Fillip smiled because he now was gaining control of the

circumstances that had brought them together. "This is not a problem, for I know this country house and it is not far from here." He drew close to her and laid his hand on her arm to emphasize his invitation. "I'll take you there."

Sarah quickly pulled her arm from his grasp. She was strangely not afraid of him. But, his touch had caused a cascade of emotions to wash over her and she didn't know how to deal with her attraction to him. Her thoughts crossed to the safety of her hostel room. "No. I'm sorry. I can't go anywhere with you. You are being kind, I am sure, but I don't know you. I don't even really know if you have ever seen the house in the painting."

Fillip quickly gave thought to his predicament and searched the gallery space about him until he saw the gallery manager. Seeing him, he excused himself. "Un momento, wait here for me, please. I must see the manager."

Sarah had wanted to protest but Fillip's long strides had already moved him some distance away before she could. She had never been the object of such an attractive man's attention before and she felt compelled to comply just to see what he would do next.

Fillip appeared to have some great charm because the couple and the manger were shaking hands with him and smiling as if he were a star. After a few moments of conversation, Fillip drew the manager aside for a private word.

Sarah couldn't help but compare the two men, her thoughts always giving Fillip the most credit. He was tall, perhaps six-foot-two. His dove-gray tailored suit looked expensive and its fit favored his broad shoulders as it tapered down over his well-developed muscular chest and torso. His eyes were so dark that in certain light they would appear black.

Sarah's thoughts caused her to blush as she imagined releasing the unopened buttons of the pale blue shirt that covered the dark hair she saw at his throat. She shook herself inwardly and then reminded herself that she was a child of God and they were strangers.

Yet, her thoughts returned to him. She liked the way his thick dark eyelashes curled naturally and sexily upward toward his hair. Her fingers trembled as she thought about caressing his soft velvety thick black hair. Again, she was shocked by her errant thoughts. She was grateful that the men were moving toward her. Surely, their presence beside her would keep her focused-on reality and not the man's sexual appeal.

"Señorita, I am Luis Lorenzana, the gallery manager, and it gives me great pleasure to introduce to you Señor Fillip Castañola. I have known Señor Castañola for many years and can assure you that he is a man of honor and knows El Alba Rosa and is most welcomed there. He can show you this house and you will be safe with him. He only seeks your company for this afternoon, but I believe he will offer you dinner too." Luis nudged Fillip in a friendly gesture. "And, now Señor it is with pleasure that I introduce you to—." Señor Lorenzana trailed off and allowed Sarah to supply her name.

"Sarah Kettering"

"Señorita Sarah Kettering who appreciates fine art." As he finished his sentence, he gestured toward the painting and smiled broadly at Fillip.

Fillip took Sarah's right hand, brought it to his lips, and gently brushed a kiss against her fingers. He nodded his thanks and Señor Lorenzana returned to his customers. Sarah blushed again and was beginning to be annoyed by her schoolgirl silliness. Without releasing her, Fillip tucked her hand into his arm and asked, "Shall we go?"

Sarah thought about protesting but not out of fear. She felt strangely drawn to him and wanted to know him. She reasoned that his appeal for her was surely an extension of the portrait El Alba Rosa and the fine art gallery's atmosphere. Stranger warnings from her childhood flashed through her thoughts along with nightly news stories of unsuspecting women being kidnapped and harmed.

She chose to ignore the warnings as vacation-Sarah wanted the offered adventure, so she could have a pleasant memory of her time in Spain. The gallery manager had after all vouched for him and her safety, so she uncharacteristically permitted Fillip to escort her to a metallic blue sports car parked at the curb.

As he unlocked the doors and opened the passenger's door for her, Sarah had to stifle a giggle. She felt like Cinderella stepping into her magic coach. She glanced into Fillip's face and her heart skipped a beat as she thought that if she were Cinderella then Fillip would be her fated handsome prince. Fillip handed her down into the leather seat and she heard her mother's voice warning about the risk of getting in a car with a stranger. But, she didn't listen. For just a little while she didn't want Fillip to be just another person she passed on her vacation.

Fillip slid comfortably into the seat beside her. "Fasten your seat belt. We must drive for forty minutes before we will see the casa."

Sarah obediently pulled and fastened the seat belt into place. The afternoon sun was beginning to fade as they left the curb and merged into the roadway. Sarah looked to the man beside her as he concentrated on the traffic around him.

How very often she'd prayed for her heavenly Father to direct her to the man he had prepared for her. She thought about the young men from church she had dated, and they were nothing like the man who now occupied her thoughts. He was much older than any of them and she had only dated those that professed knowing Jesus as their personal savior. Sarah had not chosen this dating policy for herself but had accepted it in deference to her parents' teachings.

It was not until she had grown older and seen a few of her friends dating and marrying non-Christian men that she understood her parents' wisdom. True the Bible teaches that an unsaved spouse may be saved by a believing spouse, but the intervening years had to be navigated first. And, although there certainly was love in her friends' marriages, their love had to struggle to survive instead of blossoming as she believed it would in a Christ-centered marriage like her parents.

Sarah knew the Bible well as she had started committing the word, the truth, to her mind and her heart as a small child. Even now the verses pertaining to her thinking came to mind. She looked at the man beside her. His scent was now familiar to her nostrils and the verse about not being bound to unbelievers came unbidden to her mind. Sarah reasoned however, that this was not a date, just a pleasant adventure to tell about when her vacation ended.

Fillip too mused about his actions. He had never approached any tourist before, not even one so attractive. He'd only wanted to discover her intense interest in the painting El Alba Rosa. Many who knew the house acknowledge the skill of the artist and the likeness to the estate, but no one ever felt drawn to it. Remembering her reaction to it and her sweet words warmed his feelings toward her and he glanced her way. He laughed to himself thinking this American tourist and a Spanish businessman had no future, but only a stolen afternoon. His hope for the day now included coffee and dessert, or if things went well, dinner, but his true goal was to see Sarah's reaction to the house. Then, they'd go their separate ways, but for now, his companion would have his full attention.

Fillip was now out of the narrow busy city roads and broke their long silence wanting to gather more insight into his lovely guest. "Sarah is such a lovely name. Tell me about yourself."

Hearing him say her name made it sound different. It wasn't just his accent but something, just something that made it different when he said it. "Well, let me see. American – from Columbus, Ohio. My birthday is April 17th and I just recently turned twenty-seven. I have a degree in early childhood education, but I work as an administrative assistant at the Southern Baptist Convention. I share my family home with my mother, so neither of us needs to live alone." Sarah forced herself to stop before she rambled out of sheer nervousness. But, it seemed as if Fillip wasn't satisfied and wanted to know more.

"What about your father, brothers, or sisters?"

"I'm an only child. My parents wanted other children, but mother had to have a surgery, and couldn't have any other children. Daddy always said more children weren't important because mom got well, and he had his two girls." She smiled as she thought of her father. Fillip nodded and waited for Sarah continued.

"Daddy's the one who named me. He named me for Abraham's wife, Sarah, in the Bible. It means princess." Sarah sobered. "Daddy died four years ago. A drunk driver crossed the median on the expressway and hit him head on. Wearing his seat belt that day didn't help. They said he died instantly." Sarah quieted as grief washed over her.

Fillip reached across the console and caressed her hand compassionately and his touch did more than give her comfort. "My father is dead, too. It is not easy to lose someone you love. But, you have many pleasant memories and your mother. Sí?"

Sarah's face returned to a peaceful little smile and she nodded happily in agreement. "Yes, you're right and we, mother and I, will be with him again someday. But, now tell me about yourself."

Fillip had been raised in the Catholic Church and even now he was a supportive community leader in his church, although he did not often attend. He reflected for a moment on just how serious Sarah might be about religion but decided that it was not important. For now, all he wanted to do was to answer her without revealing too much about himself.

"I am 37, Sarah, a bachelor. My birthday is October 8th. My family is local to the city here in Toledo. I operate my own business here with a partner who has also become my dear friend. My mother lives in our family home with my brother, Roberto. He is the eldest son, so he controls our family's business interests. I also have two sisters, Isabel and Rosita. They have made good marriages which help support our family's heritage and business interests."

Sarah's brow was furrowed by a frown momentarily as she thought about Fillip's sisters' marriages and then she asked, "I hope your sisters are very happy in their marriages. It sounded as if love may not have been important in their choice of husbands."

"I am sure they love their husbands well enough. But, you are right; their husbands were chosen for them based on something more important than love."

Sarah twisted in her seat to see Fillip a little better troubled by the thought of arranged marriages. Her ire raised, she challenged him. "And, why haven't you married? Is there no woman to support your business and to give you heirs, sons of course, no doubt?"

Fillip had turned off the road into a long driveway and stopped the car, but Sarah hadn't noticed. The idle of the car was so quiet that Sarah only heard a low chuckle from Fillip before he spoke. He liked her ire and looked directly in her eyes as he spoke. "I don't need a wife to support the family business as my business is my own, but, I am looking for a woman to love and have my children." He picked up Sarah's hand and turned it over to kiss her palm. "Are you interested, mi querida?"

Sarah was taken aback and blushed deeply. His question, although a tease, made her aware of her awakening sexual desires, and if she didn't understand them, she at least wanted to control them. In the confined space of his car, she was over-powered by Fillip's masculine scent, the touch of his hands and lips upon her hand, and even the wild beating of her own heart. She was so flustered, she didn't have a single word to say. She only looked at him and wondered how she could have ever permitted herself to be alone with him.

Fillip laughed pleasantly and released her hand. "Perhaps you are wise not to be interested, or perhaps I should have asked you later, over coffee. It doesn't matter; we are here at El Alba Rosa."

Fillip slipped the car into gear and edged up the circular driveway until the house came into view. He stopped the car at a distance from the house and looked at Sarah's face. The house took Sarah's breath away. It was everything the artist had painted and somehow, she believed she could feel what the artist felt about the house. Each brush stroke had brought the house to life on the canvas, and now seeing the house it was as if the casa had been painted into her heart.

"Sarah" Fillip called her back to him. "Do you still feel passionate about this house?" There was a tone of mild enjoyment in Fillip's voice, but Sarah was unaware of it.

"Sarah?"

Fillip had expected to recapture Sarah's attention, but she failed to respond to the sound of his voice. He spoke to her again. "Sarah, mi querida, where are you? Perhaps you're ready to see the inside of El Alba Rosa. Sí?"

As Fillip put the car in gear and drove to the grand entrance, Sarah suddenly sprang back to reality.

"No, no! We can't go inside! We can't intrude!" Sarah reached across the car and grasped Fillip's arm. Panic and almost hysterically, she clung to him and sobbed, "Take me back. Please, please, Fillip, I want to go back."

Fillip was at a total loss to understand such a strong and strange reaction but under the circumstances, he complied, to calm her.

"Of course. I will take you back. I will show you the house another time. Don't be alarmed."

Sarah settled back against the leather-cushioned seat and sighed in relief as they left the long circular driveway. She had expected they would merely drive past the beautiful casa. She didn't care if Fillip knew the owners; she couldn't enter their grand home uninvited on a whim. As normalcy cleared her brain, she almost wanted to laugh at her self-humiliation. She thought about trying to explain but knew she really couldn't explain herself to a man like Fillip.

It didn't really matter she decided. Fillip would drive her back to the art gallery as quickly as his luxurious car would allow. He would drop her off, shake his head in amazement at this ridiculous American woman, and then she would go back to her hostel and forget about the whole afternoon. How could she have behaved so carelessly?

Fillip had been quiet as Sarah regained her composure. He had no idea what could have caused her to become so anxious. She had been so enchanted by the painting—his painting. He had finished the painting over a year ago and hung the framed painting over his living room fireplace mantle. El Alba Rosa was his private retreat from the demands of his business and it housed his painting studio. He had designed the house and overseen the construction of his home and its surrounding acres. And, even now he remembered with a great deal of pride, as each phase of its construction was completed. No one who had seen his painting had reacted to it with her passion and he wanted to see her there. He looked at her and his imagination took flight. Maybe she belonged there chasing after *his* children.

Luis, the gallery manager, had only recently been able to persuade him to include El Alba Rosa with his paintings being shown at the gallery's summer exhibit, but it was not for sale. He had *not* been pleased to see it hang in the gallery until this afternoon when he saw it past Sarah's shoulder. It had allowed him a means to meet her. Sarah had demonstrated a depth of emotion over his home and with a little effort, he had hoped to bring some of that passion around to himself. He wasn't a man to be wrong, usually.

Dusk had settled in around them, so Sarah could not clearly see Fillip any longer, but he sounded genuinely concerned. "Sarah are you alright?"

"I'm fine. Really, I just feel silly."

"Bueno. I didn't mean to upset you." They were near the city now. "Perhaps, we can stop for coffee and talk."

Sarah needed time to put this embarrassing incident behind her and to forget about it. "No, I can't, not tonight." Not ever Sarah thought. "You have been most kind and understanding. I trust that I have not made you think too badly about American women."

"I have no reason to think badly about American women. And, there is one I would like to have dinner with this evening. Can I not persuade you with my charm? We will put El Alba Rosa behind us and start again, fresh. Sí?"

Sarah found herself once again blushing at the magnetism of her companion's many charms and she was glad that their trip would soon be over. Sarah longed for the security of what she knew. She took off her seatbelt wishing she was home. Clearly, she was out of her depth with Fillip. She believed the Lord in His time would call her to be a missionary or pastor's wife. There were people out there who needed to know the Lord she was blessed to love, and it was only right that she'd take the story of Christ's redeeming love to the lost.

Fillip pulled up in front of the gallery. He had known her for less than two hours and she was slipping from what was usually a firm and commanding spell over women.

"Sarah, there is a quiet restaurant not far from here. Surely, there is no harm in having dinner with me?"

Even in the gathering darkness with the streetlights, Sarah could see or at least sense the appeal in Fillip's eyes as he looked at her. His allure was strong, and she found it impossible to tell him no again.

"Fillip in the entire world there is nothing that I would like more—."

Fillip believed he was hearing, yes. He relaxed against the driver's seat and started the car. As the engine hummed, Sarah threw open the car door and dashed away through the other pedestrians.

Chapter 2

Fillip had always been a man of action. As the second son of an important family, he had always needed that extra drive to prove himself and to get what he wanted. Sarah's abrupt departure left him paralyzed for only a few seconds before he turned off the car and sprung out the door to find her. He ran in the direction Sarah had taken, but the people, buildings, and enveloping dusk hid her escape.

Fillip refused to let her go so easily. This woman was different, sweet and innocent, nothing like the women who knew him, his position, and wealth. She had stirred his senses, his hope, and captured his heart. He had to find her. He wanted to explore the possibilities their relationship could offer. And, he had to know why she was so intrigued yet frightened by his house. He had to know why she ran from him. He had her name and just a short time to find her before she would no doubt finish her vacation and slip away to America.

He'd call a detective service he'd used. He knew from experience if you hired the right people the job always got done promptly. They would easily locate her hotel and then he and Sarah would talk. He ran his hand through his hair and sighed. Fillip was pleased with his plan and smiled in the darkness as he returned to his car. They could start fresh with breakfast.

Sarah gained the safety of her small room and leaned her back against the door as she caught her breath. She had been doubly foolish. She had let herself be caught up in the appeal of an attractive man and had gone away with him in his car. She knew that her mother would have been appalled to see her get into Fillip's car. He had been charming, and her mind had whispered the risk was small.

How many times had her parents cautioned her against being too friendly and trusting with people? They had always wanted to know her dates before she had gone out with them. Yet, today she had heeded no caution. So, what if the gallery manager vouched for him? He was a stranger too. No, she had allowed herself to be swept away by a warm accented masculine voice and a physical attraction that she hadn't known before she'd seen Fillip.

Sarah breathed a sigh of relief. The chance meeting and her foolishness was behind her now. No harm had been done. She had regained her sanity and control. The thought to pray came to her mind, and she thanked God for His faithfulness in watching over His imprudent child. She knew too she would have to seek future guidance in controlling the desires that she had glimpsed today. Sarah laughed at herself and concluded the risk was small with the type of men around her at home.

Sarah roused herself, went into the bathroom, and rinsed her face with cool water. It didn't really matter about today she reasoned. Tomorrow night she would be on a flight home. And, since she had only one more night and one more morning left of her vacation she wasn't going to stay hidden in her room like a frightened child. Sarah patted her face dry and looked at her reflection in the mirror. She just wouldn't venture outside the hostel again this evening. A few light touches of makeup restored her appearance and she went to dinner.

Jesús had been her waiter whenever she ate dinner at the hostel and he quickly came and seated her at a small table. Sarah had enjoyed his attention, although she knew that it was a part of the hostel's service. He had given her his address and she was going to send him a postcard from home to add to his collection of cards that friendly visitors had sent him from all over the world.

She had been quite shocked to discover that his name which pronounced the 'J' with an 'H' sound was really Jesus. To her that name was the one name above all names. She would have never give a child the name she held so dear, but she was in a different culture where the name was revered and given to children.

After Sarah finished her salad, she sat back to absorb the feeling of the room and its guests. She got so busy building memories that she failed to notice Jesús' return. As he sat the soup in front of her, she was startled and the soup toppled into her lap.

Jesús was immediately alarmed and started to clear up the mess. Many other guests would have assailed him for clumsiness but not

Sarah. He wasn't surprised by Sarah's chagrin and gentle acceptance of the situation. In the time of her stay at the Hostel Auto, he noticed there was something different about her. She had a glow of true peace and love.

As Jesús handed her napkins to remedy her plight, Sarah's thoughts went back a day. Jesús had arrived at the hostel early to start his job and found her in the lobby. He had never struck up much more than a causal conversation with a guest before, but yesterday was very different. She would always remember their conversation.

"Hola, Sarah."

"Hola, Jesús. What a glorious day this has been. I have been to the Valley of the Fallen." She didn't have to tell him the valley was dedicated to the memory of those who died in Spain's civil war. Nevertheless, she had excitedly shared with him the effects of what she had seen. There was the 200-foot cross on the valley's summit with Mary holding the crucified body of her son Jesus Christ at its base. And, there was beautiful cathedral carved inside the mountain whose central altar held an exquisitely detailed crucifix. She had been delighted by the spectacular Stations of the Cross carved into the perimeter of the cathedral. She had even shared with him her feeling of exceptional compassion for the Spanish people and what they had suffered. It was her attitude of awe, which caused him to ask her that first important question.

"Sarah, what is your secret? Why are you always so happy?" Jesús asked.

Sarah smiled congenially and answered, "I am on a dream vacation, Jesús, and I have just seen your Valle de los Caidos."

Jesús shook his head sadly. He was afraid that he wouldn't be able to find the words to ask what he needed to know. "No, there must be more. You always have this glow about you. You are always so happy. Others come here on vacation, but you are so different from all of them. What is it that makes you so happy?

Sarah became solemn as she realized that now was one of those rare moments, a divine appointment, when she could share her love of Jesus Christ. "Jesús, I am a child of the King, Jesus Christ. He saved me, and His gift freed me from the bonds of sin, hell, and Satan. This relationship allows me to be different from the unsaved because they cannot have the relationship I have with the Father unless they too ask to be saved."

Her words were strange to him but not completely foreign. Raised a Catholic like many of his countrymen he knew about the crucifixion. But, there was more to her words than the sacrifice of the Savior. What she spoke of was a personal relationship and not just so much religious practice. "Tell me more, Sarah. Let me understand this way you live it. Give me the joy I see in you."

"Oh, my friend, I have nothing to give you from myself, but I can tell you how you can find it from the source. Come sit with me." Sarah patted the bench beside her and pulled out a spiritual guide from her purse to share its riches with Jesús. She cleared her mind of worldly things and silently appealed for spiritual guidance before she began.

"God made us eternal beings. At our death, our earthly bodies are given to the grave, but we who know Him, go to be with Him for all eternity. When we ask forgiveness for our sins, Christ becomes our personal Savior. When we have Christ as our Savior we do more than go to church, be good, or do good works. Look at His word in this guide."

"*For all have sinned and fall short of the glory of God.*" Romans 3:23 (ESV) "*For the wages of sin is death, but the free gift of God is eternal life in Christ Jesus our Lord.*" Romans 6:23 (ESV) "*For everyone calls upon the name of the Lord shall be saved.*" Romans 10:13 ESV)."

Then Sarah continued her explanation, "What we must do is recognize that through Adam and Eve's sin in the garden when they disobeyed by eating the forbidden fruit, we are all born into sin and thus we are sinners by nature and separated from our Holy Father. By turning to Jesus Christ and confessing our sins, we accept the gift of salvation that only He can give because His death paid the penalty for our sins. Only then can the kind of relationship I have with Him begin in you. Jesus Christ is the only way to get to heaven."

Sarah paused to see if what she had said was being understood or causing offense. Afraid that Satan would use their natural language barrier against them; Sarah lifted her eyes heavenward and silently asked that Satan be rebuked and that her words not fall short.

"Jesús, do you have any questions? Have you ever asked for God's forgiveness?" Sarah watched as her words were pondered by this man and she waited patiently for a reply.

"I have been a good man all my life. I go to church. I took catechism classes. But no one has ever said these words to me before. No, Sarah, I have not confessed my sins directly to God, nor have I asked to be forgiven. I have always gone to the priests to confess. Then, they tell me what to do. How do I make a personal relationship with God, Sarah?"

"If you want to be saved, repeat this prayer after me. It is a very simple prayer, but it will be the start of the most marvelous and satisfying friendship that you will ever have." Sarah and Jesús bowed their heads in the lobby of the youth hostel and Jesús repeated the prayer printed in the guide.

Tears filled Sarah's eyes and as she reached for her purse to find a tissue, she saw Jesús wipe his own eyes. Spiritual birth is such a joyous event that even the angels in heaven rejoice over one lost sinner coming to Christ. Sarah wiped her eyes and hugged her newfound brother in Christ.

"Jesús, our Lord Jesus Christ loves you and so do I. What you need now is to read your Bible, so you can learn more about the relationship you have just started. Ask the Holy Spirit to open your eyes to His word and be filled with it. It is only when you know His word that you will know when Satan is whispering lies to you."

She continued. "Do not let others tell you what the Bible says, but study it yourself and commit it to your heart. You should also ask the Holy Spirit to show you a church where you can fellowship with people who believe in a personal Savior, like you do."

"How do I do this, Sarah? How will I get the spirit to guide me?"

"The Holy Spirit became a part of your life the minute you prayed and received forgiveness. To grow as a Christian you need to pray, read your Bible, practice your faith with like believers, and share your faith with those who do not believe."

"I can't. I don't know how. It is too much for me. Jesús that is one of Satan's first lies. He makes us doubt the power that we have in Christ. You must ask God to rebuke him for casting doubts into your mind. Just as Christ was able to save you, He will keep you. You can memorize verses to encourage you when Satan casts doubts into your mind. Christ will not fail you. I'll give you my address, so we can write, and I'll pray for you."

Sarah patted his hand. "You are a new creature in Christ, and you must allow yourself to grow one day at a time in His grace."

Jesús left Sarah reluctantly; he had wanted to ask many more questions, but he needed to go earn his living.

Sarah brought them back to the present. Jesús also remembered the previous afternoon and how he had come to know Christ and he smiled at her with a grateful heart.

"If you bring me another bowl of soup, I promise to eat it and not wear it." Sarah's laughter at the situation caused him to laugh too as he went to the kitchen for another bowl of soup. He would be sorry to see Sarah leave, but now he was confident they would someday share eternity.

Chapter 3

Sarah stretched lazily and happily as the early morning light touched her face and aroused her from slumber. A memory of some sweet dream teased her conscious mind. Suddenly she was fully awake as an image of a tousled hair Fillip surfaced. She scolded herself for reveling in the pleasant stimulation of their meeting even if she couldn't be responsible for her dreams. She knew for certain she would carefully avoid telling anyone about Fillip when she was home. She was determined to forget him along with any feelings he had caused.

Sarah tossed back her blanket and stalked briskly to the bathroom. She had saved for this vacation for several years and she was not about to waste even one more minute letting her mind wander. She showered and dressed before she had her devotional time. Her custom while she was in Spain was to sit on the room's one small chair and have her morning quiet time. This morning after her Bible reading and meditation she placed her Bible into her overnight case and closed it for her trip home. Then, she was drawn to the window of her room by the awaking sounds of the city that had stolen her heart. As she stood watching from her window, she prayed.

"Holy Father, I come before Your throne and thank you, that as Your daughter I can come into your presence. And, I thank you that in accordance to Your word that I can in "all things, whatever I ask in prayer, believing, know that I will receive it." (Matthew 21:22 Ryrie NAS). For this people and their country, I ask for a spiritual awakening. I also ask that my heart would always be sensitive to those who are lost and hungry for the word, like Jesús. I pray for Jesús and his spiritual growth as Your son. Thank You, Father God for allowing me to lead Jesús to Your throne. Go with me this day Father and guide me. Give me a safe flight home. I ask these things in Jesus' sweet name. Amen."

Sarah put a few more things into her bag and went down to an early breakfast. This was her last breakfast in Spain, so she carefully savored her freshly baked sugar roll and café con leche. She never wanted to forget the people or their city.

After breakfast, Sarah returned to her room and finished packing her bags. The fear of running into Fillip had kept her in the hostel last night, but the morning light had restored her courage. She also figured that Fillip had forgotten about her and was tending to his business. So, she grabbed her purse, by-passed the rickety elevator, and fairly flew down the stairs to the sidewalk outside the hostel.

Turning to her right, she started to walk down the street but suddenly stopped and look back at the hostel that had been her home for two weeks. It was a weathered brownstone building in a poorer neighborhood away from the costlier hotels and stores, but she would not want any better in heaven. But, she knew that better did await her because of Christ's promises. She took a picture of it for her vacation photo album.

Her mother had been concerned for her to come here on her own. In the end, her Mom had committed Sarah to the Lord and they prayed together for their well-being while they were apart. Sarah smiled as she thought about her mother and her fear of flying. Mother tried to live according to God's word, but she still had her weaknesses.

Indeed, Sarah reflected, the walk of faith that would take one out of the boat to walk with Peter across the water to Jesus Christ was not easy. But Jesus was faithful and just. As Jesus had done for Peter, He would do for any of His children. He would rescue them when their faith failed to let them walk to Him and beside Him.

Sarah was struggling not to be anxious in her daily walk with the Lord, but she longed to find her place of service and to find that special man God had prepared for her. Thinking about the special man the Lord had prepared for her caused Fillip's image to return to her yet again. His image was strangely dear to her, so she compelled her thoughts back to the present where they belonged.

Walking on down the street, Sarah consciously tried to imprint each building, each narrow jutting street, each passing face, and each sound into her memory. She had one more tour activity scheduled, so she would soon have to get a cab and go there, but for now, even the misty rain that began to fall became a part of her vacation memories. She knew she would return when she could afford it.

Daydreaming in the present and planning for the future, she stepped down off the curb at a narrow alley without looking. Suddenly all she could see was a rain splatted windshield and the image of a startled driver desperately trying to stop on the rain slick bricks, and she froze.

It was the car's driver who first reached her. He immediately gave orders for the police and ambulance to be called. He gently covered her in his jacket and cradled her, using the power that emanated from his body, his own life force, to keep her alive. Fillip willed that their meeting would not come to such an end. "Sarah, Sarah, mi amor, do not leave me now."

Sarah was unaware of his administrations; for the pain that cascaded over her when the car struck took her to a place that was for neither the living or the dead.

The police were very courteous when they arrived for they immediately recognized Fillip Castañola. He was, in their minds, a very good man who had worked hard to bring a productive business into the city. The witnesses' interviews, completed as the medics worked on Sarah and she was taken to the hospital, were clear about the details of the accident. They described graphically how Sarah had stepped into the street and how her body hit the hood, rolled up into the windshield, before it fell to the ground in a bloody heap.

They all reported that the driver could not stop because of her sudden appearance on the rain-slicked alley, and he had quickly and responsibly responded to the emergency. The officers' report would show that the unfortunate young woman had stepped carelessly into the path of his car. When the officers looked through Sarah's purse, they shook their heads sadly at the accident. Sarah's purse contained many articles; among them were her passport, an insurance card, her return ticket home for an evening flight, and emergency information.

Fillip answered the police officers' inquiries quickly with an ear to what the medics were doing before they took her away. He copied down the information he thought would be useful but left her purse with the medics. The police were grateful that Señor Castañola knew the young woman and had decided to notify the woman's mother.

Notification duties were unpleasant and more difficult with travelers, and they sighed with relief when Fillip left to follow the ambulance to the hospital.

The hospital staff quickly moved Sarah into a trauma room and pointed Fillip to a nearby waiting area when he arrived. While he waited word of Sarah's condition, he phoned the emergency number from the card found in Sarah's purse.

Carol Kettering, Sarah's mother, was not at home and unlike many, she had no answering machine. Fillip was relieved as he had little idea what to say or what message to leave under the circumstances.

Fillip wasn't accustomed to waiting. His father had died alone before they had arrived at the hospital. Remembering that painful time standing around waiting for his doctor was still upsetting. At the least, he thought someone could come and give him some word of what was happening.

For the first time since the accident, Fillip's control broke down and he demeaned himself for the accident. He stood there alone, thinking about the 'ifs'. If only he had handled her differently, she wouldn't have darted away. Or, if he had simply let her go and forgotten about her she wouldn't be so near death. He had always gone after what he wanted and today his aggressiveness might take Sarah's sweet life.

Fillip was not unaccustomed to praying but his prayers had always been one of the traditional prayers spoken since his boyhood. Now only one thought, one prayer, filled his mind. It was a plea. "Please God, don't let Sarah die. Please be here." The words filled his mind and they repeated themselves over and over. His words were a silent prayer that came from the center of his spiritual being and reached out to the spirit of God.

Fillip was a strong-willed and confident man and after a few minutes, he regained his composure and called his office. His secretary, Gail Hernaneles, had worked for him for five years and had already cleared his morning calendar so that he could find Sarah. Briefly, he told her about the accident, instructed her to clear his afternoon appointments, and to wait for further instructions.

Within half an hour, the emergency trauma doctor, Doctor Rubio came to Fillip and explained the seriousness of Sarah's injuries. He was afraid to operate without Sarah's or a family's member consent. There were hospital regulations to be followed. His staff was working hard to contact her family. It was his hope that their efforts to stabilize would return her to consciousness soon, long enough for her to understand and sign the necessary papers. A social worker was working on getting a court order that would give them legal consent. But, each passing moment only brought Sarah closer to death.

Fillip offered to assume the responsibility as well as all her medical expenses to facilitate her care, but the doctor could not allow it since Fillip had no legal standing with his patient. Fillip was not a man to be daunted and since he intended to see Sarah well again, he turned to his good friend and attorney Javier Mora.

Javier was concerned about how quickly the social worker would be able to find a judge who could be found and persuaded to authorize the necessary surgery as most of the judges would be sitting in court this time of day. Javier paused for a moment and thought about a book he'd recently read about antiquated laws that were still in effect. One of them would allow them a creative means to circumvent the problem, so long as no one asked any questions.

Since a husband could consent for his wife's surgery, the old proxy marriage law could make Sarah Fillip's wife. The law had allowed marriages to occur when the bride couldn't travel to her new home for a time. It gave her husband access to the bride's dowry, which was often more important than the bride. When Sarah was out of danger, he could easily have the questionable marriage annulled. Fillip readily agreed to the daring plan. It was his means to assume responsibility and gain control.

Señor Mora arrived at the hospital shortly after Gail Hernaneles and he brought with him the hastily drawn papers that would permit the proxy marriage. Fillip had already apprised the hospital priest of the situation, and the priest was waiting with Sarah. Javier drew him aside for a private word.

"My friend, you have always trusted my counsel," Javier nervously started, "so I must tell you that if your marriage is questioned by anyone, it could not be proven legal."

"Javier, please put your doubts aside. You are a good friend, but not a businessman. The priest is willing to perform the ceremony. Who will question this marriage with an attorney and a priest present? The doctor will see the marriage papers and let me sign the surgery consent." Fillip patted his friend on the back and went into Sarah's room. He met the priest with a confident handshake and introduced Javier as his legal counsel. "We can get started, and we'll sign the documents when we're done." Fillip flashed the legal-size manila folder in front of the priest and handed it back to Javier for show. No one would have time to question their practically non-existent relationship, or the legality of the marriage. He would see to it.

The marriage was performed hastily without ceremony by the hospital priest. Javier and an attending nurse distracted by caring for Sarah and awed by the attractive and prominent Señor Castañola acted as witnesses. Gail Hernaneles signed the legal papers on behalf of the unconscious bride and the priest signed where he was shown. Each played their part, and no one questioned the marriage because of Javier and his legal documents. It was a drama worthy of a day time soap opera, but the bride couldn't get up and receive her accolades.

The doctor had not been deliberately uncaring but was being cautious since he was dealing with an unconscious American. The hospital had just recently settled such a lawsuit. However, he felt sure that once Sarah's spleen injury was addressed and any other internal bleeding controlled she would recover.

He assured Señor Castañola that in a day or two their finest orthopedic surgeon would be able to operate and repair Sarah's badly injured left hip and leg. There would be many scars, but she would heal given time and the proper care. Señor Castañola seemed intent on her having the very best of care provided for the young woman, and the hospital would not disappoint the Castañola family.

Fillip stood and watched the doors of the operating room slip in and out after they wheeled Sarah in, and he felt satisfied that he had opened the pathway for Sarah's recovery. As he watched the doors come to a stop, he became aware of other feelings that nagged at his weary mind.

"Fillip, it has been a long morning. Can I get you a cup of coffee?" Javier asked.

"No, I need to get to the office and work. I can do nothing here. Don't worry about me, my friend. I am fine." Fillip shook hands with his friend.

"You were just involved in a serious accident, were married to a woman you barely know, and now you are watching closed doors. You are far from fine, but you would say nothing less." Javier patted his shoulder. "Call me if you need anything." Then he left Fillip standing in the hall.

Fillip stood there for some minutes after his friend left. A passing orderly nodded as he headed down the corridor and Fillip became aware that he was still standing transfixed, still starring into space. Fillip raked his fingers through his hair, walked to the nurses' station and left his contact numbers. He also left explicit instructions that Sarah should have anything she needed. Then, he asked about their chapel and went there to pray for his *wife*, his Sarah. *Waited to hear if she would survive. Waited to see her alive again.*

Chapter 4

Sarah drifted in and out of consciousness over the next few days as she was kept heavily medicated. On the third day, she was taken to surgery and her hip and leg were repaired with metal plates and screws. As the hours passed, her bruised body and contused brain began the process of healing, but she remembered nothing. The IV's dripped and the intensive care nurses carefully observed her monitoring equipment, recorded her vital signs, and administered medications around the clock. Automatic pumps massaged her legs to prevent clots, and therapists would come and exercise her arms and uninjured leg, and the SICU nurses would shift her from side to side and prop her up with pillows to prevent sores. Sarah was not aware of them or their activities, and she would never remember struggling against them or complaining as they dealt with her physical needs and caused her pain-tortured body greater agony.

From time to time, Sarah was aware of a tall shadowy presence near the window. Occasionally, it hung above her, and she believed it to be Death. She couldn't understand why he didn't complete his job and take her away. How welcome would be his relief from her torment! She longed for the sweetness of heaven. As a child of God, she didn't fear death, but the pain and the medications left her wanting and confused.

She reached out to the shadow when he was near, trying to tell him to take her with him. She always sensed feelings of strength, warmth, and comfort coming from the shadow. It was pleasant to think of death offering those things to the dying, but she asked him to be merciful and finish quickly. The shadow seemed to linger and kiss her forehead occasionally and she remembered more than once hearing she would soon be well again.

Then she reasoned the long shadow was not death, but an angel of love sent to comfort her as she was only walking through "the valley of the shadow of death". She occasionally remembered a sweet fragrance, but before she could place it she'd drift back to a place of pleasant oblivion. Eventually she had more lucent moments, but the shadow didn't return, and she was moved to a private room, but slept through her early morning transfer.

"So, you have decided to open your eyes. How do you feel?" The nurse spoke in heavily accented English and had her wrist monitoring her pulse as she waited for a reply.

Sarah responded by studying her surroundings and trying to figure out what had brought her to this strange room. When she tried to sit up a wave of pain washed over her causing her several moments of nausea. Finally, she managed a question.

"Nurse, what's happened? Why am I in so much pain?"

The nurse smiled encouragingly and checked her temperature. "Don't worry about the pain, dear. I'm sure you don't remember much about being in SICU, but you are recovering nicely. We have reduced the dose of your scheduled pain medication, so you will not sleep so much, but we can give you more if needed. I imagine that by tomorrow we will even have you up and in a chair."

Sarah's temperature was normal. The intravenous antibiotics had prevented an infection. But she felt poorly used and abused.

"What's wrong with me? Why can't I remember?" Sarah asked. She moved her hand down to her abdomen. "I can feel bandages and my leg—."

The nurse stopped her with an upraised hand. "I am one of your three private nurses, Marguerite Castillo, and this is our first day today. The doctors have seen you many times in the SICU, but it was too much for you to remember because of your head injury and pain medication. You were in a car accident. I know you that you've had a partial splenectomy, and the injuries to your hip and leg were repaired. Anything more you will need to talk over with your doctors. I will get you some pain medicine, and tell the doctor you want to see him, mm? He will be pleased to see that you are awake and talking, Señora Castañola."

The name hung in the air between the bed and the closing door. Sarah didn't even have time to protest. Her forehead furrowed as she watched the door. The name was wrong but familiar. She drifted back to sleep before she could remember.

The nurse returned within a few minutes and plunged a syringe into the injection site of her IV. Sarah awoke again as the nurse recapped the syringe and dropped it into a red container beside her bed. Seeing Sarah open her eyes the nurse spoke reassuringly.

"There, that will help ease things soon. I have paged the doctor, so you should have some answers to your questions in a little while."

Sarah nodded, closed her eyes uncontrollably and drifted into sleep. The medication seemed to have a dulling effect not only on the sites of her injuries but even on her brain. She knew she needed to say something to the nurse, but she wasn't quite capable of figuring it out, let alone say it. Sarah continued to drift, until a doctor came into the room and touched her shoulder.

"Good morning. I am Doctor Rubio and I understand you have a few questions for me." He checked her eyes with a small flashlight, turned off the flashlight and placed it back into the breast pocket of his hospital coat. "Tell me, what you remember?"

The doctor was not a young man, but he looked at her with a great deal of satisfaction. Sarah closed her eyes and went back to the last thing she remembered. She saw herself now as if she had witnessed the events instead of living them.

"I remember eating breakfast and going for a walk. Not far from the hostel it started to rain lightly, but the rain was refreshing so I didn't mind. It was my last day to be here and I wanted to remember it all." She smiled at the memory of how she felt that morning. "So, I kept walking. Then, there was an alley— maybe. Yes, it had to be an alley because I remember the car, the eyes—the eyes of the driver."

Sarah stopped and couldn't continue. She was trying to remember how she knew those eyes. She almost had the face when the doctor patted her shoulder in a gesture of comfort and caused her to look back at him.

"You have a bad brain concussion, but no brain bleed. Your left hip and leg were seriously damaged. It required extensive restructuring. But, I will explain that a little better when you feel up to seeing your x-rays. Your most life-threatening problem was damage to your spleen. The spleen is a blood-filtering organ, so when it is injured it can cause a person to bleed heavily internally. We were able to repair it, and a few other vessels to stop your internal bleeding." The doctor's explanation was brief and simple because he'd learned that most patients still were not able to understand or remember a more complicated explanation at this point during their recovery. "Do you understand?"

"Yes, I hit a car, and you managed to fix everything." It wasn't a good medical explanation, but it was enough for now. Sarah was tired, and the medication was adding to her confusion. She knew that something wasn't quite right. She struggled hard to remember. Finally, it came to her.

"Doctor Rubio, when the nurse left earlier, she called me by the wrong name. Are you sure you have the right patient?"

Nurse Castillo was startled by her young patient's question. She had been assigned to the case when Sarah had been moved from Intensive Care to this private room. She too turned to look at the doctor.

"There is no need for you to be concerned. There has been no mistake, and everything is as it should be. Your explanation will best come from Señor Castañola. Just rest now." Doctor Rubio patted her shoulder again and departed with no further explanation.

Sarah opened her mouth to stop him, but it was too late.

"You rest now. I will be here if you need anything." Nurse Castillo was herself curious about her patient's strange question. There seemed to be a mystery surrounding her. But, her duties were more important than satisfying her inquisitiveness, so she straightened the bed covers and said, "Be patient, the answers will come. Trust me, they always do."

The nurse pulled the drapes closed over the window and her shadow reminded Sarah of the other shadow, but the assertive presence and the scent of the shadow was missing. Weariness filled her mind, so she let the memories of the shadow rest while she drifted into sleep.

Hospital routines cannot be stopped to allow for the rest of the ill or injured. Sarah's sleep was disturbed when vitals were taken, when her medications were administered, and when a laboratory technician came for a blood sample. Sarah had received two blood transfusions during her treatment. Now it was necessary to determine that her blood counts were remaining stable.

The only time Sarah was happy with the morning's interruptions came when Nurse Castillo woke her for lunch. She was given some chicken broth and a cup of weak lukewarm tea. It reminded her of home and her mother. Sarah was treated to the same fare when she had the flu. Nurse Castillo was pleased as she clucked about Sarah. Keeping her food down and regaining her strength were important goals if she was going to be free of the IV's and eventually the hospital.

Sarah suddenly became agitated. "Nurse, my mother! Has anyone called her? I was to go home days ago, I am sure. She must be worried sick."

"Now, Señora Castañola you must not disturb yourself. I am sure that your family knows. You certainly carry emergency information with you and the hospital would have called her."

"How can you be sure? My name isn't Castañola. I am Sarah Kettering. I am an American and I only came to Toledo for a vacation. And, I don't know anything about a Señora Castañola!"

"You really must be calm, or I'll have to get you a sedative." warned the nurse.

"All right, I will." Sarah pleaded as she forcibly tried to regain her calm. "But, please go check with someone about my mother, please."

"Well, if that will calm you, I'll go check with the floor supervisor. We can also get you a phone, so you can call her yourself this afternoon."

Minutes pass slowly when you are worried and alone. But, within five minutes Nurse Castillo returned to her overwrought patient. "I was told your mother has been informed of your accident and convalescence and that you have nothing to worry about. Everything is being taken care of for you by your husband." She patted her arm encouragingly.

"Your mother receives daily progress reports from Señor Castañola and she has already been notified that you are in a private room." Nurse Castillo studied her patient. She had never cared for a patient who didn't understand who she was. Her very presence in being assigned a case with private nurses around the clock spoke of the importance and wealth of her patient, or her husband.

She set those questions aside. Her nursing duties came before her curiosity and she administered her patient's pain medication and settled her down for the afternoon. The arrival of two flower arrangements in the late afternoon perked up Sarah's spirit. She was given a small cut bouquet of live flowers and she was relieved to read the card, "Trust in the Lord. He will keep you. Love and prayers, Mother."

The other flower arrangement was a large garden of live plants with a white silver dollar African violet blooming at its center. It was the most costly and beautiful gift of flowers Sarah had ever received but she preferred the bouquet sent by her own sweet mother as the card that came with the garden of flowers was signed, "Get well soon mi querida, Fillip."

His card more than the flowers made her understand something about her mistaken identify but left many unanswered questions. She was somehow married to Fillip? Nurse Castillo's shift ended, and Sarah was sorry to see her leave. The evening nurse, Teresa, was much younger and her command of English was not as good as Nurse Castillo's which limited their ability to communicate because Sarah's had only her high school Spanish.

Still she had been able to talk briefly with her mother, and she found the words to ask Teresa for a Bible; although what she received was a Spanish Bible she could not read. Sarah was not undone by the lack of a Bible. She was too tired to read anyway. So, she closed her eyes and thought of David's prayer in Psalm 86 and her heart was made glad before she slept yet again.

Her evening meal came, and she welcomed the nourishing chicken broth, plain red gelatin and weak lukewarm tea. Since she could do little more than manage a few words with Teresa, her thoughts turned to Fillip, and she wondered how he had ever got involved in her hospitalization and why everyone said they were married.

She wondered what it would be like to be Fillip's wife and giggled at the very notion. She had been overwhelmed by his virility when they had first met. To be his wife—his real wife, to be held against his chest, to be touched and kissed by him, to have him truly love her was unimaginable.

Sarah blushed at her wayward thinking and was grateful there was no monitor to register her heart rate. She looked toward Teresa to see if she had noticed her blushing. They exchanged awkward smiles and after a while, Sarah slept, and in her dreams, there was no accident, no hospital, and no pain. She dreamed of her mother, a smiling Fillip, El Alba Rosa, and dark-haired children with blue eyes.

When the night gave way to the early morning light, the night nurse Carmelita left, and Sarah barely remembered the care she administered. She was awakened by Nurse Castillo for the usual hospital routine, a sponge bath, and a light breakfast. What she found this morning was that she really wanted more than just the lukewarm tea and hard toast. She wanted to be treated more like she was well and not a convalescing hospitalized patient. She felt better except for some soreness in her abdomen, her very painful hip and leg, so she decided that she now must take control of the needs of her healing body.

"Nurse Castillo will you remove the catheter and IV this morning?"

"I believe we can remove the catheter as we will get you up today. But, you will need a bedside commode because we won't be able to get you into the bathroom easily. It is too soon to remove the IV, after all we still have your pain medication to administer." replied Nurse Castillo.

"Why can't we stop the pain medication and see if I can do without it?"

"I have been a nurse a long time now, dear. The medication is still needed, and the doctor knows this as well. He has left orders for you to have it for several more days."

Sarah didn't want to be in pain, but she also didn't want these drugs for fear that she might become addicted to them. She knew her body was the temple of God and she wanted to keep it a pure place for Him to dwell.

"Then, let's wait and see if I really need it before we use it again? Perhaps we can get the doctor to order oral medication." Sarah pleaded with her eyes as well as her words. "I promise to tell you, if I can't cope with the pain." Sarah wanted to gain some control over her recovery, and she wanted to go home.

"No, it really isn't done. You have been badly hurt. Bone injuries and the surgery to repair them are most painful. Your evening and night nurses gave you the medicine while you slept, so you do not know how much pain you can expect. And the pain will only increase as you begin to use your leg." Nurse Castillo shook her head side to side to emphasize her doubts.

Sarah looked at her nurse with respect and a developing fondness and smiled. "Our Savior experienced great pain in His very human body and He refused the bitter mixture that would have eased His suffering. And, while He endured this physical pain, His sinless nature bore the torment of the sin of all mankind, both past and present. Nurse Castillo, He understands pain and suffering, and His strength is sufficient for me. I will rely on Him and tell you when the medication is needed."

Nurse Castillo nodded in agreement slowly as it was obvious that Sarah was determined to stop the IV pain medication. She was growing fond of her most unusual patient. And, she had never thought of Christ being able to understand physical pain, from having experienced it in His own human body. She would give this more thought later.

For now, she would permit Sarah to ask for the pain medicine, but she would watch her carefully to see how she was handling the pain. Later she would talk to Doctor Rubio to see if he would prescribe something orally for this stubborn little one. It was too soon to stop the pain medication altogether. Even oral medication would still need to be something strong. She looked at the serenity in the face of her young charge and wondered at it. Sarah's body was weak, but her faith gave her a resolve that made her strong and difficult to refuse.

Sarah's first test of her resolve came when she was helped from her bed and sat in a chair while her bedding was being changed. Those few minutes out of bed were almost too much for her. She was extremely grateful when Nurse Castillo noticed her state and called the orderly to put her back into bed. Nurse Castillo gave her exhausted patient some additional pain medication, so Sarah drifted away.

Chapter 5

Nurse Castillo awakened her patient for lunch and the food was very appreciated. They brought her vegetable beef soup, plain red gelatin, a roll, tea, and a dish of orange sherbet. The afternoon's trip from bed wasn't as bad, although she was up for almost an hour. It had been hours since she had taken any pain medication and the effort to forgo it was beginning to show on her face.

"Sarah, do you want the pain medication, now? No one will think badly of you for taking it." Nurse Castillo spoke as she smoothed back Sarah's hair gently.

Sarah's smile waned, and she confessed, "I do hurt, but I would like to go a little longer."

Nurse Castillo shook her head and sighed, but she admired the effort. "It is good you want to stop the medicine, but it is not good for you to be in pain. But, I have talked to the doctor and he has agreed to give you an oral pain medication. It is not as strong and cannot work as quickly as the medication does through the IV, so it may not be enough. If it is not enough, we must use the IV medication. But, you will tell me this? Sí?"

"Oh, thank you. I will tell you. I promise." And, Sarah's gratitude showed in her smile.

Sarah took the oral medication and Nurse Castillo went to lunch, making sure that Sarah would call the floor nurses if she needed anything.

Without the dulling effect of the IV pain medication, Sarah did not feel the need to go back to sleep. She decided the next step in helping herself get well would be to start taking care of herself.

So, she elected to comb out her neglected and tangled hair. Shifting in bed she was able to search the nightstand drawer, where she found a little comb and other personal care items provided by the hospital. The movement caused her some pain, but she proceeded to work on her hair. The effort soon became too much for her as the IV tubing seemed to be constantly in her way and her arm movements caused her to pull on her incisions. She never realized what parts of her body moved when she combed her hair. She had almost decided to wait until Nurse Castillo returned to help her when the door after a brief knock opened.

Standing at the door was a woman carrying Sarah's overnight case.

"It seems I have arrived just in time. Let me help you." She took the hospital issued comb and dropped it into the trash and placed Sarah's overnight case on the bed table. She opened the case and picked up Sarah's comb and began to carefully untangle her hair.

"I am Gail Hernaneles. You can call me Gail. I am Señor Castañola's secretary. He has sent me to be sure that your needs are being met and to answer your questions if I can. He had to leave Monday for business meetings in New York or he would be here with you now."

Gail had seen her employer Monday, when he came to the office to pick up the papers he needed for his meetings. He had looked very drawn from spending so much time at the hospital over the previous six days.

Sarah knew immediately that Gail had to be a valued secretary because she was dealing with her as if her care was a part of her normal work duties. It reminded her of her own job as a secretary and she knew that someone else was still handling her duties.

"It was good of you to come and I am grateful for assistance with my hair, but, could you tell me the mystery of why I am being called Fillip's wife?" Sarah asked.

"Yes, of course." Gail started. "You remember meeting Fillip at the art gallery and then leaving him without giving him your hostel's name?"

"Yes, I remember." Sarah understood from Gail's careful choice of words that she was being kind or repeating a simpler version of what Sarah thought of as her narrow escape.

"Fillip wanted to have breakfast with you and gained your hostel location from a service he has used. It is my understanding that he was coming to see you again when the accident happened. Your injuries were serious, and the doctors did not want to treat you without the consent of a close relative. So, Fillip arranged the marriage through an outdated proxy law. You slept through the ceremony, but it was performed by the hospital's priest." Gail explained.

Nurse Castillo returned and saw that her patient had a visitor. "Excuse my interruption, please." She addressed herself in English to Gail as she heard her speaking English. "I am Nurse Castillo, Sarah's day nurse. I will be at the nurses' station and you should tell me when your visit is done, please."

Gail nodded to the departing nurse and then returned her attention to her Sarah.

"Is this marriage legal?" Sarah asked returning to their conversation.

Gail appeared to think for a minute before she answered. "I am not an attorney but Señor Mora, Fillip's attorney, drew up the papers, attended and witnessed the marriage service, and a priest presided. I would say it is quite legal, but only done so you could have the emergency treatment you needed. I signed the papers for you." She worked gently at a stubborn tangle in her hair. "But, don't worry. Señor Fillip is an honorable man and will not hold you against your will. When the time is right, Señor Mora can draw up the necessary papers and have the marriage annulled which you will sign for yourself. But for now, you are legally Fillip's wife and he is taking very good care of you."

Sarah was very quiet for a moment, but she finally managed, "I don't know what to say."

Gail replied, "You don't need to say anything more to me about your marriage or care, just let me French braid your hair to prevent more tangles."

Sarah looked at Gail and knew she was right. She must thank Fillip for her life and the excellent care she had been receiving. Her thanks would be small in comparison to all he had done. She would check with the hospital business staff to be sure her medical insurance was paying out her benefits, keeping his cost down. She turned her thoughts back to Gail and answered, "Yes, please, it needs washed, but for now a braid would be nice."

Gail's fingers started to work Sarah's hair and Sarah thoughts turned to Fillip. "I would like to thank Fillip in person. Will I be able to see him soon?"

"Yes, he is returning to our county tomorrow morning, so I expect you will see him tomorrow afternoon. He has been kept informed of your progress while he's been away and will want to see your recovery for himself."

Sarah thought of Fillip and how she could thank him. "Gail, you must know Fillip well. How can I properly thank him for my care?"

Gail had finished with Sarah's hair and returned the comb to the case before she answered. "That is for the two of you to work out. He has been very concerned for you." Gail turned the case so that Sarah could see herself in its mirror.

Sarah touched the articles in the top of the case as she marveled at the reshaping of her hair by Gail's skilled fingers. "It was good of you to bring me these things."

"Fillip had your luggage picked up from the hostel when he sent the payment to settle your lodgings. He instructed me to bring you what I thought you might need. If you need anything else, I will bring it."

Sarah sunk back against her pillow. "It appears that I owe him even more than I first imagined."

Gail turned and picked up her purse from the chair where she had left it as she prepared to leave. "Please, don't worry about it."

Sarah asked half-jokingly. "Are those my instructions from your boss?"

"Yes, they are." Gail answered pleasantly as she returned to Sarah's bedside. "Is there anything else I can do for you?"

Sarah had sobered after hearing the serious response to her light-hearted question. "If it isn't too much trouble, I would like my suitcase. It has a worn but warm robe."

"I will see that you have it. It was a pleasure to see you doing so much better. Buenos tarde, Sarah, I will send in your nurse."

"Por favor and buenos tarde." Sarah replied as Gail left the room.

Sarah pondered the things her visitor had said. Her thoughts turned to Fillip, and she smiled at the little cameo she had formed of him in her mind. She knew little about him but something about him stirred her heart and caused a warm pleasant feeling to flow out and bathe all her shimmering nerve fibers, and for a moment, she was unaware of any pain.

Always before when her thoughts went to him, she would scold herself for not controlling her emotions, this time she was not ashamed of how she felt. She wanted to remember him lovingly, once she was home. Fillip was a kind and generous man who had only wanted to show her El Alba Rosa and have dinner with her. Now he not only had assumed financial responsibility for her injuries but had made an awkward marriage commitment to her. How strange it must have been for him to be a bachelor for thirty-seven years and now be saddled with an accidental bride. For her there seemed to be many benefits to being Fillip's temporary wife and since she could do little else, she would relax and enjoy them until she became Sarah Kettering again.

Sarah's musing ended with Nurse Castillo's return with an aide carrying in a bedside-commode. "While you had your company, I was able to speak with Doctor Rubio. Since we have the commode, we will remove the catheter. He also agreed to remove the IV tomorrow if you do well on the oral medication. How would that be?"

Sarah's broad smile was enough for her nurse who chuckled at her impatient patient. Sarah was progressing remarkably, so in short order the catheter was gone. "Now, why don't you just lean back and rest before dinner?"

Sarah gave her no argument and slept until the afternoon sun gave way to shadows. Nurse Castillo watched her carefully, not for signs of distress, but for an understanding of this simple young woman and her grace. She understood from the floor nurses the story of Sarah's and Fillip's marriage. How sad she reasoned for Fillip to be responsible for Sarah's injuries. To be sure, it was an accident but nonetheless it had caused him great concern and he had gone to remarkable lengths to assume responsibility.

What a remarkable history the two already shared, she thought, as she gathered up her things to leave. Fillip was a man of money and position, and Sarah, was a young woman of great faith. *Did they share a destiny?* She wondered as she looked at her young patient. The evening nurse, Teresa, came through the door and Nurse Castillo motioned her back to the hallway so she could update her on Sarah's progress.

Teresa woke Sarah when evening trays were being delivered. After seeing to her personal needs, Sarah had a regular patient tray and the food was wonderful by any standard. She had grown fond of the way the Spanish people cooked their food in olive oil. When she got home, she was going to get a Spanish cookbook and some olive oil and learn to cook the same way. In the meantime, Sarah simply enjoyed what she could eat of the veal and its accompanying dishes. After dinner Sarah received her evening oral medication. Sarah's heart was singing thank you, Lord, thank you, when her first evening visitor arrived.

"Señora Castañola, I am Lupe Serrano, I will be doing your physical therapy. Tomorrow we will start with a few exercises for your uninjured limbs to work those muscles. We need to recondition and strengthen them. In a few days we will have you up using a walker."

"Señor Serrano, it is good of you to come to introduce yourself. I am sure you probably should be home by now."

"Please call me Lupe. We will be spending many hours together, and, my work hours vary to accommodate my patients' schedules."

Sarah responded, "Then you must call me Sarah. I will work very hard to do your exercises, so I can get better."

Lupe smiled, "Sí, Sarah. I can ask no more. Rest well tonight for we will start to work tomorrow at 10:00. Buenos noche, Sarah."

"Buenos noche, Lupe"

Sarah closed her eyes to pray and Teresa thought she was sleeping so she quietly took a book from her bag and sat down to read. There was little that required the attention of a private nurse now that Sarah was recovering so quickly, but Teresa was willing to enjoy the easy duty until she was assigned.

Sarah's heart was light with praise. *"Most Holy Father, my heart is full of your excellent greatness. Greatly do I praise you, Father, for your lovingkindness to me during this time. Continue to watch over mother while I am away and let us speak to each other again soon. Thank you for my excellent care and the great skill of the doctors and nurses who have aided my recovery. Bless Fillip and his business, Father, and grant him safety as he travels. Keep Jesús and do not let Satan undermine his position as Your new child. Let the Holy Spirit now speak for me the joy that I feel, the praise that I haven't the words to express. In Jesus' holy name I pray. Amen."*

It was not long after her prayer that Sarah had her final visitor for the evening. After a brief knock, the door opened uncertainly, and familiar head appeared. Sarah was delighted to see Jesús standing in her doorway.

"Hola, Jesús. It is so good to see you. Come in."

"Hola, Sarah. You are better now?"

"Yes, I am."

Teresa looked at Sarah's visitor and spoke to him in Spanish. Jesús interpreted Teresa's words to Sarah as the nurse left. "She said she is going to dinner while we visit."

Sarah nodded her understanding and Jesús seated himself before he continued. "It seems the Lord does answer our prayers, Sarah. I have prayed for you much since we heard of your accident. When I came to see you before, you were not awake but the nurse with you said in a few more days you would be awake and better."

"The Lord always hears and answers His children. His answers are not always what we would like or as quick as we would like. But He does always answer us."

"You are so sure, Sarah?"

Sarah stretched her muscles that ached from their long inactivity and smiled before she answered. "Jesús, our earthly fathers don't always give us what we ask for, and they do so out of love and their desire to protect us. Our Heavenly Father loves us ever so much more and He knows the future that He has in mind for us."

"One of my favorite verses is, *For I know the plans that I have for you, declares the Lord, plans for your welfare and not for calamity to give you a future and a hope. Then you will call upon Me and come and pray to Me, and I will listen to you. And you will seek Me and find Me when you search for Me with all your heart.*" (Jeremiah 29:11-13 NAS). Doesn't that excite you, Jesús?'"

"Oh, yes, Sarah. It is good to know that He has plans for me— or us. But how do you know what plans, so you can choose the right things to do?"

"Prayer, Jesús. Our Lord Jesus said to pray about everything in faith. Remember we don't have to ask for our needs for He knows these things and takes care of them."

"But, if all of this is true, why are you here and so hurt?"

Sarah laughed pleasantly. "We live in a natural world not heaven.

And, we because of our humanity and freewill make bad choices. I didn't act on the simple instruction all children receive. I didn't look both ways before I crossed the street." Sarah sobered, "But God did spare my life which means He still has a purpose for me."

Jesús asked. "Did Satan do this? I remember that Satan asked God if he could test Job's faithfulness. Satan destroyed everything Job owned including his home, livestock and family except for his wife. He even caused him to have painful boils all over his body, but through it all Job was faithful and never cursed God."

"Yes, that did happen to Job, and then God restored all that Job had and more. He even gave him ten more children too, not twenty, as the first ten were with Him in heaven. But, the Bible doesn't teach this as a typical event. I caused the accident. I was careless. My accident was a natural event, so I can't even blame the enemy for it. But when bad things happen God is not undone or surprised and He can bring good things from what appears to be only loss. Even death for the saved is gain, for the beloved one gains heaven and heaven gains another soul, whose name is written in the Book of Life." Sarah's heart hummed with praise. "God is Lord of all circumstances. He is El Shaddai, the All-Sufficient One."

"How does He do this?"

Sarah thought about her answer for a moment. "The story of Joseph is the best evidence of God's control of circumstances that I know. Joseph's brothers hated him and wanted to kill him but sold him into slavery. Joseph ended up in Egypt, a slave in the house of Potiphar and God blessed his service in the house until he was raised to the personal servant of Potiphar and placed in charge of all Potiphar's household."

"Potiphar's wife wanted Joseph to sleep with her, and after he refused she accused him of trying to rape her. Potiphar then had him thrown into the king's jail instead of killing him. I think he may have trusted Joseph more than his wife. In prison, Joseph once again rose to favor and God gave him the ability to interpret the dreams of two other prisoners. The dreams came true just as Joseph had said. But, the prisoner, the king's cupbearer forgot his promise to mention Joseph to the king and Joseph remained in prison."

Jesús nodded for Sarah to continue and brought his chair closer.

"Two years—two years later the king had two dreams that no one could interpret, until the cupbearer remembered Joseph. Joseph was brought from prison, was able to interpret the king's dream, and told him what course of action should be followed. Joseph credited God for his ability to understand the king's dream and the king made him overseer of all Egypt with only himself higher in command."

"The famine God revealed in the dreams came as predicted and, because of Joseph's leadership, Egypt was ready. Joseph's family back in Canaan was not prepared and they had to come to Egypt for grain. Joseph had been a slave and a prisoner in Egypt for thirteen years, but he recognized his brothers. Although it was a long difficult process for Joseph to forgive them, Joseph had compassion on them, and saved all of his father's family."

The room was silent for a few moments until Jesús spoke. "Sarah. What does He do with your accident?"

"I don't know." Sarah confided. "Joseph as a seventeen-year-old had dreams of ruling over his brothers before they sold him away. In Egypt as first, a slave and then a prisoner it would seem the dreams were foolish or at least ones which would never be fulfilled. But God took him to Egypt and used those thirteen years, to train him for his future position. Remember his brothers wanted to kill him, so his life was spared. But Joseph lived each day without knowing God's plan. Thirteen years seems a lot to ask from a seventeen-year-old."

"So, you will just trust God?" Jesús asked.

"More than just trust—always trust. He wants us to trust His heart that loves us when we can't know His plan. The accident for me is a place to rest in God. Later, the story of my recovery could give strength to someone with a similar injury. I don't know what God can or will do with this, but I take comfort in knowing that He is still in control. For me it is an "even so." When something bad happens, I'm going to still believe in God and trust in His plan."

"Even so, Lord." He repeated with a smile. "I like this."

Sarah was tired, and she had to stifle a yawn that was not missed by her guest. "I am sorry to have tired you, Sarah. I was enjoying our talk and forgot that you need to rest."

Sarah smiled and then laughed reassuringly. "Sharing the things of

God and His words are not tiring. It is always a pleasure. Our time together tonight is a gift from God."

"I still should be going. Your nurse will soon return and throw me out for not keeping my visit shorter." Jesús put the chair back against the wall and returned to stand over Sarah. He shyly leaned down and kissed Sarah's cheek. "Vaya con dios, my sister."

Sarah was touched by Jesús' affection and in her heart the Holy Spirit moved to thank God for him. "Vaya con dios, my brother." They each meant their words. Teresa obviously had been waiting outside the door until Jesús left as she came in immediately afterward. Sarah was indeed tired and after Teresa helped her take care of her personal needs for the night, Sarah slept. She was awakened only for her medication and vital signs.

Chapter 6

As a child, Sarah had always slept soundly and sweetly on Christmas Eve only to awaken with a great anticipation of the day's events. This morning was her third day of awakening in a general care room, but inside she felt like a child awakening to the great joy of Christmas morning. Even seeing Nurse Castillo's face instead of mother's dear face didn't quiet her anticipation. A little voice gushed inside her heart and it was saying, "Fillip is coming. Fillip is coming."

While Nurse Castillo took care of Sarah's personal needs, she noticed her patient's face was flushed. The mother in Nurse Castillo held the back of her hand against Sarah's pink cheeks and was satisfied there was no fever. A fact she later verified with a thermometer when removing her IV. When Sarah's tray came, Nurse Castillo watched her with little comment until Sarah pushed her partially eaten breakfast away.

"It may be none of my business, but I am your nurse. So, what is it that has you all flushed and bothered this morning that you could not finish your breakfast?"

Nurse Castillo's manner was now in a full-blown mother mode and Sarah was set to giggling, but the pain in her abdomen brought her up short. Sarah held her abdomen. "Oh, I am sorry. You just made me think of my own dear mother as you stood there with your hand on your hip demanding to be let in on my mental state. Mother would be pleased to see that God has not left me without a mother to safeguard me."

Nurse Castillo was pleased by the comparison because of the great fondness Sarah showed for her mother, but she was not about to be distracted. She smiled at her and crossed her arms over her ample chest as she pursued the subject. "Well then, young lady, how do you answer your mother?"

Sarah sobered and thought about her answer. "Well, nurse, it's a beautiful day and I'm to start therapy."

"The day is beautiful to be sure, but it is not the day or the start of your therapy that has put that color in your cheeks."

Sarah laughed in delight. "You are like mother. The truth is Fillip is supposed to be coming this afternoon."

"So, you blush at the approach of your husband." Nurse Castillo sighed with the memories of her own bridal days. "It is a bride indeed who blushes at the thought of her groom."

Sarah was again very still as she thought of Fillip as a groom dressed in a dove gray tuxedo with the aroma of his freshly applied cologne drifting her way. It was a tantalizing picture, so she decided to tease Nurse Castillo rather than dwell on her thoughts. "Do you have any motherly advice for a bride?"

Nurse Castillo came near the bed and stroked a loose strand of Sarah's hair back into place. "You need no advice from me. I suspect the Bible will tell you all you need to know about being a wife and a mother. But, if you were my daughter I would give you one advice. She responded first in Spanish and repeated it in English. *"Remember whose child you are, and that God loves you."*

How strange to hear those words from someone other than her own Mother. She had heard them often as a child when she would go to a friend's house to spend the night, or when she was on a trip away from her parents' counsel. The words were always said in love to remind her that she was God's child, and that she shouldn't give in to peer-pressure.

The simple phrase was to remind her that no matter where she went that God would always be with her. The only words Nurse Castillo did not include were the words Mother always added, *"and so do I."* Sarah's eyes misted as she thought of her mother and the quiet wisdom the Lord had woven into her character.

"Nurse Castillo, indeed you remind me of Mother for she has said those very words often. If I close my eyes, I can see myself a bride before the wedding. Mother would say, *"Remember whose you are, and that God loves you and so do I."* Then, she would kiss my lips and lower my veil, and it would then be lifted again for my groom."

Sarah's words stopped as she envisioned herself a bride with her veil being lifted. Then, she saw the eyes, the crystalline blue eyes of the bridegroom—Fillip's eyes. Her breath came up short and her heart was troubled by the terror she saw in those eyes and her pleasant daydream crumbled, as she now knew Fillip had been the unfortunate driver of the car.

Nurse Castillo noticed the color change from its modest blush to that of confusion, but she had no time to question Sarah. Their pleasant interlude of foster mother and daughter was stopped by the opening of the door. Lupe had come to start Sarah's rehabilitation.

"Hola, Sarah." He turned to greet Nurse Castillo in Spanish. "It is a pleasure to see you again?"

Lupe moved toward Sarah and switched to English. "You are indeed most fortunate to have Nurse Castillo, Sarah. I remember her from the days when she was a staff nurse here before she went to private care. She was the best nurse this hospital ever had."

Nurse Castillo sputtered at Lupe's compliment. "I know this one too, Sarah. His tongue is always ready with a compliment, especially if he is talking to a pretty young woman. Don't let him turn your head with flattery."

Nurse Castillo chuckled as she went to pick up her purse. Lupe responded with his hand over his heart. "Nurse Castillo, you wound me to the heart. There was never anyone prettier than you to attract my attention, and I could never turn your head with a mere compliment."

"Sarah, follow his instructions for he is a skilled therapist even if he hasn't found his match in a woman to settle his flirtatious nature." Nurse Castillo spoke to Sarah, ignoring Lupe's theatrics.

Sarah laughed at their banter. "I can tell that you two are old friends and I have already given Lupe my promise to work hard. Would you do me a favor Nurse Castillo?"

"What is it?" Nurse Castillo stopped at the door held open by Lupe.

"Would you see if you can stop the services of my other nurses Teresa and Carmelita? They have been very good to me, but someone else may be in greater need of their skills."

Nurse Castillo replied, "I am not so sure your Fillip thinks their skills are so poorly used, but I will contact Señora Hernaneles to see what I can do. Is there anything else?"

Sarah blushed noticeably because she knew what Nurse Castillo would think but she asked anyway. "Do you think we could have my hair cleaned? Señora Hernaneles sent over my suitcase last night and it would be so refreshing to be in my own things with my hair done."

"I will speak with the doctor and see if I can call beauty services for you." She looked Sarah directly in the eyes. "But, when someone you love is hurt and is recovering, you do not look at such things."

Sarah straightened up in the bed and argued. "But, it needs cleaned badly, and getting it done will make me feel better. Don't you think that will please Fillip?"

Nurse Castillo laughed and left through the open door. "Be gentle with her, Lupe. She has been through much and her pain medication is not strong."

Nurse Castillo knew Sarah was in excellent hands for Fillip had arranged for the best of health care professionals. However, she had become attached to Sarah and she intended to meet Fillip. It was the least she could do with Sarah's mother so far away. Yes, indeed, Fillip had better prove himself to be the right man for her Sarah.

Lupe closed the door behind Nurse Castillo and went to Sarah's bed. "This morning we are going to let you stay in the bed, and I will help you stretch your leg and arm muscles, then do some new exercises with you. Nurse Castillo will also work with you on these exercises. Then, I will get you a wheelchair and take you down to see the therapy room, introduce you to some of the other patients, and we will use some of the equipment there."

"Let's get started." Sarah responded with an eager heart. Lupe was gentle but the exercises even on her uninjured limbs continued to make her ache. He moved her injured limb to loosen the lower uninjured part, and gently tested her hip and upper leg. He helped her move to a chair and massaged her back and shoulders.

"What is it, Sarah? I am sorry it was painful. We could see about stronger pain medication."

"Oh, Lupe, it's not the pain. It's me. Somehow I thought my limbs would just do better." Sarah felt herself near tears with utter frustration over her stupidity and the lack of her body's function.

"Sarah, look at me." He knelt so she could look at him. "I have been a therapist for seven years. The injuries to your leg means a recovery period of three to six months before you will walk without assistance. Even then you may limp and there will be days of pain. You must not be hard on yourself. If you are to get better, you must maintain your positive attitude. A baby does not jump from its mother's lap and start to walk. You must learn to walk again with a hip and a leg that was reconstructed. Even your uninjured joints have grown weak through inactivity. But, you will get better each day." Lupe's eyes were dark brown and sincere. He waited for her to weigh his words.

Sarah finally responded, "I am sorry to give you a difficult time. I just wanted to be able to leave the hospital and go home. I saw myself walking out on crutches. Maybe you should give me a more realistic goal." Sarah's smile returned.

Lupe was pleased at the return of Sarah's good nature. "By the end of the week you should have a walker, but you will not be able to go far with it. You can only use it in a single room with a nearby bath. As for when you can go home, that depends upon the doctor. A long plane trip would be difficult and painful for some weeks yet. But, for today how about a wheelchair ride down to therapy before lunch? I will introduce you to the parallel bars."

"Ok, you got it." Lupe stood, and Sarah laughed at Lupe's puzzled raised eyebrow. "It's an expression. The children in my Sunday school class say it all the time. It means you have my full cooperation."

"Sí." Lupe nodded his head in acceptance and went for the wheelchair.

The therapy facilities were a great surprise for Sarah. Like the rest of the hospital, the room was old, but it showed recent remodeling. It was light and airy with the latest and best equipment. The surprise for Sarah was not in the facilities but in the dedication of the staff and the clients she met. Even from a wheelchair Sarah's injuries paled in comparison to some of the handicaps she saw others struggling to overcome.

Her heart was moved by a small boy with spina bifida who was learning to walk. His birth condition had been surgically corrected, but his legs were nearly useless. His upper body was being developed so that with the use of leg braces and arm crutches he would be able to mobilize his legs. With each step he successfully managed, he looked at them and grinned. The therapist and the child's mother always smiled and congratulated his successes. Sarah was also impressed by a man who had become a double amputee in a recent train accident. There was no bitterness in any of the people she saw.

Once as a child, Sarah remembered, she wanted an expensive pair of shoes like those of a girl in her class. Father had tried to explain they could not indulge her whim and she had been hurt. He told her of a man who had envied his friend's shoes, until he remembered that his neighbor had no feet. Sarah did not understand the story until now. How fortunate she was to have had her limb restored, no matter how much work and patience it took to have it whole again. Sarah was not afraid of the work, but she knew she would have to pray for patience.

When Lupe returned Sarah to her room Nurse Castillo was waiting to scold Lupe. "Well, you certainly took your time with her. Now her lunch is cold."

Sarah quickly spoke to save the two their friendly duel. "I am afraid it is my fault. I was reluctant to leave when I saw so much courage. I am sure that is why Lupe showed me the therapy room. I cannot think myself so poorly used or alone in my struggle to walk again."

Lupe beamed at Sarah as he and Nurse Castillo settled her into the lounge chair. "Gracias, Sarah. You have done well. Enjoy your lunch." To Nurse Castillo he said, "Please continue to exercise Sarah's limbs as you have time. Have a good day."

Nurse Castillo `hmpd' the closing door. "Well, let's see you do justice to your lunch?"

"Can I have my hair done?" Sarah excitedly asked as she looked over her lunch tray. "Oh, and will the other nurses be reassigned?"

"Sí, child, settle down and eat. Señora Hernaneles agreed to be responsible for relieving the other nurses when I told her that you could be easily handled by the regular staff. But I will be with you until you leave."

Sarah felt like a child opening presents and receiving all that she asked. She was especially grateful that Nurse Castillo would remain with her. After eating a respectable amount of lunch under Nurse Castillo watchful eye, Sarah had her hair carefully capped washed, dried, and curled by a hairdresser. Nurse Castillo then helped her to change into her own gown and worn comfortable robe. Sarah slept comfortably in her bed from exhaustion and pain medication after the morning's events.

Nurse Castillo did not awaken Sarah when her shift ended, but she made sure the floor nurses were aware of the shift in the responsibilities for Sarah's care. The minutes stretched into hours and the afternoon shadows fell across Sarah's sleeping form.

As Sarah's sleep lightened, she became aware of the shadow that had haunted her semiconscious moments in the SICU. Calling upon her inner strength, Sarah inhaled deeply and turned to the window to confront the shadow. Even before she was fully awake, Sarah recognized the fragrance and knew the shadow was not Death or a comforting angel but a very alive Fillip. She took in Fillip's masculine form and giggled as she realized the trick her mind had played. Fillip quickly turned, and his grim demeanor opened into an engaging smile.

"Sarah?"

Fillip could only breathe her name for he found it incredulous that she could be vibrant and giggling. She was barely aware when he last saw her in the SICU.

"Sarah, mi querida, what is it?" Fillip walked closer to her bed.

Sarah sobered as she looked at Fillip's features that had become haggard by work and worry. "I am sorry, Fillip, I shouldn't have giggled at the man I owe my life and so much more to, but it was so nice to see you there, instead of the shadow of you I remember from SICU."

Fillip took Sarah's hand and stroked her fingers tenderly. "You owe me nothing, Sarah. The doctors have told me that you were doing quite well, and Gail said the same. But, I am glad to see you for myself."

Sarah removed her hand from Fillip's hold and reached up to touch his care worn face. "Fillip, you have seen to my welfare by somehow making me your wife and providing amply for my care. I owe you a debt that cannot be paid with mere words. And, I can see in your face that you have not cared well for yourself. If these lines on your face have been caused by me, then I owe you a debt I can't repay."

Fillip's eyes watered, and he took Sarah's hand and kissed her palm. "Mi querida, your words are kind and I do not deserve them or your concern. Your spirit is so gentle, and I can see that you have already forgiven me."

"Forgiven you?" Sarah's eyes searched his face for an answer. "Why you would need my forgiveness."

Fillip took her hands. "Sarah, do you not remember?

"Remember? Forgive you? What could you have done to need my forgiveness? I was a little more than a stranger when I was injured, and you came forward and took on the responsibility of my care. You left nothing undone and you were even extravagant in seeing to my well-being and comfort."

Fillip's heart raced inside his chest with near madness. She didn't seem to know or remember. How would he tell her so that she would not hate him? "Sarah, mi dulce Sarah, the accident—do you not remember that I was driving? I caused the accident and your life-threatening injuries." Fillip rushed on. "I tried, Sarah, I tried so hard to stop, but the car slid!" Fillip stopped as the deep trauma of the accident overwhelmed him.

Sarah saw his pain and quickly pulled him into her arms and comforted him against her chest. Her fingers caressed his thick hair and the scent of his shampoo filled her nostrils. "Oh, Fillip, you aren't to blame. I was daydreaming and stepped into the alley without looking."

Sarah lifted his head gently with the palms of her hands and studied his eyes. "No one could have stopped. It never mattered to me who was driving the car, until now. It saddens me to know that it was you, only because it has caused you so much distress."

Fillip looked deep into Sarah's eyes, as if to search her heart. "You are not angry? You forgive me?"

Fillip's masculine strength and sensuality were returning. Sarah no longer saw him as a man in need of comfort. She released him and smiled brightly before she answered. "No, I am not angry, and, I will forgive you only if you will forgive me for all that I have put you through."

"Sarah, mi querida, how can you be so badly injured and ask my forgiveness?" Fillip was incredulous.

Sarah leaned toward Fillip and tentatively touched the back of his hand. "Then, neither of us needs forgiveness and we can be—" Sarah searched for the right word "friends?"

Sarah's earlier comfort and now her hand on his heightened Fillip's desires, he wanted to pull her close, lay his head against hers, stroke her hair, and then bring her lips to his lips for a light touch, a light taste, and a gentle first caress. But he held himself back. He had already scared Sarah away and he did not want to overwhelm her with open desire. So, he took her hand and kissed the back of several of her fingers. "Very special friends."

The air was heavy with unspoken desire and Sarah caught in her breath and was spared the need to respond by the arrival of her dinner tray.

Chapter 7

Fillip excused himself to go make a few phone calls while Sarah had her dinner. He first went to the nurses' station to inquire after Doctor Rubio, who had left for the day. It took him only a few minutes to convince the nurses to page the doctor. When Doctor Rubio returned his phone call, the nurses gave Señor Castañola the privacy of the station's inner-office and they conversed in Spanish.

"Dr. Rubio, thank you for calling. Sarah seems to be doing as well as I have been told. I am grateful."

"She has done well since leaving SICU, and I believe we can expect her up using a walker in a few days. Her attitude has been most unusual and refreshing and has speeded her recovery."

"When do you expect to see her released from the hospital?" Fillip questioned.

"Normally she would go home as soon as she mastered the walker, then come back for physical therapy until she could be released from care. If she will return to America, a few extra days in the hospital would be in order. She will be able to physically tolerate the trip better." Once she is back in the States, any orthopedic doctor could oversee her therapy and follow-up treatment. Within six months, I would imagine she will be completely recovered."

Fillip's response was quick and intense. "What makes you think she will be going back to America? I will remind you that she is my wife now and will be going home with me." Fillip raked his hand through his hair and composed himself. "Sorry. I have been very concerned for her recovery. What I want to know is what I need to do to make her as comfortable as possible when she comes home with me. And, I want to make arrangements for her therapy to be done at our home as well."

"I am sorry Señor Castañola. I thought she would be returning to America given the sudden circumstances of your marriage."

"Sí, Sí I understand. The accident was the catalyst for the suddenness of our marriage, but Sarah is my wife now and I will see to her needs. Our relationship is complicated, but for now, tell me what I must do to set up our home for her comfort and therapy."

Doctor Rubio outlined the need for Sarah to move about without having to use stairs, and he committed himself to assisting Fillip in arranging for the equipment needed for home therapy so that Sarah could be home within a few days. Doctor Rubio did not want to offend Fillip. He and his family had endowed a cardiac unit for their hospital.

Fillip had a great many arrangements that needed to be made so he returned to Sarah for only a few moments. He opened her room door narrowly to be sure not to intrude with any professional care. She was alone, her dinner tray gone, and she was sitting in a recliner. Fillip wanted to rush in and take her in his arms. Resisting the desire, he spoke lightly as he approached.

"Sarah, mi querida, I find that I must leave to attend to some business matters." He picked up her hand and stroked it gently as he raised it to his lips for a kiss. "Forgive me for leaving you so abruptly."

Sarah found her heart racing at his touch, but she didn't blush at his flirting. Instead she found she was saddened and disappointed that he was leaving. "Must you leave? Can't you stay a few more minutes? Time passes so slowly here in the hospital."

Sarah didn't realize her face had taken on a forlorn and a rather hard to resist womanly pout. "Sarah, you tempt me more than you know. I must leave, but, I will come back tomorrow at lunch and bring you a special dessert that no one prepares better than my housekeeper."

Sarah's face dramatically changed to a warm smile. "I don't want to put your housekeeper to any trouble."

"It will be no trouble, if it brings another smile to your face, mi querida." He knelt beside her chair and brought her hand to his lips. He held it there in an extended kiss that caused Sarah's heart to flutter and ache at the thought of his leaving. But, she knew she had no right to detain him. Fillip looked at her intently, eye to eye, as if there was more to be said or done but he said nothing more before he rose. He paused at the open door and looked back at her, and only quietly said, "mañana", and was gone.

Momentarily Sarah was sad, but then she started to look for joy, as had become her habit when things weren't going her way. The evening hours stretched before her, but she refused to allow herself to be depressed. When she pressed her call buzzer, she was delighted that nurse could speak English. She asked for help with her personal needs, and she had her retrieve a notebook from her night case once she was settled back in her bed.

Sarah updated her journal since her last entry. She wrote about Jesús' visit, confirming his salvation. Her heart filled with joy and she praised God once again for allowing her to be a part of Jesús salvation.

She wrote about the accident in a few short sentences and dwelled more on the people she had met. The best part of her hospital days she realized was the sweet anticipation of getting well and going home. She wrote about her visit with Fillip and was surprisingly more comfortable with her thoughts about him. But she did not tell the journal about how she felt about him. The feelings were new to her and they were growing rapidly, and she couldn't write about what she didn't understand.

Putting the journal aside Sarah wrote her mother a letter to assure her of her progress and in the letter, she indicated she would soon be coming home. She wanted so much to see her mother, yet the more she thought of not being in Spain the more she became aware of a special sadness. She had been in Spain for less than a month with too much of the time spent in the hospital and, yet she was beginning to think of Spain as a second home.

Sarah finished her letter and placed it in her journal. In the morning, she hoped Nurse Castillo would post it for her. One of the shift nurses came in with her medication and helped her prepare for bed. Sarah still felt at odds with her dependence on others for such matters and resolved to regain control of her own care as quickly as possible. The evening was passing quickly and quietly so Sarah removed her Bible from the nightstand and opened it to Psalms 46. She loved having her own things. She read the passage almost without looking at the words because they were so familiar to her.

The passage was David's prayer to the Lord in a time of trouble. Sarah found that these verses had a special meaning for her on this night. Closing her Bible, she returned it to the nightstand to meditate on the words prior to praying. But, tonight the peace that filled her mind and healing body lulled her to sleep, so she did not pray.

Nurse Castillo arrived for her morning shift and spent a few moments watching her young patient sleep. Asleep it was impossible to tell how badly she was injured, except for the pallor of her skin and the weight she had lost. Awake her injuries seemed to be more an annoyance to her rather than a problem and she did not complain about them or the pain she experienced. Nurse Castillo thought about the remarkable young woman she had come to love. How very much she was the picture of the Christ, she held so dear. Or perhaps Sarah was the cracked vessel she claimed to be that shone with the light of the Savior to a dark, lost, and dying world.

Nurse Castillo was a faithful practicing Catholic and yet since she had become Sarah's nurse she had stopped to look at her relationship with God. She stopped her musing and gently touched her sleeping patient to start their day together.

"Sarah, it is time to be up. Breakfast will arrive soon and then that scoundrel, Lupe, will be here to take you to your therapy."

Sarah stretched her limbs and tried to waken. "Good morning, Nurse Castillo, I wonder why it is that if I were at home my Mother would insist on my sleeping in. Something like, you need your rest to get better. And, here short of a coma you have me up at dawn so that you can prepare me to go to Lupe's torture chamber."

Nurse Castillo laughed and answered, "Mothers are known to coddle their children. Here we must make you work to help you get better. And, it was dawn when I got up. Now, half the morning is gone."

Sarah laughed too, and Nurse Castillo took her vitals and helped with her morning toilet. Together, they then managed to seat Sarah in the recliner so that she could have her breakfast out of bed. Then, they had a little time before Lupe came so Nurse Castillo pulled up a chair to chat.

"So, now tell me about your visit with your Fillip, Sarah."

"There's not much to tell you. He's the wonderful handsome man I remember." Sarah evenly replied.

"Then he doesn't make your pulse race anymore? Nurse Castillo chided.

Sarah blushed. "I think you know me too well. I do find Fillip appealing. I just don't understand why."

"This is a thing of the heart and body. They call it chemistry. I do not think that we can understand or control it. But, you must be careful, so that you are not foolish and get hurt. He is a man of experience, I fear. And, you, you are an innocent lamb."

"Fillip doesn't want to hurt me." Sarah remembered holding the sorrowful Fillip when he told her of his part in the accident. "Did you know that Fillip was the driver of the car that hit me?"

Nurse Castillo was aghast. "Oh, how horrible for him! No wonder he has been so concerned and has assumed the position of your husband." Nurse Castillo thought for a moment. "Still, I will say guard your heart, child. The bonds that have brought you together are strange, but they may strengthen if you are drawn to him because of his—manly charms. Sí?"

"Nurse Castillo, I should like for you to meet my Mother. You do not look or sound like her, but you have her heart and you give sound advice. I will guard my heart with Fillip. I am a child of the King and I can only give my heart and myself to the man He would choose. And, Fillip certainly would seek someone better suited to his needs than an inexperienced young American.

Besides, if you recall my home is in the States and that is where I will be going soon." Sarah sighed and smiled. The smile was more to encourage her belief in what she was saying rather than to reassure Nurse Castillo. "He has just been very kind, and he can't help how I feel."

"Then I shall make it a point to meet this man and see for myself." Nurse Castillo sat back and folded her arms against her ample chest in a protective gesture.

"Mother will be glad to know that you are on my personal case as well as my physical one. But, I will have to tell her in my next letter because I have already closed the one I wrote last night. It's in my journal in the nightstand. Could you get an envelope and mail it for me today? I haven't any money as my purse must be with my other things."

"I will post your letter and not be concerned for the postage. And, I might just add a note." Nurse Castillo smiled mischievously, and Sarah couldn't ask what she meant as Lupe unceremoniously opened the door and came in to retrieve her.

Nurse Castillo jumped up immediately and carefully watched as

Lupe transferred Sarah to a wheelchair. They shared their usual banter.

Sarah didn't mind going to her therapy session. After yesterday's therapy with Lupe, she had developed a rapport with him. She had already learned that he flirted with every female and that he used his charm to finagle what he wanted from the old and young. Today, she would soon discover that he was a demanding therapist who could use her desire to get better to make her give just a little more each time despite her pain.

Lupe only spoke of worldly things without any religious beliefs coming though as she worked with him. On their way back from therapy, Lupe greeted everyone they came across with his congenial air. Sarah rode quietly as she was very tired and sore. She listened to Lupe's bantering and decided that he needed to focus his life on God instead of partying. By the time they reached her door, Sarah thought of him as the brother she had always wanted, and she added him to her list of those who needed her prayers.

Back in her room, Nurse Castillo quickly assessed Sarah's state and lashed out at Lupe. "Now just look at her, all flushed and sweaty. It's one thing to give her a good therapy session but she looks as if you are trying to prepare her for the Olympics."

"Now Nurse Castillo, Sarah has worked hard and, needs your tender care, but you wouldn't want me to deny you the privilege of tending to our star patient." Lupe bantered lightly as he helped Sarah into the recliner.

"You need not tell me my job, young man. But, next time offer her a cool cloth to wipe her face or a least a little water to keep her from dehydrating. Now get on with you."

"As you wish, lovely lady. Mañana, Sarah. You have done well."

Sarah sighed, but she smiled and answered. "Sí, Lupe, mañana."

Nurse Castillo poured Sarah a glass of cool water from her bedside pitcher and placed her noon medication in the palm of her hand before she went into the bathroom to fill a basin with warm water. She gave Sarah a sponge bath.

"Such a sight you were. It is a good thing that Fillip does not see you so worn out. Now you rest before your lunch comes." Nurse Castillo covered Sarah's lap with a folded blanket and Sarah gratefully sank back in the chair with a low moan to rest and allow the pain medication to ease the cries of the thousands of nerve endings that were now protesting her morning therapy.

Sarah smiled dreamily. The morning workout had left her with little time to think about Fillip's planned visit. "Nurse Castillo can you bring me my night case, please. I want to comb through my hair and put on a little make-up."

Nurse Castillo crossed the room to retrieve the night case. "You aren't prettying yourself up for me." She teased. "You wouldn't be expecting a visit from Fillip, now would you?"

Sarah blushed, "He said that he would bring me a special dessert when he left last night."

Nurse Castillo returned with the night case, opened it up and got out a comb. "Good. I need to see him for myself."

Sarah took the comb and looked closely at her favorite nurse and foster mother. "What are you going to say to him?"

The light in Nurse Castillo's eyes twinkled and she laughed. "Nothing your mother wouldn't say." Nurse Castillo moved away to clean up Sarah's bath things while Sarah finished her hair. Sarah's lunch came, and Nurse Castillo left for her own lunch with a word of admonition.

"Now make sure he doesn't leave before I have a chance to see him."

"When he comes, I will tell him to run, if he sees you." The women laughed but silently Sarah worried that Nurse Castillo might behave more the mother than the nurse if she saw Fillip.

Chapter 8

Sarah's appetite was now diminishing with each hospital meal she ate. She enjoyed Spanish food, but hospital food was hospital food. She ate the chicken soup, salad and nibbled at the meat course but she avoided the pudding in favor of what she expected. She then rang to have the tray removed before the careful eyes of her nurse would see her tray and scold her. Her morning therapy tired her greatly and she wished she could be back in bed, so she could have a little nap.

However, she didn't want Fillip to find her asleep for fear he wouldn't stay. The pillows Nurse Castillo had installed around her were more than comfortable and resting her eyes allowed her to doze. When Nurse Castillo returned, she found her patient asleep, so she quietly slipped into the chair opposite Sarah's and read a book she had with her.

Fillip had intended to bring the promised dessert at the appropriate hour. However, his prolonged absences from the office had put him behind and he was late. When he arrived, he gently knocked on the door before entering. Nurse Castillo immediately knew who it must be. She went quickly to the door, motioned for him to be quiet and to step back outside the door.

"So, you have come at last, Señor Castañola." She continued to speak as she eyed the dessert cup in Fillip's hand. "I am Nurse Marguerite Castillo and I am glad you brought the dessert you promised. It is not good to make promises to a patient and not keep them. But, lunch is long past, and she is asleep."

Fillip looked at Nurse Castillo and did not take offense at the position she was taking in defense of her patient. "It is good to meet you. I can see why you came so highly recommended. I am late, and I will apologize to Sarah. But, it could not be helped, and I do have the promised dessert. Would it not be bad to keep the visitor and dessert away from the patient since we were both promised? I will not stay long."

Fillip caught Nurse Castillo when he played on the importance she placed on keeping promises. Still Nurse Castillo slowly looked him over to make her regard for her patient silently understood. "Yes, I believe she would be disappointed if she did not get her—dessert."

Nurse Castillo avoided telling him that Sarah was excited to see him, but she added a word of caution. "I know you understand that she has been through a serious trauma. But, perhaps you are not aware that she is a very special young Christian woman who is naive about the real world. It would not be good for anyone to hurt her, not even her *husband*."

Nurse Castillo's meaning was clear. Fillip picked up her hand and kissed it for emphasis. "No one wants to protect her more than I do, I promise."

Fillip passed through the door, stood, and took stock of what had been said and implied. While his thoughts were elsewhere, his eyes traveled to Sarah. He wanted to kiss her awake. But, he held himself in check and walked silently over to the guest chair and quietly seated himself.

Sarah's senses had become sensitive to his presence, the essence of the man and she stirred in her sleep. Fillip was startled when she suddenly opened her eyes and smiled warmly at him. Despite the joy she felt at seeing him and the dulling effects of just awakening, Sarah warned herself that there could be no future for them. Still she seemingly couldn't help herself when they were together.

"Oh, Fillip, I'm sorry. I must have fallen asleep. You should have wakened me."

"Sarah." Fillip half-whispered her name and picked up her right hand to stroke her fingers. "It is I who am sorry, for I have only just come, and it is nearly three o'clock. But, I come bearing natilla made especially for you by my housekeeper." He showed her a crystal dessert glass containing its whipped smooth custard from the bed table where he had set it.

Sarah's delight made her look like a child receiving a special gift and the look forged another link in the chain that Sarah was unknowingly wrapping around Fillip's heart. He uncovered the glass and handed it to her and she dipped her finger in it and licked it for a quick sample. "Mm, it is marvelous and even better than the hostel's."

Fillip produced a linen wrapped monogrammed spoon from his inside breast pocket, ceremoniously spread the linen napkin over her lap and placed the spoon in her hand. Sarah giggled over his deliberate formality as he smoothed the napkin into place.

"Then I am forgiven for being tardy, mi querida?"

"Certainly!" Sarah responded as she dipped her spoon into the dessert and properly took a bite. "How could I not forgive you, when I know that you are busy, and I am eating this delightful treat? Besides if you had come earlier, I would have been poor company since I was tired from my therapy. A dessert like this deserves to be eaten well after a meal to do it justice."

Shyly Sarah lifted a spoon full of the confection up to Fillip's lips. Fillip was delighted by her gesture and he permitted her to feed him the bite. It gave him hope that Sarah could be brought to respond to him the way he desired.

"What is your housekeeper's name, Fillip? I must write her a thank-you note."

"Her name is Carmen and her husband is Ramón. They are the couple I employ to manage my house. There is no need to write her a thank-you note. She is my servant and she was told to make the dessert."

"Oh Fillip! I must respectively disagree. As employees or servants, we all have one thing in common. We are all people with a full range of emotions. If you had asked her to make the dessert, would she not have made it?"

"Sí, ask or tell. It's the same."

"Wrong! Asking gives us the option to refuse, which we wouldn't. Ordering is too uncaring. As people, we want to be treated fairly and pleasantly with a fair amount of gratitude for a job well done. Then, you not only make an exceptional employee but a very loyal one as well. As an employer if you treat me, an employee, with kindness and respect, I will always give my best."

Fillip had lost his romantic demeanor at Sarah's chiding, and sharply asked. "Is this the way Americans deal with their employees?"

"No. But it is the Christ-like way to deal with employees. That is why I want to thank Carmen for making such a delightful dessert, a real Spanish treat, not something Americanized. I want to praise her expertise in preparing it."

"Alright, if it is what you want." Fillip did not care for her viewpoint, but a simple note was not worth further discussion.

"I have a notebook in my nightstand drawer. If you could get it, please, it will only take a moment to write a note."

Fillip stood and went around the bed to the nightstand to get her notebook. He noted that it was a cheap spiral affair as he handed it to her.

Sarah uncertain of his mood quietly said, "Thank you."

Fillip nodded and went to stand by the window. Sarah wrote her note and eyed Fillip periodically. She had made him angry and it saddened her more than she could understand. She wanted to make things right, but she didn't know how to go about it.

"Fillip, I've finished and I'm sorry if I offended you."

Upon hearing Sarah, Fillip turned and swiftly returned to kneel at her side. "I'm not offended. I'm just not use to having a woman offer me advice."

"It's not advice. I wasn't telling you what to do. It's just the way I live and how I treat other people." Fillip was caressing her hand between his own hands and an idea crossed Sarah's mind and she smiled. "But that means I need to thank you for bringing the dessert." Sarah teased. Should I write you a note, or will this do?"

Before he could answer, Sarah leaned over and kissed Fillip's cheek and as she slowly lifted her head, her cheek brushed his cheekbone and then his hair.

Sarah had intended the kiss to lighten the mood and restore his good humor. But, instead she felt flushed with a rush of overwhelming sensations and a part of her wanted a real kiss.

For Fillip, Sarah's unexpected kiss caught him unprepared and he stood up quickly and raked his hand through his hair. In another time, another place he would not have stopped himself, but Sarah was not just any woman, so he decided to leave.

"Sarah, mi querida," he made a point to look at his watch, "I am sorry to have to go but I am afraid business calls. Will you forgive me for coming late and leaving so quickly? I know you must be tired of being alone here in the hospital?"

Sarah looked up at Fillip and her eyelashes veiled her eyes and the mixed emotions they showed. "You must stop asking for my forgiveness when there is nothing to forgive. I understand your business comes first." Sarah raised her head and looked at him closely.

"I will always remember how you assumed the responsibility and the expense of my recovery and I know that you have been as generous with your time. As for my being alone, God has not left me friendless here in your country or in this hospital, but your company is always welcome."

Fillip saw a light in Sarah's eyes and assumed it was gratitude instead of blossoming love. He bent down and gently kissed Sarah's forehead and teased, "Then you won't mind if I come again tomorrow?"

Sarah brightened, "Not at all, and you don't even have to bribe me with a delicious dessert." She handed him the thank-you note, and the dessert cup and spoon wrapped in the napkin.

"Well then if no bribe is necessary to grant me an audience, I will be here." He bent and kissed her forehead again but this time his lips lingered. He quelled his desire to demand more. He turned and left the room, pausing at the door. And, with that almost breathless quality he had when he spoke her name he said, "Mañana, Sarah," and was gone.

Sarah sat back to take stock of their visit and was greatly puzzled as to how she had gone from complimenting the lovely dessert to angering him. Although Fillip had said he was not angry, his mood had changed. And, she questioned her own actions.

She had deliberately kissed him to attempt to restore his good humor. She chose to forgive herself just a little. He really wasn't a stranger anymore. No, not a stranger, not after all that they had been through, but she really had no right to judge his moods or to kiss him to cajole him into a different mood. She really had no right to kiss him for any reason, not that he took any notice of her kiss. And, that thought brought a scowl to her face.

Fortunately, Sarah's attempt to scrutinize and understand their visit was stopped by Nurse Castillo's return.

"It's late. I thought you might have left for today." Sarah brightened as she thought to tease her friend and nurse. "At any rate, you missed meeting Fillip."

"I met your Fillip and we have an understanding. I stayed until after he had left to be sure you got what I have for you, and to get my things."

"You saw Fillip?" Sarah bolted upright near the edge of her chair. "What does 'we have an understanding' mean...and, what do you have for me?"

Nurse Castillo raised her hand to stop her. "Too many questions, Sarah. The understanding is between me and Fillip. As for what I have for you, it is a letter from America. So, your mother has now written to you and I have mailed your letter to her." She walked over and dropped the letter into Sarah's lap and went over to pick up her things. "Now I can leave."

"But, you said you met Fillip. Tell me what you think of him?" Sarah gently asked.

"Read your letter, child. We can talk about Fillip tomorrow. And, get yourself some rest. The therapy will continue to wear you out." Nurse Castillo left without another word, although she shook her head in a negative gesture. Sarah was too young to understand she needed to pace her recovery and perhaps she was also too enamored by Fillip. At any rate, Nurse Castillo's knew her advice would not be well heeded, and she sighed as she signaled the elevator.

Sarah didn't ponder her visit with Fillip any longer, nor did she think of Nurse Castillo's reticence on the subject. Her hand held a letter from her Mother. As she opened it, the warmth of her Mother's presence flooded her with joy. Sarah looked at the handwriting and her eyes immediately misted.

My dearest child,

Forgive me for not coming. I feel as if I have neglected you because I have not been at your side, and, this was my decision because Fillip generously offered to fly me over to be with you. But, my dearest Sarah, I choose not to come as I could not be with you quickly enough. You had already had your first surgery. I feared I would be an additional burden to Fillip who has already undertaken the total responsibility of your care.

He appears to be a wonderful man. He has called me daily to tell me of your progress even when he was here in our country. I have thanked the Lord daily for Fillip, although I do not understand how he could be your husband. But, I praise our Father for His care of you and I have been comforted by the Holy Spirit from my first prayer since hearing of your accident. I have had faith that your recovery will be complete as the Father surely must have special plans for you. You have always been obedient in searching for and following His will.

I have always told you that I love you, but I have not told you of the pride that I have in the person you have become in Christ. I do not take the credit for your development but praise God for His goodness in grooming your character.

So, I pray, my sweet child that you will forgive me for not coming to you. For truly, I would have crossed the ocean to be with you if I would not have been an additional liability. I love you and do want to be with you. I look forward to your being home. Fillip has not yet said when you will be coming home. Do you have any idea yourself? And, please tell me if there are any special arrangements I need to make for your comfort. Let me hear from you soon. May the good Lord continue His care of us while we are apart.

Love you always, Mom

Dear Mother, Sarah thought, *forgive you? For what? I would have done the same, for I am your daughter. And, you are right in that Fillip has already given me, no us, so much. Oh Mother, I do wish you were here. Not to care for me, for the care I have received from the nurses, especially Nurse Castillo, has been more than you could have given me without wearing yourself out. I wish you were here so that I could hold you and say—I love you beyond the love of mother and daughter. I love you with the love that binds us together in Christ, across the years into eternity.*

I wish you were here to meet Fillip. I know you would like him. How could you not when he has been so kind to your only child? But, I find Mother that my feelings are going beyond gratitude and I am unsure of them. What would you tell me to do, if you were here?

Sarah smiled to herself. *I suppose I do know what you would say if you were here. You would say that I should listen to God. But, I am not a child any longer and my mind and body seem to be taking a course of their own when Fillip is near me. I kissed him today, Mother—just his cheek. Would you not have been shocked? Mother, dear sweet Mother, I want to follow God's will, to hear His voice. But, Mother how do I hear the voice of God, when Fillip makes my heart pound so loudly that its beating is all the sound that reaches my ears?*

Chapter 9

Sarah knew if her thoughts continued down their current path she would soon be in tears. So, she carefully folded her mother's letter and returned it to the envelope before slipping it between the pages of her Bible. As she returned the Bible to the side of her chair, a little well-worn card fell out. The card showed the three crosses of the crucifixion and lettered neatly in her Father's handwriting were the words. ***The will of God will never lead you to where the grace of God cannot keep you.***

Her father had given her the card the day she left for college. Somehow, the words on that card always lifted her spirits when she was uncertain. They fit more now than ever before, and for a moment her father was still offering her comfort. Sarah said a small *"thank you Lord"* and returned the card to her Bible. It was time to do something to distract herself.

Sarah pressed her call buzzer. She decided she should return to her bed as her body ached from sleeping in the chair. A nurse came promptly. Sarah was not a demanding patient and her physical needs and medications were easily met. Once the nurse got her settled in bed, she was once again alone with her thoughts.

Sarah stared restlessly out the window. It had been more than a week since she had been out in the fresh air and it appeared to be a lovely day. She watched the people who were coming and going from the hospital and she envied them for their freedom to move about. But, she did not envy their lives because she didn't know their relationship with God. It was just that she didn't know what God wanted her to do. She was just so uncertain. Her quiet simple life had hit an updraft and she couldn't see where she needed to land. She laughed at her thought. Gideon, looking for God's will, used a fleece. Was it too much to ask God for a little note?

Her only logical direction was to be a light during her convalescence. However, that was being complicated by her handsome benefactor. Without even saying his name, Fillip stole into her mind, and, in her mind's eye, his image formed. She smiled involuntarily as she instantly basked in the glow of a multitude of unnamed feelings. Unnamed feelings because she refused to recognize them as love in any form.

Sarah was self-schooled in the belief that sensible people do not fall in love with strangers who live in worlds outside their secure boundaries. Sarah flushed and turned to God. Her prayer was not elaborate, and she did not immediately recognize the answer she was looking for was the answer to her life-long prayer as well.

"Dear Father, the world is vast, and I am so small. What place, what plan do you have in mind for me?"

Her words were not audible as they came from her spirit and there was no closing amen. A less-than-a-minute-prayer that was not only quick, but honest and informal. A slight sound to her right drew her attention to the opened door. Sarah was drawn from her concerns to her visitor and dear friend, Jesús.

"Hola, Sarah. Have I come at a bad time?" He looked back into the hallway. "They are bringing out dinner trays. Should I come back later?"

"Jesús any time you come is a good time. The food here is not as good as the hostel's, so your company may make it easier to eat. Please come in. I really could use your company."

Jesús came in and stood beside her bed. "Are you feeling better?"

"Yes, my recovery is nothing short of a miracle." Sarah smiled. Jesús understood the smile was an acknowledgement of Sarah's faith in God's healing her. He smiled and nodded his agreement.

Sarah continued. "Please pull up the chair and visit with me. I really must be getting better. I am restless being confined to this room. Sometimes there seems to be just too much time and I get to thinking too much. Do you understand?"

"Sí, I think. You wish to go home. You are homesick?"

"No, not exactly, I do miss Mother, and, I certainly don't want to be here in the hospital. But, a part of me now will be just as homesick in

America when I leave here." Jesús looked confused.

"It sounds so ridiculous, don't even try to understand. Except to know that you," Sarah paused and hesitated as her mind pictured Fillip, "—and others here have been so good to me that, even though my Spanish is poor, and I wasn't born here, this is home now too. It's like moving into a new house. It is a little strange but exciting and wonderful."

"Perhaps God wants you to stay here." Jesús was thinking a little selfishly for he wanted Sarah to stay and be his friend and teacher. Jesús held Sarah in a place of great respect and he loved her as only a brother in Christ could. He did not wish to lose his new-found sister when he felt so dependent on her for his growth in Christ.

Sarah shook her head sadly. "It would be nice, if it were possible. But, I am an only child, Jesús. My mother needs me." A rueful laugh escaped from her throat. "Mother would never agree to live here. People get set in their ways as they grow older."

Jesús nodded his head in agreement.

"I know you didn't come here to hear me prattle. Tell me what is on your mind?"

"I am ashamed to say that I need your help. There seems to be so many things that I do not understand. Here you are, hurt and in a hospital and I come to ask your help when I should be helping you."

"Jesús, we are friends, and I have everything I need. And, when you visit me, it helps more than you know. Besides, I want to help you to grow in your Christian walk as much as you can before I go home. Tell me what you need to understand."

Before Jesús could start, Sarah's dinner tray arrived. "Let's see what I have tonight?" He waited while Sarah looked over her dinner and he bowed his head when she prayed.

"Dear Father, I thank you for this meal that has been brought before me. I ask you to be with those who prepare these meals and each of us who receive them. Let them bring nourishment to our bodies and grant us continued healing. You are Jehovah-rapha, the Lord that heals and we praise your Holy name. And, now Father, I pray that You will bless Jesús and our visit. He has become Your child. Open his mind to the truth and let him bind that truth in his heart. In Jesus' holy name and to bring God

glory. Amen."

Sarah smiled at Jesús and struck her fork into a bite of food. "Please tell me what is troubling you."

"When you prayed, you said that I was a child of God. But, I do not serve Him well. I have tried to tell my family and the people I work with about my salvation, but they just look at me strangely and my mother cried. She does not understand that I am not deserting the God of my upbringing but that I am now truly trying to serve Him. My boss has said if I want to keep my job that I must not distract my co-workers with my theology. Sarah, I want to run out on the street and tell everyone what you told me, so they too can belong to God. Yet, I cannot even convince my family or my co-workers."

Jesús' voice cracked with the burden he felt. "I have failed Sarah."

Sarah laid her fork aside and reached out to take Jesús hand. He stood and took Sarah's out-stretched hand and took in a deep breath to regain his composure. "Jesús, look at me. You haven't failed. Do you remember when you asked me how you could have a personal relationship with God?"

"Yes, of course. Then you led me to Christ, and, I have failed to lead anyone else."

"The day you were saved you fell in love with the God of love. You started a personal relationship with Him that is uniquely your own. But, it happened only because you sought Him. We all have a God-shaped void in us that only a personal relationship with God can fill, but until He is let into our lives, the void is an empty place in our hearts. People may try to fill the void in their lives with worldly things, pleasures of the flesh, alcohol or even by playing church, but only God can fill it and make them complete."

"Yes, Sarah, I understand. These are the things that we must save them from."

"No, we are called to model Christ in our lives, but only God opens their minds and their hearts to the truth."

Jesús let go of Sarah's hand and sat back in the chair. "I don't understand. We must not tell others about God?"

"Yes, Jesus Christ commissioned us to go and share the good news to a lost and dying world. But, Jesús we do not save them, God does it according to His time. You are experiencing "first love impatience". You want to share what you have found, but you can't force anyone to listen or take it. Everyone must choose Him in their own time. You can bring your guests the meals they've ordered, but you can't make them eat any of it. Yes?"

"Yes, but, Sarah since we can't save them, not even make them listen or understand, then they will die in their sins." Jesús looked grief-stricken. "How can I accept this?"

"This is the burden He gives us, and we share it with all who are His children. When I came to your hostel, I didn't run in and tell you about God. You wouldn't have accepted it. But, God opened your eyes and prepared your heart over your life time. Then He brought me into your life when you were ready. It was a divine appointment set by our loving Creator."

"Now that you are His, you must live so that others can see Him in you. You'll pray for your family and friends, and when they are ready, you or someone else will be there for them. I know you want to save the world; but remember even when Christ was here on earth there were those who refused Him."

Jesús relaxed and smiled sadly. "You are right, Sarah. People did reject Christ then. I will pray and model Christ at all times."

"That's our commission, to go and tell. The plan of salvation is opened to anyone who will call upon the name of Jesus Christ."

Jesús shook his head ruefully. "But, they must call, and many will not. It is still a very sad thing."

Sarah was quiet for a moment; she understood Jesús' grief over those who would never accept the truth. Then she said, "But we do have hope, and many will be saved. And, there is something else those who are saved have in the Lord."

"What, Sarah?" Jesús asked expectantly.

"We each have gifts of the spirit."

"Sarah, I know Jesus had special gifts and performed many miracles and His disciples did too, but that was then, in Bible times."

"That's another one of Satan's bold-face lies. He wants us to believe the age of miracles has passed. The truth is God is still a God of miracles. Jesus and His disciples worked miracles in the land where they lived.

God still does miracles, and, He gives us spiritual gifts through His power to go into the entire world and share the gospel if we act on faith and in His authority."

Jesús sat astounded. "What are these gifts?

Sarah was thoughtful. "Each of us is given a spiritual gift, of that I am sure. But all of us do not have the spirit gift. You can look at the scriptures that deal with spiritual gifts in I Corinthians 12. There is a Spanish Bible in my drawer." Sarah waited for him to get the Bible. "You need to read the entire passage but for now look at 7-11 and read it for us."

Jesús read the scripture in Spanish and asked, "How can I know my gift?"

"The Apostle Paul tells us in I Corinthians we must earnestly seek to find our spiritual gifts. Hand me the notebook from the draw, and I will write down other scriptures you can read like Romans 12:6-8 and Ephesians 4:11. As you grow in Biblical knowledge, seek your gifts and they will be revealed to you. I can think of one already. You are bi-lingual, so you can share the gospel in more than one language. We all hear, read and learn best in our native language. Your job brings you into contact with a lot of people."

Jesús nodded his head in agreement. Understanding would come later, but for now he had enough to contemplate. Sarah's thought in her spirit how nice it would be if biblical knowledge could be easily transferred from one Christian to another when people got saved. Then, a thought was whispered into Sarah's mind.

"Jesús did you get a Bible for yourself to study?"

Jesús smiled broadly. "Yes, but I don't know where to start."

"Well, start with John and read through the rest of the New Testament before you start in Genesis and read it through for the first time. If you would like, I could mark some scriptures in your Bible for you."

"Sí, Sarah. I would like this very much. I could bring my Bible tomorrow after the early dinner seating."

"Good. That will give me a special project to do tomorrow night when I am alone."

Jesús stood up to leave. "Thank-you, Sarah." He looked at Sarah's dinner tray that she had hardly touched. "Oh, look what I have done."

Sarah was confused. "What have you done?"

"I spoiled your dinner and its cold. I'm sorry, Sarah."

"Well, you shouldn't be. Sometimes the food we eat needs to be spiritual food. You have fed my spirit by permitting me to share my faith. I was falling into a state of sadness before you came. Your visit has reminded me of my special relationship to spiritual blessings. God has put joy into each of our days and your visit is one of today's joys for me."

"I liked our visit but, if you do not mind me saying so, it seems to me that your body needs real food. You are very thin."

Sarah laughed. "Everyone says eat. But it's hard when it's hospital food."

Jesús thought for a minute. "Then, perhaps I should bring you hostel food."

"Oh, no, Jesús, I didn't mean to cause you to go to any trouble for me."

"We cater food from the hostel."

Sarah smiled. "The hostel's food *was* delicious. But if you want to bring me some, could you make it food for two, and eat with me? Eating hospital food is even worse when eating it alone."

A broad smiled broke across Jesús' face. "Yes. How do you Americans say it? You have a bargain?"

"You mean, we have a deal.'"

"Sí. We have a deal."

"Thank you, Jesús. Would you do one more thing for me before you go?"

"Yes, Sarah, anything."

"Pray with me."

"You want me to pray aloud? I don't think that I can."

Sarah reached her hand out to her friend. "Yes, you can. Take my hand and pray for us. God does not honor prayers that are eloquent, but prayers that are sincere and after His will.

"I will try." Jesús prayed and God was pleased.

Chapter 10

Jesús' visit had reinvigorated Sarah and given her something to do outside herself. She spent the evening reading verses marked in her Bible and listed the ones she would mark in Jesús' Bible. In her quiet time, she asked the Lord to bless Jesús in his Christian walk and to appoint a special person to disciple him. She thanked Him for the joy she had felt when she was sharing with Jesús. At the close of visiting hours, the nurses helped her settle down for the night, and she thought about her forthcoming hostel dinner before she slept.

In the morning, Nurse Castillo was again there to help with her morning toilet and prepare her for therapy. She ate her breakfast gratefully, because she had eaten so little the night before. Even the anticipation of the visits of her two most favorite men in Spain didn't repress her appetite. After she was settled into a wheelchair to await the arrival of Lupe, she talked with her dear companion.

"Today is a special day for me." Sarah joyously shared.

"Why is that?" Nurse Castillo asked.

"I have a dinner date tonight."

"Has Dr. Rubio given Fillip permission to take you out of the hospital for dinner?"

Sarah giggled like a school girl. "No, I'm not leaving the hospital and my dinner companion isn't Fillip."

"Who's your dinner companion?"

"He's not anyone you've met but you would like him. He's a waiter from the hostel where I stayed. We became good friends at the end of my stay there because I was privileged to guide him to Christ. He has come to visit me and has taken pity on my need for food not prepared in a hospital kitchen. So tonight, he's bringing dinner for two to my room."

"It's nice that you have made a friend here in Spain. Has Fillip met him?" Nurse Castillo spoke as she pulled up a chair near Sarah's wheelchair.

Nurse Castillo's question caused a frown to appear on Sarah's face. She hadn't thought that Fillip's proposed visit might come as the same time as her dinner with Jesús. "Jesús and Fillip have never been here at the same time, so they haven't met. But I know they would be friends."

Nurse Castillo shook her head at Sarah. "I wouldn't be so sure your husband would so quickly accept this male friend of yours."

"Now Nurse Castillo, you know that Fillip is not really my husband. Jesús and I have no romantic notion about the other. Like so many I am a tourist who will be gone soon. We have a bond as children of God. But I'm afraid if they both came at dinner time, things could be awkward. Dinner for two will only go so far."

"No, it wouldn't be an easy situation." Nurse Castillo was not sure dinner made for two would be the problem. She suspected that Fillip would not like another man to be one of the two. She had met Fillip only briefly, but she was sure, Sarah was more to the man than her benefactor. "How do you plan to avoid the situation?"

Sarah reflected on the predicament. She had no idea what Fillip's schedule might be, so she couldn't predict his arrival. Her only recourse was to tell him about her dinner plans and ask if he might be able to come earlier in the day. She looked at Nurse Castillo who was still waiting for a response. "Perhaps while I'm in therapy you could call Fillip's office, and tell him about my dinner plans, and ask if it's possible for him to come earlier."

"Sí, I can call him, if that's what you want?" Nurse Castillo was not sure Fillip would be happy to work around Sarah's dinner plans.

"Yes. It's for the best. There simply wouldn't be enough food and I can't ask for more to be provided."

"No. I suppose you couldn't ask your friend to bring a third serving." Nurse Castillo smiled. Nurse Castillo speculated that Fillip wouldn't mind Sarah having a catered meal. However, she believed he would have a problem with her sharing it with an unknown male friend.

Sarah leaned back in her wheelchair and was content that she had made the right decision. She wanted to see Fillip with all her heart, but she also wanted to continue her friendship with Jesús. Sharing her

Christian experience with Jesús was critical since she would soon be able to communicate with him through letters. They had developed a sweet Christian fellowship that was as important to Jesús' Christian growth as it was to Sarah's need to be useful.

Nurse Castillo watched Sarah as she contemplated her own thoughts. Sarah was a sweet young woman and she was grateful she had been assigned to her. Sarah's faith and depth of love for God had made her look at her own life. She had become too practiced with her religion, and now her heart and spirit had been renewed.

When Lupe came whistling through the door, he was unaware he was interrupting a very ponderous silence. "Good morning, Sarah and Nurse Castillo how are the two prettiest ladies in the hospital today?"

"We are ready for you, Lupe. See to it you don't overwork my patient." Nurse Castillo picked up her bag and turned to Sarah. "I will make your phone call for you now."

"Thank you."

Nurse Castillo gave a nod of her head and walked past Lupe as she left the room.

Sarah looked to Lupe. "Good morning, Lupe, shall we go?

Lupe's congenial smiled quickly came to his face. "But of course, fair lady! Your wish is my command." He started to whistle a tune as they went to therapy but stopped at the therapy room door.

"Sarah, I know you are working hard at therapy, but you must not overdo. Nurse Castillo spends more time with you than I do, and I trust her professional judgment. If what I ask is too much, you must tell me. Ok?"

"Of course. But, I really want to get strong enough to use a walker, so I can go home."

Lupe opened the door to the therapy room. "You will get strong enough, Sarah, but if we do more harm than good, you will be delayed in getting to use a walker. You may even require more surgery."

Sarah shuddered at Lupe's last comment. She didn't reply as a chorus of therapy patients greeted their arrival.

Sarah was careful during therapy and she wasn't as exhausted as she had been the day before. However, she was still quite sore and was pleased to see Nurse Castillo when she returned to her room. Nurse

Castillo gave Sarah her pain medication and assisted her with her personal needs while the medication took effect.

"Nurse Castillo is it possible for me to stay in the wheelchair? I thought after lunch, we might be able to go for a walk in the hospital garden."

Nurse Castillo looked at her closely. "Do you really want to go for a walk in the park or are you in too much pain to be moved from the wheelchair?

Sarah laughed lightly. "I really want to get out of this hospital, but since I can't go home, a trip to the garden would be nice."

Nurse Castillo nodded her head. "Alright, it's very nice outside. But you won't be able to rest comfortably in that chair before lunch."

"It's alright. What I need now is spiritual rest. I'll just sit here and read my Bible commentary for a while. It's in my suitcase if you wouldn't mind getting it out for me."

Nurse Castillo retrieved the book from the suitcase in the closet, and read the cover, *Thru the Bible* by J. Vernon McGee. Nurse Castillo handed it to Sarah. "Why do you have a commentary book? I thought you just studied your Bible."

"I do read my Bible and meditate on it during my quiet time. But, I also find it helps to spend a little study time several times a week with a Bible commentary. There are many great Bible scholars whose study material helps me gain a better understanding of what I read in my Bible. They help you understand the time, culture, Jewish history, and the meaning of certain word translations."

Nurse Castillo had never read her Bible on her own before Sarah came. She had depended on the priests to instruct her according to its words. Now she was finding there were other materials available to help her as well. "How do you know what they teach is true?"

"You have a valid concern. We can't accept everything we are told or read no matter what the source. Even Satan quoted scripture, twisted to suit his purpose. The Holy Spirit living inside of you will tell you when something isn't right. I have found that McGee is a trustworthy source that teaches the Bible faithfully."

"Would you show me how your Bible commentary works?"

Sarah was delighted. She always felt blessed by doing a Bible study, and sharing it made it better. However, the blessings would be multiplied this morning as the study was shared with her nurse in a bond of Christian friendship.

Sarah opened their study with prayer. Because of Nurse Castillo's question on discernment and Jesús' visit the night before, they looked at the commentary on I Corinthians 12. Their discussion was barely finished when Sarah's lunch tray arrived, and Nurse Castillo prepared to leave for her own lunch. Nurse Castillo paused at the door. "Thank you. I have never looked at the word of God so closely."

"You are welcome." There was no need for further conversation as Nurse Castillo looked at Sarah, for they understood each other's heart. Sarah's face took on that special radiance that seemed to come whenever her spiritual eyes looked into someone's eyes and saw the loving eyes of her Savior looking back.

Sarah ate her lunch from the wheelchair with hardly a thought to the food. She was thinking over her study time with Nurse Castillo. If they hadn't shared the Bible study, Sarah probably would have slept in her wheelchair. The body rest she would have had would not have been as refreshing as the spiritual refreshing she now felt in her soul.

How wonderful was the mighty God she served! If it weren't for the accident, she would have been home going about her everyday life unaware of what she was now experiencing. Now God has used the accident to let her touch Him through her new friends. She didn't know what she was more excited about. Jesús' promised dinner or getting out to the garden.

After Sarah's lunch tray was removed, she maneuvered her wheelchair to the window to wait for Nurse Castillo's return.

When Sarah heard the door open, she greeted her nurse. "I am so glad you are back. I can hardly wait for our trip to the garden."

The voice that answered startled Sarah. "Then by all means we should go."

Sarah turned in the wheelchair and only half spoke, "Fillip". She had forgotten all about his coming. How could she have forgotten? She swallowed hard, regained her composure and apologized. "Fillip, I am sorry. I thought you were Nurse Castillo. She was going to take me down to the garden."

Fillip response was cool. "I understand. Perhaps I can act as your guide?"

Sarah didn't have time to respond as Nurse Castillo came back to the room. "Ah, Señor Castañola. I am so glad you were able to come earlier for your visit."

She looked at them both to see if she could judge how their visit had started. "You both should know that I just had a meeting with Dr. Rubio. He read Lupe's progress notes on your therapy, Sarah, and feels you can soon leave the hospital."

Fillip took his eyes off Sarah and turned to Nurse Castillo. "It's very kind of you to share such excellent news with us. Sarah was just saying that you and she were going to take a tour of the garden. I hope you won't mind my taking Sarah instead."

Nurse Castillo really did want to spend more time with Sarah as friends, but she said. "How can I object? Sarah wants to get some fresh air, but don't keep her out for more than an hour." Nurse Castillo took the blanket from Sarah's bed and folded it across her lap.

"An hour it shall be. Shall we go, Sarah?" Sarah noted that he had not called her "mi querida". Sarah sensed his displeasure but couldn't understand its source. They didn't speak until they were out on the hospital grounds. Fillip wheeled her over to a bench beneath a very large tree, turned her wheelchair to face the bench, and sat directly across from her. They were well away from the rest of the hospital staff, visitors, and patients.

"Sarah, who are you having dinner with tonight?" He asked the question evenly, not showing the jealously raging within him.

Sarah laughed a little nervously and tried to tease Fillip. "I can see you are worried about the type of people who have befriended me. Not to worry. Jesús is a very nice man. He's a waiter at the hostel where I stayed."

Fillip looked a little confused. "You are *seeing* a waiter from your hostel?"

"Visiting with a friend." Sarah corrected him. She was a little uncertain how to interpret Fillip's "seeing". "Jesús is a waiter. This is what he does for a living. I am seeing him because we are friends and I couldn't refuse his kind offer to have a meal made by the hostel."

"Let me understand. You are having dinner with a waiter from your hostel because you and he are friends."

Sarah was a little disturbed by Fillip's references to Jesús' job. "You seemed to have a problem with Jesús' job. Is there something wrong with having a waiter as a friend? Or, do you just object to a friend sharing dinner with me?"

Fillip laughed. He was reminded of the indignation Sarah had at their conversation over arranged marriages and thanking servants. She was certainly the defender of the underdog. Sarah now fumed. "Just what is so funny?"

Fillip's laughter had broken his tension but not Sarah's. "I'm sorry. I was only remembering how appalled you were by my sisters' arranged marriages, and thanking Carmen for her efforts on the dessert, I ordered—requested for you. You are defending your waiter as eloquently."

Sarah didn't understand the humor. "Jesús is not my waiter. He is a friend who is a waiter. And, because he is a waiter, I am going to a very nice dinner with him tonight."

Fillip sobered. "He could have brought you dinner and not shared it with you."

"True but I enjoy our visits and solitary meals are boring. So, I asked him to bring enough for us both. When you left yesterday, you didn't say when you were coming back so I didn't think to invite you. But, if I had known it might have been a bit presumptuous of me to ask for dinner for three people."

"It was your idea to share the meal?" Fillip leaned back and relaxed against the bench and folded his arms across his chest. Perhaps things weren't as bad as he had thought. Still, even if this Jesús had not invited himself to dinner, he was still going to come. "Next time you want a special meal perhaps you will permit me to bring it and share it with you?

"Oh, Fillip." Sarah said with undisguised disgust. "I didn't ask Jesús to feed me nor did I force him to come eat with me. He was just being a kind and thoughtful friend when I complained about the hospital food. The same kindness you extended yesterday when you brought me Carmen's dessert."

Fillip didn't like being cast in the role of a friend, and, he certainly thought very little of a dessert cup compared to dinner. He thought of the spoonful of dessert that she had fed him and wondered if she would feed this Jesús too. He suddenly stood to his feet, walked a short distance away, and raked his hand through his hair. How could he make Sarah see him differently from other men, if they were to argue at each meeting?

Sarah knew that she had once again said something to displease him, but she was at a loss to understand. He looked like a man who was counting to ten before he said something he would later regret. "*Please, Father,*" she silently asked, "*don't let us continue to be at odds with each other.*"

Fillip returned and seated himself on the bench next to Sarah. He picked up her hand and slowly massaged it with his thumb. "Sarah, my beautiful Sarah," he quietly breathed, and Sarah had to force her own breath to flow naturally. "How is it, mi querida, that you do not understand?" He stroked the back of her hand gently, rhythmically and lifted his eyes from their hands to look fixedly at her eyes. "We are not friends. Fate, or if you choose, God, has made us husband and wife."

He raised Sarah's right hand to his lips and purposely kissed each knuckle. Sarah closed her eyes as her pulse rose, and his kisses caused waves of new feelings to stir deep inside her injured body. Without moving his gaze from her eyes, Fillip turned her wrist over, and kissed her pulse point holding his lips against the beat of her heart, and Sarah's eyes flew open, and found his eyes, then he kissed the inside of her wrist once again. "You are my wife and I am your husband and I will let no one come between us." He released Sarah's hand and leaned over and briefly met her lips with the barest touch of his lips. Sarah without thought returned the kiss and Fillip deepened it.

When Fillip ended their kiss, silence filled the space between them. Words had no value now as their emotions were in control. Fillip had summed up their relationship for himself and fire burned in his eyes as he waited for Sarah's response. Sarah's heart leaped wildly into action. It pounded loudly in her ears and she wanted to leap into Fillip's arms and boldly, passionately kiss his compelling lips, but the wheelchair was not only a physical barrier but her protection from herself.

Sarah sat back and scrutinized the impulse and was grateful since her self-control was faint. She looked at Fillip. If he could have read her eyes quickly enough, he would have seen they were filled with love, an expression soon covered by threatening tears of emotional turmoil and frustrating naïveté.

"Fillip, I hear you use the word *wife* as if it were our true relationship. I have come to accept that I was a stranger you met at an art gallery one day and the next your wife without my consent because of an old law. But, why continue?"

Fillip pondered when she became his true wife. *Was it when he stood alone facing the closed surgery doors and went to the chapel to pray for her? Or, was it during the long hours he watched her sleep with the aid of drugs and machines fearing she would die? Was it the moment she giggled at him in her private room so alive and vibrant? Is that when he wanted to take her to his El Alba Rosa? Perhaps it was the moment she feed him the spoonful of dessert? Did it matter? God had spared her, and she was his! Being with her gave him purpose and hope for a future. How could he answer when he didn't understand?*

"Does it matter?" Fillip asked, and he knew as she trembled that it did. "Any man would be a fool to give you up, and I am not one, mi querida."

"Fillip, I know that our marriage was a heroic act on your part to save my life, not one of love." Sarah's words came more slowly now as she tried to speak against the tears. "I understand that you can dissolve the marriage as easily as you initiated it. What kind of *husband* is that?"

Fillip knew the marriage was founded in weak law, but he had stated his case, but she didn't understand, and her tears started to pour. "Sarah, mi amor, do not cry." He took his handkerchief from his pocket and tenderly blotted her tears. "Smile for me Sarah. Tell me what you want from me, your marido? Tell me how to be your husband. I have no thoughts to end our marriage. I want to make you happy."

Sarah forced a weak smile, but his questions caused her to regain her composure as she sought to please him by answering. "I have never had a mental image of the man that would be my husband." Sarah looked at Fillip and his image filled in the shadow husband in her mind. Sarah blushed slightly and laughed. "Although when I hear husband now, he looks just like you."

Fillip smiled as he liked his image merging with her thoughts of who her husband should be. Fillip relaxed against the bench and Sarah began to feel a little more at ease. "Go on. Tell me more about your ideal husband, Sarah."

"Well—." Sarah paused. "I am not sure what to tell you. When I was a teenager and started dating, my parents had "*the talk*" with me. They made me realize how important the place of husband is in a Christian woman's life. It was clear from their lives and counseling that I never take dating lightly; because dating could lead to love and marriage, and it all had to be with the right man."

Fillip interrupted. "No doubt a man like your honored father?"

Sarah nodded in agreement and Fillip frowned slightly. *How could he compete with the special image of her father?*

"But, that also means I would have to be a wife like my mother. My parents weren't perfect but what they shared made their human foibles unimportant. Their unconditional spousal love was founded in their love for God. It's God's love, nurtured in their union, which made it possible for them to disagree and even argue occasionally, but never to go to bed angry."

Sarah paused, remembering her parents' love for one another, and she looked at Fillip closely before she continued. "I want what my parents had."

Fillip looked past Sarah. "You're asking much."

Sarah touched her fingers to his cheek and turned his eyes back to her face. "It's not what I ask, Fillip. It's my birthright. It's what I'm willing to give and share."

Chapter 11

It was still an early inviting summer afternoon. The wind hadn't changed, no rain clouds had gathered, and the hour Nurse Castillo had given them was not at an end; yet it was evident their visit was over. Sarah and Fillip were married strangers who needed time to work out their feelings and their relationship. Neither wanted to part but they had nothing more to say to each other. Fillip needed time to think of what Sarah had said, and Sarah needed time to sort through the myriad of thoughts their first kiss had stirred.

Fillip stood and moved to the back of Sarah's wheelchair. "Perhaps we should return you to your room so that you can rest before your dinner." Fillip paused as he searched for the right word engagement. There was no sting to his words as there had been earlier when he spoke of Sarah's dinner plans with her waiter. The jealousy he felt had been temporarily purged by their conversation. Fillip knew he wanted Sarah, but he wasn't sure he could convince her to want him. Sarah obviously wasn't opposed to male relationships, but most likely she didn't think beyond simple friendship. He wanted so much more.

He'd had several committed relationships with captivating women, but none of them touched or captured him like Sarah. They only offered fulfilling his needs temporarily...interludes, as they looked for someone better...taking all he was willing to give but giving little and offering no future. Sarah lacked their status and breeding but offered him a future they could not. She offered a future that promised love for him and not his status and wealth and offered children to call him "Papito" and to play on El Alba Rosa's lawns. He could imagine the shared satisfaction of being a happy couple, of their frequent lovemaking, and her expanding abdomen that would be his offspring—his true legacy. He was certain a spousal relationship with him especially when it came to sexual pleasure was beyond her experience or imagination, but one she would never regret. She was unsophisticated and deeply committed to God. He was uncertain he could share her with God who seemed to hold her whole heart.

Sarah held her peace as they entered the hospital and moved to the elevators. She knew Fillip wanted to make her happy. The elevator came, and Fillip deftly backed them onto it. As the doors closed, Fillip's hand came to rest on Sarah's shoulder. She reached up, touched his hand and spoke her thoughts. "Perhaps instead of trying to make me happy, you should make yourself happy?"

Fillip leaned down to Sarah's ear as the elevator stopped at the next floor and a couple joined them. "I was hoping it would be the same thing." His breath nuzzled her ear as his words hung suggestively in her mind. "I believe we could be happy together. I can offer you most anything in the world."

The elevator opened, and Fillip stood to guide them off and down the hall to Sarah's room. He paused at the threshold for once inside Nurse Castillo would become party to their conversation. He came around and knelt in front of her wheelchair. "Think about us as a real couple, Sarah. I am not open to our marriage ending. We have something together already. We started badly, Sí, but we have our whole lives ahead of us. Don't close your mind to me and run away again. You have a place in my heart." He touched her cheek, paused to lean his forehead into hers as he stood. "I hope I have a place in yours as well."

Fillip didn't wait for a reply, but wheeled Sarah inside her room and cheerfully greeted the waiting nurse. "Nurse Castillo, as you can see I have returned your patient. I believe Sarah should have some time to rest before she meets her dinner guest."

Nurse Castillo eyed them both. "And for you, mi querida, enjoy your dinner with your friend. I look forward to meeting him sometime soon. But save your evening hours for me tomorrow." Fillip teased her. "It will be my turn to share your evening, and I will have a surprise for you, my wife."

He bent down and thumbed her cheek gently, then took Sarah's lips in a kiss that held a promise of other more meaningful kisses. With a nod to Nurse Castillo, he left.

Sarah didn't dare look at Nurse Castillo. Fillip had gone but Sarah could still feel his touch on her check, and the warmth of his lips on hers. She knew her friend would ask questions she couldn't answer. She wheeled her chair to the bathroom and Nurse Castillo followed to assist her. They only talked about Sarah's personal and medical needs until Sarah was settled in bed.

"Well, what was said? I know it's none of my business but if you need anyone to confide in, I'd like to help."

Sarah was physically and emotionally drained. "I do need to talk and to pray, but I am just too tired. Tomorrow when you come we'll talk but now I need to sleep. I hope that doesn't offend you."

"No offense taken." Without any thought Nurse Castillo smoothed Sarah's bed coverings. "You sleep, and I'll do your praying."

Sarah smiled as she closed her weary eyes. She had asked people to pray for her before, but no one had ever offered to do her praying for her. Sarah wondered sleepily if someone else could do your praying for you. Maybe not the same words, but in this case with a much clearer head. "Father," Sarah murmured sleepily, "if Nurse Castillo can pray for me, what I need to pray, hear *our* prayer."

Nurse Castillo brushed a lock of Sarah's hair back against her pillow and said, "Amen." She took her seat and prayed that Sarah would hear the Lord's footfalls and be able to follow Him where He was now taking her. When she finished her prayer, she looked at her patient.

Sarah's sweetness and naïveté would have been hard to accept if it weren't genuine, Nurse Castillo thought to herself. Sarah's biblical wisdom and childlike faith put her to shame. She knew that Sarah would have been dismayed at the comparison. She could almost hear her say that Christian growth was too personal to be compared.

Nurse Castillo realized that Sarah was a catalyst. She had changed her life for the better. And, set the soul of her friend, Jesús on fire, with the fire that failed to consume. However, it was equally as clear that the fire that burned in Fillip and the fire he wanted to kindle in Sarah was not the divine fire of God. Nurse Castillo knew Sarah would first need to see divine fire burning in the man she would allow to kindle such a fire, but, she feared it was too late for her to walk away unscathed.

Nurse Castillo quietly picked up her things to leave for the day. She looked at Sarah again before she closed the door. Clearly, she thought if Fillip and Sarah were meant to be husband and wife, *God needed to intervene.*

Sarah awoke refreshed in her mind and body and looked forward to her dinner plans. She thrust back the covers and moved her injured leg along with her good leg to leave the bed. It immediately protested. Sarah laid back and laughed at her impetuosity, then pressed her call buzzer. She was grateful she was mentally prepared to be whole again, even if her body was slower in completing the process.

The nurse who came was a willing assistant to Sarah's plans. She helped Sarah take her first shower since the accident. Sarah's dress had been stored for weeks in her suitcases, but after her shower the nurse was able to shake the wrinkles out of it. Sarah had splurged on a clearance sweater, as the travel agent had warned her of cool sometimes wet evenings, and it was perfect for her dinner plans.

The nurse's final effort for Sarah took her off to find a small table and suitable chairs for the quiet dinner party. While the nurse was out, Sarah dried and combed her hair and applied her usual touch of make-up. She felt and looked better than she had in weeks. As she waited for the table and chairs, thoughts of Fillip and their afternoon visit came to her mind. *She remembered the flood of desire his first kiss caused. She also was troubled by those feelings, and the certainty their relationship had no worthwhile foundation.*

Sarah's troubled thinking was interrupted by a nurse and orderly who arrived with a table and two chairs. Before they left, they helped Sarah into the chair facing the door. Fortunately, Sarah's troubled thinking had barely had time to return when Jesús and another man arrived. After they deposited the boxes containing the promised dinner, Jesús stopped to introduce him.

"Sarah, I want you to meet my cousin, Herman."

Sarah reached out her hand to Herman. "Herman, it's nice to meet you. I've never had anyone go to so much trouble for me."

Herman took Sarah's hand and shook it briefly. "It's good to meet you as well. I've heard a lot about you since you arrived in our country, and I was glad to help Jesús bring you dinner. I had to spend a few weeks in the hospital once and I know hospital food can be unenticing. Maybe I'll have the opportunity to get to know you better before you return to America, perhaps then you can explain the changes in my cousin."

Herman good naturedly hugged Jesús' shoulder. "Now I'll leave before your dinner gets cold." He quickly walked to the door and turned to Jesús. "Jesús, I'll return for you in two hours."

Jesús nodded to Herman and began to unpack their dinner. "Sí"

"What a thoughtful man, Jesús. I don't know how to thank him or you."

"We don't need any thanks, Sarah. This is a simple thing for a friend to do who works at a restaurant. I think God is pleased when we care for one another showing His love. I haven't been able to do much for you, so this blesses me." Jesús responded as he laid out the dishes.

Much to Sarah's delight Jesús laid out a tantalizing dinner, and then pulled out a vase with a single yellow rose. "This is for you."

"Oh, Jesús. How lovely, you really shouldn't have gone to all this trouble."

Jesús gestured toward the table. "These things are nothing in comparison to what you've done for me, and I am eating too." Jesús took his place across the table from Sarah.

"Jesús sharing the love of God with you was my pleasure. I rejoice in your acceptance of salvation. Since Jesus Christ paid for your salvation, you owe me nothing?"

"Yes, I know but I wanted what you lived in front of me. You didn't hesitate to share the gospel with me, and you've allowed me to come to you with my questions. I will always be grateful to you. And, you know I would do anything to keep you here, including bribing you with dinner and a rose."

Jesús laughed at his joke but he really did want her to stay in Spain. Sarah joined his laughter and when their laughter faded she asked, "Jesús would you ask the Lord to bless us and our meal?"

They bowed their heads as Jesús prayed. *"Our gracious heavenly Father, we thank you for Your bounty and blessings that You have provided for us this day. Bless this food and our friendship. Continue to be with Sarah as she recovers from her accident. Continue Father to use*

Sarah in my life. Amen."

Sarah heard her friend's words and they saddened her. He'd made it clear from the beginning he wanted her to disciple him. However, she couldn't begin to imagine the path God would have to clear to keep her here, so she didn't respond.

Their meal began in silence as Sarah relished the food. Jesús had brought gazpacho, veal and rice pilaf, a mixed fruit cup, hard rolls and queijadas de evora for dessert. He poured a sparkling water for Sarah since she didn't drink alcohol. For himself he poured wine but drank it sparingly.

After a good interval of eating, Jesús broke the silence. "Sarah, you look nice this evening. I'm glad you are well enough to dress."

Sarah smiled. "Thank you. It's nice to be well enough to dress for the occasion, although I needed help. The staff have been very good to me."

Jesús nodded. "Tonight, Sarah, I haven't come here with questions. We should talk just as friends. Will you begin by telling me about your life in America?"

Before Sarah could speak, there was a light rap on the door.

"Come in." Sarah responded puzzled. She had arranged for the nurses not to come until after Jesús had left. As the door opened, what gained entrance to her room was a large flowering fuchsia bonsai tree in a ceramic dish. The bonsai was followed into the room by an elderly hospital volunteer.

Jesús rescued the tree from the volunteer and placed it on the nightstand as he thanked the woman in Spanish. Sarah and the volunteer nodded in the universal language of thanks and Jesús brought Sarah the attached card. Jesús admired the expensive gift. "It certainly is beautiful."

Sarah nodded as she opened the card. She knew the gift had come from Fillip. The card was hand-written and read, "Perhaps you should allow your roots to grow here with me, Señora Castañola, Fillip."

Sarah stared at the card momentarily before she turned back to Jesús. "The bonsai came from Fillip." Sarah tucked the card under her plate and began to eat again as Jesús took his seat.

Sarah ate quietly as the underlying message of Fillip's message invaded her thoughts. The timing of his gift was ironic, if not planned.

It seemed likely that he was reminding her that they were married, and that the door was opened to their staying together. How foolish the thought was since they were worlds apart in their lifestyles and expectations. Jesús finally broke her train of thought.

"Sarah, will you not tell me about your life in America?"

"Of course, I will." Sarah wanted to remember her life, the life she would return to. She spent the next few minutes talking about her life with her job, her mother, her friends, and her church. Finally, she decided to turn the conversation back to Jesús. "Tell me something more about yourself. Do you like being a waiter? I saw you with books, are you in school? Do you have a girl friend? What are your plans?"

"I like my job because I do it well, but the hours and salary are not good. I'm dating a girl I met when we catered her sister's wedding. Her name is Marina, and I'd like to ask her to marry me, but it would be unfair to ask her to be my wife on my salary. I've been taking business classes for three years as I can pay. I would like a job at Castañola Industries but the competition for jobs there is—mucho.

"Well, perhaps we can change that. What if, I ask Fillip to review your application and see if he can find you a position?"

Jesús shook his head with uncertainty. "No, if you intervene and I am hired for your sake, then I haven't been hired on my own merit."

"No, Jesús. You're wrong. Fillip is a man of honor and his business is important to him. He wouldn't hire you if it would harm his business, not even for my sake."

Jesús appeared a little more at ease with the offer. "Yes, I know he's a man of honor and an artist. Perhaps he could look over my application."

Sarah was intrigued with her new-found knowledge of Fillip and the probable reason of how they meet. "You mean Fillip is a patron of the arts? I met him at an art gallery."

Jesús finished another bite before he shared a little more information with Sarah. "Yes, he encourages the arts but he's also an artist. I remember reading a few weeks ago that he was having a showing of some of his work at the gallery near the hostel."

Sarah could hardly contain her excitement. "Oh, Jesús, that means that I probably saw Fillip's work. Since the showing was for local artists,

I didn't pay any attention to the artists' names. Do you know what he was showing?"

"I don't know. I'm not familiar with his work. I only know his work was being shown, but I can ask at the gallery for you." Then, he laughed. "Oh, Sarah, you can ask him for yourself. No?"

Sarah smiled ruefully as she finished her dessert. Here she was married to a man, benefiting from his generosity, confused by his touch and her own desires and she really knew very little about him. She wasn't even sure what she could ask him safely without causing another bad moment between them. Yet she realized her only real concern about him was the disparity in their faith in God. Should she simply trust God to bridge the gap and pursue the man who claimed her for his own? Should she ignore the principal of being equally yoked as her human nature tempted, or remain firm in her God given desire for a faithful God-loving husband?

Sarah set her troubled thoughts aside and made up her mind to intervene for the friend at her table. "Tomorrow I will ask Fillip to look at your application. Tonight, I think we should clear the table and finish our conversation." Sarah started to stack her dinner things. "The meal was wonderful, Jesús. I nearly finished it all. It was the best gift I could have been given."

Jesús stood and started to clear the dishes. "You're welcome Sarah, but I'll clear the table, after all I'm the expert." Jesús smiled broadly at Sarah.

As Jesús efficiently repacked their used dinner things, Sarah noticed his unfinished drink. "Jesús, I am sorry I seemed to have prevented you from finishing your wine."

Jesús turned from his packing with a dampened cloth to wipe the table. "No, you didn't. Somehow I just didn't want it."

"Why? You're not sick, are you? Is your drink bad?" Sarah was concerned she had made Jesús uncomfortable about drinking.

"No, the wine and I are both fine. It's not a simple thing to explain."

Sarah reached out and stopped Jesús' hand as he wiped the table clean. "Is it because of me? Are you uncomfortable drinking around me?"

Jesús took his seat and started to play with the cloth in his hand. "Oh, no, Sarah, it's not you. It's about how I feel and tonight I don't want to make you my teacher."

Sarah was relieved. "Friends tell each other how they feel, Jesús. Christian friends often include spiritual things in their conversations. I still have much to learn."

Jesús stopped toying with the cloth and condescendingly smiled at Sarah as he shook his head in disagreement. "We are friends but you're wrong about my learning from you. I can read my Bible and learn all about the Master's teachings, but you show me how to make them come alive inside of me. You told me how to be saved, and if you teach me nothing else, then you have taught me all I need to know to live well here and for eternity later."

Sarah's breath caught in her throat as tears filled her eyes. She felt divinely blessed by such praise and knew that similar crowns waiting for her in heaven would not shine any brighter than the crown that Jesús had just laid at her feet. "You do me a great honor that is not really mine. Remember that I only gave you what I was given."

Sarah thought that perhaps now she understood why the rewards that the elect of God would receive in heaven would be taken and laid at the Lamb of God's feet. His death made it all possible and they would give back the rewards to the One where the glory was due. "If you'll share your feelings with me, friend or teacher, perhaps I can help you understand."

Jesús nodded and began. "As you know we are quite comfortable with drinking wine in my country." Sarah nodded in agreement. "Last night as I was getting off work, Herman came. He was so happy. His wife had given birth to a son. They have two daughters. So, we went to a bar to celebrate. He is with his wife and son now."

"For the first time in my life, I looked at the wine with new eyes. Honorable men of my country seldom drink to drunkenness, but Herman did last night. I took him home, helped him to bed, and spent the night. His daughters are with his wife's parents. I didn't like what I saw in him because it could so easily have been me." Jesús paused and shook his head negatively.

"I asked myself how does celebrating to drunkenness do honor to the occasion?" Jesús finished the telling of the story. "Herman wasn't in a good mood this morning. He said I was no fun. I told him of my rebirth and that I wasn't just the old me anymore."

Jesús paused again and Sarah prompted the conversation. "Did he understand what you said? Or, is that what he meant when he said we could talk about the changes in you?"

"I'm not sure he understood, but he listened and didn't laugh. He did at least agree that the joy of the birth of his son wasn't comparable to the pain of his hangover. Is it strange that I don't want to drink anymore?"

"I don't think it strange. The living spirit of God is inside of you and He'll continue to change you as you grow. You don't need to change to conform to established Christian standards, you need to change as the Spirit directs. Remember you're not trying to please man but GOD. Ephesians 4 and 5 talks about what you're asking. It's about our relationship to our former life. You can get the Bible, if you want to look at it."

Jesús retrieved the Bible and they continued their conversation, but it ended abruptly when Herman returned. Herman was embarrassed when he saw the opened Bible.

"Jesús . . . Sarah, I am sorry I interrupted." He quickly started to back out of the room.

Jesús sprinted to the door and put his arm around his cousin's shoulder and brought him back into the room. "You're not interrupting, cousin. In fact, if you'd like, you can join us?"

Herman looked at Sarah and he was obviously not at ease with Jesús' suggestion. "Jesús is right. You're not an interruption and you can join us, but, you don't have to now. The invitation is open any time you want to join us."

Herman relaxed. "Some other time I think." He turned to Jesús as he lifted the boxes with their finished dinner things. "I will take these things to the car and wait there for you."

Jesús nodded his assent and Herman said good-bye to Sarah. "It was good to meet you, and I'll keep your invitation in mind."

"It was good to meet you too, Herman. Congratulations on the birth of your son, and, thank you for helping Jesús."

"Thank you and you're welcome. Vaya con dios."

Herman left and Jesús turned back to Sarah. "I think Herman is the first person the Lord wants me to help lead to the cross. Sí?"

Sarah smiled. "I wouldn't be surprised. I'll pray for him and you. Did you bring your Bible for me to underline?"

"Of course, you are my mentor and if you won't always be with me, the word will." Jesús grinned as he picked up his Bible from where he had placed it. He put it in Sarah's hand and held it there for a moment before he turned to leave.

"Buenas noches, Jesús."

"Buenas noches, Sarah. And, I'll pray that the Lord will continue to heal you and answer the prayers of your heart."

Chapter 12

Sarah was alone once again but happy. Her spirit had touched another's and that was pure joy. A nurse from the evening shift came and helped Sarah prepare for bed. It was nearly nine o'clock, late in a hospital day when the nurse helped her into bed. After she was alone, Sarah took the Bibles from her nightstand and marked a few pages. Although Sarah's spirit was healthy and energized, her body was still healing, and it had been a long day for her. Reluctantly, she set her work aside and prayed. When her spirit was satisfied, she ended her prayer and slept.

Sarah woke before Nurse Castillo came. Her sleep had been sweet, but she still found she hated being in the hospital. If her accident had happened in America, she was convinced she'd be home. The fragrance of the bonsai's blossoms drew Sarah's attention to the tree sitting on her nightstand. Sarah removed Fillip's gift card from her Bible where she placed it.

She read the card several times, studying his handwriting, and pondering his intent. Roots the card read. Sarah thought to herself that roots were the problem. Her roots were in the word and her homeland. Yet, here was a man that could stir her heart by just the way he said her name and he was offering her a place where she could be transplanted and grow in a new environ.

Although she feared they could never have a real marriage, Spain held more for her then her feelings for Fillip. There was Jesús. Sarah had never been a part of winning someone to the Lord like she had with Jesús. He wanted her to stay in Spain to disciple him in the Lord. Looking past him, she saw Herman in her mind as well as Lupe, and many other precious faces came to mind. In the privacy of her room, Sarah looked out the window and spoke aloud to God.

"Are you calling me here to a ministry, Lord? But how can that be? I can't do this alone. I want to serve, Lord. I have always thought I'd be the helpmate of a pastor or missionary, but Fillip isn't equipped to serve You. My heart is drawn here to these people. How can I love these people and not love the man who stirs my heart, my mind and—my body? My heart is divided between home and here. And, I'm afraid to love Fillip. Show me what to do, Lord. Please show me! Amen."

Nurse Castillo had come into the room, but she had stood by quietly until Sarah had finished her prayer. Sarah was startled when Nurse Castillo spoke. "The Lord hears your prayer Sarah. But are you prepared to follow where He leads?"

Sarah sat quietly upon her bed looking at Nurse Castillo and she understood the question all too well. "No, I can't say I am. I can't see how I can stay here. I have no income, no training, and Fillip isn't the kind of man I was taught God would want me to marry."

"He would be a nice source of income, judging by the expense he has shouldered on your behalf." Nurse Castillo placed her things in the chair, went to the little tree on the nightstand, and took in its fragrance. "His gifts speak of his generosity and perhaps his love."

Sarah shook her head in agreement before she spoke. "Fillip has been monetarily blessed and generous, but that's not to say he would care to endow a mission for me here. Besides Nurse, there is more to be considered. Fillip isn't only a wealthy man but a man of the world. Surely, you can see we don't belong together."

Nurse Castillo took Sarah's wrist, counted her pulse, and then continued. "It's not I who can't see. You have a faith greater than I've ever seen and you've asked for a place to serve. Yet, when the harvest fields are made visible to you here, your spirit cringes and you say it's impossible."

Sarah was hurt and thought about a rebuttal. "You don't understand. I need to consider my mother and my heart desires a Godly husband who will serve with me."

Nurse Castillo placed a thermometer into Sarah's mouth. "I do understand. Your mother knows you need to lead your own life and I expect she wouldn't mind your being a foreign missionary's wife which would take you away from America. She wouldn't hold you back from God's plans. She can't be your excuse because you know that God doesn't need you to keep her. You're afraid for yourself Sarah. You're a stranger in our country and you're trying hard not to love a man who frightens your sense of values perhaps even your virginity. God uses you to challenge and change hearts. Do you really believe that Fillip is immune to the God you reflect?" Nurse Castillo removed the thermometer from Sarah's mouth and recorded its results.

The room was silent as Sarah couldn't answer. She felt Nurse Castillo was being harsh and not very understanding. Nurse Castillo drew back the covers to help Sarah with her morning toilet before breakfast. The next half hour was occupied with Sarah's personal care and preparation for the morning. Sarah had been hurt by her friend's candid conversation and she couldn't think of anything to say.

As they waited for Sarah's breakfast, Nurse Castillo returned to the unfinished conversation. "You think I've been unkind. Perhaps, I'm just a meddlesome old woman who has no right to speak to you. I need to remember I'm just your nurse and you're only my patient."

Sarah teared up as the rift opened between them, and she recognized the dart of the enemy used to divide Christian friends. "No, you're not just my nurse and I'm not just your patient. We're friends, good friends. I know what you're trying to tell me. You've said that because I can't clearly see how God can work out a place for me in Spain with a stranger who happens to be my husband, I'm afraid. What can I say to the truth? Why can't I be just as uncertain as anyone else when trying to know God's will when looking at the future? I know the Lord can work everything out. I just don't know if it is His will."

Nurse Castillo smiled and patted Sarah's shoulder. "You're right. I know you believe child and God can overcome your fears. He's bigger than all our fears. He'll never lead you where His grace can't keep you. Now where did I hear that?"

Sarah stopped the threatening tears, laughed, and a smile returned to her face. Nurse Castillo smiled too and leaned down to give Sarah a hug. "Remember Sarah you aren't alone. God has already given you your friend Jesús and me. And, if we're going to be more than nurse and patient perhaps it's time you started calling me, Marguerite."

"Thank you, Nur...Marguerite." Nurse Castillo moved away to change the bedding and Sarah's breakfast came. Sarah's appetite this morning was not undone by the cold eggs, hard toast, and lukewarm tea. She ate quietly and watched her friend at work.

"Dear Lord," she closed her eyes and prayed; *"I know you're bigger than my fears. You made the universe and me, and surely if You can balance the earth, the sun, the moon and the stars, I'm not so difficult. Forgive my lack of courage. I looked and prayed for a husband and a mission—on my own terms. My heart does see a mission here, but I seem to be falling in love with a man that's not committed to You. If he's not immune to Your loving Him through me, then teach him to love You as I do. Two hearts, Lord that can love as one, serve as one, and beat as one with Yours. Amen."*

Nurse Castillo wasn't aware of Sarah's prayer. Sarah had grown used to praying as the spirit moved her. Nurse Castillo removed Sarah's tray and came back to sit with her, but before she had drawn up the chair Lupe came whistling through the door. "Buenos dias, lovely ladies. Are you ready, Sarah?"

Nurse Castillo eyed Lupe. "Why are you early this morning?"

"Aye, doctor's orders. Today, Sarah must learn to use the walker."

"Isn't that rushing things a bit?" The experienced nurse questioned.

Lupe knew more than he could revel, so he deflected the question with a jaunty reply. "Not for our star patient, nurse." Then, he spoke to Sarah. "Come lovely lady, your escort and chair await." Lupe helped Sarah to transfer from her reclining chair to the wheelchair.

Sarah laughed at Lupe, "If I am such a star patient, then why are you trying to get rid of me?"

Lupe didn't reply to Sarah's banter, rather he turned to Nurse Castillo. "I've been asked to have you call Señor Castañola's office this morning while Sarah is in therapy. He wishes to talk with you."

Nurse Castillo nodded. Lupe wouldn't explain, so the answer must be with Fillip. Sarah was puzzled by what was happening and tried again. "Just what's going on, anyway?"

Nurse Castillo obviously didn't know, and Lupe only whisked her out the door and down the hall. "Lupe, what's Fillip up to?"

Sarah had been quick to guess Fillip had stirred the hospital waters with some new plan of his own and Lupe had no quick light-hearted reply. "Perhaps, it's best for you to wait and ask your husband." Sarah had wanted to probe for an answer, but she had already come to the knowledge that the hospital staff would not displease Fillip. She could call him, but the thought of calling and questioning him unnerved her.

It was probably just something about the surprise he had promised. It was beyond Sarah as to how Fillip's evening surprise could have any effect on her therapy schedule. Sarah was wheeled into the therapy room and was greeted warmly by the other patients. She didn't like not knowing what was being orchestrated around her, but she knew she would have to wait.

As Lupe assisted Sarah with warm up exercises, an errant thought suddenly stuck her. Perhaps after their conversation in the hospital garden and their meager romantic interlude, Fillip had decided to annul their marriage after all! Two kisses, one honest conversation of what she wanted from a husband, what she was willing to give as a wife, and she had struck out at bat.

Well, Sarah thought, if that's what he wants, she'd cooperate. So, Sarah worked harder, motivated by a simmering hurt she failed to appreciate. She felt rejected, and she wanted a home where there was never any sense of rejection. The parallel bars Sarah had worked on the last few days had strengthened her arms, so she was prepared to use the walker. Lupe taught her to move it ahead of herself, stabilize it, and then to walk to it with first her damaged leg and then her unimpaired leg. It was not an easy task, but by the time the therapy session ended, she saw approval in Lupe's eyes and she smiled triumphantly.

"You've worked very hard and normally I would permit you to use the walker in your room. But I'm afraid you'll over use it, so I won't bring it to you today."

Sarah was flushed and a bit out of breath as she was helped back into her wheelchair. "That's not fair. I've done what you've asked, and Fillip obviously wants me to get comfortable with the walker. So, why shouldn't I have it in my room?"

"You're right, it's not fair. But I'm the therapist. Tomorrow you may have the walker. Today, you should rest."

Suddenly, Sarah was no longer willing to be docile. "No, I want it today, Lupe. I have to have a great deal of assistance even to go the bathroom, so why shouldn't I be able to use the walker?" Sarah softened. "I promise I won't run a walker marathon. Please."

"Alright, but remember you can do yourself harm, if you do."

"Thank you, I'll remember." Sarah was delighted by her victory. "It's good to have a measure of mobility again."

Lupe knelt beside Sarah's wheelchair and added some further instructions. "The walker is to be used only for short distances, to give you mobility in your immediate surroundings. For longer trips, you still need a wheelchair. Your injuries were quite severe, and it will be some time before you will be able to walk without some assistance, or someone available just to watch in case you need help. You also have to remember that you've had major abdominal surgery and have to recover from it and regain your stamina."

"Thank you, Lupe for your assistance and kindness." Sarah leaned over and gently placed a kiss on Lupe's cheek. "I'll try to be patient, but I want to be active again. I'll think of you when I'm home and doing therapy in the States."

Lupe stood and didn't reply as he took the handles of the wheelchair. As he started pushing the wheelchair to the door, he did reply quite soberly. "Let's not say our good-byes just yet, Sarah."

Lupe's jovial spirit reappeared as he returned Sarah to her room. He chatted gaily with the hospital staff and patients, but he didn't speak directly to Sarah again. Sarah decided since Lupe was going to keep Fillip's secret she was going to get some answers out of Marguerite. Certainly, she thought Marguerite wouldn't align herself so easily with Fillip's plans, since they were now friends.

When Lupe had Sarah back in her room, he stopped to speak quietly with Nurse Castillo. "Sarah did well with the walker, but for some reason she put more into it than necessary. I'll bring a walker to her this afternoon, but she should use it only to go to the bathroom. Keep an eye on her for me."

Nurse Castillo nodded. "Of that you can rest assured. But, if she worked too hard, why didn't you stop her?"

"It wasn't the effort that concerned me, but the determination. She needs to be more patient with her recovery. Get her to rest." Lupe turned and included Sarah in his farewell. "Buenos dias, ladies."

The door had barely closed behind Lupe, when Sarah turned to her friend and companion. "What did Fillip say, Marguerite?"

Nurse Castillo's smile was bittersweet, but her voice was light. "You really must work on being more patient. It's my understanding that Fillip has promised you a surprise, and I can't tell you what I know without spoiling it for you."

Sarah looked at her for some minutes and then asked bluntly. "Is Fillip planning on giving me annulment papers tonight?"

Shock clearly registered on Marguerite's face. "Oh, Sarah, no. Whatever gave you that idea?"

Sarah wasn't ready to give up. "Would you tell me if you knew?"

Nurse Castillo moved closer and looked Sarah in the eyes. "Sarah, surely you know I would never lie to you. Now tell me, what made you think such a thing?"

Sarah relaxed back in her wheelchair. Overwhelming fatigue showed on her sweaty face but also relief. "It seemed to be the obvious reason for the sudden need to speed up my therapy, your call to Fillip, and Lupe's secrecy. I thought Fillip was planning on finishing my stay quickly, so he could send me home."

Nurse Castillo sighed in heavy resignation. "It never ceases to amaze me, how with only a few facts people can imagine such wild things. It especially surprises me to see you jump to such an assumption, Sarah."

Sarah laughed embarrassingly. "Why? Why would you be amazed to find me just as human as anyone else when it comes to adding up two and two and getting five?"

Nurse Castillo studied her patient, went into the bathroom and drew a basin of water and came back to help her bathe. "I believe you're right."

"What do you mean, Marguerite?"

"I believe you do have the right to be human. It's just I've come to expect more of you because you seem so much more in control of yourself. I forgot that you're forging into unchartered territory, feeling around in the darkness with not just your mind, but with your heart." Nurse Castillo set the basin aside and wheeled Sarah into the bathroom.

"Let's finish your toilet and get you into bed. Lupe let you work too hard."

Sarah understood what Nurse Castillo had said. She knew her feelings for Fillip were taking charge and she was failing to exercise the control she had always taken pride in before. "You can't blame, Lupe. It was my heart that worked so hard at therapy." Sarah wearily laughed at herself. "My heart said to my body. Alright, if Fillip wants your therapy finished, then finish it. My mind didn't even argue. When will I know what Fillip is up to?"

"Tonight, child. Tonight. You can wait that long. Now let's get your pain medicine so you can take a proper rest." Sarah didn't argue.

Chapter 13

Sarah slept deeply while the morning hours slipped away. She wasn't even aware of a special delivery that came to her room. To say she needed as much rest as possible was an understatement and reluctantly, Nurse Castillo awakened her when lunch arrived.

"Sarah, Sarah, it's time to wake up. You need to eat your lunch."

Sarah was reluctant to give up her sleep and pulled away from the hand that was stirring her awake. "No, just let me sleep. I can get something later."

Nurse Castillo laughed lightly. "Sarah it's Marguerite, not your mother. There's no kitchen to raid later. There's only your hospital lunch. Come on now! Sit up so you can eat. Then, I'll let you go back to sleep."

"Marguerite?" Sarah's sleepy mind focused. "Marguerite, you're supposed to be my friend. Please, let me sleep. I don't care about lunch."

"Come on, Sarah. I'm also your nurse and you need to eat to regain your strength."

Sarah was awakening unwillingly, and she moaned. "Oh, Marguerite, I probably will fall asleep in my plate."

Nurse Castillo laughed. "Sit up Sarah." As Sarah complied, Nurse Castillo handed her a washcloth. "Wipe your face. It'll make you feel better."

"I hope lunch is worth it." Sarah wiped her face and Nurse Castillo placed the tray in front of her. Nurse Castillo prepared to leave for her own lunch, while Sarah inspected her tray. "Do your best with it, Sarah. You don't have too many more hospital meals to eat. If you want to sleep before I return, call the floor nurses. Otherwise when I return I'll help you shower and prepare for Fillip's surprise."

Sarah turned her full attention to her friend and nurse, but Nurse

Castillo simply left the room. Sarah wasn't sure, but she thought that she heard a slight chuckle as the door closed. Nurse Castillo did laugh. She knew for sure that Sarah would be awake when she returned.

Sarah ate her meal with little thought to what she was eating. Her mind raced about wondering about Fillip's surprise. Her mind also turned over the bit of information that Marguerite had let slip. "You don't have too many more hospital meals to eat." Truly, she was being prepared to leave the hospital, but Marguerite had said she wasn't going to be given annulment papers and a ticket home. So, what was Fillip's surprise?

Nurse Castillo returned from lunch just after Sarah's tray had been removed, so Sarah had only to watch the door for a few minutes before it opened to admit Marguerite.

"So, will you tell me now what the surprise is going to be, or am I to die of curiosity?"

Marguerite laughed pleasantly. "You aren't practicing being patient, child. No, I'm not telling you what the surprise is, but I'll help you to be ready to receive it and I'll give you this." Nurse Castillo went to the closet and brought out a large gift box and Sarah took in her breath. "Fillip has sent me so many expensive gifts. I'm not sure I should even open this one."

Nurse Castillo brought the box to Sarah's bed and laid it across her lap. "This is no time to be refusing gifts. This isn't your surprise but when the surprise comes you'll need this to be ready. Now open it."

Sarah removed the lid from the box and Nurse Castillo set the lid on the floor while Sarah pushed back the tissue paper. First from the box she pulled an emerald blue-green cashmere sweater she held to her cheek to feel its unique softness. Next, she brought out a heavily pleated silk skirt that would fall to mid-calf. The colors of the skirt included the color of the sweater along with a brown and cream color used to make a pleasant design. As Sarah lifted the skirt from the box, a matching silk scarf fell from the folds of the skirt. The very feel of the fabrics in Sarah's hand made her realize that they were expensive. She gently laid them back in the box as she spoke. "This outfit may be a part of Fillip's surprise but it's too much for me. I couldn't wear something so expensive."

Nurse Castillo laughed and snatched the skirt, scarf and sweater from the box and hung them in the closet. "I'm afraid you have little choice it the matter. Tonight, you may feel like Sarah Kettering, but you'll be dressed like Señora Castañola."

She returned to the bed, removed the box, and stripped back the bed coverings. Come it's time to shower away the sweat of your therapy. When we're done, I'll give you a massage. She brought the wheelchair to the side of the bed. Sarah looked around. "Didn't Lupe bring the walker?"

"The walker isn't here yet Sarah, but you couldn't use it anyway. Remember the walker is for only short trips. Down the hall is too far for you."

Sarah with Nurse Castillo's help managed the transfer from the bed to the wheelchair. She was getting quite good at it. "But, I don't understand. If I'm to use the walker, why not let me use it? The shower isn't that far away."

Nurse Castillo maneuvered the wheelchair and stood in front of Sarah to answer her. "You've just been introduced to the walker. Your stamina with it isn't good, so you must use it only in this room. Any other place you go will require the wheelchair for several more weeks. You must allow yourself time to heal properly and to regain the movement you have always taken for granted. It may seem that we are being overly cautious but it's for your benefit. Do you understand?"

"Yes, but I want to do so much more."

Nurse Castillo patted Sarah's shoulder. Yes, I know, but every time you have your therapy you are exhausted. If you are to go home soon, you must learn to pace yourself. You must learn to do a little, rest, and then to do a little more. Just because you have no casts to weigh you down doesn't mean your body will heal in less than three months and due to the extent of your injuries it may take even longer."

Nurse Castillo started to move to the back of Sarah's wheelchair, but Sarah stopped her by laying a hand to her arm. "You keep saying I'm leaving the hospital, but you also said that Fillip isn't sending me home. When am I to leave the hospital and where am I to go, if not home?"

Nurse Castillo patted the hand on her arm. "Tonight Sarah. Tonight, you may ask your questions and get answers." The room was silent because no more questions could be asked for it was obvious that no more answers would be given. Nurse Castillo took charge of her patient and they went for her shower and came back to her room for a nice massage.

Later Sarah sat in the chair by the window dressed in her under garments and lounging robe, while Nurse Castillo bundled up her personal things. From the very start of Sarah's and Marguerite's relationship, Marguerite had begun taking Sarah's personal garments home to wash them. When she had Sarah's things together, she came and sat down with her.

"You're a beautiful young woman, Sarah, and I'm glad you don't wear the heavy make-up I see on so many of the American tourists. I'm going to miss you."

Sarah solemnly replied. "I'll miss you too my friend. You've been more than my nurse. You have been like a mother and a dear friend to me. Wherever I am, I will remember the time we shared and not my pain." Sarah reached out and took Marguerite's hand. "God has brought many good things out of my injury and I prize our friendship as one of His gifts."

Tears came to the eyes of each of the women, but they were not ashamed. Marguerite patted the hand that held hers. "When you leave here, it will be a good thing and our friendship will not end. Even though the time may come when we can't see each other, I'll look forward to the time when eternity opens our eyes in our heavenly bodies and we see each other again."

"As a nurse, I have seen many people die and have been grieved in my spirit because I could not alter their fate. As a Catholic, I've believed in the resurrection of our Lord. When I have been afraid of my own mortality, I have taken hope from His resurrection for my own, but because of you I am more certain and satisfied in my eternal destination."

Sarah drew some tissues from her pocket and the women dabbed at the tears in their eyes. "When daddy died, we were sorely grieved by our loss. But we found comfort in a note he'd left for us in his Bible. He'd called it "My last will and spiritual testament." In it, he spoke of our spiritual bonds, as well as our love for each other. Then it pointed us to 2 Corinthians 5."

"I think Sarah that you have supporting Biblical evidence for everything you believe."

Sarah laughed. "I don't, but rather God has given us all the evidence we need to support our faith. Father's Bible had the first verse of that passage underlined and, in the days, following his death, when I repeated it, I was comforted." Sarah quoted the familiar scripture. *"For we know that if the earthly tent which is our house is torn down, we have a building from God, a house not made with hands, eternal in the heavens.* We are sisters in Christ and He has provided that we should be together eternally with all those who share in His righteousness."

"Thank you, Sarah, for opening my eyes to the word. It's hard to accept that I've never read the Bible for myself."

Sarah received the thank you with a nod. The minutes had slipped away, and it was time for Nurse Castillo to leave. "Sarah I'll see you tomorrow but for now I want to give you some advice. When the answers to your questions come, remember opportunities exist for you that will never be opened again. Don't let the safety of your former life keep you from going forward for fear of tomorrow. Each new day belongs to the Lord and You are always in His sight."

Sarah thought about her advice as Marguerite kissed her cheek. "Remember Sarah, the Lord that kept you through all your yesterdays, will keep you through all your tomorrows."

For a moment, their eyes held, and the spoken message was brought home. Marguerite turned to leave and walked a few steps away before she turned back to Sarah. "Enjoy the evening, Sarah." She paused. "No, pardon me. Enjoy the evening, Señor Castañola."

"Thank you, Marguerite. I think." The ladies laughed, and Marguerite left.

Marguerite stopped at the desk on her way out, instructed the nurses to hold Sarah's dinner, and to help Sarah dress for Fillip's arrival. Dr. Rubio's permission for Sarah to spend the evening outside the hospital was recorded in her chart.

Sarah leaned back in her chair and decided not to waste the rest of the afternoon wondering about Fillip's surprise. Sarah thought about how welcomed the walker would be when a familiar whistle sounded outside her door.

Sarah laughed at Lupe's timing as he entered the door. "I was just thinking about how useful a walker would be to get to my nightstand."

Lupe smiled and set the promised walker down. "And, what do you need from the nightstand, lovely lady."

"I was going to get the Bibles, so I can finish marking my friend's Bible with the scriptures I have marked in my own."

"I see." Lupe went to the nightstand and picked up the Bibles and brought them to Sarah." Did you think about how you would carry them and move with the walker at the same time? To the bathroom and back, remember. That was our agreement. You can't carry things and manage the walker at the same time. You could cause yourself to fall, Sarah."

"Oh, Lupe. You came too soon for me to think of how I would manage it. What about one of those little bags that loop around the bars, like they use in the nursing homes I visit. Now that you've brought me the walker, I can get one of those little bags so that I can carry things without having to use my hands. Would that satisfy you?"

"No. You're missing the point. The walker is to help in your therapy, to help you to learn to walk again. It isn't to help put you back to work. But you'll use it anyway. I only hope you'll not overdo. Promise?"

Lupe was right. Sarah wasn't used to being idle while someone else did the work. Sarah needed the walker to regain her sense of usefulness. "I promise, Lupe. I've no intention of causing myself any harm. I'll pace myself and my activities, but I won't permit myself to sit and grow lazy."

Lupe shook his head good naturedly. "Alright then, I'll tell you what I'll do for you, lovely lady. I'll go to occupational therapy and get you a walker bag and give it to you at therapy tomorrow."

Sarah smiled broadly. Her victories in managing her recovery were small but they were victories all the same. "Lupe, I don't care what Marguerite says, you're a true gentleman."

"Nurse Castillo is the best, but she does see me as a wayward son. It surprises me that you call her by her first name. It's not a privilege she grants to many. She must be very fond of you, Sarah."

Lupe laughed. "No doubt she thinks of you as the "perfect" daughter. Who knows, perhaps someday her opinion of me will change. Then, I will be "perfect" too." Lupe reflected on this for a moment and his thoughts caused him to smile. "Well, I'm off for home." He picked up the walker and sat it near Sarah. "Behave yourself lovely lady and have a good evening."

"You behave yourself too, Lupe. I can see you as a "perfect" brother in Christ." Lupe winked at Sarah as he started for the door. Almost immediately, Sarah heard Lupe start to whistle. Sarah spent an hour marking Jesús' Bible. When she finished, she felt her first sense of accomplishment in what seemed a long time. She read a portion of the scripture from her Bible, mediated on it, and then closed it for a time of prayer. She finished her prayer with a great sense of peace.

Sarah relaxed in her chair and her eyes came to rest on the walker. It was some hours before Fillip would come, so she decided that a little trip to the bathroom to test her new freedom would be appropriate before she took a nap in the chair. Sarah removed her lap blanket and pulled the walker in front of the chair. It took some effort for her to stand and maneuver herself into the bathroom. Tending to her own needs without assistance was a gratifying accomplishment, but by the time Sarah returned to her chair, she better appreciated the caution of her nurse and therapist. Sarah spent the rest of the afternoon sleeping fitfully in the chair.

The hospital routines continued around her and soon a nurse popped in to take her vitals, deliver her pain medication, and help her dress for her visit with Fillip. The fabrics of Sarah's outfit caressed her skin and she understood at least one of the comforts that money could provide. Sarah looked at her feet and the little black loafers she wore. They were the shoes of a tourist, bought for the comfort they could provide while walking. Her outfit she mused would look best with a pair of high-heeled leather boots. But, Sarah knew it would be some time before she would be able to walk in a pair of heels, even if Fillip had sent a pair along.

Sarah looked at her watch and saw that it was nearly 7:00. Suddenly, she was struck by a thought. Fillip was coming to take her out to dinner. How strange, she hadn't thought of this before. She hadn't even missed her dinner tray. It was like Fillip was playing a game of one-upmanship. Jesús had brought her dinner and now Fillip was coming to take her out.

She had guessed the surprise.

Sarah's eyes moved to the door. How very pleasant it would be to leave the hospital, even if it was for only a little while. But why did Lupe put the rush on the walker, and then not want her to have it in her room this afternoon? There was more to Fillip's surprise than dinner. Sarah's thoughts moved on. Marguerite had said her questions would be answered tonight. Sarah's calculation of the facts came to an abrupt halt as the door opened and Fillip filled the doorway.

"Sarah." Fillip carefully studied her appearance and he obviously approved. "You grow lovelier, each time I see you." He walked closer to her.

"Once again I find that I need to thank you for the gifts you have sent. The bonsai fills my room with its color and fragrance. And, if I am lovelier," Sarah blushed, "I must credit the clothes you sent."

Fillip leaned over and kissed Sarah's cheek. "No, you make the clothes lovely. I chose them for you because when I spoke with Nurse Castillo about my plans for this evening, she reminded me that your clothing has been in suitcases."

"You chose this outfit yourself and had it here by lunch time?"

Fillip pulled the straight back visitor chair over to Sarah's chair. "It wasn't difficult. I had a meeting in town and I stopped at a shop my mother and sisters use. I liked the outfit the moment the saleswoman brought it out for me to see, and delivery is a part of their service." Fillip ran his hand over the sleeve of the sweater. "Do you like it?"

Fillip's touch on the clothing he had selected caused shivers to run through her. Holding herself in check, Sarah smiled nervously. "Your gift is more than I deserve, or I'm used to. I can't help loving it." Sarah heard herself say the word love and the fragrance of Fillip's cologne stirred the cauldron of her emotions. She wished she hadn't said "love" to Fillip, even if she was only talking about the outfit. She changed the subject. "Just what do my new clothes have to do with your plans for me this evening?"

Fillip smiled. He had obviously taken the time to shower and change for this evening. He smelled of soap, shampoo, and the cologne that Sarah had come to associate with him. He wore a tailored dark blue suit, white shirt, with a marbled silk tie. Fillip's eyes glowed with delight. He looked like a small boy about to give what he thought was the best gift of his life. "Dr. Rubio has given me permission to escort you to the dinner I offered you so many weeks ago. If you're ready, I'll call the nurse and she'll bring you down to my car." Fillip paused with uncertainty, remembering Sarah's abrupt departure at his last invitation. "You will accompany me?"

Sarah smiled. "It would be my pleasure."

Fillip's face relaxed as he stood up and his boy-like grin returned. "I'll bring the car around." Fillip stopped and crouched down beside Sarah's chair. "Tonight, Sarah, we must agree to agree. We will have a good evening together, with no misunderstandings. Tonight, mi querida, we go to dinner as husband and wife. We will celebrate our marriage and your recovery." He leaned over and kissed Sarah gently and Sarah felt as if he had pulled from her lips a part of her will.

Fillip left without waiting for her to agree. Tonight, they were husband and wife celebrating her impending release. Sarah wouldn't think beyond tonight or the possibility of remaining his wife.

Chapter 14

Sarah's first awkward moment came when she tried to maneuver from the wheelchair into Fillip's car. She wanted to appear graceful as Fillip stood by and held the door for her. He had carefully parked the car near the wheelchair ramp and he had expertly judged the distance to allow for the wheelchair to be stopped at the passenger's door. After the nurse prepared the wheelchair for Sarah's transfer, she assisted Sarah into the car the way Sarah had been trained by Lupe. Her transfer to the car wasn't exactly graceful but it was accomplished without mishap.

Fillip thanked the nurse in Spanish and told her when he would return Sarah to the hospital. She nodded and bid Sarah a good evening. She moved the wheelchair to the opened trunk of the car, while Fillip turned to Sarah. "Are you alright?"

"Yes, I'm fine." Fillip closed the door. Sarah snuggled into the comfort of the leather seats she remembered as Fillip loaded the wheelchair into the trunk. As she fastened her seatbelt, she listened to a conversation from the rear of the car on how to properly open and close the wheelchair. Sarah realized the challenge of taking her out to dinner, however Fillip joined her in a few minutes without complaint, fastened his seat belt, and started the car. The silence in the car was comfortable, like that of a married couple accustomed to driving together. Sarah studied Fillip's profile and remembered how afraid she was of his overt masculinity just a few short weeks before.

Fillip turned and looked at Sarah briefly before he turned his attention back to the road and Sarah was not embarrassed to have been caught looking at him. "The restaurant where we're eating tonight is not the one where I would have taken you the night we met. It's not quite as casual and caters mostly to local taste. With your approval, I thought we could start with a shrimp and lobster salad appetizer, Salpicon de Mariscos. The main course could be their Trouxa de Vitela.

It is a veal roast served with green beans, and for dessert I thought we should have Queijadas de Evora, a sweet cherry tart."

Sarah felt blessed to be offered such a meal, especially with Fillip. "The menu you have suggested sounds delightful, especially in Spanish. The Spanish language is lovely, almost musical. I took several years of Spanish in high school, but I'm afraid I've had little occasion to use it since." Sarah laughed lightly. "I've almost worn out my English/Spanish dictionary since I've been here. The people here have been delighted by my attempts to speak the language and have been very patient and helpful."

"Your attempts at our language would be appreciated by the people of my country who deal with many tourists. No one would ever offend a guest in our country, especially one as sweet as you. It pleases us when someone tries our language instead of acting as if English were the only language. I'm surprised though that you haven't been propositioned by a few of my countrymen. Regrettably, American women seem much more..." Fillip paused to look for a word, "shall we say accessible than some of the women of our country. Proper women of our country are protected by their families."

Sarah laughed. "I think the word you are looking for is easy. I had a few offers, when I was out on my own, but Jose, our tour guide, explained to me the first afternoon how to handle such offers."

Fillip turned into the parking lot of the restaurant, put the car in neutral, and pulled on the parking brake. A valet immediately open Sarah's door, Fillip pulled a lever on the car's dash and opened the trunk. Sarah released her seat belt and looked at the valet. "Un momento, por favor." Fillip turned to Sarah and smiled his approval before he left the car. "When we are seated, please remember to tell me how Jose instructed you to deal with such offers."

With that Fillip was out of the car getting her chair. She heard him say something about the Señora being in a car accident, and he would help her from the car. When Fillip had the wheelchair opened beside the car door, Sarah was puzzled on how to get out of the low-slung bucket seat. Lupe's lessons hadn't covered this, but Fillip short changed the dilemma. He moved the wheelchair away from the door, then leaned into the car and swiftly lifted her up into his arms. "If you don't mind, Sarah."

Sarah's natural reaction was to fasten her arms around his neck and she found that she liked the nearness of his chest to her body. She felt as if she had enjoyed his arms around her forever. She felt the same peace that she had experienced at the end of her prayer earlier in the day. He moved Sarah to the wheelchair and gently lowered her into the seat. Reluctantly, Sarah released her hold from around his neck and straightened her silk skirt, as Fillip spoke. "Are you alright? Did I hurt you?"

Sarah smiled into Fillip's eyes, remembering the feel of his arm beneath the silk of her skirt. "No, but I'm starving."

Fillip laughed and propelled the wheelchair forward. "Then, by all means let's not keep you from your dinner."

Some departing dinner customers held the door for Fillip and Sarah and once inside it became obvious that Fillip had made them aware of Sarah's special needs. They were quickly taken to a table that had been set for two, although one of the chairs had been removed. When they were seated, Fillip refused the menus and placed their order. "I placed the order we discussed in the car, and they'll be bringing you sparkling water. Dr. Rubio insisted that you not drink, although I suspect you would prefer the water anyway."

"Yes, thank you."

Fillip nodded and turned their conversation back to the unfinished one from the car. "Tell me what did your guide tell you to do with such offers?"

"He said I should look very shocked, which wasn't difficult, wave my ring finger, and say, "No, gracias. No quiremos ofender a mi esposo." ("No, thank you. We don't want to offend my husband.") Apparently, the men of your country don't like to deal with angry husbands."

Fillip laughed, and the waiter came with their drinks, rolls, and salads. Sarah bowed her head and silently gave thanks for their meal. Fillip bowed his head in reverence and waited respectfully before he spoke again.

"It is more than dealing with angry husbands, Sarah. In my country, we respect marriage and although there is adultery, it's certainly not something most men would indulge in easily." The subject sparked a tangent in Fillip's mind, so he turned the conversation to Sarah's previous night's dinner. "So, how was your dinner with your friend, Jesús, last evening?"

Sarah smiled warmly at her memories. A frown creased Fillip's lips, although Sarah was unaware of it. "The dinner was excellent. The nurses helped me to dress for the evening and they set up a little table in my room. Jesús' cousin, Herman, helped him to bring in a full service. Herman's wife just had their third child, a son. She was a patient in the hospital too. At any rate, Herman came back in a few hours to help remove the dinner things. Everyone I've met in your country has been very generous and kind to me."

"Did you talk about anything special?" Fillip gently pried.

"I told Jesús about my life in America and he talked about his life here. He has a girlfriend he would like to ask to marry him, except he feels he couldn't adequately support her. He said he keeps an updated application at Castañola Industries, but he hasn't been able to get hired on there. He has been taking business classes for several years although he hasn't earned a degree. Fillip, I told him I would ask you to have his application reviewed."

Fillip's jealousy had cooled at the mention of a girlfriend and marriage," but his expression hardened as he spoke. "So, he's using you to try and get a job with Castañola. Interesting?"

Sarah quickly tried to rectify the impression she had made. "No, he didn't ask, but I volunteered. He tried to stop me from saying anything because he doesn't want a job except on his own merit."

Fillip snickered. "But, because you insisted he let you ask anyway."

"No, Fillip. You're wrong. Jesús is a Christian and a very honorable man. I don't know him well enough to understand his job skills. I don't even know what your company or employees do. I assured him that your business was very important, and you wouldn't hire him, if he was not suitable for the work, no matter who asks."

Sarah was interrupted by the waiter as he cleared away their salad plates and brought out their main course. He refilled Fillip's wine glass and her own glaseoso. When the waiter finished, Sarah concluded before returning her attention to the meal.

"It would be better for Jesús and men like him to be told their skills are not suitable for employment in your company, instead of letting them keep an application on file and never be called. I and I mean "I" am asking that his application be reviewed. It doesn't even need your personal attention. And, if you can't use him maybe he'll finally know to look elsewhere to improve his life."

Sarah was shaking from her impassioned speech. Slowly, she collected herself and started to eat her veal roast.

"I'm sorry, Sarah. I said that tonight we would agree, and I seem to have already broken that pledge. You've made it clear that I've misjudged your friend's motives in dining with you. I will look at Jesús' application personally, and I'll see how such applications are dealt with at my company. Perhaps a new personnel policy is in order. Will that satisfy you?"

"Yes, and thank you." Sarah answered in relief.

The two ate silently for some minutes. Fillip was coming to terms with the idea that Sarah could have a male friend without any romantic involvement. He looked at her and somehow couldn't understand how any man could not fall in love with her, but there she sat, unmarried until their unfortunate accident.

Sarah moved in her chair and the silk of her skirt rustle against her slip as she looked at the man who had given her so many things and she was grateful they were together. A part of her mind said to her, "Tell him how you feel." Sarah blushed at her thoughts and started a safe conversation to block her impulsive and dangerous thoughts.

"I never told you, but Jesús is the first person who I've ever had the privilege of leading to salvation."

Fillip didn't like the direction of the conversation. "I'm not sure that I understand. What do you mean by salvation?"

"Salvation is a personal identification with the death, burial, and resurrection of Jesus Christ. Being raised a Catholic, I believe, you are assumed saved when you go through your catechism classes, get confirmed, and take your first communion. Being raised a Protestant there must come a time when you recognize you are a sinner and that Christ died for sinners. Then, you turn to Him, ask for forgiveness, and you're saved from your sins."

Fillip didn't quite follow what Sarah was saying. "I can't imagine that you were much of a sinner."

"There are no small sins, or no small sinners. God is holy and therefore must separate Himself from any sin. Sin isn't something we can measure or compare. Sin isn't only something you can do that displeases and separates you from Him. It's the state in which we are born as children of Adam and Eve. Jesus Christ came so we could be reborn into the family of God. It's our choice. We can stay in our lineage as descendants of Adam and in sin, or we can accept redemption and be adopted into everlasting life. Listen to me. It's no wonder Jesús thinks of me as his teacher. It just seems so easy for me to talk about what I believe."

"You say these things quite well and what you say is very interesting." Fillip paused for a moment to think about what he had just heard. "And these things are what you've said to Jesús and he has accepted this salvation, and why you now say he is saved?"

"Yes. And, that's why he's now my brother in Christ. We believe in God and His plan of salvation."

Fillip finished his dinner and leaned back in his chair to think about what he should say so he wouldn't offend her. "What you say is new to me and I need time to think about it, when I'm less distracted."

Sarah was a little disappointed. She had hoped he would want to hear more. "I understand. We can talk about it later."

The waiter came and cleared their table and Fillip ordered coffee to complement their dessert.

When they had been served, Fillip reopened the conversation that she thought he'd closed. "This salvation you speak of, is it what you've said must be shared in marriage?"

Sarah was delighted to find they could continue their conversation about God. "If any man is to be the husband that God would have him be then he must be saved first. The husband is the spiritual leader of the family and he can't lead properly if he doesn't have God to follow."

"I understand." Fillip frowned. "This acceptance of salvation would make Jesús an acceptable husband for you?"

"Yes and no." Sarah saw the frown furrow Fillip's forehead. "Yes, because my husband should be saved before he is my husband. No, because Jesús and I don't share the kind of love required for marriage.

The love of God is the basis of a Christian marriage. That's why I felt bad about your sisters' arranged marriages. I'm a romantic. I believe in love and I'm not willing to settle for anything less than what my parents shared."

Fillip breathed a sigh of relief. Sarah didn't see Jesús as an acceptable husband, but he wasn't sure he would be able to satisfy her demands for such a husband either. But, he did have one advantage. He had a marriage document, and no one seemed to question its validity.

The waiter came and cleared away their dessert dishes and brought them more coffee. Sarah had enjoyed her dinner out with Fillip. Fillip was obviously well known at the restaurant and their service had been excellent. Sarah absentmindedly stirred her coffee to cool it. "I want to thank you for this lovely dinner and time with you. It was truly a very special surprise."

"I too have enjoyed our evening. I'm glad we've been able to agree as well." Sarah continued to stir her coffee and tried to hide a yawn with the back of her hand. "I think though your first evening out has been long enough."

Fillip signaled the waiter and after a few words, the waiter laid the dinner bill on the table. Fillip pulled his wallet from his breast pocket and laid down a generous sum of money. Sarah savored the last of her cooled coffee.

"The waiter is having the car brought around." Fillip finished his coffee.

Sarah was saddened that their time together was coming to an end. She decided to tease her dinner companion. "I'm sorry to have been such an early date for you. I know the people in your country tend to stay out much later."

Fillip picked up on Sarah's attempt at humor. "For our date to end early is not such a bad thing." Fillip picked up her hand and caressed it in his own before he gave it a meaningful kiss. "It is only sad that I am returning you to the hospital instead of taking you home with me. At home, our time together would not have ended so soon."

Sarah had lost this round of teasing and she blushed noticeably. Fillip laughed. "Well, I'm convinced you are returning to health. This is the first time I've made you blush so deeply, since our last evening together."

The waiter came back and signaled to Fillip. Fillip released her hand and stood up and came around to stand behind her chair. He nuzzled her hair behind her ear and whispered into it. "I am glad to see my bride blush again." He kissed her cheek, "I truly wish I could take you home." Then, he pulled her chair from the table.

The valet had the trunk opened and was holding the car door when they got outside and Fillip without a word lifted her from the wheelchair and placed her in the passenger's seat. Fillip quickly tipped the valet, deftly loaded the wheelchair, and joined Sarah in the car.

Sarah smiled at Fillip as he put the car in gear and drove from the restaurant. Sarah hadn't planned on falling asleep, but she was tired, well fed and the car hummed gently with little road sound, so Sarah nodded off without ever saying a word.

Fillip glanced at Sarah as he maneuvered the car and he knew she was asleep. He relaxed a little and thought about how he would tell Sarah about his plans. He had meant to tell her in the restaurant, but he really didn't want their dinner spoiled by a disagreement. But, once they were back at the hospital, he would have to tell her. He looked at her again. He had truly meant what he had said about taking her home.

As the car stopped in front of the hospital, Fillip turned to Sarah and gently kissed her cheek to wake her up. Sarah stirred, opened her eyes, and smiled at him. "Fillip, I'm sorry. Not only am I an early date, I'm poor company as well." Sarah straightened in her seat. "Thank you again, for the evening and these beautiful clothes."

Fillip was aware of the nurse approaching the car and he released the trunk lid. "You're most welcome, mi querida, but the evening isn't quite at an end. If you will permit, I will park the car and come to your room for one more surprise.'" Fillip left the car before Sarah could respond. He helped the nurse with Sarah's wheelchair and spoke with her briefly before he came and lifted Sarah out of the car into the wheelchair. As Sarah settled into the wheelchair, Fillip caressed her shoulder. "I'll see you in a few minutes." Sarah only nodded her head in response as the nurse started off with her.

The night air was cool and refreshing for one who had napped briefly in the comfort of a warm sports car, but Sarah was unaware of the air, her mind was once again puzzling out what surprise could be left. The nurse left Sarah in her room saying she would return when Señor Castañola had gone.

The minute the door opened Sarah raised the question that had troubled her all day. "Fillip what's going on?"

Fillip came and sat in the chair nearest Sarah and pulled her chair into him. "Dr. Rubio has agreed to release you from the hospital tomorrow. It's time for you to go home."

Sarah sat numbed. She knew the day of her release was near, but she hadn't expected it to be tomorrow. She understood now that the evening out was a farewell dinner. Fillip watched carefully as Sarah took in the news. Finally, she spoke. "Well that's wonderful. Does mother know I'm coming home?"

Fillip shook his head, picked up Sarah's hand, and kissed her fingers. "I've spoken with your mother and she's looking forward to hearing from you tomorrow when you're home. But, tomorrow home is with me, to our home."

A chill swept up through Sarah's fingers and caused her heart to pause. For a moment Sarah felt frightened, but when she looked into Fillip's eyes her fear left. He continued to hold her hand and his touch warmed her senses.

Sarah protested as she felt she must. "You've been kind, Fillip, but I need to go home to my job and mother."

"No, Sarah." Fillip stopped her. "You must finish your convalescence. I've readied our home and Lupe will come twice a week to continue your therapy. How can you think of going home until you can walk again?" Fillip needed time to get Sarah to think of El Alba Rosa as home.

"I've made arrangements to take care of your mother and she knows she can come here anytime to be with you, to live with us. Your job placed you on extended leave. You see your mother and I have become well acquainted through our many conversations. When you're able, we'll go see her. Perhaps then she'll fly back with us and make her home here." Fillip paused and then made his point. "We need time to see what the future holds, Sarah."

Sarah sat quietly. Fillip had opened a door to a future very different from the one she'd imagined. What was it Marguerite had said?

"Remember opportunities exist for you that will never be opened again."

Fillip had grown anxious at Sarah's prolonged silence. "Certainly, Sarah you should at least see what we can have before you run off." Fillip studied Sarah but couldn't read her thoughts. "Come home Sarah. Give us a chance—." he paused. He heard himself plead. "Please, Sarah, a short time."

Fillip caressed her hand, his eyes never wavered from hers, and he silently appealed to God. *"Please God, I know she's yours, but I need her."*

Sarah nodded her head in acceptance with a smile. Fillip sighed in relief and captured Sarah's lips. His kiss promised she wouldn't be sorry. And, Sarah returned his kiss.

Chapter 15

Sarah slept restlessly. She wasn't troubled by dreams but her subconscious mind thinking about the implications and the possibilities of living in Fillip's house. He had said "our" home was ready for her convalescence. He even indicated a future where her mother would live with them. He always spoke of them as a real couple, living together as man and wife. He certainly had the financial resources to take care of her and her mother, and his lips and touch promised to take care of the more personal, more intimate needs he stirred.

Hour after hour, her thoughts kept interrupting her body's need for rest. She would open her eyes to find that the long hours of the night still lingered. Sleep would not come and offer her any peace. Finally, the long night ended. She restlessly turned her head to the slits of the window's blinds and saw the light of a new day. Each day when Sarah awoke and looked at the day's new light, she always spoke true words of praise to God for the giving of a new day. Today she considered the spreading light as if she could somehow in the dawning see God's face and know His will.

In her heart's eye a picture of Jesús and his cousin Herman formed. Then she saw Nurse Castillo and the light-hearted Lupe, and a parade of other nameless faces. And, a voice from the spirit brought a message to her ears, "Feed my sheep."

Her spirit understood the message and she responded, "Here I am, Lord."

Sarah relaxed against her pillows and smiled. The road had been chosen and because she no longer struggled against the command, she was filled with a sweet peace. The fragrance of the bonsai caught her attention and she reached out and touched its petals. She thought about the bonsai, a tree that if left to grow in nature could reach generous heights. She marveled at the lesson growing on her nightstand.

The beautiful bonsai had been touched by a master horticulturist and had acquiesced to having its roots and branches pruned and trained, so it could grow and flower in a dish away from its home soil. Being pruned and wired to come to its present state had not been easy or done quickly. She realized that its shaping had taken time and patience, but the final effect was worth it all.

She knew Fillip couldn't have known the spiritual significance of his gift she now saw. Her heart was light with a joy that was almost giddy with pure revelation. God spoke to her. Fillip's gift card spoke of establishing roots with him at her side. Sarah now understood. If her roots were to be pruned and established on foreign soil with Fillip, then Fillip's roots were subject to the same care by the Master horticulturist. Her thoughts again soared to new possibilities and her heart saw Fillip differently. Her heart sang a familiar tune. "*What a Mighty God we Serve.*"

Nurse Castillo came, set down Sarah's laundry and her own things, put down the bed's side rails, and studied her. She was uncertain how she would find Sarah this morning and looking at her she couldn't tell.

"Well, child, how was your evening? How are things going to be?"

Sarah swept back her blankets and aiding her injured leg she swung her legs around to sit on the edge of the bed. She immediately encircled her friend in a generous hug and almost sang with the joy she felt. "I understand."

Nurse Castillo stiffly returned the hug and then removed Sarah's arms. "Understand what, Sarah?"

"I understand that I am to stay here in Spain. God does want me here. I have waited all my life to find my place of service and now I know it's here."

Nurse Castillo relaxed a little as she began to understand Sarah's euphoria. She hadn't doubted that God could use Sarah in Toledo. She had already experienced the touch of God from Sarah's hand. But, what she remembered was Sarah's fear of staying as Fillip's wife. "You are no longer troubled to be Señora Castañola?"

Sarah quieted as she thought of Fillip, but the spirit of her revelation bolstered her faith. "You said that God wouldn't take me where He couldn't keep me and that He could overcome all my fears." She thought about the warning sirens that went off inside of her each time Fillip touched or kissed her. "I believe, my dear friend, that Fillip Castañola will experience God for himself." Sarah paused and looked at Marguerite. "Somehow!"

She reflected quietly on the size of the task. There was not only the matter of Fillip's salvation, their need to be spiritual partners in a real marriage, but all the steps of establishing a new ministry in a foreign country. She smiled to herself. The country wasn't foreign to Fillip or God and if God wanted a ministry here He would direct their steps.

Nurse Castillo was satisfied. "Well alright then, let's get this day started." She went to get Sarah's wheelchair as had become her habit.

"Marguerite, how about the walker? Let me show you how well I can manage."

Nurse Castillo brought the walker, but Sarah did not reach out to take it. Instead she reached out to touch her nurse's arm. "I'll miss you, Marguerite."

Marguerite's nurse's demeanor softened. "I'll miss you too, child. But, since you're going to be here, we can see each other. I have your address and phone number and a standing offer from Fillip to come by and see you anytime. He said his servant, Ramón, would drive me anytime I called." Sarah brightened at the thought of their friendship continuing outside the hospital. It pleased her too that Fillip was going to such effort to make her happy in her, no "their" new home.

Marguerite shifted back into her Nurse Castillo mode and bristled. "Besides you haven't needed a nurse for many days. Fillip has just indulged you, so you wouldn't be alone." Nurse Castillo bumped the walker with the toe of her shoe. "So, are you going to show me how you get about with this thing or not?"

Sarah laughed. It was clear that there was no room for sentiment. "Alright, alright, I'm ready. Just stand back."

Sarah's movements were slow, but she was on her way back to some form of independence. Marguerite was pleased. Fillip had asked her to look after Sarah at home. He'd even offered to keep her at her full salary, but Marguerite had refused. Sarah didn't need a nurse and there were others who did. She would miss Sarah, but they were no longer nurse and patient. Maybe—she reasoned, the Lord would use her in this new ministry that made Sarah glow when she talked of it.

When Sarah finished her morning toilet and hospital routine, Nurse Castillo helped her to dress in the outfit she'd worn for her dinner with Jesús. This morning she wanted to go to therapy dressed to say good-bye to all her friends. Sarah's efforts to care and dress herself left them without any time to talk as Sarah's breakfast arrived. Sarah had little appetite as the expectations of the day made her too excited to eat properly, but Nurse Castillo didn't scold her this morning.

Sarah's thoughts centered on Fillip's arrival to take her home. "Do you know what time I'm being released from the hospital?"

"Sí, Sarah. You have just picked over your last meal here. Fillip is coming for you before noon. So, while you are at therapy, I'll prepare your things." Nurse Castillo picked up Sarah's tray and took it out to the cart in the hall.

Sarah got up and went to her nightstand and pulled out her journal. When Nurse Castillo returned, Sarah handed her the journal. Since you have my address and phone number, I thought I should get yours too."

Marguerite took the journal and wrote the information. "This isn't such a nice area now. I was raised there, and I raised my children there. My husband and I wouldn't live anywhere else. It's a good neighborhood, but sometimes a bit rough after dark."

Sarah understood what Marguerite was trying to tell her. Her neighborhood, like many in America, was neglected, not for pride or ability to repair but for the money needed to keep it up. Crime and violence seemed to prey on people who struggled to live in such conditions. But, that was where the message of hope was needed most. Perhaps that is where the Lord would have their mission start. "Do you have any vacant buildings there that could be used as a mission?"

"Sí. There are empty buildings, but I don't know what a mission would need."

Sarah laughed. "Neither do I, but a place to start. You think about it. Maybe the Lord will speak to your heart and give you the perfect place for us to start."

Lupe came and greeted the ladies. "Time to go, Sarah. The other patients know you are leaving today." Sarah obediently moved to the wheelchair and sat down.

Nurse Castillo spoke to Lupe. "Now you see to it the Sarah doesn't work up a sweat today. She's going to see her home for the first time and she wants to look presentable."

Lupe smiled. "There's no need to fear, dear Nurse. Today, we have little to prove and many goodbyes to say. Sarah has made many friends among the other patients and staff. Besides there's no hurry because I'll be working twice a week with Sarah at home, until she no longer needs therapy. But, I'll miss seeing you." He took her hand and lightly kissed her cheek. "Until we see each other again."

Nurse Castillo withdrew her hand as if it had been burnt and blustered at such frivolous treatment. "You can save that nonsense for someone who is more likely to fall for it. Watch him Sarah." She laughed as she walked over and opened the door. "Now out with you both. I have things do, if Sarah is to go home today."

Lupe collapsed Sarah's walker and handed it to her. "Isn't it marvelous, Sarah? I finally figured out how to get to her. I do believe she loves me."

Nurse Castillo shook her head and held her peace, not wanting to give Lupe anything more to play with for his game. Lupe sensed that his victory was slipping so he wheeled Sarah to the door.

At the door, Nurse Castillo stayed the wheelchair with her hand on Lupe's arm. She leaned down and kissed Sarah's cheek. "Sarah, you are a sweet child and I have come to love you as a daughter. If ever you need me, I am only a phone call away."

Before Sarah could answer, Nurse Castillo motioned for Lupe to move on. Sarah looked back at her friend and felt sad. Surely, it was not time for them to say goodbye. Yet, she felt that Marguerite had just done that.

"Lupe will Marguerite be gone when we get back?"

"I can't say Sarah. All I know is that you are going home with your husband before noon. But, then you know this, too."

"Yes. Fillip told me last night and Marguerite supplied the time."

Lupe began to whistle but stopped. "Señor Castañola would be a hard man to disappoint." Lupe continued his whistling. Sarah had learned that Lupe whistled as an invasive tool, so he wouldn't have to talk when he wasn't comfortable. So, she said nothing more.

When Lupe opened the therapy room door, Sarah heard the sound of party whistles. Today, Sarah wasn't to work. She would party with the patients and hospital staff she would be leaving behind. Many of these faces had been a part of her vision as the day first dawned. Lupe opened Sarah's walker and she used it to make her way to each of them as they worked out or enjoyed the cake and punch that had been provided by the therapy staff. Sarah had bonded with them in the brief time she spent with them, and she had each of them write down their addresses, so she could follow their recoveries. In her heart, she saw their need for a personal Savior, and knew she had understood her call.

Finally, the moment came for Lupe to take her back to her room. Sarah sat back into the wheelchair and Lupe collapsed the walker and handed it to her. Sarah tearfully said her final goodbye to these hard-working therapy patients.

"I have come to know and admire each of you. Each day when I awake and have my quiet time with God, I will speak your names to Him." Lupe repeated this in Spanish for those who would understand it best in their own language. "Vaya con, dios, mi amigos." Her friends responded in a mixture of goodbyes and Sarah started to cry mistily as Lupe took her from the room.

The ride back to her room seemed unbearable. A chapter in her life had ended and she was a little apprehensive. The hospital was a place of refuge where she'd made new friends, people she'd come to respect for their courage. Now she had a new life waiting for her and she wasn't sure what was going to happen, but she breathed a silent sigh of relief as she remembered that God would not leave her to face it alone.

Lupe opened the door and Sarah expected to be greeted by Marguerite. But, Fillip was standing by the window. At the sound of their arrival, he turned, looked at them, and smiled when his eyes met Sarah's.

Fillip spoke first. "Sarah, you look lovely this morning."

Sarah smiled in returned. "Lupe, I would like for you to meet Fillip and Fillip, I would like you to meet Lupe. It's time the two of you met since you both have worked so hard to get me back on my feet."

Fillip crossed the room and shook hands with Lupe. "Dr. Rubio gives you the highest praise for your skill as a therapist. I'm surprised you're not older."

Lupe took Sarah's walker and set it against the wall. "Señor Castañola it is good to meet you and I can assure you that my skill is not dependent on my age. Sarah is the kind of patient that makes a therapist's job easy. You are a very lucky man to have Sarah for your wife. She's been taken into the heart of many here and will be missed."

Fillip didn't respond although his attention was still on Lupe. Lupe quickly grew uncomfortable. "Well Sarah, I must be seeing to my other patients. I won't say goodbye since I will be seeing you on Tuesdays and Fridays." He nodded to Fillip. "Buenos dias, Señor Castañola, and thank-you for permitting me to see Sarah's therapy through."

Sarah nodded her farewell to Lupe and he departed quickly. Her attention returned to the room that had been stripped of her possessions.

Fillip walked toward her and said. "I have signed your discharge papers. You have an appointment with Rubio on the seventeenth. And, Nurse Castillo left your last dose of pain medication for you on the table."

"Fillip where's Marguerite and all my things?"

"My car wasn't suitable to take your things, so Ramón came and picked them up. He also gave Nurse Castillo a ride home, so she wouldn't have to take the metro. He will also fill your pain prescription. Nurse Castillo insisted too that I make sure you take it as scheduled. But, I do have a personal message for you. She said, "Not to worry for you haven't seen the last of her and she will look for your building." She wouldn't explain to me about the building. Do you understand her message?"

Sarah smiled. "Yes, I understand." Sarah didn't want to explain it either, so she made a statement that was sure to distract Fillip from inquiring about it further. "You know you didn't have to leave work for me, since Ramón had to come by to take my things, I could have gone with him."

Fillip smiled ruefully and put his hands on either side of Sarah's wheelchair. "Now what kind of a proper home coming would that be, sending you home with a servant? No, you must go home with me. I want to show you our home and see you settled before I finish at the office today."

Fillip crouched now in front of the wheelchair and his eyes darkened with a look of passion. "With your permission, Señora Castañola, I will get the car and have the nurse bring you down, so we can go home." His hands moved from the arms of the wheelchair and came to hold Sarah's face before he took her lips.

As Sarah responded and their kiss deepened, Sarah found she wanted to be held and caressed, but fortunately her injury and the wheelchair prevented what her body willfully demanded. At last Fillip released her lips, although he still held a certain enchantment over her, as well as her gaze. Fillip was aware of Sarah's new response to his kiss. He stood to his feet, leaned back down, and kissed Sarah's forehead at her hairline. He moved his head only inches away from hers as he spoke. "We should be going, our future waits – impatiently."

Sarah didn't respond but she didn't have to. Fillip and her body had said it all.

Chapter 16

The trip home to live with Fillip started the moment his strong arms lifted her out of the wheelchair and into the car. After being kissed so warmly by Fillip only moments earlier, being in his arms felt alarmingly exciting and she was reluctant for him to release her. Alone for only a few moments as Fillip loaded her wheelchair and walker into the car's trunk, Sarah sternly warned herself against allowing such feelings to take advantage of her.

She was coming to terms with her own expanding thoughts and feelings, but she was unsure Fillip would come to accept salvation. True her heart told her she belonged here in Spain which meant Fillip, but her mind still warned her of her school-girl fears of loving unwisely, being used, and then being rejected.

Fillip opened his door and Sarah's thoughts were brought back from their reverie. His manner with her had always been forthright and Sarah suddenly was ashamed of casting him in a villainous self-serving role. She avoided looking at him for fear he might understand her thoughts, and carefully put her seat belt on and looked out her window at the hospital. Only when he said nothing and started driving the car, did she look at him. Sarah relaxed against the plush seat and chided herself for being foolish enough to think he might be able to read her thoughts.

Sarah broke the silence to salve her conscience. "Tell me about your house and servants."

Fillip didn't answer immediately as he wasn't sure how to tell her about the house that had captivated her in oil and frightened her in person. He started with the servants. "We have Ramón and Carmen who are married. Carmen is my housekeeper and cook. When I was first able to afford a housekeeper, Carmen was recommended by Raúl, my business partner and friend. After I designed and built my house, I needed to hire additional help. I needed someone who could do heavy work as well as oversee the landscaping, so I hired Ramón. I can't imagine how I would keep our house without them."

Sarah heard his natural use of "our house". She hadn't seen his house, but she understood the pride he took in a house he had designed and built.

Fillip continued. "And, today they are joined by a new servant. I hired a young woman, María Vargas, who will be your personal maid and help Carmen and Ramón as she is able."

"Fillip, you hired someone to help me. Why? I've been released from the hospital. I'm certainly not helpless. My being a part of your life has cost you a fortune from the day we met."

Fillip laughed pleasantly. "Actually, getting to know you didn't get expensive until the second day." Fillip quickly sobered. He didn't like remembering the accident. "Carmen and Ramón have needed help for quite some time and whenever you don't need María, she will be helping them."

"Besides she's Gail's niece. You remember Gail Hernaneles, my secretary?" Sarah nodded and remembered how much she'd liked her. "So, now there are two less applicants wanting jobs at Castañola Industries. She's very inexperienced so you and Carmen will have to train her in all her duties."

"I've never had a maid, so I'm not the one who can train her." Sarah had caught the word two less applicants. "Wait! What do you mean two less applicants?"

"María had applied to be a secretary at Castañola, but we have no opening. So, when I mentioned looking for a new maid at my house, Gail suggested María. She said she is deeply religious, so I believe you will like her."

Sarah prodded Fillip. "And, what of the second applicant?"

"I looked at Jesús' application. We have no factory openings, but there's a need for additional office help now. Since he has had several years of business classes, he is qualified. The pay is only slightly better than the unskilled factory workers, but he'll work day shift hours. Personnel offered him the job first thing this morning and he's agreed to start in two weeks."

Sarah was just beaming. "If you didn't do it just for me and you weren't driving, I'd give you a big hug and kiss."

Fillip continued as if he hadn't heard her. "The current office assistant, Raphael, came from the factory staff and has taken night classes for several years and has earned a business degree. He has been helping Raúl, my partner, who has not been well for a long time now in addition to his regular duties. He's earned his new position. With Raphael's promotion and Jesús taking his place I will have more time for my bride who I want to spoil." Fillip's eyes briefly left the road and held Sarah's eyes. "As for the hug and kiss, I'll call for full payment later."

Sarah blushed as Fillip's words caused her nerve endings to tingle. "It seems everything is working out. Everyone has a job to do." Sarah paused. "Everyone but me – let's see, Raphael assists Raúl and Jesús assists your office. María takes care of me, and Carmen, Ramón, and María take care of the house. So, what do I do?"

Fillip had cleared the city traffic and normally he would have permitted his sports car to roar down the country road, but he held it back as he had not yet prepared Sarah to see the house. "Why you have the most important job. Your job is to get well and to take care of me. And, I've been sadly neglected for a long time now, Sarah, so you might have to work at your job day and *night.*"

Sarah blushed at what Fillip implied. "I'm not so sure that I will be able to handle such a demanding job."

Fillip released his right hand from the steering wheel and touched her cheek. "You need not worry for I, mi querida, I am looking forward to being your most patient and dedicated teacher."

Sarah's blush drained to pallor as she sat stunned by the depth of Fillip's words. Sarah suddenly was confronted by her virginity and the realization that she was going to live with the man who could claim it. Fillip had meant his words to reassure her, so he returned his hand to the steering wheel and laughed.

He turned the subject to the one thing that was becoming increasingly important as the miles past. "Sarah, I need to tell you about our house."

Sarah was relieved to have the subject changed, although going to live in Fillip's house was a part of what had just frightened her. "I'd like to hear about it."

"The house I built Sarah, our home, you've seen in a painting and have been in its driveway. Our house is El Alba Rosa." He looked at Sarah to see if he could read her reaction to what he had said but she showed no emotion.

"I don't know what frightened you so much that day I took you there, but I hope you will not be shocked today. I want you to love the house as I do. I have altered it slightly to make you comfortable and I want you to add to my life the things you said were missing from the painting." Fillip stopped at the entrance of the driveway that Sarah remembered. "Sarah won't you say something? Are you alright?"

Sarah took a deep breath, nodded and forced a smile. Surely, she thought that the Lord had called her to this place. She had felt strongly about the painting. "Yes, I'm fine. I feel a little foolish though. I made such a fuss because I didn't want to disturb the owners." She took another deep breath and laughed lightly. "Will you show me your home now, please?"

Fillip moved the car down the driveway, but before Fillip stopped the car at the stairway, the door of the house opened, and Ramón came down the steps to them. Fillip got out of the car, tossed the keys to Ramón and spoke to him in Spanish. Sarah released her seat belt and opened the car door, looked at Ramón and then the house. Fillip scooped Sarah up out of the car and introduced her to Ramón.

"Sarah this is Ramón and Ramón this is your mistress, Señora Sarah Castañola." Fillip said her name with a sound of pride she had only heard before when he spoke about El Alba Rosa.

Sarah thought that Ramón looked to be a man in his late fifties. He was a man of short stature and medium built with slightly greying dark hair. "Hola, Ramón. It's good to meet you. Thank you for picking up my things, getting my pain medication, and taking Nurse Castillo home.

"Da nada, Señora Castañola and welcome to your new home. If you need anything, please do not hesitate to call on me."

Fillip shifted Sarah's weight in his arms a little impatiently as if to say their pleasantries could wait until later. Sarah tightened her hold around Fillip as he started up the wide white stone stairway to the opened door. At the doorway, he stopped and grinned at her a little breathlessly. "I'll carry you over the threshold again when you can walk on your own."

He carried her over the threshold and in the great foyer stood Carmen and María to meet her. Ramón came in quickly behind the couple and opened Sarah's wheelchair. Sarah was not heavy but the constant burden of her weight and carrying her up the stairs had taken its toll on Fillip, who gratefully lowered Sarah into her wheelchair.

Sarah gave Fillip a little time to catch his breath, as she introduced herself to Carmen and María. She first extended her hand out to the older woman. Carmen looked well suited to be the wife of Ramón. Sarah thought she was younger than Ramón, petite, but heavy boned. Her dark hair showed only a little grey.

"I'm looking forward to tasting more of your cooking, although I probably should be careful about how often I let myself eat your elegant desserts."

"You are most kind Señor Castañola."

Sarah extended her hand to María. Sarah judged her to be about twenty, blonde and very pretty. Sarah smiled at her broadly when she thought about the impact such a lovely and devoted girl might have on the blithe Lupe. "María it is good to meet you. It's nice not to be the only new person here. I'll try not to give you too much trouble."

María's faced relaxed as Sarah spoke. "Oh, no Señora Castañola, you can be no trouble. I am very grateful to be working for you. My aunt has said that we are very much alike."

Sarah smiled at the lovely girl who was obviously not vain about her looks as she spoke of their heart for God.

Sarah sat back in her chair and looked at Fillip before she spoke. She knew that Fillip had taken on a sense of pride hearing her called Señora Castañola, but she was not comfortable with the name. "I look forward to getting to know each of you, and I hope to learn your language, so I'll need your patience with my attempts. I'm not used to being served, so I'll probably not make a good mistress. So, I think we should all agree now that we shouldn't be formal. I would like you all to call me Sarah, so we can be at ease with each other from the beginning."

The servants looked at Fillip and then each other. Finally, Ramón answered for them. "Sí, Señora Sarah. We look forward to serving you."

Sarah's gentle manner and graciousness had already opened the door to a relationship with the servants that Fillip could not readily understand. Sarah planned on being their friend and she wouldn't have them wait on her for long.

"Well, now that you've all met, how about a tour of the downstairs?" Fillip asked.

The servants moved away to tend to their duties while Sarah took in the grandeur of the two-story entrance and dual curved oak stairway that formed the upper gallery. Fillip took Sarah to the first room at the right of the hallway. "This is our formal living room." The room appeared to be near the size of Sarah's whole first floor and it was fashionably decorated with a grand piano near the room's front floor to ceiling alcove window. The room also had a massive stone fireplace directly across from its double hung sliding panel doors and the portrait El Alba Rosa hung above it.

"What a magnificent room. It looks as if the fireplace was built just to display that painting."

Fillip pushed Sarah to the door at the far end of the room. Sarah looked back at the plush rug they were traversing, and she saw no wheel tracks. "I'm glad you like it. Back here is the formal dining room." The room was half-paneled in a light oak and a three-pane window allowed ample light in to reflect off the room's chandelier. The room included a massive serving buffet and two matching china cabinets.

"Do you have enough company to fill all these chairs?"

Fillip laughed. "We can fill those chairs and more with my brother and sisters and their families. Once you're well, I expect we will host some business dinners. I have needed a wife to do justice to such dinners." Fillip leaned down and kissed the top of Sarah's head as they exited the door at the left of the room. The door opened into a hallway at the rear of the foyer. Fillip opened a door in the hall. "This is our guest bathroom. I am afraid that it was not built with wheelchair access."

The bathroom was large and neutrally decorated in shades of green and gold. "This house is pleasantly decorated, light, and cheery. Did you do the decorating as well?"

"No, my sisters helped to make many of the choices through the decorating service I used. However, I choose the decor for the master suite and your rooms. You can change anything you like, although I would like to be consulted."

"I haven't seen anything I'd want to change. This house is beyond any skill I would have to decorate it." Fillip turned the wheelchair back into the foyer without taking her down the hall that ran beneath the gallery. "What's down that hallway?"

"The hall leads to the kitchen and servants' bath. They are preparing lunch, so I won't take you in there yet."

Sarah thought it was probably a room he didn't visit much but she felt it was probably the place where she would prefer to eat. She hoped that Carmen would teach her to cook Fillip's favorite foods in that kitchen. She thought that preparing his meals might in a small way let him know her appreciation for all he had done, and, maybe let him know her growing feelings for him.

Fillip stopped in the front hallway and opened the doors, first to his den and then to what Sarah thought would be a family room. The hall also contained another bathroom. The end of the hall had double hung doors that Fillip opened to show her what she thought must be the master bedroom suite. As Fillip wheeled her into the room Sarah was pleased to see that the room wasn't heavily masculine, although she thought it could use a few personal touches.

"This is your suite, until you can manage the stairs. Lupe will do your therapy here and it will be your private sitting area. It has a whirlpool, so you can soak after therapy. The bedroom is through this door and the bath connects with an easily accessed shower and a jetted garden tub."

He allowed her a moment to check out the bedroom before he took her into the bathroom which was flooded with the natural light that came from the opaque floor to ceiling window at the rear of the garden tub. The bedroom had a walk-in closet.

Sarah was astounded by the suite's suitability to her needs. "Fillip this bedroom is incredible. You had to have completely redone this just for me. I can't believe that after all my hospital expenses you did all this."

"You worry too much about the money. This suite was originally designed for my mother who chose to stay with my brother and his family. She adores his home and children. They keep her busy. So, these rooms just became an unused guest suite, until now. When you are well, perhaps it can become a mother-in-law suite. The therapy room equipment is only rented so that area would just normally be a part of the sitting area for your mother and her quests. The furniture that was there is in storage in the garage for now."

Sarah was relieved that the therapy equipment was rented, and she was pleased that Fillip's desire to have her mother live with them was genuine enough that he had thought about these rooms being used by her. "I can't imagine mother in these rooms. She always said that all she wanted was one room in heaven. And here you are offering her splendor above what we've ever seen, let alone lived in."

Fillip brought Sarah back into the sitting area and knelt in front of her wheelchair as had become his habit when he wanted to talk. "This is my house, Sarah. I built it without knowing you or your mother... to fit a life style that I thought I wanted. But, from the moment I saw you looking at the portrait of my house, I knew it was built for you. You've finally come now and it's yours as much as mine and I want you to make it the home that captured your heart."

Sarah remembered her feelings when she saw the house in oil. Fillip saw the beginning tears. "Sarah what did I say? You're not going to cry, are you?"

Sarah responded by taking his head in her hands, leaning over and kissing him briefly but squarely on the mouth. She released him and laughed. "These aren't sad tears. I'm just so overwhelmed that you could have unknowingly created this for me that my eyes are relieving the fullness of my heart."

Sarah saw, for the first time, French doors and she pointed to them as she dug in her dress pocket for a tissue. "So, if you don't want real and abundant tears, why don't you show me where those doors go?"

Fillip had wanted to kiss away her tears but since he didn't understand them and wanted them to stop, he moved to take her to the doors. He swung them open to a small private patio that had been set for lunch, but what Sarah saw was the splendor of the garden that rose behind the stone walls and railing of the patio. "Oh, Fillip. It's incredible. I've never seen such a garden. If human hands can create such beauty, how truly magnificent the Garden of Eden must be."

Fillip took her to the railing, so she could take a closer look. He was very pleased by her response. "This garden was planned by the university's horticultural department. I got your bonsai from them as well. The area was swampy and there was often stagnant water standing were we now have the pond. We had the pond dug deeper and it has underwater drains that siphon the water away from the house. Some of those shrubs hide a pump and filter system which keeps the water clear. The other plants and flowers are species plants and were planted to look natural and to give color most of the year."

As Fillip finished his proud narrative, Sarah used the rail to pull herself to her feet to look at it without the rail in her line of vision. Fillip was not prepared for Sarah's reaction and he quickly pulled the chair back out of the way, so he could stand behind her and lock his arms around her for support. With his arms around her, his body warmth penetrating her skin, Sarah melted against his body. But, even as her body betrayed her, she forced her mind to converse evenly.

"Does the pond have fish?"

Sarah didn't see the smile that lit up Fillip's face as she snuggled up against him. Releasing his hold briefly, he stepped to the side and turned her in his arms until she could see his face. Losing the support of the railing, Sarah's arms encircled Fillip's back, and she stood being held by him for the first time. He had long desired to hold her in his arms, to feel her breasts against his chest. He answered her question with little thought. "The pond was designed to keep fish, but there has been no one to enjoy them until now." Fillip looked at Sarah intently, holding her attention with the clear desire that shone from his eyes, until they forgot about fish. Standing in their own private Eden, their lips yielded to their united desire as they joined in a kiss that fueled their passion until there had to be a release.

Fillip released their kiss, to take in a composing breath and Sarah tightened her hold around his back to bring his lips back to her own. Fillip brought his face back to within fractions of an inch from her face and began to speak. "Sarah, mi amor—." He interrupted himself to feather kisses along Sarah's neck, and cheek, and lips. When his lips touched hers, she moved her lips against his to encourage him to hold and lengthen the kiss, but she met with some resistance to her rising passion. "Sarah, mi amor, we must be patient—."

Fillip couldn't finish his thought as he was interrupted by Ramón as he quietly sat down a tray and started to withdraw. "It's alright, Ramón, we're ready for lunch."

Fillip kissed Sarah slowly and teasingly one more time. "I like the way you paid your promise to reward me with a hug and kiss. I'm looking forward to keeping your favor." Since her chair was not within reach, Fillip scooped her up in his arms and turned with her in several circles before he seated her in the wheelchair.

Sarah felt the same exuberance and joy but with the fresh air and separation from Fillip, she began to feel alarm by her response to him. As Fillip wheeled her to the table, she tried to lighten the ardor of her response. "I trust then the payment was satisfactory and met in full."

Ramón set out salads, bowls of hot chicken soup and rolls. María appeared with their drinks, and desserts, and then they left quickly. Sarah suspected that Fillip had ordered their lunch and privacy. Fillip laughed at Sarah joyfully as he settled her at the table and took his seat. "I suppose that I should be satisfied by the payment, but I'm feeling quite greedy and I'm escalating the debt." Fillip's voice quieted as he looked at Sarah's flushed cheeks. "I'll enjoy being your banker and receiving your payments."

Sarah blushed to full color and took a spoonful of soup without praying.

Chapter 17

Their first few hours together would become memories Sarah would always treasure. She would forget what they had for lunch, but she would remember Fillip's apparent happiness and the ease of their time together in his home.

"I must be getting back to my office." He looked at his watch. "I have a few matters to attend to this afternoon and if I don't leave now I'll be late." He laid aside his linen napkin, came around the table, and sat on the edge before he leaned down and briefly kissed Sarah. "I'll be home by six." He kissed her again a little more leisurely and took her hand and held it between his own.

"I'll need to see that Raphael learns to assist Raúl quickly in a few other areas, now that I have you to draw me home at night." He kissed her again to add emphasis to his words and stood up to leave but Sarah held her gaze on his lips. Fillip kissed her hand mockingly and let it go. "Don't look at me like that or I won't be able to leave you at all."

Sarah continued to hold his eyes with her own, but she smiled mischievously. "Perhaps that's what I am trying to do. I don't know what I'll do here without you."

"I'm not so sure you'd know what to do with me, if I stay." Sarah blushed, and Fillip smiled broadly. He kissed her forehead and turned to leave. A few feet away from the table he stopped. "Don't worry Sarah. We'll not rush that part of our relationship. In the meantime, keep my promise to Mother Carol."

"What promise?"

"Call her this afternoon. She wants to talk to you. Then you can take a rest and explore the house. Open all the doors and drawers and get to know the house. By then I'll be home, and we'll have dinner together."

The idea of exploring the house appealed to Sarah. "Can I explore upstairs?"

"I'm afraid I have not installed an elevator yet, so your exploration upstairs will need to wait until another time when I can take you up. You'll have to contend yourself with the first floor. Now I must run. Call your mother soon and don't worry about costs. I will send María to you, and you can get to know her." Fillip winked and left.

Sarah sat comfortably in her wheelchair absorbing the pleasantness of her new opulent surroundings. It was good to feel the sun on her face again, to hear the wind in the trees and the song of the native birds. Her musing was stopped by the appearance of a few ants on the linen tablecloth that had come to enjoy the remnants of their lunch. Sarah was stacking the assorted dishes when María appeared to clear the table.

María hurriedly sat down her tray and started to load it with the dishes that Sarah had stacked. "Señora Sarah, you must leave these things for me to do. It's my job."

Sarah understood her position. "María, I know you want to do a good job but it's not natural for me to be waited on by others. My injuries are healing, and I no longer need special care, but I do need to be useful. If I live in this house and you work here, you must get use to my being involved. I'm not used to servants, but I can take care of a house," she paused to look around and laughed, "just not one this big."

María stopped and looked at her new mistress and appeared close to tears. Sarah reached out and touched María's arm. "Please don't be upset. I need you, so I can learn about your country, your customs, and your language."

María's eyes cleared as she looked at Sarah and dragged a chair over to sit beside her. "You're homesick for America?"

"Yes. I came here for a vacation, had an accident, was married to Fillip, was in the hospital, and now I'm here. At home, I work in an office and I share a small house with my mother. I miss her, my job, my church, and the people at work. This house is as new to me as it is to you."

María nodded in understanding. "We will be friends and I'll teach you, but now can I do my work?"

Sarah laughed. "I have an idea." Sarah pushed her wheelchair back from the table. "Hand me the tray."

María looked confused but she handed the tray to Sarah. "Now let's go to the kitchen. I haven't been there yet."

Sarah laughed and María joined her as she pushed the wheelchair to the open door. "I'm not sure Carmen will approve."

Sarah giggled. "She doesn't have to approve, and I promise I won't ask to dry the dishes, today. If I am to live here, then I need to work here too, even if it is only in small ways."

Carmen was finishing her lunch when María and Sarah swept through the kitchen door and she spilled her coffee on her apron when she saw them. She quickly toweled off her blouse and ran over to remove the tray from Sarah's wheelchair. The shock of Sarah's arrival with the tray turned to displeasure as she looked at María who was no longer laughing.

Sarah had sobered too. "Carmen, I came to thank you for a wonderful meal and to tell you how much I'm looking forward to eating more of your cooking. I was just telling María that I have no intention of being treated like an invalid. I don't want to interfere with any of your jobs, but I'd like to be useful. As we get used to one another, I hope you'll teach me to cook some of the wonderful dishes of your country. I'm willing to start as an apprentice. I'll help prepare vegetables or anything else that will prove useful."

Carmen looked a little awed. "I'd be pleased to teach you whatever dishes you'd like to prepare. But, you can't work in the kitchen. Señor Castañola wouldn't approve."

Sarah smiled at the women. "It'll be a few more days before I can be truly useful to you, but then it will not be for Fillip's approval since he wants me to be happy here. You are not used to being idle and neither am I. I refuse to be. If this is truly to be my home and I'm to be happy here, then we must be friends first and then I hope a family."

Sarah levered herself out of the chair and supported herself my holding on to the kitchen island. Then she put her arms around Carmen and gave her a hug. Powerless to do anything else and to Sarah's delight Carmen returned the hug. Carmen and María then helped Sarah to reseat herself in the wheelchair. Sarah was becoming very tired, but she added a little more. "I'm sincere. I know Fillip and my ideas differ, but he does want me to be happy here. He's told me to explore and get use to the house. He'll always be the head of this house but if I am to be here I hope to be its heart."

The women were silent, but the house seemed to sigh in relief, as it was clear that the life force needed to change the house into a home had finally come. Carmen smiled at her young mistress. Life at El Alba Rosa had taken on a little spice. "Can I get anything else for you Señora Sarah?"

"Only my pain medicine. Fillip suggested a nap and I think he was right. I need to call a friend first and tell him I am no longer in the hospital, so he won't come to see me there. But, when I've rested I'll be calling home to speak with my mother. Then, if we have time before dinner, perhaps you can acquaint María and me with the house and its contents."

"Sí, Señora Sarah. There's a phone in your sitting room and another one on the bedside table. I'll show you and María the house whenever you are ready. Is there anything you'd like for dinner?"

"No, I'll not upset your menus and I have no diet restrictions. But, thank you for asking."

María wheeled Sarah back to her room and showed her the bedside intercom that was connected to the kitchen and to the servants' apartment above the four-car garage.

"María, I'd like to use the bathroom before I take a nap. I can manage it on my own, so, while I do, would you find my walker for me? It will make moving around in my room easier?"

When Sarah returned from the bathroom, the bed was turned neatly down, the room's drapes were drawn, and the walker was beside the bed. María gave Sarah a glass of water and her pain medicine, then Sarah called the hostel and left Jesús a message. María helped Sarah into bed and then returned to the kitchen to help Carmen.

Sarah stretched out comfortably on the queen bed and took pleasure in the sweet aroma of the coverings. She thanked God for her sweet homecoming, asked for His presence to fill the house, and for Him to use it for His glory. Sweet peace filled her mind as she said amen and gave her body to sleep.

María finished clearing the patio table from the outside garden path and helped with the dishes. The atmosphere in the kitchen was quiet as the ladies thought about their new mistress and started the task of learning to work together in the friendship that Sarah thought so important.

Ramón had finished his outside duties and returned to the kitchen for his afternoon coffee. The staff spoke to each other in Spanish. He heard the report of Sarah's visit to the kitchen and gave it some thought as he finished his coffee. He took his cup to the sink, wrapped his arms around his wife, and gave her a hug. "I've always told you that Fillip needed a good wife. I was only afraid that I had the good fortune of finding the last one."

Carmen was delighted by her husband's flattery. The years had not changed his attitude toward his wife and he still took pleasure in making her aware of his love for her. She replied in kind to his comment. "And, Sarah no doubt will find herself challenged to change Fillip into a husband such as I found."

María watched the exchange without embarrassment but she added a comment of her own. "Is it really the role of a wife to change the man she marries?"

Ramón had not released Carmen, but he responded to the young woman who reminded him of his own daughter. "A woman cannot hope to change a man but when a good woman marries, she changes. And a man cannot hope to change a woman but when he marries a good woman, he changes. But, it is hard to find a good spouse."

Carmen looked into her husband's eyes and kissed him somewhat uncomfortably with María present. But, when she had kissed him soundly she turned to look at María and added to her husband's wisdom. "Look long and carefully before you choose and seek God's approval and you will find him."

Sarah slept unmindful of the stir that her presence had caused in the love shared by Ramón and Carmen. She dreamed of blue eyes looking at her across flickering candles and they were filled with desires that were becoming familiar to her. She awoke saddened to realize that they had never spoken about love. Dark afternoon shadows draped her room and it took a few moments for her to realize she was no longer in the hospital.

Awake she realized where she was. But, sitting up in bed her mind focused on love. She was becoming accustomed to looking at eyes darkened by passion, but that wasn't love. A cloud of doubt entered her heart. Perhaps she was building a marriage based on Fillip's desire and the desire he was stirring in her. *"Dear Lord,"* she sighed into the air, *"can't there be love?"*

Somewhere in the distance Sarah heard the prelude of a chiming clock and she counted out five strikes of its movement. She tossed back her covers and called her mother. Fillip would be home soon, and she really needed to talk to her mother.

Sarah hoped that with the six-hour time difference her mother would be home since she worked part-time. The phone rang six times and Sarah was beginning to fear she wouldn't get to speak to her mother.

Her mother's voice was bright and cheery. "Hello, Kettering residence."

Sarah's voice choked with tears and she was unable to answer so her mother repeated her greeting. "Hello, Kettering residence. Is anyone there?"

Sarah finally choked out her own greeting fearful. "Oh Mother, it's me."

This time the silence was on the other end of the line while Sarah's mother absorbed the thrill of hearing her daughter's voice. "Oh Sarah, it's good to hear from you. Are you really out of the hospital?"

"Yes, I am. Fillip brought me home about noon today. I missed you so much Mom, and I have so much to tell you. Although from Fillip, I gather you've been kept well informed."

"He's been quite wonderful and has called me every day. He even repeated his offer to fly me to Spain, but I was reluctant to abuse his generosity."

"I know what you mean, Mom. But, the money he spends seems to be of little concern to him. He even hired a girl, who started today, to be my personal maid."

"Do you still require that much care? Perhaps I have been a very poor mother and I should arrange to come and be with you."

Sarah got more comfortable on the bed and relaxed as the sound of her mother's voice still brought her the same comfort it had when she had been a child. "No Mom, I don't need that much care. I'm beginning to get along with a walker, although I can't get far with it. You wouldn't believe the size of his house. It's so big it has its own name. It's called El Alba Rosa. It means the daybreak or dawn rose. He says that María..."

Sarah trailed off at what she started to say. "Sarah, what is it? I'm your mother and I can tell something is wrong."

Sarah felt like a little girl and she poured out her heart for Fillip, the people of the country, and what she thought might be her call to serve God in Spain.

"But, Mom, Fillip and I have never spoken of love. How can we be husband and wife without love? He speaks of our future together like we're truly married. I'm sitting in a first-floor bedroom suite he had changed for me and plans to give to you if you come to live here with us. It's all too much for me!"

Fillip's phone conversations with Mother Carol had given her first-hand knowledge of Sarah's physical condition. Sarah's confession to her mother informed her of vistas that Carol had never contemplated. Carol had believed in an easily annulled marriage to a man that had extended himself for her daughter out of compassion not passion. And, whereas she knew that God could call her daughter into service she had always hoped it would be as a pastor's wife, somewhere in America. She needed time to sort out everything Sarah had said.

"Sarah, I wish I had an answer for you. As your mother, I want to protect you and tell you to come home, but as Fillip is your husband and has done nothing wrong, I can't give such advice. And, as for God's call, Sarah, isn't it the answer to your prayers? I heard in your voice a real concern for the lives of the people whom you've come to know. If He has truly called you there, we know He can work it all out."

Carol paused as she searched her mind for what to say. "From the time you turned from being a child and I had to admit you were becoming a young woman, I prayed for you and the man you would marry. The importance of that commitment was so important to your father and me that we bought your promise ring."

Sarah looked at the ring that encircled her engagement finger. She hadn't thought of it during the past few weeks.

"If your promise is to end with Fillip, then I trust God it is right. You must give yourself and Fillip time and I will pray for you but—."

"But, what mother?"

"I don't want you to be hurt Sarah. I always warned you about loving too easily, but it wouldn't be right for me to tell you not to love the man you've married."

Sarah closed her eyes in pain. Her mother wasn't there to see it, but she heard it in her response. "But, our marriage wasn't out of love, we'd only just met. I never heard the vows Fillip spoke and I took none myself. We met one day, and he married me dying the next. Does a legal document make us husband and wife?"

"Most marriages start off better than yours, child, but if I understand what I am hearing it sounds as if there is more between you and Fillip than a certificate of marriage. I'm afraid you'll have to decide for yourself. Call me in a few days and tell me how things are going. In the meantime, I'll add my prayers to yours and we'll continue to leave things with God."

Sarah knew the call had been long and she really couldn't expect her mother to tell her what was right or what to do, but she asked only one more thing from her mother. "Mom pray for us now."

Carol Kettering's voice called out to the throne of God. Sarah was comforted by her mother's prayer. "Thank you, Mom. I love you. Good-bye."

Across the vastness of the earth and ocean, a familiar goodbye reached Sarah's ears. "Remember whose you are child and that God loves you and so do I."

Chapter 18

Sarah sat and looked at her ring for some minutes after she'd cradled the phone. Technically the ring was no longer hers, but for a time unknown to her she could still wear it. In the distance, Sarah heard a clock chime and she knew another half hour had past. If she had explored the house with María, she would have seen the massive grandfather clock. Hearing the chime, Sarah realized that Fillip would soon be home, and she needed to freshen up. She struggled to her feet and maneuvered the walker to the bathroom. In the first vanity drawer she opened, she found all the toiletry items that had been in her night case. Sarah brushed her teeth, applied fresh lipstick, combed through her hair, and caught the right side of her hair up in a pretty barrette. Her face only bore faint bruises, and she saw a healthy glow and maybe the excitement of a woman expecting to see her new husband.

As she left the bathroom, she thought about going to meet Fillip in the entry hall, but her attention was drawn to a book on the bottom of the table next to the settee. When she had seated herself on the settee, she pulled the book up from the table and immediately knew she still had Jesús' Bible. Sarah's departure from the hospital had not given her time to return the Bible or to tell Jesús she was staying in Spain. Since it was late in the day, Sarah decided to send the Bible with a note to Jesús in the morning with Ramón. She had just laid the Bible next to the phone to look for her journal when Fillip quietly opened the door. When he saw Sarah on the settee, he went to her, pulled her into his arms, and kissed her before he spoke.

"María said you were still sleeping." He let her pull back. "You don't have to stay in your room."

Sarah was attracted to the warmth and comfort of Fillip's arms and chest and her body of its own volition snuggled against his shoulder. "I slept until five then talked to Mom. I wanted to meet you in the foyer, but I was too late. I'm sorry I slept so long. I'll have to explore through all the nooks and crannies tomorrow after breakfast."

Fillip moved Sarah from his shoulder, so he could look into her face. "You owe me no apology, me querida. You need to rest whenever and as long as necessary. The house will wait for you. Is it everything you imagined?"

"Just as you painted it, although I never imagined having my own luxurious room in it."

Sarah smiled happily, and Fillip took the opportunity to pull her into his arms. "Ah, but this room is only temporary. As soon as you are well you will join me in our master suite." He held her close and softly rained kisses on her lips and whispered in her ear. "It's wonderful to be near you like this."

As he spoke, his hand traveled beneath the softness of her sweater and stopped to gently caress her breast through the fabric of her dress and bra. His lips continued to extol kisses on hers and just as his fingers managed to touch her bare flesh, Sarah's virgin senses demurred, and she pulled herself away.

"I thought we were going to have dinner at six."

Fillip chuckled softly and pulled Sarah back into his arms. "I said I would be home by six and we would have dinner. I was just enjoying a little appetizer, first." But, before Sarah could respond, he was nibbling at her lips and then kissing her soundly. Once again, she responded to his embrace and his kisses, much to his delight, but he didn't take any further liberties. He released her to retrieve the wheelchair, and Sarah suddenly felt deprived of his touch.

Fillip was pleased. Sarah no longer resisted his kisses or his embrace. In time she would accept his touch and her body's natural response to his increasing demands.

He stopped the chair in front of Sarah and looked at her innocently. "Your chair, mujer, dinner waits."

Sarah moved to the chair without comment and Fillip moved her thorough the lighted corridors to the foyer. At the foyer, Sarah asked Fillip to stop.

"What is it, mi querida?"

"I was looking for the clock that chimes the hour and the half hour, but I don't see it."

Fillip moved the wheelchair near the front door and turned Sarah to the stairway. "The clock is in the gallery on the second floor. Do you see it?"

The second floor was not lighted, but Sarah couldn't miss the clock that had been placed at the center of the gallery. Behind the clock the walls were barren. "Those walls could use a few family portraits. Do you have any photographs that could be hung there?"

Fillip stroked the back of Sarah's neck with his fingers providing a warm gentle massage. "Mother has a few she might allow copied to hang there. But perhaps soon we can supply our own pictures. We'll have a picture of us together, then our babies, and then us with the children."

Sarah looked back at Fillip. He rolled his eyes and shrugged his shoulders as if to say, "What?"

Sarah shook her head. "Might we have dinner first?"

Fillip laughed. "Of course, mi querida."

Fillip propelled Sarah into the dining room where the table had been set for two near the kitchen door. "Just the two of us are going to eat in here?"

Fillip was surprised. "Yes, where else would we eat dinner tonight? We lunched on the patio for privacy and the fresh afternoon air, so you should enjoy the dining room this evening. We wouldn't eat in the kitchen with the servants?"

Sarah hadn't given it much thought. At home, she and mother always ate in the kitchen when there was just the two of them, but they had no servants. "Did you eat in here when you were alone?"

Fillip pressed an intercom and their salad and rolls were brought. Sarah thanked Ramón. Fillip didn't answer, and Sarah knew he was waiting for her to offer a silent prayer for her evening meal. Sarah surprised him by taking his hand and praying aloud.

"Gracious, Father. We thank you for the bounty of this home and the food that has been prepared for us this evening. We ask your blessing on it for ourselves and our servants. Nourish us with this food and let us work to your glory. Amen."

Sarah released Fillip's hand and placed her napkin in her lap and offered him the breadbasket. He remained quiet until he had taken a roll from the basket. "I believe you asked if I took my meals here. The answer is, yes. I was never lonely, though, at least I wasn't aware of it until now." Sarah stopped buttering her roll and looked at him to see he was still looking at her. "Do you often hold hands to say grace?"

Sarah laid down her roll and knife. "When we sat down as a family, we always did. Father said that holding hands not only united us in prayer, but it gave us an opportunity to touch one another. Families too often permit themselves to become distant from such simple gestures like hugging and kissing one another."

Fillip thought of his own childhood and understood what Sarah had said. It was difficult to think of touching her without showing her the building passion he felt.

They ate silently for a time before Ramón returned with the main course. Ramón set before Sarah a plate of sirloin tips in onions and green peppers with a baked potato dripping with butter, cheese, and bacon.

Sarah's face beamed seeing her favorite American meal. "Muchas gracias, Ramón."

"Da nada, Señora Sarah. Señor Castañola found out from your mother some of your favorite dishes. It was very simple to prepare."

Sarah reached across the table and squeezed Fillip's hand. Her gesture pleased him.

"It seemed only right to welcome you with your favorite meal. We have two countries to unite."

"Please, thank Carmen for me too. You all have made me feel accepted here. And, I think if you can call me Señora Sarah you all should call Fillip, Señor Fillip. Isn't that right, Fillip?"

Fillip smiled at her and nodded. He decided not to challenge Sarah's concept of equality. "Yes, Ramón, I do believe it's time." He reached out, shook Ramón's hand, and looked meaningfully at Sarah. "I think it's the first of many changes that Sarah will bring to our house."

Ramón picked up their salad plates and returned to the kitchen to share the conversation with his wife. For dessert that evening, Carmen prepared Natillas with lady fingers. So, their first dinner at home as husband and wife was a blend of Spanish and American food. After dinner, Sarah persuaded Fillip to take her to the kitchen, so she could personally thank Carmen for her selection and preparation of their first dinner. She also took the opportunity to apologize for sleeping the afternoon away.

"Oh, no Señora Sarah. You needn't apologize. You have been in the hospital and I understand. You will see the house as you are able."

Fillip gave her an "I told you so look", but Sarah's sincerity strengthened her bond with Carmen and Ramón. Before they left the kitchen, Sarah told Fillip of her kitchen plans. "I think it only fair to tell you Fillip that Carmen has agreed to let me help in the kitchen from time to time so she can teach me the art of cooking in this house. So, at some time you will be subject to my cooking."

Here was another point to which Fillip knew he would concede. He didn't want Sarah to work in the kitchen, but he knew she would and it would make her happy. It's what she would want to do as a wife. He knelt beside her chair and kissed her hands. "I'll be pleased to eat anything your hands prepare."

The kitchen was filled that evening with a warmth and familiarity it had never known before. Fillip took Sarah into the family room, helped her to the couch, and turned on the television. He came back and sat beside her and draped his arm over her shoulders.

"I usually watch the news after dinner. I hope it won't bore you."

Sarah sat tensely beside Fillip, waiting for him to press his romantic overtures, but they simply watched the television together comfortably with Fillip providing needed translations. Despite Sarah's nap and her companion's attentions, Sarah fell asleep on his shoulder sometime after nine. Sarah was only slightly disturbed when Fillip picked her up and carried her to her room. She didn't stir until she was laid on her rumpled bed.

She smiled at Fillip sleepily. "I'm sorry. It seems I'm making a habit of falling asleep on you."

Fillip sat beside her on her bed. He stroked her hair back against the pillows and leaned down ever so slowly, looking into her eyes, down to kiss her, once, twice, and then passionately. When all her will ebbed, she locked her arms around him to hold him against her. Fillip's breathing became ragged and with a great deal of effort he removed Sarah's arm from around his neck as he sat up. "I want you to fall asleep beside me every night for the rest of our lives, but you're not ready for what will come first."

He brushed her cheek with his fingertips. "I want there to be no regrets, Sarah, no recriminations, no guilt." He smiled at her and feathered a kiss against her lips. "Make no mistake it's difficult to be patient, but I'll give you time." He pulled her into his arms. His kiss was hard and demanding, as if that one kiss would release and satisfy the desire in his body. Failing he released her and she fell back against her pillow as he walked purposely toward the door. "Forgive me, Sarah, I'm not a patient man. I won't be able to keep my promise if I help you change."

Then, he was gone.

Sarah laid thoroughly awake against her pillow and touched her lips. She still felt the hard pressure of his lips against hers as she fingered the tender tissue. She looked into the cold fireplace at the end of the room and knew if he hadn't stopped she would have let him continue, although she wasn't sure she could have seen it thorough to its natural conclusion. All she knew now was that without his body touching hers was she felt bereft. She touched the empty pillow beside her and was joyless.

She reasoned with herself. *If this is what my husband wants, and my body wants it too, how can it be wrong? Fillip had awakened a part of her that had been dormant, an untouched part no other's kisses had even faintly stirred. But she knew it wasn't right for her. Fillip was right. They both could want it and it still could be wrong.* The room was dark and chilly and offered her no comfort. Sarah sat up in bed and looked for her walker or wheelchair. The walker was out of her reach near the settee and the wheelchair was still in the family room. She wasn't sure of the time, but she had no alternative but to use the intercom. María answered.

Ramón and Carmen had retired to their apartment but María was working on the morning breakfast and hadn't left yet.

"Sí, Señora Sarah. Do you need something?"

"Yes. I'm sorry to disturb you but I can't reach my walker, so I can prepare for bed."

"I'll be there soon."

In a few minutes, there was a light knock on the door and María entered. She went to the settee and brought the walker to Sarah's bed.

Sarah tried to explain to María. "I fell asleep while Fillip and I was watching the television. When he carried me to bed, he forgot about my walker."

Sarah's appearance said a little more had happened, but María only nodded. "I'll get your night things for you. While you slept this afternoon, Carmen and I cleaned and pressed your clothing. You didn't bring many things with you. I think you'll need to buy more things. Fillip has a household account for us at the department store in the city. You can make a list of the things you need, and Carmen said Ramón can take me to buy them for you."

Inexplicably, Sarah began to cry. At first, María stood helplessly at Sarah's closet door. She had draped Sarah's nightgown and robe over her arm. After a moment, she went to her new mistress. She took Sarah in her arms and held her while the tears turned to sobs. She patted and stroked her back and murmured words of comfort in Spanish. María never tried to stop the tears, but when Sarah had quieted, she handed her several tissues from the box on her nightstand.

"Thank you." Sarah wiped her eyes and blew her nose. "I'm sorry to trouble you like this. I don't often burst into tears for no apparent reason."

"I don't think you are crying without reason now. You have been through many things and they have not been easy. Then, today you came home to a new house full of strangers. Even Fillip is still new to you, I think. I wouldn't like to go through an accident and hospitalization in a strange country."

"But, everyone has been so kind to me. I miss my mother, but it would have been difficult for her to come to a strange country especially without knowing the language. Even without her here, I don't feel alone. María I trust in God and He has not left me without comfort here. Even now He has provided you to comfort me."

María smiled. "I have only known you a few hours, but I'm glad your difference is due to your trust in God. I trust God, too. I go to early mass every Sunday."

"Does Fillip go to mass on Sunday?"

María shook her head. "I know Carmen and Ramón go. My Aunt Gail has said that Fillip is good to the church, but he has not gone much since the death of his father. He works hard at his business. But, I think you will change this."

"I don't think it's wise for a person to marry, believing they can change the other person."

María patted Sarah's hand. "I think you are wise as well as pretty. You're not going to change Fillip, but I think he will change for loving you."

Sarah shook her head sadly. "That's the problem. I don't believe what we have is love. How can he love me when we've only known each other for a short time? For most of our relationship I have been in the hospital or asleep. I don't even understand my own feelings. When I am with him I feel so wonderful yet confused, and without him I feel alone and uncertain. Is that love?"

"Have you ever felt this way before?"

Sarah took in a sudden deep breath and let it out slowly while she thought of her answer. "No. There's never been joy, like what I feel when I am with him, and there's never been sadness like what I feel when we don't agree. I have never desired any other man."

María laughed lightly. "It sounds like love to me or at least a worthy imitation. But, since it's new and you and Fillip are not well acquainted, like a seed you may need to let it have time to grow and blossom before you'll be able to call it love."

Sarah closed her eyes as if in pain and María reached out a hand to touch Sarah's. "What is it? Does your leg hurt?"

"My leg always seems to hurt, but it's not my leg, although I could use my pain medicine, it's my heart, María. I'm afraid that if love is the seed planted here that it may be unwise to let it continue to root and grow, let alone permit it to blossom."

María withdrew her hand. Fillip was Sarah's husband and was known to be kind and generous employer and she didn't like what Sarah said. Sarah understood María's withdrawal.

"Perhaps because you love God, you can understand my reluctance to love someone who doesn't share my trust in God or my desire to serve Him."

María remained unmoved, not certain of what Sarah meant by her service to God. "I always pictured myself a minister's wife. And, now I find my husband is not a minister, not reared in my faith, and not even serving in the faith of his family."

María eyes registered her understanding. "Sí, he is none of these things, but you trust in God and He has allowed this marriage to come about." She patted Sarah's hand. "My grandmother has said to my married siblings that they must work for their marriages, and she quoted her in Spanish and then in English, *"Love is not an easy road to travel but when God sets the yoke and guides the team who can declare the team unsuitable?"*

Chapter 19

After sharing her burden with María, Sarah prepared for bed. María found her pain meds and brought Sarah a glass and a fresh pitcher of water. She put the bottle on her night table and vowed to do a better job taking them on schedule as instructed by Nurse Castillo. Then, María left and Sarah slept. The long night hours passed quietly for Sarah after her cry and conversation with María.

In the master bedroom suite on the second floor, the night hours were long and marred by restless turnings and time spent staring out the balcony doors into the night. Fillip dressed and dutifully suffered a portion of his normal breakfast before he went to his study to work on some of the papers he had brought home. His concentration was broken from time to time as he listened for sounds from the bedroom suite at the end of the corridor.

Sarah was disconcerted by her surroundings when she first awakened but when she realized she was in Fillip's house she smiled and relaxed in the comfort of the bed. She wasn't sure of the time as her travel alarm hadn't been placed on her nightstand but the light peeping through her drapes made her decide to get up. Using her walker, she opened drawers and discovered the locations of her things, including the alarm clock. She tucked the alarm and her under things in the walker bag, went to the closet, and selected a pair of dark green slacks, a white polyester blouse and light green cardigan. She prepared for the day slowly, using the walker to support herself, but finally she was dressed and combed on her own.

When she was done, she went to the nightstand to get the two Bibles and placed them in her walker bag. Sarah remembered the alarm in her bag and took it and set it on the nightstand with a little pat. She was being to feel at home although she hadn't managed to clean up after herself. She decided that for a little while the task of making her bed, opening the drapes, and tidying up would have to be done by María. She wasn't happy with the thought, but she had little choice, so she moved back to the settee to have her personal time. When she was done, she left her Bible on the table for her next quiet time.

Sarah sat on the settee for a while, uncertain as to what she should do next. She wondered where Fillip might spend his Saturday morning and what the normal routine of the staff might be. She knew she could summon help by pressing the intercom, but she didn't want to interrupt anyone to get to the kitchen. After a few minutes of indecision, Sarah decided to ignore her stomach's mild complaints in favor of a visit to the garden.

When she opened the patio doors the sunshine and fresh air made her glad about her decision. Sarah left the door ajar and cautiously moved to the edge of the patio and down the incline of the garden path. Her progress around the garden path was slow and tiring but eventually she came to a little bench beside the pond and gratefully sat down. As she rested from her efforts, she was appreciative of the warmth of her sweater as the morning air was cool. She also understood the wise restrictions of her use of the walker and knew she would have to spend some time in the garden before she could even attempt the return to her room.

When the gallery clock stuck ten, Fillip decided it was time to make sure that Sarah was alright. He didn't knock on her door but peaked in and saw her empty bed and unkempt room. He stepped into the room and called her name. When she didn't respond, he checked the bathroom. He went to the intercom to call the kitchen when he noticed that the patio door was slightly opened.

He went to the door, saw no one on the patio, and started to close and lock the door, but as he pushed the door closed a new sound came to his ears. He opened the door and went to the balcony railing to listen. Sarah had found the peace of the garden nourishing to her soul and the words to a favorite hymn had come to her mind. Sarah's voice was pleasant and what it lacked in greatness was more than compensated for by the heart felt meaning she gave to the words of, "In the Garden", as she sang. Fillip stood at the railing taking in the sound and beauty filling him.

When Sarah finished, her spirit continued its praise and sweet fellowship unaware that she had been heard or that her song had stirred another heart. The beauty of the garden was not lost to Fillip, but this morning it had been buoyed by Sarah and her gift of praise. The hours of his long night and his displeasure with Sarah for causing him such misery had been displaced and he moved quietly down the path to join her.

Sarah looked up at him and smiled when he was several yards away. If her song hadn't melted away his angst from his restless night her smile would have, and he breathed her name.

"Sarah."

Sarah returned his greeting in the same tone. "Fillip." Without another word between them, Fillip joined her on the bench and enfolded her in his arms and their lips were drawn together. When Fillip released her, the tranquility of the garden was strained for neither knew what to say to the other. Sarah's tummy grumbled, and she laughed in embarrassment as she placed her hand on it to quiet it down.

Fillip looked at her with concern. "Sarah, have you had breakfast?"

"No. After I dressed, I didn't think I could manage to get to the kitchen. I know I probably should have called the kitchen, but I didn't want to bother anyone." Sarah laughed at herself. "Lupe warned me not to go too far, but the beauty of the garden called me here. Now I'm afraid I can't get back to my room, let alone the kitchen without help."

Fillip took Sarah's hand and caressed and kissed it lightly. He had hired María to look after Sarah, and she hadn't done her job properly. He would be having a serious talk with the girl about her responsibilities. But, for now there was Sarah. "Then, permit me to assist you lovely lady. Where's your wheelchair?"

Sarah shrugged her shoulders. "I imagine it is in the family room—." Sarah started to add a comment about him carrying her to her room, but she was reluctant to remind him.

Fillip looked at her quizzically. "Family room? Oh, you mean the den." He now remembered carrying her to her room and laying her on her bed. But, he pushed the memories and his unquenched desires aside. "Then, we best be off to retrieve it." He swept Sarah into his arms in a now familiar style, and Sarah draped her arms around his shoulders and laid her head comfortably against his neck. She hadn't planned to take advantage of his nearness, but her body was responding on its own accord and Fillip groaned in response. Fillip stalked off purposely, but in his mind sighed, *"Oh, Sarah, please don't touch me, unless you're ready to be loved."*

He marched them through her bedroom and Sarah opened the door to the den when they arrived at the door. Fillip lowered her into the chair with some undisguised relief and took her to the dining room. He rang the intercom.

"Fillip, really, why don't I just go eat in the kitchen. It would be much easier for them and I wouldn't be eating alone. Unless you haven't eaten, either?"

Fillip patted her hand. "The staff is prepared to serve our meals here and I've eaten but I'll have coffee with you."

Ramón came into the room and Fillip spoke to him. "Sarah needs her breakfast and I'll have coffee. What would you like for breakfast, Sarah?"

Sarah directed her attention to Ramón. "Good morning, Ramón. Could I have a scrambled egg, toast, and tea, if it is no bother?"

Ramón smiled at Sarah encouragingly. "Good morning, Señora Sarah. It's no bother; it's our job to serve you."

Ramón turned to leave when Fillip added. "Ramón ask María to come here please."

Fillip turned to Sarah. "You must learn that our servants are here to deal with the house and not to be so uncomfortable with giving them your— requests." Fillip had started to say orders, but he thought better of it remembering how Sarah felt about employees and servants.

Before Sarah could respond, María joined them in the dining room, bringing Fillip's coffee and cream, and her tea. "Good morning Señor Fillip and Señora Sarah."

"Good morning, María. I wanted to clarify your duties." Fillip immediately started to address his concern. "Sarah has been up for some time now. She dressed without assistance, but—." Sarah cut Fillip off unceremoniously. María looked frightened and Sarah was disturbed that María was being unfairly reprimanded for not coming to her when she hadn't been given the opportunity.

"Yes, I did, and it felt quite good, but it was perhaps a little unwise on my part. I left the bath and the bedroom in a total state of disarray and I'm sorry since you must now set things right. Tomorrow when I get up I'll call you and with your assistance I'm sure things will go better. If you could make up my room now, I'd be grateful and I'm afraid that I left my walker in the garden. Would you bring it in and put it near the settee? Oh, I almost forgot. In the little bag on my walker, is the Bible of a friend of mine. If you could give it to Ramón for me, I will ask him to take it to my friend when he brings me breakfast."

The fear in María's eyes vanished when she had turned to hear Sarah. She nodded quickly and smiled. "Sí, Señora Sarah. I will clean your room and take care of the walker and Bible." María looked to Fillip a little fearfully who was stirring cream into his coffee patiently. "You may go, María." María left the room quickly.

"Sarah, you do have a way about you, don't you?" Fillip laughed. "I wasn't going to dismiss her or eat her."

Sarah laughed. "I know, but I doubt that María did. Besides, she didn't do anything wrong. She can't be responsible for not helping if she wasn't asked."

Fillip drank from his coffee. "True, but she could have checked on you."

Sarah shook her head and laughed. "Like you did? Even you were too late to spare the room, but I do appreciate your rescuing me from the garden." Sarah became pensive. "I wish it weren't true, but Lupe and Marguerite are right. I'm afraid that I am too impatient to walk, and that the wheelchair is still my best mode of transportation. "Although...," Sarah paused, not certain she should finish her thought. She looked up at Fillip innocently, "being carried in your arms is quite pleasant for me, even if it is hard on you."

Fillip sat down his coffee cup, took Sarah's hand, and looked warmly into her eyes. Sarah was now sure she shouldn't have finished her thought. As Fillip had rescued her from the garden, now Ramón bringing her breakfast rescued her from Fillip's response.

Fillip released her hand as Ramón set down her breakfast. Fillip was grateful that Ramón had come too. After what had almost happened last night, he had decided he would control his desires for Sarah until she was physically better. He wanted to be sure she was fully aware that he wanted more than passionate foreplay, and her body needed to not only be able to physically respond to his attention, but to enjoy it without pain.

Sarah looked at Ramón. "Thank you, Ramón. This looks delightful." Ramón nodded and refilled his cup. "Ramón, I'd like to ask a favor from you."

"Sí, Señora Sarah. What is it?"

"I have the Bible of a friend that was left with me at the hospital. I need to return it to him. I can give you his business address. Would you be able to take it to him today?"

Ramón nodded and added his thoughts. "Sí, Señora Sarah. I can do it when I take Carmen out to pick up the things you need."

Ramón withdrew, and Fillip looked at her questionably. "What things, Sarah?"

Sarah paused to give thanks for her breakfast and Fillip waited for her response. "María helped me prepare for bed last night and we talked a little. She said she noticed that I needed some things since I had only packed for a two-week vacation. But, I really don't need anything."

"No, Sarah. María is probably right. You'll need more clothes and personal items. I'll open some accounts for you at the stores where my sisters' shop, and when you are able you can go and choose a new wardrobe, suitable for your life here. In the meantime, we'll permit Carmen to shop for the things you need sooner. I'm sorry I didn't think of it. It'll take me awhile to think in terms of your needs now that you are out of the hospital."

Sarah had taken a few bites of her meal while Fillip spoke. "I have no complaints about how my needs are being met. I know you have no problems with the expense, but I do. I'm unhappy that I'm such a financial burden to you."

Fillip leaned over and kissed her cheek. His lips had been warmed by the coffee and her cheek registered the additional warmth. "Sarah, mi querida. Money's not a problem for us. You are not a burden but my delight. And, your health insurance plan is covering much of your expenses according to the hospital business office. You must accept that you are the wife of a man of wealth and I want no other woman to have my name. All I ask is that you allow us the chance to fulfill our future together."

Sarah continued to eat quietly. Her breakfast wasn't going down easily, and she looked to the man who offered her a lifetime of comfort and togetherness but who hadn't said he loved her. She thought of the great mansion that surrounded them and the servants who would come when she called. It wasn't enough. She needed the sense of God's presence in this house, to know that their union was holy and blessed.

Finally, she slowly turned and looked at Fillip and put down her fork. She extended her hand. "I want to see the future with hope, Fillip. God has brought me here and I'm willing to pray together about the future."

Sarah's response was not what Fillip had expected or wanted. "You mean you want to pray now and together?"

"Yes. I'm comfortable with prayer. Praying as a husband and wife will be new for me and perhaps difficult, but I feel we need to learn to pray together if we are to be together."

Sarah hadn't spoken in terms of an ultimatum, but Fillip understood it as such and had no argument. He nodded his head as if to say, alright. "How should we do this?"

Sarah took both of Fillip's hands. "Perhaps until we are comfortable praying together, we should both pray silently but I can open and close our prayer.

Without waiting for consent Sarah opened their first prayer. *"Our most kind Heavenly Father, we come to you sharing a new experience. We are your children and now husband and wife. Hear and answer our prayers according to Your will."*

The room grew silent around them and the grandeur of their surroundings dimmed. Fillip's words were awkward, but God knew his heart. Fillip was a man treading a road of wealth and comfort, whose life had been touched by a strange young woman he desired more than understood. He married her without thought of a real union. She was supposed to be a temporary wife. He'd asked God for her life at the hospital, and he wanted to share her life. His family was uncertain of his sanity. After all who marries a woman he has known for less than a day, and who is unconscious?

So, Fillip prayed for her to loosen some of her religious drive and settle down and become the wife *he envisioned.* He told God that he didn't mind softening his approach with his servants or employees, but he wanted Sarah to accept their position in the community. He asked that they be able to put the accident behind them and to forge a real life together. He reminded God that he hadn't ask for a wife like Sarah, but He had brought her into his life. He perhaps then unwisely asked God to let her become all he *needed.*

Sarah's prayer wasn't as awkward. His hands warmed hers and Sarah was buoyed by their unity. Her prayer was for a real Christian marriage. After Fillip finished his prayer, he looked briefly into her face before her eyes met his.

"Father," she closed her eyes and prayed out loud; *"I know You are willing to be Fillip's personal Savior but won't force him."* Sarah swallowed her nervousness and confessed. *"He touches my heart as no other man has ever done. And his touch causes desires in me that I don't understand. I understand it's a part of the sexual nature You made a part of me and I shouldn't be ashamed of it. But, it's new to me and, I'm not sure that we should be together."* Sarah paused and then plunged forward. *"Father, if this marriage isn't pleasing to you, then let the desires of our flesh go unsatisfied. Let our marriage be annulled and let us part as friends. We seek your will Father in Jesus' holy name, Amen."*

Sarah looked at Fillip and when he met her eyes, Sarah saw the same warmth and longing, and Fillip saw the same glow of sweetness and eagerness to please. *Fillip had been pleased to hear her confession of a physical desire for him. However, he was not pleased to hear her pray that their physical desires go unrequited, or for their marriage to be annulled if it wasn't pleasing to God. He wanted to make Sarah trust him. Surely that would please God.*

The room was awkwardly silent as they released their hands. Sarah added timidly. "I could use a hug."

Fillip came over and hugged her, and Sarah returned his hug. It was awkward and lacked any sexual tension.

"Thank you, Fillip. I know that praying with me wasn't easy, but I know it's a good and powerful tool against the enemy. It will get easier over time."

Fillip didn't respond in kind but observed. "Your breakfast is cold.

We can have it warmed, or a new breakfast made."

Sarah stopped him from calling the servants. "I don't need it warmed, or a new breakfast." She laughed lightly and took a bite. "I've been eating hospital food, and it comes this way.

Fillip didn't argue but finished his coffee. Sarah had been right about the demons of hell being opposed to united prayer, especially that of a husband and wife. They had much to fear if Fillip and Sarah became a successful God-fearing couple.

Satan heard his second and more disturbing report about the *wretched Christian woman in Toledo*. He'd remembered she had led a waiter to his enemy, but the report hadn't disturbed him. He assumed the *waiter's* flame might be easily extinguished by resistance from those naturally involved in his life. Or, a few fiery darts from a lower demon skilled in discouragement would at least stop his growth and service to God. Satan paused after using *His* name, but then grinned. Since there wasn't a local gathering placed in Toledo for *her* kind of faith in *Him* the waiter would soon falter without the support of like believers. The waiter had little chance to grow and therefore wasn't a threat.

The wretched disciple of Christ was the problem and she should have gone home to America. There she could have only supported the waiter through phone calls and written letters. But, *He* was turning the unfortunate accident into something good.

The demon of Warning fairly choked while reporting to him about Sarah's influence on the waiter's cousin, her nurse, her therapist, and other therapy patients. Worse, Satan crumbled the written report in his hands; she was heard praying with her husband, a man of wealth who wanted the woman to remain in Spain.

Warning's report hinted that the man might be persuaded to seek his enemy himself. Then, with his resources the "building" the nurse was seeking could become a mission, a local beacon for *Him and restoration to His divine plan*. She had to be stopped before she could wreak havoc on the people and the city.

Satan called for his elite squad of demons and ordered them to act quickly and stop the union. He ordered Desire to fuel Fillip's sexual desires for Sarah. He wanted the recovering innocent and faithful woman to run home to American in fear. He ordered Doubt and Discord to come between them.

Discord asked, "Can a demon of Jealousy be spared to help us?

"Yes. Take whoever is available, but DO NOT disappointment me." He hissed. "His Son cannot get such a foothold in this community."

Chapter 20

Sarah and Fillip finished their breakfast unaware of the call out of demons to fight against them. The demons' mission was to prevent the fallout of a successful marriage succeeding spiritually not just within their family and friends, but the city of Toledo, Spain, and maybe Spain itself over the coming generations.

Fillip's thoughts dwelled on keeping him and Sarah together on neutral ground, which meant he had to stall his desire for his lovely young wife. He needed to give Sarah time to heal further, and time to accept him as her true husband. He also needed to dampen her desire to be involved in religious service. Sarah's thoughts stayed on Fillip accepting Jesus Christ, or ending their relationship as friends, before their natural desires made it impossible.

Finally, Fillip broke their reflection and momentary silence. "I know you need to rest and I want you to whenever you feel the need, but if you have anything you want to do, I'm ready for a suggestion. I try to avoid office matters on the weekends."

"I can rest this afternoon, but, for now could we visit the second floor?"

"Of course. We'll tour upstairs and then you can prepare your shopping list for Carmen. We won't have lunch until one since it's the weekend, and it can be later if you need. Dinner will be at seven or later."

Fillip pressed the intercom to signal Ramón.

"Aren't the long days and nights hard on Ramón and Carmen? And, what are María's hours?"

Fillip shook his head wearily at Sarah. "They are servants not employees, they don't have shifts, they come and go as their duties allow. They also have a day off during the week as well as Sundays, and more time as they need it. Basically, they live their own lives as I don't require much of them. I spend long hours at the office. Carmen complains when I don't stop for breakfast during the week. She is cooking for her and Ramón anyway. They have their own two-bedroom apartment and María has a studio apartment over the garage. It isn't a bad life for them, Sarah."

Ramón came, and Fillip stood up. "Sarah and I'll be touring upstairs. I'll carry her up the stairs, but I'll need you to bring the wheelchair up, please." The word please was not lost on Ramón who had seldom heard it from his employer. Sarah smiled at the use of the common pleasantry.

Fillip looked at Sarah. "Ready?"

"Please." Sarah rejoiced at the feel of Fillip's arms encircling her body. She would certainly miss this when she could walk again. Fillip took Sarah up the front stairs and Ramón brought the wheelchair up the back stairway. Sarah wasn't heavy but moving her up the long stairway made Fillip breathe heavily and he leaned her against the railing to catch his breath. The slight bump caused her to catch her breath and wince in pain. Her pain didn't go unnoticed.

"Sarah, I'm sorry...are you alright?"

Fillip's setting her against the rail had been natural and the pain he'd caused added to his sense of guilt. Sarah released her breath and smiled reassuringly. "Yes, I'm fine and looking forward to seeing the upstairs. Fillip as I heal, I am bound to suffer a few bumps. We can't let my recovery stop us from enjoying life. Lupe certainly doesn't let my pain stop my therapy. I took a pain pill earlier this morning, but I probably should have another one soon."

Ramón brought the chair and Fillip gently lowered her into it. "Thank you, Ramón. Have María bring Sarah's pain medicine. I'll call you when we come back downstairs." Ramón nodded and left, and Fillip turned back to Sarah. "Lupe causes you pain? I will talk to Dr. Rubio and we'll get someone else."

"No Fillip, please, you don't understand." Sarah hadn't intended her comment as an accusation against Lupe's skills. She had only said it to relieve Fillip's concern for her discomfort.

"Lupe is very good, and I like him. Any therapist would cause me the same pain, it's a natural part of the therapy process. For now, I need

Lupe's help, so I can be rid of my wheelchair and walker. You want that, yes?"

Fillip wanted desperately for Sarah to be healed. He still woke up nights in a cold sweat remembering seeing her through the windshield of his car, the feel of his car not stopping on the wet bricks, and the sounds of the impact of her body against his car. He'd see her battered bleeding body with the rain rinsing her blood out onto the bricks, his breath coming hard as he tried to block out the memory.

He was grateful there had been no pictures taken of his injured bride during their quick ceremony. He watched her for hours in the SICU after her surgeries, amazed she was even still alive. He'd never seen a face so badly swollen, bruised, and scraped. He could still hear the equipment beeping, see IV bags hanging and running, and most disturbing of all to him, blood being transfused.

Worse he would always remember the times she had asked him to let her die – to take away the unbearable pain. So, how could he tolerate her having any more pain, not from him or from the therapist she defended so readily? "Of course, I want you to be well. That's why I brought you here and why El Alba Rosa has a therapy room. I just don't want you to have any more pain. I want you out on El Alba Rosa's lawn chasing our children, mi querida."

Sarah cupped his face and pulled him down to her. "Oh, me too, Fillip, but it would take longer to heal without Lupe's instruction and it would be more painful, at least in my heart, if you stopped holding me, carrying me, and stopped sharing your life with me. If we are to have a life together, then we must put the accident behind us, as well as the pain it caused or will cause, and we must concentrate on the future. I can't promise you the future you want, but I want to try."

As Sarah spoke, Fillip's head instinctively drew near to her own. He nuzzled her face and the tip of his nose brushed against her cheeks and nose until he kissed her. A little voice criticized him for breaking his new rule of neutrality, but he kissed Sarah until they were breathless. Her arms had encircled his neck, and she allowed her fingers to stroke his hair.

He looked at her for a few moments, took in a deep breath, and calculated the distance to his bedroom. Sarah released him and smiled beguilingly. She wanted his kisses, but she feared where they might lead as she remembered the previous evening. She pushed him back playfully. "When does the tour start?"

Fillip laughed and raked his hand though his hair and stood up. Neutrality he thought. *"Neutrality, a little time, and a little patience".* He wheeled her off to the master suite with a different purpose than what desire had placed in his mind. María joined them there with a glass of water and her pain medicine.

The master suite occupied the space over the living and dining rooms. It had pale yellow walls and dark blue carpeting. Sarah liked the comforter that covered the king size pillared bed. Sailboats covered the comforter and the bold use of white, blue, and black to draw the design would have dwarfed a smaller bed and room. The master suite contained a large sitting area, a master bath, and his and her walk-in closets.

The gallery contained two bedrooms that shared a bath. The two bedrooms above Sarah's also shared a bath and one of the rooms was being used for storage. The other room delighted Sarah for it was Fillip's art studio. Its southern wall was covered with windows and overlooked the garden. The room was cluttered with books, art supplies, and canvases leaning against a wall. It was clear that Carmen wasn't allowed to clean this room.

"I imagine you're thinking it needs a good cleaning in here. I hadn't realized that it has been so neglected. I haven't been in here much over the last year and it certainly could use a dusting but otherwise I like things to be left untouched."

Sarah propelled her wheelchair over to a stack of painted canvases. She looked at him for permission before she looked through them. They were paintings of the garden and surrounding hillside. "Why have you left these on the floor? I think they should be framed and hung."

Fillip laughed at her. "You really don't know much about art. They really aren't very good. The garden changes so rapidly, it's hard to capture."

Sarah picked up her favorite canvas and balanced it on her lap. "I imagine I'm like most people. I know what I like. There's a place for this in my room and I'd like to send one to mother. I think you should frame and show your lovely garden landscapes."

"You're a treasure. I believe when you were young Mother Carol must have hung up all your drawings."

Sarah responded brightly. "Not all of them but most of them. She kept a scrapbook of them and the little certificates, awards, and ribbons I won. It was always a special moment for me to rush home with one of my newly created masterpieces, to be greeted by a warm hug, and have my genius displayed on the refrigerator. And, daddy always took pride in my efforts when he got home. He would set me on his lap and let me explain the development of the picture in detail and didn't rush me."

Fillip questioned. "On the refrigerator, Sarah?"

Sarah's head bobbed up and down in response. "I'm not sure of Spanish homes but in American homes the kitchen refrigerator is used for displays of art as well as grocery lists and reminders. Magnets easily hold such things and they can be taken down without damage to the *art.*"

Fillip's growing image of Mother Carol was vastly different from the reality of his own mother. She was not a soft and gentle woman and as their fortune had improved, she had little time for her children, as church, charities, and social commitments edged out her time. Even Fillip's budding skills as an artist had been rewarded with private lessons and little parental praise.

"If you really like it, I'll have it framed and hung in your room. Choose one for Mother Carol as well. You can send it as a gift from *us.*"

Sarah's smile brightened the room. "Has anyone ever told you how marvelous and generous you are?"

Fillip blushed slightly. He was not used to sentimental praise over his art. "Not recently, that I can remember, besides these paintings are worthless."

Sarah shook her head negatively. "That's not true, Fillip. Your art was on display in a prestigious gallery, and not everyone has that honor. I only knew you painted the canvas El Alba Rosa, when we toured the living room, and I recognized that what I felt when I saw the painting came from you. Seeing the garden was confirmation, seeing these canvases confirms your talent, seeing all this shows me a part of you that you think is hidden. Since beauty is in the eye of the beholder, true

~ 177 ~

value can't be measured in dollars. I see your heart in your paintings." Sarah placed a canvas in front of the one she had previously balanced on her lap. "My mother will display this fall garden over our living room sofa and she will proudly tell everyone that the artist is her very own son-in-law."

Fillip sat on the corner of a table and smiled down at Sarah. "Sarah, you make me proud. I am glad that you are the only one who can see my heart." He moved to her chair and set the paintings aside and kissed her gently without his normal passion to thank her, touching his forehead against hers relishing her and her praise. "To keep my place in Mother Carol's heart growing, I'll have the painting you selected framed and shipped immediately. You can write her a little note from us." Fillip stood and removed the paintings from where he had placed them and sat them near the door. "Now I think it's time for you to rest." He pressed the room's intercom and Carmen answered. "Tell Ramón, we're ready to come downstairs and send María to meet us in the foyer. Uh, thank you."

Fillip hadn't said "please" but he had said "thank you" and Sarah was pleased. He strolled back over and picked Sarah up. Sarah took the opportunity to quickly kiss him. "Thank you, Fillip."

"What for?"

"For changing your approach to the servants, for the gift of your paintings, for the time you shared with me."

"You're welcome, Sarah." Fillip started from the room with Sarah and she enjoyed the nearness of his body. He took pleasure in her words of praise and ardent snuggling and as he took the stairs down, he rehearsed the words, neutrality and time, with each step. His desire for her was growing alarmingly. María was waiting at the bottom of the stairs and he spoke to her briefly while they waited for the wheelchair.

"Sarah needs to rest before lunch and you can help her prepare a list of things she needs. You can go with Ramón and Carmen this afternoon after lunch to pick them up." Ramón came and opened the wheelchair. Fillip lowered Sarah into it with practiced ease. He kissed Sarah on the cheek in a rather fatherly absentminded gesture. "Have a good rest, Sarah." He turned to Ramón. "Come with me, *please*."

María and Sarah went down the corridor to her room while Fillip and

Ramón headed back up the stairs. Fillip instructed Ramón to dust the studio, rather than letting the women do it. He assured his servant that he only wanted it dusted and not cleaned to Carmen's usual standard. Ramón smiled as he understood his employer.

Fillip also showed him the paintings which needed to be framed. Fillip thanked Ramón and patted him on the back and left to call the frame shop. He was a man of action and he worked best by taking care of things quickly.

Fillip decided to present Sarah's painting to her in a few weeks when she was well enough to preside over a family dinner. He thought about his mother. She was a hard woman, but she was his mother and Sarah would have to learn to deal with her. He wondered how her sweet naïveté would deal with a proud aristocratic overbearing woman.

He chuckled to himself. More he wondered how his mother would deal with someone so genuinely sweet and honest. He was sure his brother and sisters would like her and accept her as his wife, but his mother was a different matter. After all, Sarah was an American and not Catholic. He was sure it would be an interesting evening for all concerned. His thoughts brought Sarah's image to his mind, and he smiled. Her spirit even injured now was remarkable, and would no doubt win them all over in time. His smile faded as he knew they already had their hearts set against her. A beautiful and intelligent woman who had won his heart and all the hearts of those she'd met and they without even meeting her wanted her gone from his life. He dismissed them from his thoughts. Sarah was all he needed to give him a future filled with happiness and joy.

After he invited his family to dinner, he called Raúl and invited him and his daughter, Elena. Elena was close to Sarah's age and he thought it wouldn't hurt for them to become friends, since he and Raúl were business partners. With his business complete instead of calling the kitchen, he went there to inform Carmen of the upcoming event.

The kitchen was filled with the aroma of the afternoon meal and for some reason Fillip looked at the gourmet size kitchen refrigerator. It was void of any artwork, as he knew it would be, yet he saw there was ample room for <u>little</u> masterpieces. He wondered if they would have a child that would be a budding artist. He smiled as he left the kitchen, and Carmen wondered at the changes in her employer.

Sarah was grateful for the comfort of her bed as she slid beneath its comforter for a brief nap. Her morning excursion to the garden had been quite a workout. María pulled out a pad to add to the list of things that Carmen had noted that Sarah would need when Sarah motioned for her to set with her on the bed.

"Tomorrow is Sunday. Will you be going to mass?"

"Sí, Señora Sarah. Ramón and Carmen go to the seven o'clock mass and I can go with them if I am not needed here."

"If today is any example of the time I'll be up, you'll have time for mass and I'll wait until you're back to dress."

María wasn't sure that Señor Fillip would tolerate her inattention to Sarah two days in a row. "But, what about your breakfast? Today, you could have eaten much sooner, if I had known you were awake?"

"Today was my fault. I can be stubborn. No one was to blame for today. Although I'll need your help to dress for a time, I'll eat in the kitchen when Fillip is not here. I think your major job will be to be my friend and to help educate me. Even though Fillip thinks your life is bound to mine all the time, I know that you have a private life as well. So, whenever you need to be gone, you tell me, and you go. Tomorrow go to mass. Do you understand?"

"Sí, but what if Señor Fillip wants his breakfast. I could stay and prepare it for him."

Sarah shook her head. "I don't know what Fillip does for breakfast on Sunday, but its Ramón and Carmen's day off. So, he must be capable of taking care of himself." Sarah's face brightened with mischief. "As a matter of fact, if Carmen and you could have things all prepared, I could finish and serve breakfast to Fillip in the kitchen at nine. Wouldn't that be a nice surprise?"

"I'm not so sure that Señor Fillip would approve."

"He will accept it. For us to become a family, María, many things will need to change. You and I will just believe and pray that the changes will ultimately bring God glory and fulfill His will in each of our lives." Sarah finished and turned the conversation back to María.

"Fillip told me you are thinking about being a nun. As we grow more comfortable with each other, I hope you'll be able to share your feelings with me." Sarah reached out and hugged her new friend and yawned.

"But, I'm really tired now and I'm probably keeping you from something. I remember too that I have a date with you to rummage through our new home. I hope you'll forgive me until I can manage it better."

"Of course, Señora Sarah but what of the list of things?"

Sarah had started to fade into sleep. "I can't think of anything I need. You and Carmen can shop for me."

María slipped the notepad back into her pocket and quietly left the room to its sleeper. Sarah slept soundly while the household hummed around her and her new maid checked on her before they went shopping. Then, Fillip checked on her. Sometime after the great clock struck two, Sarah awakened.

She was startled by the hour displayed on her travel alarm, quickly tossed back her comforter, and reached for her walker María had placed in easy reach. The adrenalin coursing through her veins had completely eradicated the normal sleep induced sluggishness from her body.

Sarah hadn't wanted the lunch meal to be delayed for her, and she scolded herself for not thinking to set the alarm. After she had her balance, she turned and smoothed the comforter back into place and pressed the intercom. María responded promptly and Sarah made off to the bathroom. María was waiting for Sarah when she'd finished and carefully held the wheelchair while Sarah seated herself. "I'm sorry to be keeping everyone waiting. Fillip said that lunch was served at one on Saturdays. I wish you had awakened me."

"Oh, no, Señora Sarah. Señor Fillip said that no one was to disturb you unless you were still asleep by dinner tonight. He told us that you are to sleep and eat as you choose."

Sarah thought about the difference in Fillip's philosophy of healing over Marguerite's. From now on, she would set her little clock to be on time. She was not used to leisure and she didn't want to use her injuries as an excuse to sleep away the day. She had no responsibilities here, so she would at least be on time for meals.

Fillip was waiting for Sarah in the foyer and he kissed her cheek lightly before he took command of the wheelchair. "María, please, tell Carmen that we're ready for lunch."

As María scurried away, Sarah looked up at Fillip. "I'm sorry to have kept you waiting."

"Don't apologize. I told you we'd eat when you were ready. I never realized how lonely eating a meal could be until I started sharing them with you." He kissed her earlobe to emphasize his meaning.

Chapter 21

Sarah didn't know what had happened during the hours of her nap, but a change in Fillip was apparent. Even their Sunday breakfast rolls and coffee in the kitchen together failed to have the effect Sarah had intended. Oh, he'd been surprised when he had walked into the kitchen for coffee and found Sarah there. But, he failed to enjoy the moment or even take advantage of it.

He was still wonderfully gentle and caring, but he seemed to have built a wall around himself. He touched her less often and his kisses didn't hint of intimacy. He avoided her room and any of his former references to her status as his wife. As the days past, the wall grew stronger as did Sarah. And Sarah didn't know how to ask him about the change. She and María had become an efficient team.

He left for work early each day and when she offered to get up in time to share breakfast with him, he'd refused, pleasantly of course. He came home after long hours at the office tired and drained. Sarah would share a little of her day and her therapy sessions with Fillip. He would ask a few questions here and there but shared little of his day. Then they would watch television and talk about current events. He took her out to dinner a few times, and even to a movie.

Finally, one night, she asked him if he shouldn't be getting more rest. They were watching television in the den, and the former more intimate Fillip pulled her into his arms. "I'm sorry, mi querida, that I'm not better company for you, but Raúl is growing weaker and Raphael has much to learn. And, Jesús has just started."

He kissed her lips repeatedly, savoring what seemed to be forbidden fruit. "Just a few more weeks, Sarah." The ardor of his kisses grew, and Sarah was revived by his touch and warmth. "For now, mi querida, know that you're my fountain of life in a very difficult time. Even when we are apart, I'm content because I know you are here waiting for me." Fillip's hands began to wander when Ramón came to call him to the phone.

For a few savored minutes, love touched their time together. When Fillip returned from his phone call, it was only to tell her good night. Raúl had been taken to the hospital, and he went to be with his friend and his daughter. Sarah said a prayer for Raúl and his treatment and waited for Fillip as long as she could. Finally, she'd permitted María to help her prepare for bed, and they'd prayed together for Raúl.

Sarah made a point to be up early the next day to share breakfast with Fillip. He seemed grateful to be with her as he shared the long hours in the emergency room with her. "Raúl's medication has stopped keeping his heart beat regular. The doctors say that with a pacemaker and semi-retirement from the company, Raúl may live to see his daughter married and to play with his grandchildren."

Sarah nodded and poured Fillip another cup of coffee from the carafe that had been left by María. Dark circles rimmed his eyes and she was concerned for his health. "What does that mean to you?"

Fillip patted her hand. "Don't worry about me, Sarah. Raphael is doing well at work. I'll need to spend some time at the hospital now with Raúl and Elena, but I shouldn't be home much later. Remember too that Jesús is working in the office. Let's hope Raúl will be well enough to make our dinner party."

Sarah was startled. "What dinner party?"

Fillip leaned over and pecked her cheek playfully. "The inevitable, mi querida. I wasn't going to tell you until a little nearer the event, but I've arranged a dinner for you to meet my family, Raúl, and Elena in another week."

Sarah was dumbfounded. "You've made arrangements for me to meet your whole family?"

Fillip took her hand and kissed it in his old style. "Sí, unless you say you are not up to it. We could have had several different dinners, but it seemed better to have you meet them all at once. They're very anxious to meet my beautiful wife." He looked at her closely and continued.

"You're not really upset? It's time for you to become a part of the family and hopefully develop some close relationships among your new relatives. Mother can be trying, but I'm convinced you'll win her over."

Sarah didn't respond immediately, and Fillip stroked her hand and kissed it again and looked at her pleadingly. His dark-rimmed eyes and pleading look, stole her heart. "I'm not upset, but I want you to promise to be near me all the time."

Fillip laughed and kissed her warmly with a little of his true nature showing. "But, of course, mi mujer, isn't that what I've offered all along."

Sarah inclined her head in thought. "Not very often the last few weeks."

The sound of Fillip's laughter filled the dining room and his response made her blush. "Sarah, I'm shocked. I thought my husbandly advances made you uncomfortable."

Fillip stood up and put on his jacket, while Sarah answered. "I'm happier with you behaving like yourself, stealing kisses and saying passionate things, even if they do make me a little bit uncomfortable."

If Sarah could have heard Fillip's heart, she would have known it was beating faster. Restraining himself for nearly two weeks had wrecked as much havoc as had his long hours at work. "Then, be prepared for my ardor, for your wish is my command."

Fillip pushed back Sarah's wheelchair and pulled her up into his arms. Hearing the return of his romantic banter, being held tightly against his chest, and having his lips tantalize her own was an answer to her unspoken prayer. Fillip released her and lowered her to the chair. "Regrettably, I have to go to work now." He touched a finger to her lips and she kissed it. "Save these lips for me." At the dining room door, he stopped.

"I should tell you though. If you change your mind today, I won't hold it against you. But, don't let us start something you'll regret finishing. I can be driven to a point of no turning back. I want the promised intimacy not only consummated but frequently shared." He closed his eyes savoring the thought then opened them quickly as he finished. "I want you but, *you* need to be sure. In the morning I don't want there to be any regrets or recriminations only satisfaction and happiness."

Sarah's heart beat rapidly as she took stock of what Fillip had said. He studied her for a moment gauging her understanding then left. Throughout the rest of the day she thought about Fillip's parting words.

She understood that he wanted more than romantic banter and a few kisses, and she hadn't promised more, and her mind bulked at what her heart and body wanted.

María shared a morning devotional time with her and tutored her in Spanish. Sarah tried to only communicate in her new language with the staff and they encouraged her efforts. Her command of the language was growing without Fillip's knowledge of her efforts. Because of her success with high school Spanish it was a matter of working on her grammar and vocabulary and learning local expressions.

Sarah ate lunch in the kitchen as was her habit when Fillip wasn't home. Carmen had slowly let Sarah do the things she could handle sitting down at the kitchen table. So, she helped prepare vegetables for the evening meal. Sarah enjoyed her time in the kitchen each day as she learned about Spanish cooking and Carmen didn't seem to mind her Americanizing some of the dishes.

Ramón interacted with Sarah much less than the women, but he chatted briefly with her when he brought her mail from home. Late in the afternoon Ramón and Carmen's three-year old grandson, Paulo, was dropped off for a few hours. Sarah held the squirming child on her lap and read him a little children's book.

When he asked why she spoke so funny she didn't taken offense but explained to him in careful Spanish about growing up in another country where they spoke differently. Even when his squirming caused her pain she was not ill-tempered.

Sarah felt comfortable and at home with her new family. She called her mother because she was on unpaid leave now, her savings spent on her trip, and her mother would be without enough income to make their mortgage payment. Carol Kettering reminded Sarah that Fillip was helping out. He was actually providing her an ample allowance, despite her protests. Sarah came to appreciate just how faithful Fillip was to all his promises for her and her mother.

As the day drew to an end, a delivery truck brought a bouquet of long-stemmed red roses. Sarah had been surprised when Ramón brought them to her room just after her call home. She examined the petals and breathed in their bouquet before she permitted Ramón to take them away to put them in water. The card reminded her of the evening's potential outcome, "For my lovely bride" and it was signed, "Always yours, Fillip". His message was simple and clear. She wandered how he even had time to think to send them, let alone order them. The arrival of the roses troubled her and when she was troubled she sought the solace of her Heavenly Father. Sarah sought Him in the comfort she'd found in the garden.

The effort to walk toward the bench was not as strained as it had been two weeks earlier. When Sarah gained the bench, she was grateful for the rest, but she wasn't exhausted. She reviewed her life at El Alba Rosa. It was beyond anything she could have dreamed. She could have anything money could buy, and El Alba Rosa was amazing. She had servants to wait on her she adored. And, there was a special man responsible for her new status in life who promised her the joy of a marital relationship. Her life could be changed forever tonight, and Fillip had left her the decision.

The song of a bird brought her out of her musings, and as she watched another more brightly colored bird of its species join it. She watched the interaction of their courtship. As the sun faded the male bird flew off, and the female called for him to return, but he didn't come back. The female's song was not sad and when she ended her solo Sarah heard a similar sound from farther in the garden. Within the first few sounds of his song; the female flew off to join him.

Sarah smiled into the final rays of the day's sun. How perfect a picture God had shown her of courtship and union. She remembered that David had captured these feelings in Psalm 8. She had learned it as a child to please her father and to earn a dollar to buy her mother a birthday gift. Reciting it had become a part of her gift to her mother. Today she used the words to please her Heavenly Father.

She still was afraid to decide about her and Fillip. How many times had she walked down a receiving line and looked into the joy filled face of a friend on her wedding day and wished her well, knowing that the marriage was not well fortified against the storms of life. Could she now convince herself that she and Fillip would be the exception to a marriage that was not equally yoked? Would she tell herself that Fillip would get saved? God was faithful, and she prayed for Fillip's salvation, but would Fillip choose it?

Yesterday she didn't have the problem. If anyone had asked, she would have said that Fillip was only marking time until he could decently annul their marriage and send her home. How miserable she'd been through the days of his withdrawal from her. But, Doubt still whispered. "How can he love you?" Her head counseled stop and her heart and body counseled go. Sarah closed her eyes and rolled her head to clear her mind only to be distracted by her surroundings.

Sarah watched the sunset as it revealed the approach of evening with a brilliant display of pink and blue hues, and gauzy white shadows. She was so captured by the ever-changing canvas in front of her that she was startled when Fillip wrapped his arm around her and kissed her brow.

He lowered himself to sit on the bench. He said nothing to her but searched her face, his eyes probing for an answer. Sarah thought he looked totally exhausted, more in need of a bed than a wife, but remembered he wanted both. To hide her blush from his steady gaze Sarah lowered her head into his left shoulder. Fillip cradled her in his arm and then lifted her chin with his fingers. Before he could bring his lips to hers or demand a decision, she delayed him with a question.

"How are Raúl and Elena?"

Fillip was pleased that she continued to show concern for Raúl and Elena, especially since they had never met. "Raúl tolerated the pacemaker placement well and is resting comfortably. The pacemaker is working well, and the cardiologist is pleased considering his age. His previous two heart attacks, and the angina he experiences is a real concern. I persuaded Elena to go home and rest. She's been with her father since last night. Raphael was taking her home, but he will first see she gets a nice dinner. The hospital will call if anything changes."

"That's so wonderful. Tonight, I'll thank God for answering my prayers for Raúl." Sarah turned away from Fillip's steady gaze and looked into the brilliant sunset. "Have you ever taken the time to watch a sunset from your garden?"

Fillip looked at the view and breathed in the fragrance of the Sarah's perfume. It was called Seduction and it had come with the first of Carmen's purchases for her. His head was near her earlobe as he continued to enjoy her perfume and nearness. "I designed the garden, so it could be seen privately, but I've never the taken time. I never had anyone want to share it with me, but this is only the beginning of the new things we'll share."

Sarah felt her breath depart as she understood his meaning and his lips drew near to draw his answer from them. Sarah could feel his breath on her lips as she closed her eyes. His kiss asked the question and understood only her surrender. He broke off his kiss although he felt an *overwhelming desire* to rush her, so their marriage could be consummated.

"The beauty of the garden and sunset are not lost to me. They're a perfect canopy to sanction our marriage and with them as my witness, I promise you a life time—" Sarah's heart beat erratically as she strained to hear his commitment to love and fidelity that she hadn't heard on their wedding day. But, he finished with the words. "of wedded joy." As his promised ended, she compressed her eyes to prevent tears. How could God give her more than she had ever dreamed possible, and not give her Fillip's love?

At the head of the garden path, the sound of a throat being cleared caused Fillip to release her as he turned to look at the approaching Ramón. Sarah used the diversion to blot her eyes. "I'm sorry to disturb you, sir, there's a call from Raphael. He sounds most disconcerted." He looked quite uncomfortable and added. "And, we can serve dinner whenever you're ready."

"Thank you, Ramón. I'll take the call in my study." He stood up, looked back at Sarah, picked her up, and cradled her in his arms. "Please bring Sarah's walker along and ask María to bring Sarah's wheelchair to the study. We can have dinner as soon as I finish my call."

He moved with Sarah down the path and across the little patio. When they went through the opened door to her room, he paused at the bed. He sighed and whispered into her ear. "Such a shame as we should be stopping here."

Sarah giggled as he moved on past the bed. "Surely we would have dinner first?"

He looked at her with an expression of mock shock. "Mi querida, you have much to learn about setting priorities." He laughed, and Sarah joined him. At the door to his office, he paused, and Sarah obliged by opening the door. After he sat her down in the chair near the door, he went to answer the phone. Sarah pondered their time in the garden and their conversation.

Chapter 22

Fillip's call to Raphael was in rapid Spanish. Sarah's time with María made it possible for her to understand Fillip's side of the underlying conversation, although she didn't intend to eavesdrop. Apparently, Elena was finding it impossible to rest and wanted to return to the hospital. Fillip instructed Raphael to see if he could locate some sleeping pills in the house, or to call the family physician and have something appropriate sent from the pharmacy. Fillip's tone of voice suddenly changed as it was obvious that Elena now had the phone.

María had come to help Sarah into her wheelchair. As she transferred, Sarah heard a familiar endearment. "Elena, mi querida, you must listen to Raphael for me." "No." "Sleep now, for me." As they left the room Sarah heard a little more. "You know I do, but I have Sarah now. Tomorrow, Elena. I'll come tomorrow."

As Sarah was wheeled toward the dining room, she thought about Elena and Fillip. Carmen had described Elena as a lovely young woman who had graduated from college with a degree in business. She'd never mentioned what type of relationship Fillip might have shared with Elena before she came, and Sarah had never asked. Sarah's heart filled with pain. Elena was young, beautiful, well-educated in business, and her heritage was totally Spanish. Doubt quickly filled in Elena's side of the conversation. What if Elena had said to Fillip, "Don't you love me?" Then, Fillip had answered that he did, and Sarah was now a problem in *their* relationship.

Sarah was desolated by the thought. Doubt had supplied the possible question and consequentially the fear that gripped her heart. She took in a deep breath and released it slowly to regain her peace. She reminded herself, "I am a child of God. In Him I have nothing to fear." She chided herself as nothing good could come from speculation and she had to keep her guard up. She knew that lies and deception were weapons that Satan and his fallen angels used well.

Fillip joined her a few minutes later. A new line seemed to have creased his brow and he looked near total exhaustion. He rang the intercom as he spoke. "Elena is refusing to sleep and Raphael didn't know how to cope. Raphael will get her something to help her sleep and tomorrow things will be better for everyone."

"It's difficult for Elena now. It's understandable why she wants to stay at the hospital, but without rest she won't be much good to her father." Sarah included Fillip in her assessment of those who needed rest as María and Ramón brought in their dinner.

Sarah voiced the thought after the servants left. "When are you going to get some rest?"

Fillip smiled at Sarah and laced their fingers together. "I am a little tired, but I have other matters to tend to before I sleep tonight."

Sarah understood, and her heart tightened up. He believed she agreed with his desires, but she still wasn't sure. What if her coming was driving a wedge between Fillip and Elena? Fillip had made her well aware of what her body wanted. He had understood the language of her body in the garden earlier. But, what if she betrayed her body when Fillip took her to bed and she suddenly screamed for him to leave her alone? She thought of only one possible escape. "Perhaps, you would be better letting these other matters wait until you have slept. After all, you said you wanted no regrets in the morning."

Fillip smiled at her warmly and leaned over and licked a little sauce from her lips. "Don't worry Sarah, I won't fall asleep. Our first time together is too important."

The rest of Sarah's meal seemed to stick mostly in her throat and she refused the flan that had been prepared for dessert. Fillip had eaten heartily, and he also refused dessert in favor of a third glass of wine. After dinner, Fillip took Sarah to the den and turned on the news program for her and excused himself to make a few phone calls. "I want to make sure that our evening won't be interrupted." Sarah tried to concentrate on the broadcast, but she found herself nervously awaiting Fillip's return. Secretly, she hoped he would be called away, although she didn't want him to go to Elena.

When he returned he seemed less tired or at least a little more relaxed. He joined her on the couch and pulled her into his arms. "Our friends are doing well and are resting comfortably this evening, so we should be able to enjoy our evening." Sarah thought his kiss was the opening salvo to their love-making and her response was tense and disappointing. Fillip released his hold and laughed. "Mi querida, I understand your nervousness, but I only want to make love to you. I won't hurt you."

Sarah smiled sheepishly and leaned over and brushed Fillip's lips with a kiss of her own rare instigation. "I'm sorry, Fillip. I know you believe that I'm being childish, but I can't help myself."

Fillip pulled Sarah against his shoulder and she instinctively rested her head against it. "It's alright, mi poco Sarah. I'm a patient man when it comes to you. I want our first time together to be the beginning of a lifetime of fulfillment."

He used his free hand to lift her chin up and kissed her with a quiet ardor. He quietly said. "I'll give you a few more days, princess. But, I won't wait much longer for you to come to me and our bed."

He kissed her again and she was able to respond without fear. She had a few more days to play at being the woman of the house before she would have to prove she was the wife of the house. Fillip stroked her shoulder as they sat together on the couch.

Sarah was grateful that the evening would end differently than she feared. Fillip was still stroking her arm, but he wasn't making any other advances. After a few minutes, the number of strokes of Fillip's hand lessened and Sarah became aware that Fillip's breathing had altered. She strained her neck to look at him without disturbing him and found him sleeping with his head tilted back slightly. A peculiar smiled creased his lips and she was tempted to kiss him.

She resisted the urge out of fear for rekindling a flame she couldn't yet know wouldn't burn her. She shifted herself a little more to look at him better. Asleep he seemed more like a little boy than a man who threatened all her concepts of love, marriage, and fidelity.

She looked at his thick dark eyelashes as they curled up. They were one of his nicest features. Sarah had babysat for a little boy baby with such eyelashes. Mother had called them bedroom eyes to break the heart of unwise girls. Being with Fillip now she had finally understood what mother had been saying.

If she had to describe Fillip, she would have called him ruggedly good looking, not modelish handsome. Sarah smiled at herself. She would never win any beauty contest either. But, if beauty was in the eye of the beholder, then Fillip was all she wanted. His shirt was opened at the neck and she remembered how she felt when she had first seen the hint of his chest. Today she thought of not only touching the hair on his chest, but she imagined rubbing the muscled torso as well.

Sarah felt a sudden wave of _jealousy_. _Her hands would not be the first to wander through the hair on his chest and she would not be the first to feel his chest lying bare against her own. Sarah's body flushed warm and she blanched at the vision she had of his bare chest touching her own bare breasts._ She moved away from him and sat up straight. Her eyes looked at the television and she was aware that some evening programming had replaced the news.

The demon of jealousy mocked her. Fillip had been with other women, probably many other women, maybe even Elena. She looked at him accusingly. The smile had left his face and he was sleeping soundly. Doubt joined in, and she wandered what he would bring to their marriage bed besides experience.

Sarah remembered a long-ago afternoon when she had learned the reality of lust. She was a few months short of her sixteenth birthday and had gone to the mall with a friend. They'd been dropped off by her friend's mother for a day of shopping and a movie. Her friend, Brenda, was what her father referred to as a "crummy buddy".

A crummy buddy was a friend who was not yet saved but whose friendship although worldly was not harmful to Sarah. Precisely at noon, her friend had insisted they stop for lunch at one of the mall food shops. They were joined there by Brenda's boyfriend.

Brenda had used her to meet a boy her parents had refused to let her date. He was a high school dropout just short of his twentieth birthday. Brenda begged her to go along with them and Sarah unwisely went to the movies with them. Their behavior disturbed Sarah's morals and she left to call her mother for a ride home.

Sarah's mother came to the mall and picked her up without questioning Sarah's sudden departure from her plans. During the silence of the unquestioned ride home, Sarah decided to tell her mother the whole story. She remembered her mother's response now as if they were together in the car.

"I'm sorry your friend used your friendship to meet someone that could cause her harm. Your father and I have never prevented you from making friends with those that our not saved because we can't shield you from the reality of the world. You must live in this world and yet be separate from it. I'm glad you didn't accept her behavior. Hopefully she will rethink her own actions from your witness."

"Your father and I have never spoken to you much on the subject of sexual sin, and perhaps we have neglected you in this. Your friend's disobedience, I am afraid, can only lead to heartbreak. Young people, as well as many older people, don't count the consequences of disobedience and sin. Your friend like many others may become involved in worldly pleasures of the flesh. She will convince herself that it is right because they are in love. But, pre-marital sex is a sin, Sarah. It may lead to an unwanted pregnancy and the destruction of a precious new life if the pregnancy ends in an abortion."

Her mother glanced at her to check her understanding. "Unprotected sex also can lead to the spread of disease. Your generation is faced with the sexual diseases of the past, and the threat of a new disease readily recognized by its initials. AIDS isn't just spread by shared drug paraphernalia, or through contaminated blood transfusions, but by unprotected sex."

"Why does God let so many innocent people suffer from AIDS?"

"God didn't bring AIDS about to punish His wayward children. AIDS developed because God's abhorrence of sexual perversion and reverence for the human body was not regarded by mankind. Careful testing is reviving the faith in our blood supply and with the information available it is reasonable to hope that drug users will stop sharing needles. There is also hope for the babies of HIV positive mothers."

Her mother stopped at a light and looked at her. "People look at their sexual partners through colored lenses. They believe they are in love and in bed with just the one person, but they really are in bed with all of that person's sexual partners. A person infected with the AIDS virus can spread it to another without ever appearing ill. And, if your friend escapes these problems, there is one she cannot escape."

Sarah had thought that she meant God's punishment for those who sin and don't seek salvation. But, her mother didn't mention God's judgement. "People who have premarital sex defile their marriage bed. A shroud hangs like a canopy over them. They sometimes cannot be satisfied by their spouse as they compare them to a previous lover or a potential new lover."

"Premarital sex can cause what might have otherwise been a successful marriage to fail. Remember it is just as easy to fall in love with someone who is not saved as it to fall in love with someone who is saved. You'll soon be allowed to date and although we'll want to meet all your dates, you'll be the one who has to decide if the relationship is right."

———————◆———————

Back from the past, Sarah looked down at her hand and straightened the ring that wrapped her wedding finger. It wasn't a wedding ring. She didn't have one. She smiled as she remembered the special dinner prepared to honor her sixteenth birthday. Her parents had offered her the promise ring with all its responsibilities and she had accepted it. She had promised to remain sexually pure until she was married. Marriage was the only event that could release her from her commitment to virginity. It was to be her gift to her husband. The gift only she could give him.

A soft moan escaped from Fillip's lips and her attention was drawn to him. Fillip stirred in his sleep and Sarah looked at the lips that brought her so much joy and torment and wondered at all the other women who had touched them. *"Dear Lord,"* she silently breathed, *"if I lie in a marriage bed with Fillip, who else will share it?"*

This time Fillip's moan was louder, and he stirred from his sleep. "I'm sorry Sarah. I'm not much company tonight."

Sarah smiled at the weary man. "That's because you shouldn't be company. If you listen, I do believe there is a comfortable bed calling you from just off the north gallery."

Fillip stood up, stretched, and yawned. "I do believe you're right." He stooped down in front of her, took her hands, and looked in her eyes. "I must say it was a pleasure to wake-up at your side. Next time—," he paused and kissed her warmly. "I trust we will enjoy sleeping together in a much more comfortable and— satisfied manner." He kissed her once again. "Good-night, mi mujer. Dream of me. Soon, very soon, you will have reason to dream of me, of us, together for we will be together. I will send María to you."

The evening hours had shifted to night and Sarah sat in the darkness of the room with only the flickering light from the television. The only thing she knew for sure was that given a choice, she would never have chosen a relationship with Fillip.

Doubt shifted to a new tactic and regret filled her thoughts. She should have stayed hidden in her hostel until it had been time to catch her plane. Now instead of being safely at home with her mother, she was still in Spain desperately falling in love with a man that was a "crummy husband".

Sarah didn't laugh at the altered version of her father's term but thought about how the word "desperate" seemed to fit her own feelings. She knew she had to keep such thoughts out of her mind. She hadn't inventoried her thought closet in a while, and it was clear that negative thoughts had been allowed in, and they weren't gathering any dust.

María entered the room quietly and would have taken Sarah directly to her room, but Sarah asked her to turn off the television, light the room, and spend some time talking to her. Sarah wouldn't have slept so early in the night, especially with her mind filled with so many disturbing thoughts.

Sarah opened a general conversation with María in Spanish to direct her thoughts away from herself. However, their conversation switched to English as the need for the conversation was more important than language instruction. "Tell me, if you weren't trapped in this house with me, what would you be doing tonight?"

María and Sarah had become good friends in the brief time of their relationship. María giggled a little nervously. "If I were not here now, I imagine I would be at a convent studying for my vows."

Sarah and María had never talked about her desire to be a nun or why Gail had intervened and sought this job for María. "And, are you sorry you aren't studying for your vows?"

María quietly shook her head no. "I would be at the convent to please my parents not to please myself or God. I am the youngest of three daughters and perhaps the best candidate to be a nun. Ever since I was a young child my parents have spoken to me about my becoming a nun and serving God as does my Aunt Mary, my father's oldest sister."

"When I graduated from school, she came to our home to celebrate with us. My Aunt Gail and I have always been close. She never believed I was called to be a nun and she told my Aunt Mary as much. My parents were very angry with my Aunt Gail for her interference, but my Aunt Mary convinced my parents that it needed to be my choice. My parents gave me a year to decide, and I've lived with Aunt Gail for almost a year now and worked at a daycare. In that time, I've prayed for God to show me His will, but I still don't know what I am to do."

Sarah knew exactly how María was feeling and she understood now why God had brought them together. "I too have been seeking God's will and I'm afraid that I'm failing to discover what His will is for me."

María looked very puzzled. "You're not sure you love Señor Fillip and want to be his wife?"

The color in Sarah's cheeks rose at her young maid's intuition. Sarah felt compelled to be honest with María and herself. "I'm sure that I do love Fillip, María. I'm just not sure it would be right for me to stay his wife." The puzzled expression on María's face hadn't changed, so Sarah tried to explain by an example. "It's just like you. You're sure you love God, and yet you aren't sure it's right for you to be a nun."

María asked, "You're not happy to be the wife of Fillip Castañola?"

"It is not a question of happiness." Sarah recognized the prejudice that any woman should be proud to be Señora Castañola. "I've been raised to believe that the husband is the spiritual leader of the family. Unfortunately Fillip and I do not share the same belief."

This María understood. "It is because Señor Fillip is Catholic, and you are Protestant. You can take classes and become Catholic, then you and Fillip will be the same."

"No." Sarah had failed to communicate her indecision about the wisdom of maintaining the marriage. "I can't become Catholic. My relationship with God goes beyond religion. I identify with a protestant church of like believers, but I don't practice a religion. Practicing a religion, going through rituals and rules, is a distraction from a true relationship with Christ. I am a disciple of Christ not just a member of a church. Remember Jesus Christ calls us to be His followers. Nowhere in the Bible does He promote a religion. He denounced the religious leaders in His day and called them "white washed tombs" and they were Jewish as He certainly had been reared. He wants an intimate relationship with us which is why He left the Holy Spirit in the world when He returned to heaven to advocate for us at His Father's throne."

María didn't answer, so Sarah continued. "I've always believed that I would marry a man who believes in God the way I do and that together we would evangelize the world or at least our little part of it with Christ's gift of salvation. I don't see how that can be Fillip."

María looked at Sarah questionably and gathered her courage to speak her mind. "Then perhaps your belief is wrong. To me, you seem to fill a void in the life of a man I greatly respect. Perhaps it should be enough for you to be married to him, to love him, and to have his children."

María's opinion had summed it all up in one neat simple package and Sarah had no easy reply. She looked at María and asked a similar question. "If God hasn't chosen you to be a nun, then is it possible that you can serve Him as a wife and mother?"

Sarah hadn't been prepared for María's opinion but María didn't suffer the want of an answer. "Since I have come here, I have thought of such a thing, seeing Carmen and Ramón and how you and Fillip love each other."

Sarah wished she could accept María's judgement that Fillip loved her, but he had never said it. She wondered if he had said it to any other woman – maybe Elena? He had clearly had relationships with other women, but she needed to be more to him then what they had been. Needed to be what they couldn't ever be. She needed a lifetime of one man loving her as he loved the Lord. She had confided her feelings for Fillip to María, but she knew that Fillip would never have taken María into his confidence.

María blushed and continued. "I want to ask you, but I have been afraid to ask. I know you've known him only a short time but tell me what you know about Lupe."

Sarah rolled her eyes heavenward. Lupe was a friend but hardly the person she would choose for María. Now Jesús was different but he had a girlfriend and Sarah couldn't choose for María any more than her mother could choose for her. As Sarah talked about Lupe, María's eyes began to glow and Sarah knew she'd have to commend them to God in her nightly prayers.

Chapter 23

Sarah did remember María and Lupe in prayer prior to sleeping that night. She had promised María she would ask Lupe with subtleness, if he had any interest in her. Knowing the beguiling Lupe, she had no doubt he would. And, she was going to make it clear to him that María was not just another girl to add to his list of lady loves, but one that he would have to treat with great respect. She was a woman who deserved true love with a man of faith.

Sarah awakened before dawn and stretched in the morning light that came through her curtains. Sarah assumed that Fillip was probably already dressed and seated at breakfast. She could have joined him, but she was reluctant to go to breakfast and have him see her dressed in her night things and, by the time María could be summoned to help her change into something suitable, he would be gone. Still sleep had forsaken her, so she arose to greet the day the Lord had made and to thank Him for it.

Sarah made a quick stop in the bathroom. Once her face had been washed, her hair combed, and her teeth brushed she felt truly revived. She selected her blue flannel robe from the back of her closet where Carmen had purposely stored it. The robe was old, but it belonged to her mother and Sarah had brought in to Spain as insurance against the possible loss of heat in her little hostel room. This morning she chose it to prevent a chill when she went to greet the sunrise over her patio railing.

The sun had been up for a while when Sarah got to the railing. She carefully held it for support as she set her walker aside and pulled her Bible from the pocket of the walker. As Sarah struggled to open the Bible and maintain her balance, a little morning breeze caught the opened pages of the Bible and it opened to Psalm 9. Sarah read the words to the morning and she took to heart verse 10 as it stood out in her mind as a message from the Lord. She read it aloud, one more time.

"And those who know Your name will put their trust in You; For You, O Lord, have not forsaken those who seek You."

Sarah's mind turned to thank God for the day and the verse He had given her, but she realized she wasn't alone. Fillip had been disappointed that Sarah hadn't joined him for breakfast, so he'd gone to her room to sit on the edge of her bed and kiss her awake. But, he found no sleeping beauty to be awakened by his kisses. So, he went in search of her and found her reading scripture.

His first instinct was not to interrupt her private time but a part of him rebelled. Discord reminded him that Sarah spent far too much time on religious things. She was his wife and he needed some of her time. So, he asked her somewhat crossly, "Do you always read to the birds?"

Discord snickered at the anger he had stirred in the man. Fillip quickly crossed the small patio and took the Bible from her hand and Sarah answered him sweetly. "No, but the garden draws me in, and its beauty and wildlife always make me want to praise God."

Fillip didn't want to provoke an argument, but Discord pushed another thought that parted his lips without censure. "You can't credit the beauty of the garden to God, it was designed by men." Once he had said it, he regretted the words, for fear of Sarah's dismay, and an argument. To his surprise she only laughed.

"I'm not wrong to credit God for this garden. I do believe that he had it designed and planted, by men, for us, but he clearly gives the sunlight and rain that keeps it. Imagine when God formed the earth and moved about it, He created a poorly drained area right here, so your horticulturists could place this here for us." Sarah was suddenly struck with a revelation of the Spirit. "Even when He planned the Garden of Gethsemane where His Son went to pray and was later betrayed by Judas, He planned this for us."

Fillip was silent in the face of the fallout of the Spirit that he had come to accept from Sarah. She saw things so differently than He did. Fillip knew that the Spirit of the Lord had joined them in this place and he took Sarah in his arms. He was never surer that God was real and that He dwelt inside his wife, his Sarah.

Sarah had never felt a greater joy than she did in the presence of the Lord that morning with Fillip's arms wrapped tightly around her waist with her Bible in his right hand. Her spirit heard the words intoned, "Who God hath joined together, let no man break asunder." And, of her own volition Sarah kissed her groom.

Fillip responded without the passion Sarah had expected but he didn't release her. "I think you're right about this garden. Surely, God did plan this for us." He kissed her lightly and pulled her walker closer, slipped the Bible into the walker's pocket, and guided it to her for support. "Have a good day, Sarah."

Fillip moved to the French doors as Sarah said good-bye. "Vaya con dios Fillip." He turned and nodded to Sarah in response, confused by his feelings for her, the movement of the spirit inside of him, and despite her old robe, she looked like an angel in his garden.

Sarah felt as if she had spouted wings and she hardly minded the inconvenience of her walker. As she went through the day, she found that everything seemed to be touched by a special feeling. On therapy days, Sarah had adjusted her schedule to include an abbreviated Spanish lesson, so she could rest in the early afternoon just after lunch before Lupe came. Today Sarah's routine was interrupted by an unexpected but welcomed visitor.

Sarah found a nervous Jesús waiting for her in the living room where he had been seated by Ramón. Jesús' coming added to the total joy of Sarah's day and she laughed in sheer delight when she approached her fidgeting friend. "Jesús, how wonderful to see you. I am so happy you came."

Jesús stood up quickly when Sarah spoke. "It's good to see you up and moving around. I didn't know you could walk."

Sarah sat down on the couch and motioned for Jesús to join her. "I'm not up to winning any races but I'm quite pleased with the stamina I'm gaining even if I'm dependant on this extra set of legs."

As Sarah moved her walker to the side of the couch, Jesús grinned. "I'm glad you haven't changed."

Sarah was puzzled. "What do you mean?"

Jesús looked a little embarrassed by his statement. "I saw Nurse Castillo, at the open market and I asked her how you were getting along. She said I should find out for the both of us. But, I told her I would be ashamed to come to see you at your new fine home with your servants.

She got angry and she said, "Don't be a child, Jesús. Sarah will always be Sarah in a fine house or a dog house. You go tomorrow." Jesús hung his head. "I probably should've called first, but I am on an errand for the office, and thought I'd stop here on my lunch."

Sarah leaned over and touched Jesús' hand and he looked up at her. "She's right, Jesús. You should never be ashamed to come to see me, for you will always be welcomed wherever I am. You're my friend and my brother, and I need both in this country."

Jesús face broke out in a broad smile. "Then you are staying in Spain?"

Sarah thought about the few days of indulgence that Fillip had granted her, and she smiled. "It would seem so." Sarah didn't want to think about Fillip and her discomfort about that area of their relationship, so she brought the subject back to her guest. "How do you like your new job? Are you excited?"

"Yes, I'm very excited and grateful, Sarah. Marina and I have set our wedding day. We'll be married next April. You're my first invited guest."

"Jesús I'm so happy for you and Marina." Sarah glowed with a wonderful thought. "Fillip is having a dinner soon, so I can meet his family. So, why don't you ask Marina what her plans are for three weeks from this Friday? You and she can be my first dinner quests in my new home."

Ramón came in and brought Sarah and Jesús some glasses of Sangria. Carmen didn't add rum to the common mixed fruit drink and Sarah was very partial to it. Jesús waited for Ramón to leave before he answered. "I will ask Marina tonight. I've told her all about you."

"Does she understand and accept your relationship with God?" Jesús' eyes filled with a deep sadness. "She has listened to me and is willing to accept my faith, but she doesn't understand it, Sarah. I've agreed not to discuss my faith with her family and I've promised we'll raise our children to be Catholics. Will she ever understand?"

Sarah didn't have an answer and took a sip of her drink before she spoke. "God speaks to all of us. His voice is the voice of a family member, a friend, and sometimes a stranger, even perhaps an angel. But, just as we must choose our spouse and our friends, so we too must choose God.

When you are with Marina, she'll be able to see your relationship to Jesus Christ and through your witness to His lordship and our prayers she may choose Him as Lord of her life too. I can't say she will, but I will pray for it for both of you."

Sarah reached out and closed her arms around Jesús and gave him a hug. "What I know for sure is she's getting the best kind of husband in the world. The kind of husband, I have prayed about for myself." Sarah sat back and looked into Jesús' questioning eyes. "Only a husband, who loves the Lord, knows how to love a wife. If you love her with the love of the Lord, she will be truly loved and that is a blessing straight from God."

Jesús looked back into Sarah's eyes. "Thank you, Sarah. I always find comfort from the things you say to me."

"I can only give you the comfort that I've been given." For a moment the friends were quiet and they each thought about the people they loved. Sarah broke their silence. "If you'd like, I can show you the downstairs of El Alba Rosa? I'm afraid I can't get up the stairs yet."

Jesús stood up and set his unfinished drink down. "No, I need to return to work."

Sarah stood up slowly, set her glass down and reached for her walker to see him out.

"I've not heard from Nurse Castillo since I came home from the hospital. Is she well?"

"Yes, she was fine when I saw her yesterday, but she is very busy with her latest case. She said to tell you she has noticed several vacant buildings, old restaurants, that might be of use to you, but she hasn't had time to inquire about them."

Sarah was surprised that a case could occupy so much of Marguerite's time as she had only worked with her on a regular shift. "Did she say much about her new case?"

Jesús wasn't certain that Sarah should be told about Nurse Castillo's new patient, but he relayed what he had been told. "She said that if you asked about her patient I should ask you to pray for the child and his family. Her patient is an eleven-year old boy that has leukemia. The doctors can do no more for him and he will probably die in the next few weeks. Nurse Castillo is spending a lot of time with them to help with the boy's care, so he can stay at home. Although there is another nurse who comes, she looked very tired."

Sarah's heart, as Jesús feared, went out to the little boy and his family as well as for her friend, Marguerite. She thought about how awful it must be to have your child become so ill and to be unable to stop the disease. "What's his name?"

"Jaime Molina. Is his name important?"

Sarah nodded her head and explained. "Our Father knows everything, including that this little boy is so desperately ill. But, I like to write names in my prayer journal to remember them later, and the journal helps me to focus, and I can record outcomes and praise."

Jesús seemed amazed. "A prayer journal is something I should think about then. Would you want to see this child?"

God had given Sarah a tender heart where it concerned the physical needs and well-being of others. "Yes. It's what I did in America. In my church, I had two prayer partners, two men whose hearts I came to know through our intercessory prayer. When we were contacted by the pastor or a family about a need, we would meet at the church and pray together. Or, we would go to a home or hospital room and pray there. The Prayer Partners didn't meet just to pray for the sick but to pray for any need that was called to our attention. Praise is a wonderful reason to meet in prayer and each of our meetings ended with hugs all around."

"This must take a lot of time and be difficult to do. I'm not sure I could do this."

Sarah smiled as she remembered the feeling she had when she met with her friends in intercessory prayer. "We weren't half as busy as we could've been even in a church the size of ours. And, I expect if we had gotten too busy that God would have called other prayer partners to meet the need. I never left a prayer time no matter the prayer concern that I didn't feel rewarded or empowered by the Spirit, even if I felt tired when we started."

Jesús was awed by what he heard. "So, you believe this thing you call intercessory prayer is important? Is this something we should do?"

"Christ taught intercessory prayer and it's something that should be done whenever there is a need. Marguerite has asked for it for Jaime and his family."

Jesús pointed to a bench in the great foyer and they sat down together. "Then we must do this for the child." Jesús took Sarah's hands and a prayer partnership was formed as they brought Jaime, his family, and Marguerite to the Lord. Jesús prayer was music to Sarah's spirit and she internalized her own prayer for them.

At the close of the prayer, Sarah thanked the Lord for His care of Jesús. She remembered a few weeks past when Jesús had to be encouraged to pray aloud and now he wasn't afraid to lead. After the prayer ended, Sarah leaned over and hugged her friend. "Do you feel the power?"

Jesús felt the glow in himself he had witnessed in Sarah. "Yes. Thank you for sharing this with me. This will be my first entry in a prayer journal."

Jesús would have said more except he became aware of María standing nearby. "I'm sorry to interrupt Señora Sarah but Lupe will be here soon for your therapy and you must change."

Jesús jumped to his feet and apologized. "I'm sorry. I've stayed too long."

Sarah laughed and put out her hand to stop Jesús from leaving. "I'm not sorry and I won't let you leave until you promise to come again soon, and don't forget to ask Marina about dinner."

Jesús leaned over and kissed Sarah's cheek. "I'll come soon, and I'll phone you tomorrow with Marina's answer."

Sarah released Jesús' hand. "Alright, you can go. And, I'll pray that Marina will come to understand and accept the Savior as we do. Adiós, Jesús."

As Jesús walked away, Sarah got to her feet and started to her bedroom and María followed. Her spirit soared but her body was weary.

Sarah was ready by the time María returned with Lupe and Sarah noticed how María watched the man who had caught her attention. Lupe was a tireless taskmaster, but Sarah just couldn't keep up with him today. "I'm afraid I just don't seem to have the energy for my workout today."

"I can see that the fair lady is not at her usual drive. Is there a problem, Sarah?"

"No, I don't think so. I used my walker a lot today, and I had a visitor, so I skipped the rest I usually take before you come to make me jump through your routines."

Lupe laughed. "Then, I'll let you rest today and give you a massage. When I'm finished, you should take your rest."

"Thank you, Lupe. I don't care what Marguerite thinks. I believe you're a true gentleman."

Lupe helped Sarah unto the massage table. As he started Sarah's rub down, he asked about Marguerite. "And, have you heard from our good friend and nurse?"

"No, not directly. My friend, Jesús, who was here earlier, saw her yesterday and he said she is working with a terminally ill child."

Lupe's trained massage brought a groan of pleasure to Sarah's lips. "I'm sorry to hear that. She almost gave up nursing a few years ago after caring for an older patient that died after a long battle with cancer. I believe that is why she went to work with orthopedic patients like you."

Sarah thought about Marguerite and understood how her friend's dispassionate front hid a very loving and compassionate heart and why Marguerite had sent Jesús with her request for prayer. "Sometimes Lupe, God uses us because of our weakness. He is then clearly seen and we in turn are made stronger for our next service."

Lupe's hands stilled momentarily. "Do you think that God would have a use for someone, like me?"

Sarah turned on her side. "I think God has a use for all His children, when they are ready to recognize that their lives are not their own but His. Take María for example. Her parents want her to be a nun and I am sure she would be a good nun, but she is unsure that this is her calling."

Sarah rolled back onto her back. María had now been included in their conversation and Sarah waited for Lupe to respond. "I've only seen María a few times, but I think it would be a shame for her to be hidden away in a habit."

Sarah laughed, and Lupe stopped the massage. As Lupe helped Sarah sit up, she continued her mirth. "I think you sound like a man who is looking at María's outward beauty, but we were talking about the inner beauty that God sees and uses."

Lupe looked a little sheepish. "She is quite pretty, and she has a delicate sweetness that is a part of her inner beauty. Can't God use her without her being a nun?"

"That is between her and God, but so far she hasn't had the experience to judge between the devoted-life her parents want for her or a life of service that might include a husband and a family. Rearing children and being a loving wife is a very high calling." Sarah had a thought. "Perhaps it would be helpful for her decision if she saw a little of what goes on at the hospital. Maybe you could arrange to show her the hospital and let her talk to a few of the staff."

Lupe thought about this for a moment. "I could certainly show her around the hospital. I'm sure a good many people would talk to her about their jobs. Then, we could discuss it over coffee."

Sarah smiled. "I would ask you to be very considerate with her Lupe. She has lived a very sheltered life."

Lupe looked a little dismayed. "You don't think I should take her out for coffee?"

Sarah laughed and put her arms around Lupe's neck and gave him a hug, unaware that Fillip was standing at the opened door. Sarah spoke softly in the ear that was near her mouth. "I know for a fact she would enjoy it but be gentle with her. I don't want her to get hurt."

Sarah released Lupe and he kissed her cheek lightly. "I promise, Sarah."

Fillip's hand moved through his hair in a familiar gesture. Jealousy encouraged Fillip to strike him fast and hard. A small inner voice reminded him of Sarah's loving spirit and the life he wanted with her.

He slammed his fisted hand into the opposing palm, and turned away from the door, Sarah's laughter reached his ears. He had a strong urge to go back to confront them, but he chose to move away quickly and give himself some time to think, so he didn't hear Sarah's response.

"In that case Lupe, help me into the whirlpool and go find María. She can go with you this afternoon, if she would like, but please remember to make sure Carmen comes to help me out of the whirlpool."

Chapter 24

Sarah stripped to her bathing suit, and Lupe helped her into the water with his usual skill and gentleness and then quickly left to find María. Sarah was glad that Lupe was gone but she was troubled that he was with María. They were both of age, but Sarah was still concerned for her part in bringing them together.

The warmth of the whirlpool soothed her aching muscles and she relaxed. She thought about the glorious day the Lord had given her from her cherished moments in the garden with Fillip, to her visit with Jesús and yes, even the time spent with Lupe. The Lord had blessed her day and in less than two hours Fillip would be home and she could share her joy with him.

Sarah heard the door open behind her and she assumed Carmen had come for her. "Thank you for coming. Lupe left a towel for me on the therapy table." Sarah lifted herself out of the water and sat on the edge of the whirlpool. "If you can hand it to me, I'll dry off a little before I drip all over the floor you keep so nice and clean. I want to rest before Fillip gets home."

Fillip had watched her slip from the pool. He walked to her quietly not wanting to frighten her, pleased that she was thinking of him. He'd never seen that much of her body, and Lust used it to fuel his passion for her. He picked up her towel and reminded himself that she was to have a few more days. When Sarah became aware of him, she turned and smiled. Fillip's gaze never left her as he draped the towel around her shoulders, and quickly took possession of her mouth.

Sarah's hands instinctively grasped the towel to keep it from falling into the water. And Fillip intertwined his fingers in her hair to hold her mouth against his. Sarah's navy-blue thigh high cut swimsuit had been bought by Carmen and was a size smaller than Sarah would have bought. When Fillip released his hard-demanding kiss, the heaving of her breasts was evident to him. Sarah pulled the towel across her breasts and tried to quell the storm rising inside her. "I was expecting Carmen to help me. I didn't know you were home."

Fillip leaned his head toward Sarah's and made no attempt to control the passion stirring inside of him as he ran his hands down her shoulders and kept her close. "I wanted to surprise you. We haven't had much time together and everything is good at work today." He kissed her lips lightly, followed by her cheeks and forehead, teasing her to respond.

Despite the pleasure he now was experiencing, Fillip thoughts suddenly went to the scene he had encountered when he arrived home. He could still see Sarah leaning into Lupe's arms and being kissed by the therapist *he paid*. He sought no explanation. He was only aware of his *jealousy* and his deepening desire to be the only man to feel Sarah's arms and to kiss her. He moved his attention to kissing her exposed breasts.

The edge of the whirlpool was uncomfortable, and Sarah wiggled about to get more comfortable, but Fillip was unaware. Her towel slipped as her arms clung to him, and she returned his kisses. Sarah remembered his promise for another few days.

Her own mounting desires were hard to deny, and Sarah remembered Fillip's warning about his point of no turning back She wasn't afraid, but gently pushed him back and looked into his face, hoping to dispel his desire. "Aren't you going to help me from the whirlpool?"

Fillip paused briefly to consider his next action.

He swept Sarah into his arms with a practiced ease. "Your wish is my command, mi mujer." Sarah noticed his endearment had changed to wife, but she had no time to comment. Holding her wet and skimpily glad body, he kissed her with a new urgency. Fillip carried her through the therapy room and laid her down on her bed and took off his wet shirt and threw it aside before he sat on the bed bedside her. "Fillip I got you wet, and I'm soaking the bed as well." She was hoping they could go out to the garden. "If you get my walker, I can get out of this wet suit and change into some clothes."

As Sarah sat up, Fillip fingered her shoulder straps one at a time, and pulled them off her shoulders, and took her in. "You are so beautiful,

Sarah." Since Fillip didn't move to get her walker, Sarah moved back against her pillows.

"Fillip, you're frightening me...a little." She counted on more time. "We are supposed to wait a few more days."

Fillip leaned down and kissed her lips without controlling the passion he felt. He breathed, "I don't want you to be afraid of me Sarah or to be afraid of making love with me." He began to feather kiss down her neck, and down the curve of her exposed chest, and before he pressed his passion on her breast he breathlessly added. "I know I promised you another few days, but I was wrong. It's better this way." He began kissing one swollen nipple. "I won't hurt you Sarah. I couldn't do that."

Sarah's uncertainty and fear became lost in her awareness of him. She was lost in a swirl of new sensations, lost in her desire to please the man she loved. "You are so beautiful, mi mujer." And, before the words faded from his lips he kissed her lips briefly before he went to her other breast.

Sarah found a part of her was very disturbed by her exposure. She was fascinated by the hair on his bare chest, and she explored its contour with her hands soon forgetting her near nakedness.

Fillip took his own pleasure from her unskilled touch and guided her hands to massage his nipples. As Sarah's hands heeded his bidding, his own were not idle as they explored the length of her body. He gently explored the scars on her leg. In his own time, he stopped Sarah's hands and reclaimed her lips in a kiss that spoke about a hunger she didn't understand. When he ended his kiss, he stripped the swimsuit down off her hips and tossed it aside. He directed Sarah's hands to release his trousers and then he stood while Sarah watched as removed and discarded his remaining clothes.

In the few moments, it took for Fillip to finish removing his clothing, Sarah had time to separate herself from her the experience. Her uncertainty about the rightness of what they were doing, made her want to stop. But, seeing Fillip standing naked beside her bed she understood what he meant about a point where he wouldn't be able to stop. Sarah closed her eyes, but the image of Fillip's arousal didn't leave her mind.

As Fillip laid down bedside her, he laughed pleasantly and kissed each of her eyelids. "It is alright, mi amor. I understand, but soon you won't be shocked to see me ready to make love to you." Fillip kissed her lips and then his kisses trailed down her neck, her breast, the scar on her abdomen, and then he trailed kisses down the tracks that the surgeon had left on her hip and leg. And, when he finished his hands explored her virginity and he directed her hands to feel his maleness.

Sarah would always remember their first union as husband and wife. She would remember his careful thrust into her softness. How he kissed away her pain and paused to allow her to adjust to his fullness before he took her in a rhythm to a euphoric world she couldn't have imagined. For Sarah the novels were wrong when they spoke of indescribable ecstasy and lusty fulfillment from being loved by a skilled man. Sarah felt warm, languid, and *complete*. She felt a deep satisfaction in being the one to bring Fillip to his release.

When Fillip finally moved out of her, he pulled her to his chest and cradled her in his arms. He kissed her face repeatedly. "Sarah, mi amor, talk to me. It's not always so easy the first time. Did I not give you any satisfaction?"

Sarah propped herself up on her elbow and looked in the eyes of the man who was her husband and *lover*. She understood the unique oneness in a man and woman joining in love and giving the hidden part of them to the other. She trailed a finger up his abdomen, over his breast and kissed him with a mischievous grin on her lips. "I think you ask too many questions for a man who has just had what he's desired for some time."

Fillip looked stricken as Sarah tilted her head back and waited for his kisses or banter. "Sarah, mi amor..."

Sarah was still not certain of the rightness of their relationship, but she couldn't let Fillip suffer. She pushed him deep into the pillows and kissed his lips until he returned the pleasure. She liked the feel of being on top of him, naked. She had a unique taste of just what real intimacy meant, and a little pride of ownership.

"Oh, Fillip this has been most—enlightening." She stroked his chest. "And if, I'm a little tender, isn't that to be expected? You said you wanted no regrets, so don't make any for us." Sarah laid her head on his chest and listened to the sound of his heart beating as his chest rose and fell.

"Just hold me, Fillip. Just hold me."

Fillip's arms came around her and he held her tight and she forbade her mind to analyze the how and why and the right and wrong of things as they were now. She listened to the sound of his beating heart and fell asleep in the security of his arms.

As Sarah slept on his chest, Fillip tormented himself with his impatience for not waiting but taking what he wanted. *Why had he permitted jealousy, over what was surely only a friendly hug and a quick kiss on the cheek, to overrule his plan to allow Sarah more time? He'd broke his promise. Could she ever want him as badly as he still wanted her?*

She had come to him so genuinely innocent and he had chosen to make her obedient to *vows she had not taken.* He had said he wanted to hear no regrets...his words to her only yesterday. Surely, since he couldn't turn back the clock, he could find a way to make it up to her.

Even seeing her scars hadn't cooled his desire but made him rein in his passion enough to cause no harm to her leg. Fillip began to stroke Sarah's soft damp hair to fulfill his need to comfort her. He thought it was good that she didn't have more time to worry about them coming together. He smothered a laugh. She didn't have time to escape back to America. And, thankfully she didn't know his jealousy had stolen away his efforts to be patient and forced their first union.

Sarah awakened to the feel of Fillip's fingers stroking her hair and she leaned back against her pillows and smiled at him dreamily before she remembered her nakedness and their lovemaking.

"I'm sorry Sarah; I didn't mean to disturb you."

Sarah rose on her elbow and teased her hand through his rumbled hair. "I don't think you should be sorry. I'm not sure though that it's good manners for a wife to fall asleep the first time her husband makes love to her."

Fillip laughed. "I think it is only poor—technique if she falls asleep while he's making love to her." He smiled hopefully. "It seems I have satisfied my bride?"

Sarah smiled. She was relaxed now that everything she feared about the first time was behind her. She kissed his lips and feathered kisses down his chest. "Was I a disappointment to you, Fillip?"

~ 215 ~

Fillip kissed her with uncompromising ardor and then answered. "Oh no, mi amor. I enjoyed your innocence as well as your efforts." He kissed her again and placed her hand low on his abdomen. "For an innocent Sarah, you show great promise. I'm looking forward to teaching you to enjoy your body as well as mine." He kissed her again. "I'll be a most thorough and attentive teacher, mi amor."

"Fillip I—." Sarah shook her head as she couldn't find the words she wanted.

"What is it, Sarah? Tell me, we must always be honest with each other."

She spoke to his chest. "I'm not so naive to believe that your knowledge came from anywhere but experience, but have you always been—careful?"

Sarah was relieved that Fillip didn't laugh at her question. "You have nothing to worry about Sarah. I doubt you would want a discourse of my experience, but I'll assure you that there are no children running about who look like me."

Sarah wasn't quite satisfied by his answer. "I may be wrong; Fillip, but you took no safe sex precautions with me."

Fillip brought his head close and gave her a reassuring kiss. He was sure if he had waited he wouldn't have planned any precautions either. "You're not wrong, mi amor, but you're my wife. You are the only woman who has come to my bed a virgin and you are the only one I want for all my life. I'm Catholic, Sarah, and I've waited thirty-seven years for this moment. We need no precautions, only time."

Sarah thought about all the learning about each other they still had in front of them. "If we take no precautions, Fillip, how much time will we have?"

Fillip drew her into his arms and laughed. "At least nine months." He cradled her face and stroked her hair. "We will leave that up to God for now. My religion is opposed to birth control, but we can talk about it." He kissed her passionately and she responded.

"I must say you are a good student, but I think I should feed you before I make love to you again. And, I want to again—tonight." He ran his hands down her body and caressed her womanhood. "Many times, so long as your leg tolerates our—efforts."

Sarah blushed and turned her face into his chest hair. Fillip laughed and pushed himself away to the edge of the bed and stood up. Sarah resettled herself and drew the comforter over her nakedness. He turned to her and grinned at her shyness. "I'll run you a hot bath to soak away any soreness I may have caused and then we'll have dinner."

Sarah watched as he strolled naked into her bathroom. She liked the trim of his departing backside, more since she had touched it. She smiled to herself and thought about her new role. She had either become a wayward woman, or she was discovering the God given sexuality of a wife. It was new to her, both thrilling and a little disturbing. When Fillip returned wrapped in a towel, he scooped Sarah off the bed and carried her into her waiting bath and helped her get settled safely. He sat on the edge of the tub for some minutes and watched her until she blushed deeply. "I thought you were going to go see about dinner."

Fillip leaned down and kissed her. "If I must, but I was hoping for an offer to join you."

Sarah laughed at his departing figure and was surprised by her response. "I think dinner would be delayed. Another time—maybe?"

Fillip looked at her and smiled. "Many more times, Sarah, many more times."

When Fillip returned he had evidently showered and was wearing a silk dressing robe and slippers. He had one of Sarah's newly purchased nightgowns and robes draped over his arm. "If I leave you in there much longer, I'm afraid you'll turn into a lovely prune."

Sarah released the water from the bath with her toes and pulled herself up to the edge of the tub. Fillip sat beside her and slowly and seductively dried the water from her back. She responded, "You know, I can do this myself."

"Oh, but this is so much more fun, especially since you banned me from sharing your bath."

Sarah took the towel from him because she couldn't stand the thought of letting him dry her more intimate parts. She was shamefully aware that she'd lose her desire for the meal that was being prepared. She pushed Fillip away. Fillip permitted her to take the towel, but he didn't overt his eyes and his pleasure was evident. Sarah finally threw the towel over his head. "I think you watching me dry off and dress should be a banned activity too, if I am to get any dinner."

Fillip removed the towel, laughed, and threw his hands up in the air and shook his head in a gesture of innocence. Sarah slid the nightgown over her head and shoulders and it fell to her waist. As she struggled into her robe, she lost her balance and fell backwards; Fillip immediately grabbed her by her arms and pulled her up to her feet away from the danger of the tub. Then turned her around and folded her into the safety of his arms. "Sarah, are you alright?"

Sarah laid her head against his chest. "I'm always alright when I'm in your arms."

The apricot shift gown was a simple blend of inexpensive fabric with a halter-top that accentuated her breasts. The gown fell to her knees and had short capped sleeves. The white terry cloth robe was one of Carmen's practical purchases too because Sarah had only brought along the blue robe. Sarah was aware of the poor quality of her attire in comparison to the expense of Fillip's dressing robe, but the ladies wore the type of things they'd hung in her closet. Fillip had recognized the simplicity of Sarah's things when he selected them for her, but he only made a passing note of them. Clothing wasn't on his mind. Fillip kissed her, relieved she wasn't hurt, and then he swept her up into his arms. "Let's go eat."

Fillip carried Sarah through her room. The pile of wet and discarded clothing was gone, and the disheveled and wet bed had been freshly made. Fillip carried her to the patio and sat her at the table that had been set for their dinner. "When I thought of our first time together, I envisioned us having a dinner like this first, although, I wasn't sure how to get you dressed in something intimate without frightening you."

Fillip seated himself and pressed the intercom. Ramón immediately appeared with their drinks, soup, salad, and rolls. Sarah looked to see if Ramón was as uncomfortable as she was with the apparent prelude to their dinner, but his mannerisms were unchanged. Sarah chided herself. Ramón was a married man with grandchildren; he wouldn't think anything of their *time* together.

Sarah had shared many dinners with Fillip but tonight things had changed. She had changed. She still loved the garden, the dinner they'd be eating would be excellent, but now Fillip was truly her husband.

"You're not saying much tonight, Sarah. Is there something wrong? Would you have preferred my romantic dinner and careful seduction to my unplanned assault?"

Sarah smiled and looked at Fillip. "You're being hard on yourself, Fillip. You were right, you know. If you had waited, and had me dress for your romantic dinner, I would have been afraid and may have bolted." Sarah touched her leg and laughed. "At least, I would have tried."

"Then, if you have no regrets, why are you so pensive?"

Sarah took a drink of her sangria and sat back in her chair. "Pensive is a good word. I was thinking about the what "if's". "If' is such a small but powerful word, don't you think? What if I had never come to Toledo? What if you hadn't shown your paintings, if I hadn't gone to the gallery, or went for a walk the morning of the accident? But, we did, and it completely altered our lives forever."

Fillip winced inwardly when Sarah mentioned the accident. "Aren't "if's" a form of regret? I'd like to believe we would have still met." Fillip reached across the table, took Sarah's hand, and kissed it. "If not, mi amor, at my life's end, it would have been the biggest regret of my life. I may have never had a wife or children, waiting for you."

Sarah was touched by Fillip's answer and she hoped it would be followed by a confession of love. But, Ramón came to clear the table and to bring out their main course, and Sarah wasn't to hear the words she longed to hear. "I only wish that our second meeting was the one I planned. Did you ever stop to think about why I was driving in the street near your hostel that morning?"

Sarah was disappointed by his question, but she answered. "No, I can't say it ever came to mind. Why were you there?"

Fillip released her hand and took a bite of his scallops before he answered. "I was coming for you. I located your hostel and I was going to take you to breakfast so we could talk." His mind leaped to the moment of the accident, but he blocked it out and continued.

"Your life touched mine for only a few hours and then you ran away frightened. I couldn't let you go. I had to know what frightened you so badly. I wanted to understand and a chance to touch you, and for that you paid an awful price in pain and suffering. Until the day I die, I'll regret that I caused you so much harm."

Sarah was surprised to hear that Fillip had been coming for her. But she was even more surprised and grieved by his revelation that the accident was still an unhealed wound in his life. If Sarah had been able, she would have left her chair and gone and sat in Fillip's lap and taken him into her arms. But, where the accident had opened new horizons for her, it also had left her with temporary limitations.

Sarah smiled at Fillip warmly to reassure him. "It's somehow pleasing, sitting across from you now, to know that you were coming to see me that morning. But, whatever instincts or drives caused you to come that morning are the same ones that caused me to act like a frightened child and run away. Don't misunderstand. I was attracted to you and frightened by the same things. Meeting you stole my common sense, so I went with you, and you stole my sense of commonness and security in all that I thought I was. You made me aware of myself like I have never known."

The garden was alive with the reassuring sounds of night and Sarah's voice melted into those sounds as she lifted her sangria and took a sip. The flickering candlelight glinted off the promise ring on her left ring finger and her attention was drawn to it as she finished her confession.

"If you truly have no regrets, about having me here with you now, then you'll have to stop regretting the accident and count it as a blessing instead. For there is one I'm sure about. If there had been no accident, I'd be at home with mother now."

Fillip ate a bite more before he replied and smiled a little mischievously. "Are you so sure, that I wouldn't have been able to persuade you with my many charms, to extend your trip and give us time to come to this night?"

Sarah had difficulty swallowing the food in her mouth since she started to giggle. As she wiped her mouth with her napkin, she was still smothering her desire to giggle. "It's your attractiveness and persuasive charms that frightened me. I would have reminded you that I was a working woman on vacation. And I would have counted my job as a blessing since it would have been my excuse to escape *you and your charms.*"

Fillip rang for Ramón and smiled at her. "I may have to think about our accident a little differently, since it has brought us to this day—." Ramón was approaching the table with coffee and dessert, so Fillip finished his sentence with a glint in his eyes and a different choice of words, "of no regrets."

Sarah blushed noticeably to Fillip's delight as Ramón served them and removed the unwanted dishes. As Ramón left, Fillip lifted his wine glass to his lips and toasted Sarah. "Your innocence is a delight to me, I'll regret the day when you no longer blush at the thought of our intimacy, but I'll cherish growing old together."

Sarah toyed with the ring on her finger. His words almost sounded like love, but she wanted to actually hear the words. Sarah pulled the ring from her finger. She had worn it for eleven years and now it no longer belonged there. She looked at Fillip for the ring now belonged to him along with her innocence. He had started to eat his dessert, but Sarah had no appetite for hers. The ring felt heavy in her palm as she closed her fingers over it, shut her eyes, and prayed. "Give me the words, Father." Fillip had educated her about physical desire and possession, but she would now have to teach him about commitment.

She looked up into Fillip's face and saw that his eyes had become fixed upon her. "My parents could never have imagined my wedding day, but they did plan for my wedding—night." Sarah smiled as she remembered.

"For my sixteenth birthday, my parents took me to a nice restaurant. Later that night, we talked about sexual maturity, sexual responsibility, and God. The things that they shared with me were not new concepts. They were a summary of all the things they'd taught me. That night though, they asked me to make a commitment to sexual purity until the time of my marriage to the man God would choose for me. I accepted their concepts and I made that commitment and sealed it with a prayer out of my love for them, for God, and for the man I would someday marry."

Sarah paused, opened her palm, took the ring, and held it up. The ring was made from 10k yellow gold and it had been fashioned to show two hands exchanging a ring. "They gave me this ring to remind me of my pledge, so that no matter where I was, or who I was with, or how I felt, I would be reminded of my pledge until I exchanged it for a wedding ring. I kept that pledge to them, to God, and to you. Tonight, Fillip Castañola, my husband, I give you my promise ring as this afternoon I gave you my innocence."

The night sounds of the garden seemed to have stopped to bear a silent witness to the giving of the ring and completion of the pledge. Sarah handed the ring to Fillip and he took in his breath as he fingered the small ring in his fingers. It looked out of place in his large fingers and then it was Sarah's turn to take in her breath as he brought the ring to his lips and kissed it. And, then he got to his feet and came around the table and pulled her up gently into his arms.

"Sarah, mi amor, you take my breath away. I have seen your ring and thought it was a ring of friendship and thought no more of it. Tonight, you have explained its symbolism and significance and I feel like a bandit, unworthy of what you have given. When my father died, I was angry with God. I am no longer angry, for he has given me a treasure beyond any that I could have asked."

Fillip kissed Sarah's lips in a tender reverence and Sarah answered from her heart. She opened her eyes and looked into his and tears filled her eyes to the brim as she thought to herself. *"Oh Fillip, say the words. Tell me that you love me."*

Fillip smiled at Sarah and kissed each eye. "Sarah, you are truly my treasure without any measurable value. I can't tell you what your gift means to me, but I will spend the rest of my life showing you."

Sarah found her lips being caressed by the lips that failed to speak the simple word love. She needed more than physical love, and more than the endearment mi amor. She needed to hear those words and to say them in response, but this would not be that night.

———◆———

Satan twisted Warning's report in his hands and roared in disgust. "You have all failed me. This *infectious Christian* not only strengthens her *waiter* but has wrapped her husband around *her* wedding finger.

Warning tried to defend, "Lust, Doubt, and Discord as well as Jealousy are doing all they can. But Master, Sarah has hidden the divine truth of the Bible in her heart and only sees the good in the man, her husband. Despite all that has happened to her she is content as *His'* beloved daughter. Doubt cannot thwart her position and faith in our enemy."

Satan stepped angrily toward Warning with piercing eyes of hate. "Doubt can gain no ground on the *pious Christian*," he spat on the words, "but what of the husband. Doubt tore him away from God at his father's death?

Warning bobbed up and down in agreement. As a demon he only knew the past, not the softening of Fillip's heart toward God concerning his father's death. "Yes Master, he is angry with Him—but has not denounced Him." Warning wished that Doubt was here to answer and bear their master's wrath. He stays away from his parish home, but still contributes to its welfare."

"So, why hasn't Lust used the man's feelings for the woman? Or, why hasn't Jealousy been useful in tearing them apart. Doubt asked for one of them? Isn't the man an easy target? "Master do not be angry with your trustworthy servants. Lust and Jealousy worked hand in hand today, but the man held his jealousy and didn't harm his perceived competition as hoped, for he sees the virtue in the woman. But, Lust was successful." Warning hedged to downplay the truth.

Satan grabbed him by his neck and glared into his face. "Then, why haven't you reported that the woman is packing?"

Satan flung him into a chair.

"Master the man did act on his feelings, but just prematurely, and he was gentle and considerate with her. The man just took her without giving her the time he promised to allow her to come to him. Doubt and Discord can still use this?"

"But—!" Satan waited impatiently. He knew there was more.

"But, she loves the man and is coming to terms with their marriage, their uh...martial union was not unpleasant. She prays ardently for his salvation and their marriage. I fear she won't leave him."

Satan roared. "Bring me all the demons on their case. And, tell them I want solutions not excuses! Warning rose and crept toward the door glad they he would not have to suffer Satan's anger alone.

Satan struck the table and knocked over the chair in full view of

Warning who paused. "Must I do everything myself?"

Warning stole away and thought to himself. "*Master you did not prevail against Christ after His forty days in the wilderness. If you had master, you would be at least equal to God on earth, and your servants wouldn't be feeling your rage over an infectious Christian woman.*"

Chapter 25

The morning light had long since entered her room when Sarah awakened to find the pillow next to her head empty. Sarah picked up the pillow and breathed in Fillip's essence. Fillip had made good on his promise to make love to her again and had spent the rest of the night in her bed. She finally slept spooning with him on her good side.

Sometime before dawn, he drew her awake loving her when he was still sleeping himself. There was little time spent on seduction or encouragement, but he drew her in with a raw need also new to her. She revealed in his urgency and matched it with her own. Awakened by his climax, he whispered in Spanish his pleasure in needing her as much in his sleep as he did when he was awake. She turned on her back and he leaned over to kiss her, and she almost said the *word* she wanted to hear herself. But said, "I will pray that you, my husband, will always need me, but in more ways than just this."

"You," he kissed her nose. "I will always need in every part of my life, our life, but for now I am a newlywed, and you must feed the appetites you stir, yes?

"Sí, siempre y cuando usted ayda acrecer el mio. "(Yes, so long as you help to grow mine.) Sarah slowly and carefully answered as she rolled back to her side.

"Con placer, mi esposa". (With pleasure my wife.) Fillip answered without noticing her Spanish as he nuzzled and kissed her ear. Sarah pondered her husband's passion as she listened to his breathing. First, he slept, and she soon followed.

Remembering their night of lovemaking, Sarah shifted the pillow to her chest, and reveled in the daylight streaming in around her. She looked to see if the light bore the warmth of God.

"Dear Father, I come to Your throne different than I have ever been and

even more unsure and confused. First, I lost control of my heart, and now my body, to a man of whose choosing? How can I be married to a man who isn't Your child? Speak to my heart and give me understanding as to what I am supposed to do now?

Silence filled the room as Sarah strained to hear God answer. As she waited, Sarah thoughts turned to the story of Esther. *Esther, a very young and beautiful Jewish woman, had been kidnapped along with many others and taken to the palace in Susa as candidates for the king's new queen. King Xerxes had divorced his current Queen because she would not scantily dance at his command at a drunken feast. Each kidnapped candidate was given a year of beauty treatments and training, then they each got one night with the king to win his favor. Failure left the candidate one of the king's many concubines for the rest of her life.* This certainly was a situation Sarah didn't envy.

But Sarah knew that Esther won Xerxes favor on her night by being herself, a virtuous daughter of God. So, she went from being an orphaned young woman living amongst the other captives in a foreign land to being Queen of the Medians and Persians, who had conquered her people in a brutal war. Being Queen hadn't been her vision for her life and it wasn't easy, but from her position of Queen, through the insistence of her cousin and guardian, Mordecai, she was at last obedient to God's divine plan to save all the Jewish people throughout the land.

Sarah remembered more details of the story. *Haman the chief minister to King Xerxes had wanted Mordecai dead. So, he plotted to kill Mordecai by killing <u>all</u> the Jews throughout the land. Haman had King Xerxes unwittingly sign a royal edict to allow all the Jewish people killed by their neighbors for their possessions because of a lie he created. The very evil Haman had told Xerxes that the Jews were plotting to overthrow him. Haman's hatred and jealously would see Mordecai die on a gallows Haman had especially built for him.*

Esther had been reluctant to seek the king's intervention for herself and her people because the king hadn't called to see her in a month, but through prayer and fasting she faced her fear and went to the King. King Xerxes, as was his right and power, could have her killed for coming to him without being called. However, when he saw the beautiful Esther, his queen, standing in his court, he was pleased with her and held out his gold scepter to her. So, Esther approached and touched the tip of the scepter and was spared.

The infatuated Xerxes then offered her up to half his kingdom, but she procrastinated in fear and only asked for him to come to a feast she wanted to give in his honor. Sarah had some mirth at Esther's' expense for Esther who held two dinner parties for the King, the evil Haman, and other guests before she told Xerxes of the plot against her and her people.

Once the King knew about the plot and realized that the Jewish people in his land were no threat he had an edict written that allowed Esther's people the power to defend and save themselves, and, Haman was hung on his own extra tall gallows.

Sarah pondered the story. God had not only foreseen Esther's kidnapping with the other young beautiful virgins of the kingdom, but he had seen the evil heart and intent of Haman. God had positioned her ahead of time to save the captive Jewish nation.

Sarah's thoughts then ran to the story of Joseph. His own brothers had turned against him and sold him into slavery. Their betrayal placed Joseph in a position of authority to save Egypt and his father's family from a great famine. However, God's path to gain him that position included thirteen years as first a slave in a foreign land and then a prisoner in jail for a rape he <u>hadn't</u> committed. He had turned down his mistress' advances, and her indigent cries of rape could have resulted in his death!

Sarah pondered how very different their outcomes might have been without God's intervention. Sarah was amused at herself. Her life now could hardly compare to these two Bible heroes. Her only suffering had come at her own hands because of falling in love with a city and a people and daydreaming instead of safely crossing an alley, and she too now lived in a palace.

Sarah couldn't help thinking about Esther's reluctance to use her position to intercede and her fear. Sarah knew she had nothing to really fear from Fillip, but like Esther she was uncertain and reluctant to be in her position as Fillip's wife. Mordecai hadn't let Esther whine her way out of her responsibility! He had sent her a message in face of her reluctance, **""Do not think to yourself that in the king's palace you will escape any more than all the other Jews. For if you keep silent at this time, relief and deliverance will rise for the Jews from another place, but** you and your father's house will perish. And who knows whether you have not come to the kingdom for such a time as this?"?" (Esther 4:13-14 ESV)

Maybe she thought that God had brought her to this marriage and had a plan despite her uncertainties and reluctance. She was joyfully reminded that God had a plan for each of his children!

"I can't say Lord, that I understand Your plan, but I will believe in it each day with hope. Thank You Lord. Grant me the patience to trust in Your plan, and the patience to wait and see when I'd like a written detailed plan. Be with Fillip. I am grateful that You have a plan for him too, a plan to see him saved. In Jesus' victorious name. Amen.

Sarah laid the pillow aside and turned to get out of bed. Fillip had evidently thought of her need for the walker because it was within reach. María came at her call, helped her dress for the day, and they spoke only of Maria's afternoon with Lupe at the hospital.

"Sarah, I never knew there was so much I could do to help people without becoming a nun. It will require a lot of schooling and hard work, but Lupe says that the hospital always can use a trained occupational therapist. I like the ideal of helping people recover, adjust to their new limitations, or to train for a new way of life—." She smiled sheepishly. "And, to be a spiritual aide too!"

Sarah made her way to the settee. She was dressed but not willing to go to the kitchen. "Are you so sure you want to help people or are you just admiring what Lupe and the others do?"

María joined her and looked a little hurt. "It is an answer to our prayers, at least my prayers. I know I find Lupe and what he does appealing. He helps you. And, I love you, but it is more than admiration. I have a sense of release. The long dark shadow of a nun's habit no longer hangs over my thoughts."

Sarah patted María's hand. "I'm glad you have new dreams but guard your heart wisely. I believe Lupe is a man who enjoys a woman then moves on to the next one."

"Señora Sarah are you still not happy with Fillip?"

Sarah avoided the question with her reply. "My thoughts are only for you. Lupe has a very jaded reputation at the hospital. I don't want to see you get hurt."

María understood and nodded her head, not wanting to hear more about Lupe, or to press her mistress about her marriage. At her silence, Sarah had breakfast brought to her room and when she completed a simple breakfast of rolls and tea, María and Sarah shared their morning quiet time.

"Sarah how is it that you study the Bible on your own, and don't go to a priest for confession? María asked.

"When I asked Jesus into my heart to be my Savior, we began a personal relationship." She paused and reflected on how to answer and sent up a silent plead for help.

"When Jesus came into our world as our infant King, the Jewish priest offered different animal sacrifices at different prescribed times to atone for the sins of individual believers or the nation. But Jesus was the only perfect sacrifice, and when He died for us, no sacrifice was ever required again."

"Yes, I understand." María responded.

"The Bible tells us that at the time of Jesus' death the heavy sixty-foot high curtain that separated the Holy of Holies from the common area where only the high priest could go just once a year was divinely cut from the top to the bottom. Divinely cut, María. God did this to show us that we could go to Him directly without a human intercessor. The people of Jesus' day and now us no longer need a priest to make sacrifices or pray for us."

"But, your pastors pray for you?"

"Yes, they pray for us and with us, but we can pray for ourselves alone. Throughout the New Testament in scriptures like Romans 8:34 and Hebrews 7:25 we are taught that Jesus is our intercessor in the throne room of God, but we can pray directly to God our Father. I read God's word and do Bible studies to grow in God and pray directly to Him because Jesus' death for me gave me that freedom and privilege. When I sin, I can directly confess to Him without delay or an intercessor. And, we don't need to pray through Mary either, because she needed a Savior as much as we did. Remember God, Jesus, and the Holy Spirit are Triune, the great three in one. God is our Father, Jesus our Savior and Intercessor, and the Holy Spirit indwells each of us to guide us in "paths of righteousness."

María had listened carefully and understood what Sarah said, but found it difficult to reconcile with her religious training and practice.

"Then, how is it my faith teaches confession and atonement though priests?"

Sarah felt uncertain how to answer her sincere friend without sounding judgmental. She had extended family members who were devout Catholics like Carmen and Ramón, and Marguerite.

"There are over 4200 religions in our world and many don't teach faith in Jesus at all. We are fortunate to trust and believe in Jesus, for Jesus Christ himself says, "I am the only way to the Father and our eternal home.""

"Satan uses the multitude of religions even within Christianity to distract and confuse God's beloved children from finding a personal relationship with the Trinity. The Bible doesn't call us to religious practices, or to a specific religion, but to be followers of Christ. That's why the early followers of "The Way", faith in Jesus Christ were called Christians."

"There won't be any Catholics, Methodists, Presbyterians, Nazarenes, Baptists, or any other religion in heaven. Heaven will be filled with the saved. It is a matter of our hearts for Christ and Christ living in our hearts." Sarah studied her friend. "I hope I haven't offended you."

"I am not offended, Sarah, but I must think this through." María nodded to herself. "I wish to speak about this to Ramón and Carmen."

"You are very wise. We need to test all new information to see if the Spirit says it is true and seek Godly counsel from our believing friends. Believing in Christ being the only way to heaven isn't being intolerant. We accept each person's freewill to choose what they believe, but we cannot stop telling them the truth, or growing in the truth ourselves."

"Knowing what we believe and defending our belief with truth isn't intolerance, it is following the commission God gave to all His disciples to take the gospel to everyone. But as our friend Jesús has discovered, we cannot save anyone with our faith, but must rely on the Holy Spirit to convince and save." Sarah paused. "Are we still friends?"

"Of course. I know you love me and want only good for me. I just need time to think on this."

"Of course." Sarah patted her hand and they ended their time in silent prayer. Sarah's prayer included understanding for María as well as her protection from her womanizing therapist. She prayed that the Holy Spirit would convince Lupe of his need for Christ. She also remembered to include her dear friends Jesús and Marina's relationship as they approached marriage as an unequaled couple.

Sarah was restless and preoccupied the rest of the morning and found little solace in the garden. She ate lunch in the kitchen with her household friends but couldn't confide her troubling thoughts about her marriage to them. They all seemed absorbed by their own thoughts.

She did seek her bed for her usual respite but found her tumultuous thoughts interfering with her sleep. Doubt kept piercing her thoughts with random dark thoughts. She heard "fallen woman", "living in sin", and her favorite because it was close to the truth "kept woman". She had waited eleven years for marriage to a man of her own faith, a man who placed God first in his life. She had waited for the man who would be the true spiritual leader of their household.

She drifted into sleep to have sleep torn from her by a voice that mocked her in a singsong of "unequally yoked".

She thumped her pillows and propped herself up trying to stop the unbidden thoughts. She knew they weren't really her own. She prayed for the faith to trust God's plan in her life, in Fillip's life.

If only Fillip would say that he loved her, she would feel better about their relationship. It would be easier to believe that Fillip would come to Christ in time. But, he only spoke about a lifetime of their being together. She feared it was really a lifetime of penance for him because of the accident.

She never placed any blame on Fillip, even if she still had the daily pain, the limitations of her injuries, and scars to remind her. He was the truly innocent victim in the accident.

Sarah found it useless to stay in bed with her mind a jumble of thoughts, so she went to search out María for a Spanish lesson. Carmen was alone in the kitchen sweetly singing a familiar hymn in Spanish but turned at the sound of Sarah's walker. "Señora Sarah, you didn't sleep long this afternoon and you do not look rested. Is there something wrong?"

Sarah took a seat at the kitchen table. "There's nothing wrong. I just found it difficult to sleep. I'm restless today. Perhaps all I need is to be out of this house or be of some real use. I miss my old life in America."

Carmen joined her at the table. "Sí, I believe I understand. You are house bound too long now. Perhaps you should have Señor Fillip take you out to dinner."

Sarah had to laugh. They all wanted to make her well and happy. "I don't think the answer to my problem lies in eating food outside of this house. Besides you have already started dinner preparations. Maybe you should just let me help?"

María came into the kitchen with an arm load of soiled linens and stopped when she saw Sarah. "Señora Sarah, I must tell Ramón you are awake. You had a phone call earlier and he didn't wish to disturb you."

Sarah knew they would have awakened her for Fillip or for her mother, so she had to ask. Who was it María?"

María shrugged her shoulders. "Ramón only said to tell him when you were awake. I'll go find him then you'll know."

María headed out and Carmen left the table. "Let me get you a cup of tea."

Sarah didn't say no so Carmen prepared the tea. Shortly, after the tea was set before her María returned with Ramón. "Señora Sarah, while you were asleep Marguerite Castillo called. She said to tell you to call her at this number as soon as you were awake."

Sarah took the offered paper. "Thank you, Ramón."

He nodded. "Do you want me to call the number for you?"

Sarah smiled at Ramón. No, thank you. I think I'll try my Spanish on Marguerite." Sarah slowly made her way to Fillip's den to use the phone.

The phone was answered by an unfamiliar male voice and Sarah gave her name and asked for Marguerite. Marguerite hadn't called for a chat and she got right to her point. "Sarah, I'm glad you didn't sleep the afternoon away. Jesús called me last night and told me about your Prayer Partners and your desire to be useful here. I have a little boy who is quite ill, Jamie Molina. His parents are at the end of their strength. You need to come Sarah. See if Jesús can come with you too. Ramón can pick him up at work and bring you all. I gave him my address."

Marguerite's directness was not new to Sarah, but her request came as a surprise. "Are you sure the Molina's want us to come?"

"I have spoken to them about your faith, Sarah. They want you to come. They need you to touch their lives with your faith."

Sarah sat dazed with the phone in her ear. She had been called to prayer unexpectedly before but never without her prayer partners. Sarah switched to English. "Do they believe that prayer can save Jaime?'

Marguerite was silent for a moment. "I have told them that God hears your prayers and that you believe He is still a God of miracles. You are all they have left, Sarah. Whether you pray, and God grants them a miracle or not, they need your faith and the comfort of your presence."

"I don't know what to say to them Marguerite. You want me to come late into a difficult situation and I'm not prepared. They are strangers to me, and I to them. I don't even have my prayer partners here."

Marguerite answered someone in Spanish and Sarah understood. "Sí, she will come."

"Sarah the situation here is difficult, but surely that will not stop you. And, Jesús and I will be your prayer partners. Surely God is calling you to come."

Discouragement brought excuses to her mind. She was tired. The Molina's were strangers. Her recovery might be at risk. But, she had never turned her back on a request for prayer. "I'll call Jesús, but he is new to his job, and may not be able to leave it. But, I'll come."

Sarah called Jesús at his office, and after a quick conversation with Raphael, Jesús agreed. It was late in the afternoon when Jesús would normally have finished, and Sarah was their employers' wife. Shortly, after Sarah finished her call to Jesús, María knocked on the door and came in with Sarah's warmed, untouched tea.

"Is something wrong? Sí, I can see it in your face. How can I help?"

"Please tell Ramón to bring the car. We are going to the address Marguerite gave him. She wants me to come and pray at the home of a very sick child she is nursing." María nodded and turned to go and Sarah's mind flashed to them praying together. "María I want you to come too. We pray well together, and this child needs all of us."

María looked startled but agreed. Sarah took a moment to search her heart and to pray for the challenge ahead of them. Her tea remained untouched. As she got up and struggled to the front door, she thought of God's timing. She was restless in her new role as a recovering patient and uncertain wife. And, she had spoken about her prayer partner service only yesterday as if it was behind her. Today, God had contracted a new partnership, and had called her to serve where she now lived.

———————◆———————

Warning stuck his latest news about the infectious Christian woman into some bigger more successful reports, and quickly left before his master returned from a state summit of leaders in Europe. Jealousy had been removed and reassigned for his failure, although Warning felt he had done all he could under the circumstances. The unsaved husband had after all been a decent man, and the infectious Christian woman deserved his trust. He only hoped that Deceit who was on site at the El Alba Rosa battleground could be more effective in his efforts to keep the man from salvation.

Chapter 26

Ramón, Sarah, and María didn't return home until well past the usual dinner time and Fillip was waiting in the foyer. Sarah was exhausted by the events of the past two days and her lack of true rest. She had spent too much time on her walker, but, she couldn't imagine how Ramón could have gotten her past the stairs in her wheelchair. He certainly couldn't carry her as Fillip did, but they were home now, and the wheelchair was waiting.

Fillip came to her and she hoped he saw the something in her eyes that hadn't been there since her last outing with her old prayer partners. However, the special energy of the spirit that followed such prayer wasn't enough to strengthen her physical body and she collapsed into Fillip's arms.

"Sarah, mi amor what have you done?"

Sarah relaxed against the comfort of Fillip's familiar body. "We went to pray for Jaime, he is a very ill child and his family. It's beyond anything I can explain now."

Fillip picked Sarah up in his arms and shook his head at his exhausted wife, as Ramón brought the wheelchair close. "And, I suppose I can't be angry with Jesús, Ramón or María for helping you with this *thing*?"

"You can be angry with only me and you know that won't do you any good. I was needed and would have gone in a cab, but I am grateful they came with me."

Fillip laughed. "I expected as much when Carmen told me you left after a phone call from Marguerite to pray. I only wish mi amor that you didn't look so exhausted."

Sarah didn't respond but closed her eyes and rested in Fillip's arms. "María go turn down Sarah's bed." He looked at Ramón with displeasure. "I think it's time we let your mistress rest."

María ran ahead and had the bed turned down and Fillip carefully laid her down, removed her shoes, and brought the covers up to her shoulders. Sarah spoke weakly. "I won't be good company tonight. You deserve more."

Fillip playfully kissed the tip of her nose. "No, you won't be, but we both have other needs this evening. You rest, and I'll go to the hospital and see Raúl and Elena. If you awake, call for your dinner. María can serve you in bed. I don't want you to leave your bed. I know what you did this afternoon was important to you, an activity of your old life, but you shouldn't exhaust yourself."

Sarah stirred herself wanting to give Fillip some of the attention he deserved. "You're right. I'll leave becoming exhausted for when you are with me." Sarah giggled, and Fillip smiled at her attempt. "Tell them I am praying for them and perhaps Ramón will take me to see them tomorrow."

"Sleep, Sarah." Fillip leaned down and kissed her lips to which she didn't respond, and then he kissed her forehead like a beloved child. Her eyes were barely open, but she nodded weakly. "Tomorrow is Saturday and I will take you myself."

Fillip pondered his beloved wife, and how he could change her as he drove to the hospital. She wasn't as beautiful as some of the other women he had dated but was refreshingly sweet in her beauty. And, from their first meeting he liked that she didn't wear heavy makeup. Even near death in the hospital when she reached out to him, he saw her beauty. And, healthy she always had this special radiance that was so much more than reflected light. Better clothing from the right stores and designers would easily fix the problem. But, she was too deeply religious to suit their life together. It was something she would have to leave behind with the rest of her American life. Deceit found his opening. He couldn't force her compliance but easing her into it slowly over time would work. It worked on their intimacy, he smiled to himself, *and she wanted to please him.* A new thought entered his mind. *She'd want to please his family too; after all he'd already established himself with her mother. Marriage was about compromise, and she would surely compromise and become the woman he had waited for.* Fillip became aware of the increase in traffic, reduced his speed, and focused on his drive to be with his friends.

Sarah slept fitfully for hours without the pain medicine her body needed before a cyclic conversation stole into her sleep. Her dream state was an endless cycle of prayers for Jaime and his family or she was endlessly trying to explain to Fillip why such prayer was needed. She desperately wanted him to understand the responsibility and the privilege of being called to pray for the sick and those in any need.

She drifted close enough to wakefulness that she forced herself to move her limbs to escape the endless restless praying for Jaime and the unfruitful conversation with Fillip. Sarah was groggy pulling herself away from the sleep she needed, but her conscious mind knew that type of sleeping was more harmful to her brain than rewarding. Not fully awake it took her a few minutes to comprehend her surroundings and her circumstances. She pulled herself up to the edge of the bed and called for María. Her sweet maid came immediately with her walker and helped her to properly prepare for bed. And, Carmen brought her a thick potato soup, crackers, and tea for a late meal.

———————◆———————

Warning anxiously prepared Doubt's report for Satan. He had indeed been successful in the woman's unconscious mind. Doubt really hadn't planted any new seeds of doubt but more the stirring of the age-old question about whether God would answer their prayers with a miracle of healing for the sick child. Warning knew the child and his family were no threat for God would readily receive the child into heaven, and a demon of Doubt could then prey on the family's grief and it would either strengthen their resolve to believe or less likely damage or destroy it.

Fillip's unbelief and discomfort with the deep prayers of the faithful for healing was the real target Doubt was trying to stir. The man would have to be pushed harder to claim his wife's attentions and thus remove her from the ministry she served at home and would facilitate here. The others would quit if she was denied and drawn away by her husband.

But, Warning knew that Doubt really had no right to claim any victory. For the conscious mind of the woman, or more an angel whispering reason had pushed her to wakefulness. And awake the woman no doubt shook off the vague memory of her restless sleep state and by now had dismissed it altogether. Warning decided this meager report of Doubt would wait until it could be a footnote to a real victory. Warning had other reports to leave that would no doubt please his master. He would wait to see if Doubts trifling with the unconscious mind of the woman would bear any conscious fruit.

Eighty percent or better of the human population were no threat to his master or his plans to see them perish with him in the hell prepared for him and his demonic servants. Satan had convinced a third of the angels of heaven to leave God to serve him, and centuries of effort by Greed, Lust, Carnality, Vice, and the newly titled demons of Road Rage and Electronic Distraction had sewn up in the civilized world. Missionaries were a threat in the third world countries where they served, but even there their bustling cities had little time for God's son. His master couldn't *un-save* those who had asked and received salvation, but he could certainly have them troubled by his unholy servants, steal their joy, if allowed, and certainly thwart their actions to get others saved. Warning sighed. All this trouble over one unsaved man, but it was what the master wanted. He knew stopping the salvation of one man had stopped many from getting saved before, stopped salvation from coming to whole families.

Warning thought that it would be better to let this one man go. He had a praying infectious Christian wife, a praying mother-in-law, a praying American church, and Christ faithful servants in his home. Demonic effort had never prevailed against that much prayerful opposition. Maybe they had already lost, but it was their job to fight these special battles for a human soul. Only *He* knew what the man would decide, and the battle for this one man seemed as important to his master *as the enemy.*

Sarah wasn't very hungry, but her light meal made by the wise motherly Carmen was well received by her ill-abused body, and she had María stay to keep her company. María pulled up a chair and before long they were talking.

"My parents always made me feel like it was my duty to be a nun, so I could serve God and pray for people the way you did this afternoon. I see now that God doesn't need to have me in a nun's habit or even a therapist's uniform to bring His comfort and love to people."

Sarah took her friend's hands like they did when they prayed. "We prayed this afternoon María. I was not alone. We, Marguerite, Jesús, Ramón, Jaime's parents and other family members, and *you* beseeched God in His throne room for Jaime's life. Remember Jesus Christ is our advocate who intercedes for us at His father's throne. We should do the Bible study, *What Love is* by Kelly Minter together. I loved it and learned so much from it. Mother can send it to us. But, tomorrow I will show you the scriptures in John that speaks to this. John tells us that because we have the Holy Spirit living in us and Jesus is our advocate in the Trinity we actually have access to God in His throne room. We have great power through Jesus Christ, María. Power we often fail to appreciate or call on. Who could we trust more to defend us and to love us unconditionally than the One who died for us?"

María's face lit with excitement. "So, you really believe Jaime will be healed."

Sarah teared at the thought of all the sweet child had been though and his current state. "María, we shouldn't be surprised if we get the miracle we have prayed for, but we can't know God's will in this for little Jaime, but death is not the _end_. It just ends what we know and understand. It is just so hard when death takes someone from us. But, it is in no way final, just a doorway to another eternal world. It is the loss for all we could have had with our loved one here that causes us to grief. Even then God has given us the gift of tears to relieve the grief. He says that He gathers our tears, and to do that means He is near when we cry."

"If you look at death from God's perspective, death is the time we leave behind this world of sin, pain, and sorrow to be received forever in Heaven, our true eternal home. We struggle against death because we were created to live eternally. Sin in our world has stripped away our eternal physical design, but not the eternal design of our souls. God's plan for eternity in heaven restores our eternal physical design when we are received in heaven and are given our eternal glorified bodies. If God receives Jamie home to be with Him in eternal joy, he will not be lost to his family, but only separated from them until it is time for them to step through eternity's door."

"To live here on earth, we have temporary bodies suited to this environment. I remember a pastor once, who called our bodies "earth suits". Once we step away from our earth suit, and put on our glorified bodies, we will never face sickness, death, or even aging again. Our grief at the passing of a loved one in Christ Jesus is tempered by the hope of sharing in Jesus' resurrection from the dead."

Sarah released María's hands and they sat quietly together. When María didn't speak again Sarah said, "I'm sorry María, I didn't mean to lecture, and now I've done it twice in one day."

María laughed. "I like your speeches. I am learning a lot from you, and Señor Castañola pays me."

"And...you are worth every penny dear friend. But, I'm done with dinner and speeches for tonight." Sarah answered and hugged her maid and friend.

María started to rise but stopped. "Sarah, you didn't ask, but I want you to know that I liked being with Lupe." María's face was mostly hidden as she spoke. "I will sound foolish, but because you can be obedient to the Lord and be Fillip's wife, I hope I can have a future with him."

Sarah was dumbstruck by María's confession. Sarah moved the tray from her lap and placed it on the other side of the bed and struggled to sit on the edge of the bed. She had in less than twenty-four hours gone from being the Sarah she thought she knew, to being intimate with a man, her husband, that didn't fit her image of a Godly husband, to once again being the Sarah who could respond to intercessory prayer with others. And, now she had the shock of María's confession. Sarah liked Lupe, but she couldn't imagine him married to her devout friend.

María went to pick up her tray. "I will leave you now. Is there more I can do for you?"

Sarah knew they weren't done, but she needed some alone time with God. "Please bring me some water, so I can take some pain medicine. I have sorely neglected this. And, will you stay for just a little bit? I won't keep you long."

María assented with a nod of her head and quietly left the room.

Sarah had come to a physical and mental low point. Doubt threw a fiery dart. For some weeks now, she had seen herself in a small boat in a heavy sea. But, she hadn't been afraid because she knew the Master of the Sea was with her. The day and now the night had seen the storm intensify, and she was now keenly aware that there were other souls in the boat with her. Along with the Holy Spirit her spirit grieved for all who didn't know the Lord. She couldn't kneel, but she took her walker and went to the garden door. Her grieved soul turned her grief for the lost to praise for her Father. The night sky, the moon and the stars, always reminded her that God was in charge. He called all the stars in all the galaxies by name, and He knew not only her name, but His plan. She spoke to Him out audibly.

"Thank you for reminding me that I am not alone. I know that by Your might not one star is missing. Tonight, I have been crushed by the great burden of Lupe and María, *as well as all the lost around me. My little boat in what was a weakening storm has become a crowded ship. Bring us all safely to shore, for it is more than I can do. These lives crowding into my boat are precious to me because they belong to You, those who acknowledge You as Lord and those who do not. Protect María and her vulnerable heart, and if Lupe is to be her helpmate finish the work You have started in him before she becomes hurt. For Jaime and his family bring comfort and healing. His healing is* not *too much for You. And, Lord, I can't even imagine the impact of such of miracle, where the doctors have failed. Yet, I know that death for this sweet child might be the right answer for him. And, will You Father finish the work in Fillip too? Teach Him that all He has is meaningless without You guiding him. He has done well on his own, but oh how much more he could do following You. I thank you for my own healing Father and Your constant presence with my mother. We are a handful here in Toledo. I don't know why we are important to You, to Your Son, and to the Holy Spirit. I am just grateful that we are. Bind the enemy from any victory here, in Jesus precious name. Amen."*

María had slipped in and heard much of her mistress's prayer. Sarah watched the sky as if the stars would form an answer to her prayer. María cleared her throat and Sarah indicated the settee and María met her there with her pain medicine and the water.

Sarah sighed heavily. "Please don't be offended but I want to share my feelings with you as your friend, and my words are my own and not God's."

María nodded and Sarah spoke. "I have been very confused over the past few weeks when it comes to understanding God's plan for my own life. But, I'm so very grateful, that He gave me you. Just don't blindly fall in love with Lupe...if it isn't too late. Seek God's plan. Lupe doesn't share your heart for God. God is so important in a marriage and an unbelieving spouse can hinder the believing spouse's service to God. I've prayed from the beginning that Lupe will receive the light, but he hasn't yet."

"I understand Señora Sarah, but must I crush my feelings for Lupe, when you do not crush yours for Señor Fillip." María had once again given a human voice to the very question that tormented her, and Sarah blanched white. "I'm sorry, Señora Sarah, I spoke out of turn."

"Don't apologize. My mind troubles me with the same question. But, I didn't come to this marriage through a conscious choice. As a matter of fact, when it was my choice, I planned to go home and never see Fillip again."

María shook her head in understanding but pursued the truth. "But, you chose to live it when you could have gone home to America annulled."

Sarah's heart ached hearing the truth and she became pensive. *When she first came to El Alba Rosa, she was too weak and in too much pain for the trip home. And, in just those few weeks she had lost her heart to Fillip and his staff. She had prayed for guidance.* Doubt threw another fiery dart. *Had she not listened to hear her Father's voice? Had He said "go"?* Another dart struck. *Had she allowed her desire for Fillip to block the Father's guidance? Yet, another dart. Could she have stopped Fillip before they left the therapy room?*

Sarah whimpered in her trouble soul for the doubts to cease. *If I failed to hear You, forgive me, but weren't Esther's and Joseph's stories recalled as Your direction for me to stay?"*

Sarah addressed the patient María. "I did choose, but not without prayer. And, I still have my doubts. But, I have given myself to Fillip,

~ 242 ~

and even now, if I am wrong to be here and leave, I will remain Fillip's wife in my heart for my lifetime even if he divorces me. But, you still have time to choose rightfully for yourself though prayer before there are others to consider. Don't run to Lupe to escape a convent. You have other options."

María took Sarah's hand and squeezed it gently. "I've not understood before that you are torn in your love for Señor Fillip and God." She nodded in understanding to herself but spoke to Sarah. "Yes, it is clear. If Fillip shared your heart for God, then Satan would have something to fear in the strength of your love for each other and God. Together you would be powerful servants for God. We must pray that our enemy is bound so you and Señor Fillip can become one in love and service. This is what we must do, Sí?

"Sí, my wise friend and sister." Sarah began as was their habit.

"We come to Your throne room Father as sisters. Thank You for Your mercy, grace, and lovingkindness. The day stretched new before us and is now ending, but so much happened in between. We bring Jaime to You this evening once again, not because You didn't meet with us or hear us this afternoon, but because in Jesus we have the freedom to come to You whenever our hearts seek You. Christ came into our lost and dying world and had compassion on the people in His day, and He healed the sick, cast out demons, restored limbs, restored sight and paralyzed bodies, and even death released its hold at His command. Our Jesus is the same today as He was then. Restore, precious Lord, Jaime to his family. We agree that this miracle is not too much for You. And, for Fillip and Lupe who are now in our lives we pray for a finish work of faith in them. We know that the Spirit has long before us worked in their lives, now rebuke Satan and any demons that would interfere with this work of salvation. Let the healing blood of Christ be applied to their spirits and save them for all eternity. We seek Your divine will in Jesus' holy name."

Sarah squeezed her sister's hand. *"Our Dear Heavenly Father, thank You for opening my eyes to see that You have a plan for me that would allow me to serve You without being a nun. I thank You for the opportunity to join in a united prayer for Jaime and his family. Call me again and again for this, Lord, but answer this prayer with a miracle for this little boy."* María paused in brief uncertainty, and then plunged in without timidity. *"Please open Fillip's eyes, so he can see Sarah and what they can have in You. They are a married couple despite their unusual wedding. Bind Satan and allow what has started to finish and bring You glory. Bless my friend, Sarah and her husband Fillip so they share a common heart in love, marriage, and service to You. I know Sarah wasn't sent to Spain, to answer my prayer about my service to You, but You have used her in this, and through her I am learning much. And, Lupe, Father, You know he has a little piece of my heart but let him give his whole heart to You whether we ever become a couple. Seal these two men to Your service, and then to us, if this is Your will. Give Sarah the rest she needs tonight, rest to meet the challenges of tomorrow and continued healing. In Jesus' holy name we pray with praise. Amen."*

María left after helping Sarah to bed. The demons were rebuked and forced to retreat as an answer to prayer and Sarah slept restfully without Doubt's repeated tormenting refrains.

Chapter 27

Raúl was responding well with his new pacemaker and although weak he was alert and talking throughout the course of Fillip's visit. At the end of visiting hours, he insisted that Elena allow Fillip to drive her home. Raphael had come with her that morning before work and she'd refused to let him come back for her as she'd wanted to spend the night. Raúl's home was on the opposite side of town in an older development. Fillip stayed with her and shared a glass of wine while she talked about her father's health and her fears. The hour was late by the time he got home and remembering Sarah's exhaustion from her day's activities and his own need for her in his sleep the previous evening, he went to his own room.

Much to Sarah's surprise after her morning toilet, when she called for María, a familiar freshly showered dark head popped open her door and brought in a heavily loaded breakfast tray. "I wasn't sure how you would feel this morning, so I decided we could share breakfast in bed." He smiled at her and raised his eyebrows suggestively. "If not, maybe at your settee."

Sarah laughed at him warmly. "I am well rested, and I could have eaten in the kitchen, but your offer sounds good, if there are no strings attached."

Fillip stood with the tray in hand and looked at Sarah sitting on the side of the bed. She looked refreshed and delightfully tempting in her nightie, but he understood her unstated reluctance to share breakfast in bed with him. "No strings this morning as I will work on satisfying my hunger with breakfast, mi amor, but maybe you could put on a robe and join me at the settee.

Sarah struggled into her robe as Fillip put the tray on the coffee table. She joined him at the settee, and he readily took her hands while she prayed a blessing over the food. They each took a plate of eggs and bacon and started to enjoy the food. Sarah was hungry this morning and relaxed as they ate.

They spoke randomly over the meal, and Fillip filled her in on Raúl's condition and Elena's reluctance to leave him alone in the hospital. Sarah suggested that a special duty night nurse might offer her the opportunity to feel good about getting some rest at night. Fillip readily agreed and planned to arrange for a night nurse quickly.

Fillip decided he would let her have mealtime prayers as well as church attendance, but he would draw the line at this prayer partner business. Sarah was too fragile for it now, and he would discourage Ramón from participating as he had María just this morning.

Sarah had finished her breakfast and juice, and decided she deserved a little of Carmen's iced pecan cinnamon roll with her cup of tea.

"Sarah, I talked with María and she told me about your prayer visitation for the Molina family. I understand you did this in America, but I'm not sure you should continue here. You are a married woman now with a new home and new responsibilities. And you were totally exhausted last night when you got home." He drove his point home. "You collapsed in my arms and I had to carry you to bed. I'm sure this is not good for your recovery." He could see Sarah's displeasure, and toned down his demand. "You should at least recover your ability to walk before you do this again, please."

———◆———

Deceit beamed at the man's opening volley and Doubt stirred the woman's fears. The demons had come with Fillip into her room. They'd been kicked out last night because of the women's prayer, but back again this morning and so far, there were no angels in sight.

———◆———

Sarah took another sip of tea and set down her cup. This was what she feared. He couldn't understand the need or the meaning of her prayer ministry. Marriage with Fillip couldn't work for either of them unless he understood. More she wanted him to be a part of her work. "My exhaustion can't be blamed entirely on my sick call."

Fillip immediately thought of her "no strings comment" and was suddenly bitter about her denying him his right to make love to her this morning, since he had forgone it last night due to her exhaustion. He angrily questioned her. "So, you blame your exhaustion on *my making love* to you."

Sarah reached across the settee and caressed his cheek. "Let me finish husband. I don't regret *our* lovemaking and you were the one that didn't sleep late. But, I wasn't able to sleep when I rested yesterday afternoon." She refrained from commenting on her restless mind. "In time, my body will be completely healed, and I'll not tire so easily."

Sarah decided to make her stand for God clear. "But, you need to understand my prayer ministry in America is a part of who I am in Christ. With my recovery and all the changes in my life, I hadn't thought about it. But, yesterday God showed me I can still be a part of a prayer ministry here."

"When Marguerite, Jesús, Ramón, and I prayed together with the Molina family we had the same anointing I felt in America. I would love for you to be involved in this with us. But, make no mistake; I can't be anything less than what God calls me to be. I want your approval and support, but if that is not possible, I'm not the right woman to share your life."

Sarah sat back quietly and toyed with her roll. Fillip stared at his coffee cup, as he thought about his response. *He could demand her obedience, but with God behind her desire for this ministry, she'd made it clear that she would leave him. He had told her that he didn't need a woman to share his life to secure his business and wealth, but he did want her. He'd just have to be subtler in slowly changing her. Certainly, she wouldn't be called out to pray often, so he softened his approach.* "I didn't mean to forbid your service to God but was just looking to protect you from harm. Will you forgive me?"

"Yes, of course." Sarah broke off a piece of the delightful cinnamon roll and stuffed it in her mouth to give herself more time. *It wasn't a simple argument. She saw her fragile world at El Alba Rosa collapsing.*

She couldn't be herself here without alienating her husband which made her a wife she didn't want to be. She thought of her conversation with María about Lupe, and clearly saw the wisdom of crushing her feelings before they could crush her life. She looked at her husband struggling with his own thoughts and hated the dark thought of leaving him. She knew too that if the time came to leave, her heart would remain with him.

Fillip pondered his plan to wean Sarah away from her religious beliefs. *There was no harm in them. It would just make it harder for him to groom her into the wife he desired. He would call Marguerite and tell her of Sarah's collapse after the sick call. He would appeal to her sense of duties as a nurse and ask her to allow Sarah more time to recover. By then the subject might never be brought up again.*

For now, he would cajole his bride. Deceit was delighted by how quickly the man followed his directions. "I didn't mean to minimize the importance of what you do. I only want you well, so we can build our future together."

Sarah's fingers had become sticky from the sweet roll and she brought them to her mouth to clean them off. Fillip grabbed her hand and teasingly licked each finger. "I think we are going to have to agree to agree again. And, I know the perfect ending to our first argument."

"What do you mean?" She liked the return to his sexual undertone but was uncertain of his sudden change of his attitude.

Fillip kissed her quickly on the lips. "If we are finished with breakfast, I can show you." Fillip smiled and without waiting for a reply, picked up the tray and started out of the room. "Wait, here."

Sarah waited somewhat anxiously for Fillip. She knew sooner or later they would make love again, and although the mystery behind the physical union was behind her, she feared the spiraling effect on her. It was some minutes before Fillip returned and he came back with two large boxes. "I was planning to give these to you last night, but today is better." Fillip almost mentioned Sarah's outing and exhaustion but caught himself. He needed to let that go and work more subtlety. He leaned down and kissed her. "Open this one first."

"Oh, Fillip, you have already given me too much. I think I should be the one giving you a present."

Fillip put the other box on the floor and sat beside her. "They aren't

retrieved later by Ramón or delivered. Doubt tumbled through her mind. *Servants, special services, buying expensive things were Fillip's life. Sarah had adjusted to the servants because they were friends, the extra service was livable, but spending a month's salary on a few items? How could she become accustomed to such a life style? He was giving her everything and all he had to show for it was one night of lovemaking. She wasn't the woman to fulfill his fantasy. He obviously hadn't been lonely for female companionship during his adulthood, so why settle for an unsophisticated virgin now? All she saw were obstacles and doubts to her marriage with Fillip.*

Fillip took her to lunch at a sidewalk café, and the air and passing shoppers were refreshing for someone who had developed a case of mansion fever. They talked after they ordered.

"I wanted to let you know that I invited Jesús and his girlfriend Marina to dinner three weeks from yesterday."

"Good, it is nice you are making friends here." He also thought a fuller social life would distract her from all her praying for others.

"And, you should know, I am going to be graduating from Lupe's torture at the end of the month. So, except for the exercise bike, the equipment can be removed then. Since I am doing well, I will switch to a cane soon after receiving my instruction. So, I'll use the cane around the house and the walker for longer ventures, like the garden and shopping. I should be free of my wheels altogether."

"This is wonderful news." Fillip's fleeting smile left as he remembered Lupe holding Sarah, and his kiss to her cheek. Jealousy promoted his question. "Won't you *miss your therapist?*"

"I will miss my friend who has seen me through a rough time, but not my therapist. I will need to go to the hospital a few times after my graduation for him to check my progress." Sarah touched his hand and looked into his eyes and she smiled like a Cheshire cat. "But, I'm afraid it is María who will miss his visits to the kitchen after my therapy, but their dating will soothe that over, don't you think?"

"María and Lupe are involved?" Fillip was incredulous.

"I'm afraid so. Preparing for the nunnery hasn't prepared her for an experienced charming man like Lupe, but we've talked and prayed about her being careful with her heart." Sarah shared.

"Wait, Gail's niece, your maid was preparing to be a nun, and now she is dating your therapist." Fillip asked. "How did I miss this?"

Sarah laughed at him boldly. "You must not have asked the right interview questions before you hired María and you certainly aren't privileged to our girl talk."

"I only hired her because she was Gail's niece and spoke English. You needed a maid quickly, and I trusted Gail. You've been happy with her? Si?"

"Si. I love the girl. I'd adopt her if she needed it." Sarah laughed. "You did her a real service hiring her and giving her a chance to see what life could be outside a nunnery. Her parents were pressing her hard, and Gail saved her from choosing a life to please her parents because you brought me home and spoiled me with her care." Sarah became pensive.

"But, I'm afraid Lupe has stolen into her heart, much the same as you stole into mine. I want her to think with her head and not her heart, but when it comes to such matters, it seems the heart rules."

Fillip kissed her fingers. "In this I am glad, if I'm in your heart, mi amor. I'm sure the head will see the wisdom in it soon, as does mine."

The arrival of their food allowed Sarah to take back her hand, and not respond.

After lunch they stopped at the hospital and Sarah met Raúl and Elena. Elena despite the stress and sleepless nights with her father's hospitalization was even lovelier than Carmen had described. Sarah felt a moment of jealously when she compared herself to a woman who obviously was more suited to be Señora Fillip Castañola, but she dismissed it. Elena had been available to Fillip, maybe even a lover, but he hadn't married her. Sarah found both Elena and Raúl charming and receptive of her as Fillip's wife.

By the end of their visit, Sarah felt a yearning to pray with Elena and Raúl. But, she wasn't sure how her new friends would feel about her praying at Raúl's bedside, and she felt certain Fillip would disapprove. On impulse when saying good-bye, she stood up from her wheelchair and kissed Raúl's cheek and whispered in his ear. "I will keep you in my prayers."

Sarah sat back down in the chair, and Fillip moved her to shake hands with his friend, but Raúl held his grasp and spoke to him in Spanish. Sarah understood what he said but didn't give herself away. Her time each day with María and conversing with the staff in Spanish was making understanding easier if the conversation wasn't too fast.

"I'm not certain how you gained the chance for such a woman to be your wife. You don't deserve her, but you need her, and you are a most fortunate man. You would lose my respect if you do anything to cause her harm or have her leave you. Don't crush her sweet spirit, Fillip."

Raúl released his hand to cover his cough. He smiled at Sarah and spoke to her in English. "I know you are praying for this man too. He is stubborn and used to having his own way. It will be interesting to see what you and God can do with him."

Sarah smiled back and nodded. Raúl understood her heart and mission with Fillip. "God hears and answers our prayers but only changes people when they allow. When you are well enough, please come to dinner with us. It is an open invitation and you know Carmen's food is worth the drive. It was a pleasure to meet you both, and I hope to see you out of the hospital soon."

Elena thanked Sarah and turned her attention back to making her father more comfortable. Shopping, lunch, and the hospital visit had tired her, and she didn't even have the joy of the spirit that filled her after a sick call to carry her home. Even though traveling in her wheelchair Sarah's state was approaching exhaustion, and the pain medicine she took for her adventure had worn off. Fillip knew she was hurting, and once seated in the car with her wheelchair stored by the valet, Fillip headed home.

"I'm sorry, mi amor. I scolded others for over-taxing your strength and now I've done it just as carelessly."

Sarah had been studying Fillip's profile, carefully memorizing his outline and smiled wearily. "No one has been careless or inconsiderate of my recovery, especially you." She laughed. "You chauffeured me about today. I'm grateful to have been out with you."

Fillip reached over and massaged Sarah's aching leg. "When we get home, I want you to take some pain medication and nap before dinner. Tonight, we'll have a quiet evening and you can have an early night."

Sarah leaned back against the soft leather and closed her eyes. No doubt if her leg and hip and other parts weren't protesting vigorously she would be asleep. She opened her eyes and shared her morning plans. "I could use an early night. I've promised to attend mass tomorrow with Ramón, Carmen, and María, although they are going to the nine o'clock because of me."

Fillip was surprised. "I didn't think you'd be willing to go to a Catholic mass."

Sarah smiled broadly remembering Carmen's surprise when she asked to join them. "I haven't been to church in a long time now. I'm going to church to fellowship with God's people, not to become Catholic. I hope you might come too. It would be good to go as a couple and worship God for all He's done for us."

Fillip left the city behind, but concentrated on his driving, delaying his response. "It's been a long time for me too. I haven't been to church since my father's funeral."

Sarah leaned over and placed her hand on his arm. "It's not unusual for someone to become angry with God when death takes a love one. It would please me, if I could be the reason for your return. I know God has missed you."

Fillip watched the road as he thought about what Sarah had said. *He knew his grief had seemed best focused on God. It seemed foolish for a grown man to be angry with God because death had been impartial and taken his father. Yet, if he had abandoned his habit of attending mass because of his father's death, then he had gone only to please his father, and he knew that wasn't true.*

He wondered if you could shake your fist at God in anger, and then go back to Him? He didn't feel angry now, just a lingering sorrow. Looking at Sarah he knew God had not left him in his grief, but he had left God.

Sarah was reclining quietly in her seat praying he would go with them.

Looking at her he had no doubt God would be pleased to see him in church. Perhaps he would attend again, at least occasionally. Hadn't God sent him an angel to ease his sorrow, and to give him hope for a family? How could he not attend tomorrow with her?

"It would be a pleasure to be your escort, mi amor."

Sarah's angel praised God for the growing hope in Fillip's coming salvation. Satan's elite squad of demons had gained no ground today in the battle for Fillip's soul, or in the destruction of the fragile uncertain marriage.

Warning paced outside his master's chambers. He really had no choice. He would again downplay the demons' failures, after all the man hadn't made it through the church's doors. A lot could happen overnight, but he knew there were angels quietly working in the home where an infectious Christian woman only had to smile. He sighed.

He decided his friends weren't to blame for failing. Lust fired a few darts, but the man once again exercised patience. No, the woman and the man were basically good and their loving feelings for one another a salve for the emotions being stirred. And, Deceit's efforts were too long range to bring about the results needed quickly.

The man needed a lot of attention from several demons successful in frustration and impatience. Certainly, his sexual needs weren't being fulfilled by his little *prudish virgin* as compared to his past lovers. And just how long-suffering did he need to be for the woman to heal? He knew just the demon who could join Deceit and Doubt already assigned to the case. His friend could easily work on the man as well as the woman.

Although it wasn't his job, he could insidiously suggest that Doubt remind the woman that the man was only keeping her because of his guilt; because her scars reminded him of the accident whenever he touched her; and because she was too pathetic for another man to want now. With so many demons working together his master would see the union destroyed before it could flourish and cause them any more issues.

Chapter 28

Sarah willingly went to bed after taking her pain medication. As the throbbing in her hip and leg eased, she drifted into sleep with praise in her heart for a quickly answered prayer. Fillip would attend church in the morning.

With Sarah tucked safely in bed Fillip went to his study to arrange nurses for Raúl to relieve Elena from her constant vigil. When the arrangements were confirmed he called the hospital to let Elena know she would be spending her nights at home despite her protests. He assured her that the hospital would call if she was needed. He also called Raphael who was going to evening visiting hours, so he would take her home.

Then, he called Javier to manage a legal request. Javier was home and delighted to hear from Fillip. They conversed in their native language. "It is good to hear from you my friend. How is Sarah getting along?"

She's doing quite well. The doctor and therapist are both pleased. She tires easily if she leaves the house for an extended time. I took her shopping this morning, to lunch, and to the hospital to see Raúl, so she is sleeping now with the aid of pain medication."

"It sounds like a rather full day for someone so recently hospitalized with a bad injury. I take it that Raúl is doing better?"

Fillip winced at the reminder of the seriousness of Sarah's accident. Living with Sarah daily, he had grown accustomed to her limitations. For the most part he was able to put the reason why out of his mind. He only saw her as his wife now, and the challenge of making her the wife he wanted. "Raúl is recovering, although the doctors are not sure of his prognosis yet. It seems that even with the pacemaker his heart may fail. Elena understands, but I'm afraid she's not willing to accept it. Raúl has made his peace and is remaining hopeful."

"Is Raphael assuming Raúl's duties as you expected?"

"Raphael is doing well. Since he finished his business degree earlier this year while working fulltime, he deserves his advancement in the company. Raúl saw this day coming and didn't hide from it and has trained him well. Thanks for asking about our friend, but I called to talk about my marriage."

Javier sighed. At last he could undo what he probably should never had done. "I take it that you and Sarah are ready for the annulment?"

Fillip was not angry that Javier thought he was sending Sarah home. "Sarah is well enough to go home, but she can't be annulled. I have made her my wife, Javier. I want you to see that no one can question the legality of our marriage."

Javier's initial silence confirmed his surprised. "Congratulations, my friend, I always believed it would take an unusual woman to hold your attention. I assume she shares your feelings?"

Fillip knew she wasn't certain about their marriage, but he also knew it wouldn't be easy for her to leave him now that they had shared a bed. The power of her own convictions would cause her to sign a marriage agreement. "Sarah has accepted our marriage, and it has been consummated. We are hosting a dinner party for my family Monday night. I know it gives you very little time, but I want you to come and bring with you a document we can sign that will make it clear that Sarah and I are man and wife."

Javier shook his head woefully before he replied. "I can prepare a nuptial agreement, but I doubt it will validate a proxy marriage, if scrutinized. My best council is to marry your bride properly. A simple civil ceremony would do, although I favor a religious ceremony."

Fillip pondered a proper ceremony but explaining the need to Sarah would be admitting they weren't properly married, which he knew would cause her great concern. Sarah wouldn't accept their continued intimacy, and he didn't want a moral dilemma to spoil their marriage. She'd run home to her mother in shame, and their relationship would be hard to rebuild. For him his marriage was as real as any other for legalities didn't make a marriage. His marriage was about Sarah and their future together. Priests and judges could preside, a marriage license and certificate are nice, but they didn't need those things to confirm his commitment.

"We'd go from an unconscious bride to one using a walker. Perhaps we should wait and have a renewal ceremony with a fully recovered bride to celebrate our first anniversary. By then Raúl will be well enough to give the bride away, you can be my best man, and the mother of the bride will be living here. But, for now prepare a nuptial agreement."

"Alright, I'll specify that you both agree that despite the unusual and urgent timing of your proxy marriage you find it legal and binding. Do you want any restriction clauses about the length of your marriage regarding financial settlements in case of divorce?"

"No. You'll find such clauses are unnecessary. Sarah doesn't believe in divorce. You can add our vow renewal to celebrate our first anniversary. Sarah would like that." *He would like it too. Any man would be proud to wed a woman such as his Sarah, although a late stage pregnancy would make it a little more awkward. Maybe a few precautions would be good for a time.* "Can I count on you for dinner?"

"Don't you always?"

"Yes, I do. But, I don't thank you enough. We'll see you at church tomorrow, so please don't mention the agreement. I want to see it myself before I show it to her."

"Of course, since that is what you want. I'll come prepared Monday night." Javier chuckled. "And, I'll look forward to seeing you and your bride in church tomorrow."

"Good-night, Javier."

Javier thought long about the conversation. *The agreement would be easy enough to prepare, and would reinforce the unusual marriage, and no one would ever question Fillip. Still another ceremony with a conscious bride and guests would be better. He was looking forward to meeting this young woman who had so dramatically entered and altered Fillip's life. He chuckled to himself. Fillip would be in church in the morning for the first time in a long time with an American bride. He doubted the other parishioners would be discussing the service.*

Javier went to his study to start working on the agreement.

◆

Fillip sat back in his chair and Deceit joined him entering his thoughts. *Fillip went over the conversation he would have with Sarah about the nuptial. He would explain that Javier felt it necessary for them to secure their marriage, but that he had no concerns. There anniversary ceremony would be an opportunity for them to share their marriage with their family and friends. His wife would make a beautiful bride.*

His thoughts turned to Sarah's promise ring that now rested in his jewelry case. On Monday, he would have a jeweler come to his office with a selection of engagement rings and wedding bands. He would see that her promise ring was properly replaced when they talked about the nuptial agreement.

He smiled as he thought about his wife. His mother had wanted him to take Elena for his wife. His strong-willed mother refused to understand that he had no romantic interest in her. And, he didn't need to marry Elena for his business. He never wanted Elena as anything more than a friend. He never thought he'd have a virgin American wife who was so deeply religious, but that same faith would see her stay with him. He'd claimed her virginity and over time he'd see that she distant herself from practicing things like her prayer ministry.

Sarah was young, sweet, naïve, and beautiful. And, he loved her more with each passing breath. Strange he never felt like he would be a man whose heart could be won by a woman. Fillip laughed. Sarah was not just a woman. No, she was a woman cut from the cloth of an angel. He liked the realization that he loved her and didn't just want her.

The problem was getting Sarah to love him in return and be the wife he wanted. Her body, even injured, warmed to his invasion, although her mind was more reluctant. Time was the problem. They had only known each other only a short time. And she made it clear she had wanted a Christian husband. Sex was easy enough for many dating couples, but Sarah needed the full commitment of loving for a lifetime.

The phone broke into his introspection and after finishing the call, he spent some time catching up on the paperwork he brought home.

Sarah woke as the afternoon light gave way to evening shadows. The extra dose of pain medication had eased her pain but left her feeling groggy. She hated the dulling effect of the pain medication and resisted the urge to go back to sleep. Getting better meant taking back her life and she didn't take naps.

However, because of the pain medicine and her over confidence with the walker, Sarah planted the legs of the walker poorly at the transition between the bedroom and bathroom floors and fell to her buttocks on her good side. Pain shot thought her body and made her immobile just inside the bathroom door on the hard tile. After a short time, she knew that she wasn't really hurt, but she couldn't get up. She was frustrated with herself and hurting but had to remain on the floor until help came.

She chided herself, "Why couldn't she have called and waited for María, so she wasn't alone?" At home she could have called out and her mother would have been able to hear her and come, but not here in Fillip's towering El Alba Rosa.

As the time passed Sarah became certain that she was only bruised and shaken, and she was able to push the walker off and pull herself up against the door frame. After no more than fifteen minutes that seemed like hours, María found her. Poor María immediately panicked and rushed to kneel beside her. "Oh no! Señora Sarah! Are you alright? Oh, Father help us?" María made the sign of the cross and was so distraught she didn't wait to hear Sarah's answer. "Don't move. I'll get help."

María ran out the door screaming for Fillip who was out the door of his den before María could get to him. "Señor Fillip, you must hurry. Sarah has fallen and is hurt. Come, come quickly"

María was in tears and wringing her hands by the time they got to Sarah. Sarah sat quietly waiting for help to get her off the floor. She wished María hadn't panicked and called the whole house down on them. Fillip knelt beside her in alarm.

"Please, Fillip. I'm not hurt. Everyone just needs to be calm. I just can't get up on my own." She laughed, "Maybe Lupe should be working with me on that." No sooner had the words left her mouth then Ramón and Carmen appeared.

"Are you sure?" Fillip asked taking her hands. He felt sick remembering the accident.

"Yes, my pride is significantly wounded, but I'm intact. See no bleeding." She waved her hand around her. "I just would like to be off the floor, I've finished admiring your tile work."

"Alright, you heard her." Fillip directed. "Carmen do something with

María and Ramón page Dr. Rubio." Carmen took the sobbing María and they all left for their assignments.

"Sarah what happened? Are you really alright?"

"I just lost my balance and fell. I'm not hurt just bruised. I fell mostly on my behind and good leg. My legs simply won't allow me to stand without something to hold on to properly like my very strong husband. Please just help me to my feet."

Fillip nodded and gently cradled and lifted her from her non-surgical side by habit. "For now, let's put you on the bed."

Fillip laid her on the bed and sat beside her. Sarah kissed him. "I'd prefer you to try and take advantage of the situation than to look so worried."

Fillip kissed her back less heartily. Ramón came and motioned to the bedside phone. "Dr. Rubio is on the phone."

He spoke in English for Sarah. "Dr. Rubio, Fillip Castañola, thank you for calling so promptly."

"You're welcome. I understand Sarah has fallen. How is she?"

Fillip touched Sarah's cheek and she turned into his hand and smiled. "She says she is merely shaken and bruised. She fell on her uninjured hip, but she gave us all quite a fright."

"I understand. If you would like, I can meet you at the hospital for some x-rays."

"Just a moment doctor." Fillip covered the receiver and spoke with Sarah. "Would you like to go to the hospital for some x-rays?"

What she wanted to do was to scream that she was fine and would only like to go to the bathroom, but she answered reasonably. "I don't need any fuss. I'm scheduled to see Dr. Rubio Friday. We should leave it at that."

Fillip looked at her closely but returned to the phone. "Sarah said she doesn't need a trip to the hospital. She just wants to keep her Friday appointment."

Dr. Rubio answered, "Let's trust her judgement about the hospital, but call the office Monday and bring her in, so I can see her. In the meantime, have her exercise good judgment, and if she experiences any further pain or difficulty call me immediately."

"Alright doctor. Thank you for your time."

Fillip hung up the phone and looked steadily at her. "The doctor will see you Monday, but you need to stay out of trouble."

"I'm sorry for the scare. And I am still going to church in the morning."

Fillip started to protest but Sarah kissed him. "Please, don't make me an invalid. A less adventurous trip to the bathroom, a quiet evening, and church in the morning is all I need." She sat up gingerly and kissed him more boldly, and he relaxed and returned her kisses. She whispered a sweet threat in his ear. "Don't make me show you my new underthings."

Fillip laughed. She leaned back against her pillows satisfied with Fillip's reaction. "And if we are done with the chaos, I wonder if dinner might be served?"

Fillip ran his hand through his hair that she had just ruffled. "Ok, I'll send María to you if she has regained her composure, but don't get up without help. I'll have dinner served to you in bed."

Fillip got up to leave, but Sarah stopped him. "Will you eat with me?"

Fillip looked out the French doors. "It's been raining all afternoon, so the patio is wet, but I have a table in the studio we can use. I'll build a fire in the fireplace and we can eat in front of it. How does that sound?" He gave her a wicked smile and kissed her and whispered in her ear. "Maybe after dinner you'll show me your new underthings."

"Yes, to dinner, but a quiet evening precludes you seeing your purchases, sir." She pushed him away. "Quickly to work, sir. I still need the bathroom."

Fillip laughed, swept her up in his arms and carried her to the toilet that had been equipped with hand rails. "Stay put until María gets here. I'll see to dinner."

Their fireside dinner wasn't the romantic evening Fillip wanted but Sarah enjoyed their dinner, easy conversation, and his unthreatening company. She made it a point to eat heartily to quell any lingering doubts about her wellbeing. She lingered over her tea to extend their pleasant evening, but Fillip had other plans.

"Either you're a wonderful actress or you weren't injured, but I still want you to have a good hot soak and an early night. I can use the time in my den since my morning schedule is filled."

Sarah was a little disappointed, but she didn't want him to use her as an excuse to forgo church. "I'm not an actress. I'm not in severe pain, although I will take more pain medicine before I sleep tonight. So, you can leave me without giving me a second thought."

Fillip came around and scooped her up and for a moment she hoped he'd changed his mind about working. "I don't have to give you second thoughts, mi amor, because you always have my first thoughts."

Fillip carried her into the bath and set her down on the chair now placed in the bathroom for her. He went to the tub, started the water, and returned to her. He removed her shoes and then started to undo her blouse. Sarah stilled his hand. "What are you doing?" Fillip smiled mischievously.

"Just what you asked. I'm treating you like you're not an invalid. I'm seeing to your need for a good soak, and a brief showing of your new underthings."

"And, if you see my new things will you work in your den tonight?"

Fillip didn't answer immediately, but removed her blouse, smiled fingering the lacy strap of her new bra. "Regrettably, I must. You, mi amor, need a quiet night and I have work to finish so we can have Sunday together without interruption." He leaned down and kissed the tops of each of her breasts and kissed her lips. Sarah responded, and she felt his fingers working the claps of her bra and pulling it away, but as her breast spilled out he pulled back.

His voice was quite husky. "I'll send María to you". He turned off the water faucets. "Don't get into the tub without her."

He came back to her as she tried to pull her blouse back on to cover her breasts. He brushed her hands away. "Another time, Sarah, we'll share your tub." His hand reached out and brushed her nipple with his thumb, and it immediately responded. She reached up to cup his head and brought him down to her, but he pulled away. "You tempt me princess, but my passion for you tonight would not be easily held in check." He touched her other breast and smiled. "But, tomorrow you and I will have the whole day and you can prove you are able." He kissed her lips and tasted her moan of frustration, and it didn't begin to match his own.

Sarah sat partially undressed after he left. She was aware of an ache deep within her that had nothing to do with her fall. Her heart ached too, and she wanted to call him back. *He was the one who said not to start something you couldn't finish. She felt very unfinished.*

María came and helped her into the bath and left to clear up the dishes while she soaked. As she relaxed in the hot water with the water jets following, she became aware of how dissatisfied she felt, and it shocked her. She wasn't sure what complete sexual gratification with Fillip would be like, but she knew frustration and unrequited desire and she was shocked, more she was angry with Fillip. Her head might say she shouldn't be learning to enjoy a very physical relationship with Fillip, but her heart and body had other ideas.

She wrung her washcloth between her fingers. If El Alba Rosa had an elevator she'd surprise him by climbing into his bed in the negligee he'd picked out. But, there was her leg, her leg, her leg, the walker, and the hulking mansion! She'd have María bring her the negligee. Maybe Fillip would return—but she knew he'd give her a quiet night despite his own desires. But, tomorrow leg or no leg she was going to coax some action!

Chapter 29

After María helped her from her bath, Sarah did put on the negligee and then checked herself out in the mirror. It made her pause. She had never seen anything so lovely or revealing. Without the walker in her reflection she felt sexy. She knew this was one of the benefits of being Fillip's wife. She tossed her head at the errant thought. She wasn't seeing anything that didn't come from God. She couldn't lose herself in fine things, El Alba Rosa, or Fillip. She was a beloved daughter of God. She said a brief prayer for forgiveness and asked God to keep her humble, and never let her become a worldly Christian.

Sarah asked Maria to sit with her on the settee, but she politely refused. It was clear that María had been instructed to let Sarah sleep, and she resented Fillip interfering with a choice that should have been hers. So, she reluctantly took her pain medicine and went to bed, so María could leave.

She turned her mind over to praying, but after a while she drifted into sleep. A log in the fireplace burnt through and the sudden thud startled her awake. She apologized for falling asleep to her Father and ended her prayer with just one more plead. *"If we are a couple, Lord, please make it right for us to be together and to serve you faithfully "*

She never heard anymore sounds from the fireplace, nor did she see Fillip come and still the remaining embers. Sarah's quiet unassisted breathing drew him to her bed and he watched her sleep with relief. He had spent many anxious hours at her hospital bedside, praying she would awaken and be herself. The pampered weeks of her recovery had replaced some of the weight she had lost and had returned a healthy glow to her cheeks. He saw the top of her exposed breasts and the negligee they had purchased that day and was tempted to join her. He recognized that the gown was an invitation. How easy it would be to remove his clothes and slide in beside her. He knew she had worn it to lure him. He smiled. He also knew she would respond to him hesitantly.

He watched her sleep and when she stirred, he silently bid her to stay asleep. Then, he kissed her cheek ever so gently, and went reluctantly to his master bedroom. He knew it was the right thing to do. *But, as he undressed, he kicked the bedpost in frustration. His bachelor days where behind him and this wasn't right. Soon very soon his days of sleeping alone would end too.*

By morning the skies had cleared and Sarah with María's help was dressed despite some stiffness and mild bruising before she joined Fillip for breakfast. Her gait with the walker was considerably slower, but her spirit was soaring.

Going to mass was the fellowship Sarah needed, although Javier was right about the congregation's reaction to the Castañola's' appearance in church that morning. Sarah met God there as well as many God-loving people. Her spirit had found a much-needed sanctuary.

After their return from church, Fillip insisted that Sarah lie down and rest. Sarah obediently stretched across her bed, but she was too rested and restless to sleep. It was now second nature to Sarah to seek the solace of her garden sanctuary, although she had the foresight to only go as far as the patio. After wiping off one of the table chairs with a towel she had thought to take out with her, she sat down to enjoy the peace of the garden. She had taken pictures of the changing scenery and sent them to her mother, but the real image before her was even better than Fillip's paintings.

Her fall the previous evening was a clear reminder to her that she still had a long way to go with her recovery. She had really wanted to be more useful by now and not such a burden to Carmen and María. Of course, she never planned to still be at El Alba Rosa learning to be Fillip's wife.

Sarah began to wonder again about God's plan for her life. She wanted to follow His will but looking ahead she saw no clear direction. She felt as if she was living someone else's life, certainly not the one she had long envisioned for herself.

"I thought you were resting tucked safely in your bed?"

Fillip had startled her, and she felt like a child caught sneaking a cookie before supper. "I'm safe. A person can only rest so much, and then they are all slept out. Yes, I tire easily, but I'm tired of resting, tired of becoming tired, and tired of taking it easy while everyone else works. I'm used to earning my keep, and here I do nothing. And, I have help doing that."

Fillip came and sat on the edge of the damp table. "As my wife, you'll never need to work again. When you've recovered you can volunteer at the hospital, until we have children. Then, you'll be needed by them as well as me. If you want money, you only have to say how much. Actually, we should open a checking account for you. Then, you'd have your own money."

"It would still be your money." Sarah pointed out.

Fillip took her hands. "There's no job for you outside our home. Your job is Señora Castañola and the challenges of having me as your husband and that will grow as you recover, and you make your place here." Fillip touched her cheek and thought of watching her sleep the previous night, smiled at her, and confessed. "I won't turn down another invitation such as the removal of the negligee you wore for me last night." He caressed her cheek. "Do you really not like your job or its benefits?"

Sarah turned Fillip's hand over and kissed his palm. "I don't think my qualifications match the job requirements, or that I can handle all the benefits. You deserve much more and I'm afraid I'm a disappointment."

"Sarah, mi amor, what can I do to make your happy? I know it isn't easy for you now. You're in a strange country, you don't speak the language, your mother's not here, and your recovery isolates you. But, you are making friends and you have an adoring husband. I always seem to be asking you to be patient, to give us a little more time. Tomorrow you'll meet my family and they'll expand your possible activities as you get to know them."

"Sarah, I need you to want to stay. We've had a rough start no doubt, but that doesn't mean it won't be good. I understand that you didn't choose me, but I believe God chose you for me."

He pulled her into his arms and steadied her before he kissed her and then teased her. "Admit it; I am an answer to your prayers for the perfect husband. I'll tell you something I've never said to any other woman." Sarah held her breath. "I need you Sarah. You make my life complete."

Sarah's heart begged to hear the word "love" and to repeat it. *Was "love" the same as "need"? She didn't believe so, but she thought his confession would be a prelude to his making love with her again. Last night under the circumstances she had wanted him, today she would yield because she was his wife and he wanted her.*

Fillip released her mouth. "Since you have cabin fever and you like this garden so much, I know something that will make you happy, if you don't mind a late lunch?"

Sarah looked into Fillip's face. "Eating is the second thing that recovering people are forced to do excessively by those who are attempting to make them get well."

Fillip's face glowed like a little boy. "I'll have a picnic lunch ready for us and we'll leave in twenty minutes. Your clothes are good, but you'll need a sweater and a scarf." Fillip lowered her back into the chair and raced to the door. "Meet me at the front door in twenty minutes."

Sarah sat dumbfounded and she slowly began to smile. She was pleased that she wasn't being carried to bed. An intimate time should be anticipated with joy like last night, not a wifely duty. If they were to sustain a husband and wife relationship, she wanted their intimate relationship to be lovemaking and not sex. Whatever he was planning really pleased him and that somehow excited her. She pulled herself up and slowly made her way back into her bedroom and María joined her.

By the designated time, Sarah sat in the foyer and when Fillip joined her he had changed into a pair of nice fitting jeans, a white long sleeve shirt, and a V-neck yellow pullover sweater. He also wore a Cheshire cat smile that glowed all about the edges until the very second, she lost sight of it as his lips claimed hers. Ramón and Carmen entered from the kitchen bearing a large picnic basket, a thermos, and a blanket. "It looks like we're all set. Are you ready?'

Sarah giggled. "As directed. Are you going to tell me where we are going?"

Fillip leaned down and kissed her lightly on the nose. "No." Then, without another word, he swept her up into his arms and set out for the door, gesturing for Carmen and Ramón to follow. It took only a few minutes to load Sarah, their lunch, and her walker. As they drove, Fillip talked to her about his sisters and their families, and his brother and his family. He gave her no clues as to their destination.

About an hour's drive away from El Alba Rosa, Fillip turned onto a graveled side road and told her to close your eyes. Sarah obeyed but her excitement was evident. At last, the car came to a stop, although the engine still hummed. Fillip turned in his seat to look at her. "Open your eyes now."

The beauty of the garden had stolen into her heart but now it had to share the grandeur of an unspoiled clearing with a small lake and well-built cabin. Sarah sat spellbound.

"I haven't been here for a long time. Perhaps now that I can share it with you, I'll find more time to visit here."

Sarah looked at Fillip. "This is yours?"

Fillip smiled. Her reaction was as he expected, yet seeing it added a certain satisfaction to the moment. "I'm not sure a place like this can be truly owned, but it does belong to my family. When I was a small boy, Father would bring us here. Mother and my sisters never liked roughing it out here. My brother wasn't an outdoorsman, so as we grew older, I had the privilege of coming here alone with my father. We fished for our supper, swam, hiked, even camped out under the stars. In his will, he spoke of this place and our memories, and he left it to me to be its caretaker for the family."

Fillip put the car in gear and edged up to the cabin. The skies were slightly overcast, but there was no clear threat of rain. "Let me show you the cabin then we can eat." Fillip brought Sarah her walker and she made her way up to the wide front porch of the cabin that faced the lake. She paused and looked back at the lake and the little dock.

When Fillip opened the door, the air of the cabin smelled stale but everything in view was orderly and covered with a heavy layer of dust. Fillip let Sarah inspect the cabin without saying a word. The cabin appeared to be one open room divided by a central fireplace that soared past the loft and play area above the kitchen. There were two private bedrooms on each side of the great room, and they each shared a bath. The cabin had electricity and running water from a well and generator. Sarah sat on a kitchen chair. "So, you don't come here because of losing your dad. You lost your connection to the cabin?"

Sarah's insight was accurate. "You're right. If I hadn't brought you here on impulse, I would have had the cabin dusted and aired out. Then, you would see it the way I remember. I've been a poor caregiver."

They sat on a comfortable couch and he put his arm around her shoulder. "Since you have entered my life, I'm seeing things differently. I have neglected my painting, not used the garden, or even taken the time to come here to relax and remember my father. Isn't that proof of how vital you are to my life?"

Sarah touched his face and shook her head. "You could use me as another reason to neglect your talent and life."

Fillip kissed her tempting lips. "In just a short time now, things will be settled at work and we will have more time. *We* will establish a balance in our lives that will include all these things."

Sarah looked into his eyes and she hoped he was right. She also prayed his need for her would be balanced by love for her as well as God. "Can we eat down by the lake?"

"Sure. The weather looks like it should cooperate."

Sarah slowly made her way to a spot under a tree and Fillip followed with the picnic things. It was difficult for Sarah to sit on the ground and Fillip had to help her down, but she smiled not letting on to her discomfort. The sun and the wind blessed their picnic and Sarah relished each moment of their informal meal. Then a mist began to gently fall on them. The mist felt good, but Fillip insisted they take no chances. He had to help her to stand up, packed up their picnic remnants, and they headed to the car. Sarah's progress was slow as she regained her circulation. Fillip eyed her. "Perhaps we should have eaten in the dusty cabin?"

"When I have full use of my legs again, I'll only remember the special time we had together on our picnic by the lake." She stopped and kissed him, and he returned her kiss, but heavy clouds moved in and opened up. Fillip dropped his cargo, picked her up, and ran to the wide porch. Sarah started to giggle and Fillip breathing heavily laughed with her. "I'll likely remember our drenching too. I think we could use a warm fire."

Fillip took her inside and set her on the couch. "I hope you don't add an illness to your day's memories." Fillip quickly got the fire started and came back to her. "You need to get out of your wet things. I'll look for a change of clothes."

"I hope that concern is for my well-being and not a convenient excuse to get me out of my clothes." Sarah laughed as she stood up and removed her wet sweater and scarf. The scarf hadn't spared her hair. Fillip didn't seem to enjoy her attempt at humor. He most likely had heard her but was being very serious all of a sudden. She had loosened her blouse from her slacks and had most of the buttons undone when Fillip returned empty handed except for a few towels. "I'm regretting more my impulse to bring you here today."

Sarah tugged his sweater up and encouraged him to remove his wet clothes. He removed his sweater and shirt. "I don't. We can put our clothes by the fire on chairs and they'll dry. There's no real harm. This is the first time we've really been alone."

Sarah took a towel and wrapped it around her hair, pulled off her blouse that revealed a lacy beige bra which was almost transparent from the rain. She shivered and leaned into him wrapping her arms around his neck. Sarah hadn't intended to initiate any intimacy, but it felt right in this little cabin with her bare-chested husband holding her. "We could add to our special private memories"

"Sarah, don't start something you don't want me to finish."

She quivered against his chest and ran her hand over his thick chest hairs and touched his nipples as he had done to her. "Like you did to me last night?"

Fillip pulled her chin up with his fingertips and kissed her and she responded. He hadn't planned this for their afternoon, but he wasn't opposed to encouraging her first attempt to initiate lovemaking. "My apologies for disappointing you. I'll do better today."

Sarah laughed, and her fingers fumbled with Fillip's belt and zipper, but she managed to release his jeans. He removed them and then her slacks. Fillip diligently went to the kitchen and brought back a bench. Laid out their clothes and came back to her. She wrapped her arms around him again and offered him her lips. "Oh, Sarah, mi amor." He pulled off her wet towel and ran his hands into her wet hair and gently pulled back her head and kissed her neck, slowly working his way up to her ear, her checks and her eyes before he took her lips. He lifted her into his arms and carried her to the first bedroom. She pulled back the comforter.

Fillip laid her on the bed and followed her down into her open arms. He liked the look of expectancy on her face. She snuggled against him for warmth and pulled the comforter over them before she kissed him as he escalated her kiss. Sarah felt her bra being released as Fillip undid the front fastener. He released her lips and began to rain kisses down her breast. "I think this is where I stopped last night."

"Yes, it was." She giggled. "And, if you stop today it is likely to end in pain."

"Oh, yours or mine?" He asked huskily.

"Mostly definitely yours." She lifted his head and kissed him, but she could not delay the direction of his actions. He massaged her soft yielding tissue before he sucked her nipple into a hardened peak. Then, he turned his attention to her other breast. Satisfied at last, he leaned back against the coverless pillow and invited her to do the same for him. Sarah shyly followed his lead until he stopped her, pushing her back into her pillow. "You are taking to your new lessons well, mi mujer."

Fillip's hand travelled down her abdomen and slid beneath the lacy film of her underwear, and she soon realized the pleasure he sought for her. He easily removed her panties and his own underwear followed. Then, he rolled to his back and taught her how to touch him and bring him pleasure although her efforts where awkward. When he stopped her, she laid against the comfort of his broad chest, and felt the quick beating of his heart. He spoke to her thickly, bringing her head up kissing her. "I am ready to come inside you, mi amor, but I am uncertain you will be able to be on top yet."

She answered him with a kiss and then rolled to her back inviting him to come to her. He quickly took possession of her body, filling the ache inside her, and Sarah moved with him in rhythm. Her body ached from her fall and injuries, but she searched for the release her body wanted. She was pleased when he finished and found her greatest release was bringing him the gratification he sought. Fillip nuzzled her hair and she raised her face to look at him. "Soon, mi amor, your injuries won't steal from your pleasure in our union. You will find your full climax *with me* and you will have the same intense pleasure."

She moved her fingers over his chest and he moved out of her bringing her to his chest kissing her. She blushed but looked at him as she answered. "I look forward to being with you not because you promise me greater pleasures, but because I am with you, and you are teaching me about my body as well as yours. I always and only want to be with you like this. To be one with you is a gift of the heart, mind and body that brings joy because I can open the gift over and over again, discovering new delights."

He answered her with a groan and kissed her repeatedly and passionately until they slept in the comfort of their isolation, warmth, and spent passion.

------------◆------------

Fillip drifted awake first softly stroking Sarah's inner thighs before moving on to suggestive touching of her more intimate core. But, Frustration saw an opening and moved in to attack Fillip's sleepy, gratified mind. The cunning demon planted the thought, *it would be pointless to stir their passions again. Sarah no doubt would respond, but she lacked the experience to give him the simple pleasures others had provided without instruction, hesitation, and awkwardness. And, he always had to be considerate of her injured leg and now her careless fall.*

Doubt joined the attack, *suggesting there had been no fall, only a stage performance to thwart his making love to her as was his right. He had given her his entire day, and she denied them their night, and he'd even had to sleep alone in the master to restrain his natural desires.*

But, Sarah wasn't unprotected. Sarah's angel protected her virtue rightfully arguing, *she had been the catalyst for their afternoon of passion. Her virginity was an underserved gift that had already warmed and delighted him. She had been spoiled by no other man. His skill and teaching would bring them a lifetime of pleasure and the children he always wanted. No one could be a better mother than the woman he had given his name. And, what a foolish thought that she had faked a fall. Sarah was not a liar!*

------------◆------------

Sarah woke because Fillip was gently stroking her inner thighs. She moved to his side, looked into his clouded eyes, and smiled as he turned his attention to touching her scars. She thought about him making love to her in his sleep their first night together. She thought they would come together again. But, Fillip's eyes cleared, and his hand stilled before moving to touch the area that ached for him. Without thinking why, he felt compelled to leave their little oasis. "The rain must have stopped, and we need to go home. We have been gone longer than I planned."

His words had broken the mood he had been creating. Sarah didn't want to leave. Despite the complaints of her healing body parts, the parts he had wakened from dormancy wanted more time with him. "Can't we have just five more minutes?"

Fillip sat up on the side of the bed and pulled on his underwear as Sarah watched. "No. We need to get back." He handed her the dainty things he had discarded. "I'll check on our clothes."

Sarah pondered what he didn't say or do. She heard what she thought were her own thoughts tell her that she had failed to please him. She, really Doubt, ticked off the proof of her failed miserable efforts. *There was no kiss or light touch. He hadn't even said mi amor, or an endearing tease like, "sweet temptress". She had tried hard to please him, and she thought he had enjoyed her efforts.* Her hackles rose. *And although she was receiving pleasure, surely there was more she should be experiencing based on the less risqué movies she had seen. Now he was a cold, and on a mission to get away from their only romantic interlude where they had been truly alone.*

Sarah threw back the comforter and put on her dandies. They were pretty and expensive, and had made her feel sexy, now they sicken her.

Fillip returned dressed and handed her things to her. "They're still a little damp, but I'll go warm the car and get your walker." He leaned down and kissed her forehead as he did when he limited their contact. "Get dressed and wait till I get back. I don't want you to fall again."

She tried to cajole herself into feeling better. *He had said or done nothing wrong. His words were gentle, but there was something cold in them she just couldn't make out.*

When he came back she was dressed and her damp clothes clung to her dainty lingerie. He handed her the walker and left without a word or gesture. She followed him out of the bedroom and as he stilled the fire, she longed for her old life. She thought of her life without being inadvertently responsible for Fillip's ill moods as she walked passed him to the front door.

She suddenly felt ashamed. As Fillip walked toward her, Doubt fired another dart. *Fillip's presents weren't for his bride to dress her in fine apparel, but to keep her from embarrassing him. She even had to have a new dress to have a simple family dinner! He was treating her, the same as any other mistress he had kept! He had married her to save her life, and then what—kept her out of guilt. He was staying married to her to punish himself?*

Fillip broke into her introspection. "Sarah I'll put your walker in the car with our other things and come back for you. The porch is slippery." She nodded as he took the walker and reached to balance herself against the door frame.

Her mind raced on and she thought logic was the voice she was hearing. *It was no doubt time to end their ill-advised marriage before Fillip grew tired of his unsophisticated plaything. He could easily annul their marriage and she wouldn't protest, although an annulment would not end it honestly. She wanted nothing from him even if he divorced her; she had already cost him enough.*

Fillip came back and picked her up without any banter or conversation. So, she returned to thinking. *She knew Ramón would be dispatched to right the cabin and he would know how their picnic had ended, so much for a private interlude with her husband. She sighed as Fillip seated her in the car, and he didn't ask after her.*

She'd should just make the arrangements to go home. She just needed a way to make Fillip understand that she had appreciated his care, but she couldn't stay in a relationship that didn't include God as their united focus.

Chapter 30

The car's heater was efficient, and Sarah became comfortable despite her damp clothing. She couldn't think of a way to approach the topic of her return home. The miles slipped by quickly until Fillip broke their long silence. "You're very quiet and tense." It was a true statement that spoke of the growing familiarity between them. Away from the cabin, he seemed less distant now. "Is there something troubling you?"

"No, I was just thinking. Isn't that what overcast and rainy days are about?" She couldn't bring herself to laugh.

"Tell me what you are thinking? We should have no secrets, as lovers. Sí? Did our lovemaking make you unhappy?"

Sarah found it interesting that his thoughts were on their lovemaking which he had ended so uncharacteristically. "I'm not experienced enough to judge such matters, but I enjoyed this afternoon —our lovemaking." Sarah found it hurtful to be described as a lover when she was trying to be his wife. "I was thinking I should go home, before I learn too much more."

Fillip turned and looked at her darkly before turning his attention back to the road. He hurled angry questions at her. "Home means back to America and your old life?" Fillip was hurt by her desire to leave him after all he had done for her. "Are you unhappy here or is it just me that doesn't satisfy you? Is it because I caused your injuries, or do you simply not like me touching you?"

"I don't' blame you or me for the accident." Sarah quieted her initial tone although she wanted to release her pent-up anger and hurt in her response. "The accident happened because I fell in love with Toledo and was day-dreaming and stepped into an alley without looking. No one could have stopped. I'm probably only alive now because you were the driver. Fillip, I am healing. Yes, I have physical scars, but they will fade, but you've been hurt more and aren't healing. Giving up your life to make amends isn't necessary." She touched is arm and drew his attention to her momentarily. Blushing in the fading light she spoke truthfully. "Your touch has become a desire for me. It brings me fulfillment and want at the same time. It is more than I understand, and I want it from no other man."

Fillip was incredulous. "You want me, and yet you talk about leaving me?

"You gave me my life back, now I want to give you your life back. I have in my own way taken advantage of all you have offered me. You've bought me fine things, to dress me in style so I wouldn't shame you. I'm not especially beautiful or talented. My degree in childhood development and elementary education is unused. I have little business knowledge. We don't share the same faith and our practice is very different. We weren't even taught the same language. I'm not the best wife for you, especially if you've chosen to remain married to me out of some sense of quilt."

Fillip felt a little ashamed about how he had tried to change her, but he rebelled at the thought. He'd only asked her to tone down her ardor for God, not to leave Him. Frustration ebbed away at his control and he raised his voice. "Is it wrong to give you the best I can afford? I don't think so, Sarah. And I could never be ashamed of you. You are beautiful and talented. If I had needed a wife with a business degree I could have found one by now, or I could have married a woman and sent her to school."

He raked his hand through his hair and continued in his raised voice. "I speak your language and so does our staff. And, I can get you a tutor if you want to learn mine. And, as far as our faith, we worship the same God as Christians. Sí, you are more ardent and have a ministry of service, but you shouldn't condemn *me* for it."

Silence hung in the car after Fillip's angry response. Sarah answered quietly. "I am not judging your faith. God has not given me the right to judge anyone. Your acceptance of who I am doesn't mean you don't deserve better. Improving my dress and making me bi-lingual doesn't mean I'll emerge from my cocoon a butterfly. I am more likely a moth."

Fillip didn't seem to be getting through to her, so he tried a gentler approach. "Sarah, mi amor, I could have annulled our marriage weeks ago, but I have never wanted any other woman. I've only ever had unprotected sex with you. You gave me your promise ring and your virginity. Could you so easily leave my life and deny me what you may have conceived?"

Sarah hadn't thought of the possibility of a child. "I hadn't considered it, but it doesn't seem likely in our few times together, and it won't happen if we stop now."

They were now only minutes from El Alba Rosa. Fillip had come to the end of his patience and more uncontrolled anger than he had ever known spewed from his lips. "Sarah, you are my wife. Tomorrow you'll go see Dr. Rubio, meet my family, and you'll still be my wife. Tuesday you'll go shopping with María, have your therapy with Lupe, and you'll still be my wife. And, if you haven't conceived this month, then it will be the next month, or the month after that, and *you'll still be my wife*. El Alba Rosa is your home. I am your husband! We won't be divorced!"

The car filled with a deadly silence that was permeated with Fillip's frustration and anger. Sarah couldn't find a gentle argument to persuade him. They turned into the long drive of their home and Fillip looked at the deadly pallor of his unwilling wife.

Fillip tried to understand how the mad man inside his head had gained control and spewed out his anger and frustration on the woman he loved and wanted. *Would he look weak if he apologized? If he capitulated, would she want to stay? No, he would just need to be gentler, control his sexual desire for her, and cajole her like they were in their best moments together. Then she would stay, and they could work toward a real marriage—one that would be good for both of them.*

Fillip turned off the engine of the car and looked at Sarah. Nothing came to either of them to say. He opened the car door and got out, slamming the door harder than he wanted. *"Please God don't let me ruin my chance with Sarah. Give us the time we need to be a real couple."*

As he removed her walker from the truck, Ramón flew down the stairs. "Señor Fillip Raphael called. "It's Señor Raúl. He has suffered another heart failure and they don't think he will come through the next twenty-four hours."

Fillip stood stunned momentarily then moved into action. "Get the

walker and picnic things. Call the hospital and tell them I'm on my way."
As Ramón and Carmen moved to the trunk of the car, Fillip swept Sarah
into his arms, and carried her into the house. "I am sorry to leave things
so poorly, mi amor. I don't want us to argue." He set her down in the
foyer and steadied her and lifted her chin, so she would look at him.
"You didn't marry a monster." He touched his forehead to hers. "I'm
only desperate for you. But, now I need to go and be with Raúl and
Elena. We will be ok. Just give us a little more time. Please."

"I understand. Please go to your friends. And, tell them I am praying
for them."

Ramón placed the walker within Sarah's reach and discreetly left.
Fillip looked as if he wanted to say something more, but merely leaned
over and kissed her briefly but passionately. He made sure Sarah had
gained her balance with the walker then left with only one more
comment. "Don't wait up for me."

María joined Sarah in the foyer but said nothing. When Sarah
became aware of her, she turned and thinly smiled. "We need to go and
pray for Raúl and Elena."

María nodded and they went to Sarah's room settee. They called out
to Jehovah-rapha, the God who heals, in intercessory prayer, and it was
all Sarah could do to prevent her own troubles from spilling out in her
prayer.

After their prayer together, María helped Sarah with a soothing bath
instead of Sarah seeking the Lord for her own situation. For the first
time at an important junction she failed to bring her burdens to the Lord
and seek his will. She wished she could have joined Fillip at the hospital
to be with their friends. Although she felt left out of this area of his
personal life, she knew he was only protecting her strength from
spending a long evening and perhaps night at the hospital. She hated
her weakness. She felt useless in his life.

After her bath when she was alone, Sarah called the airlines and
booked a flight home for Tuesday, taking the only remaining seat, which
was first class to New York, with a flight change in New York, and one
stop before getting home. She decided against calling her mom for fear
of her advice. Hurt and emotionally distraught, she took a pain pill and
cried until she slept.

Fillip called from the hospital as Sarah slept and she wasn't disturbed. When she awakened she dressed in one of the slack outfits she had brought to Spain and went to the kitchen without calling for assistance. Entering the kitchen with its warmth and seeing Carmen caused her spirits to lift slightly. "I have dinner ready for you. Fillip called and said Señor Raúl is stable, but they don't know the extent of the damage. He is staying with Raúl, so Elena can rest in a room at the hospital and Raphael is going home to rest. Once he returns to the hospital, Fillip will be home, but it will be late, or early in the morning."

Carmen set a bowl of her delicious potato soup Sarah favored in front of her as if everything was normal. She followed that with some warm rolls, beef, green beans, and a mug of hot tea. "You eat and stay well. Señor Fillip told us that you were drenched at the picnic, and it won't do for you to get sick now that you are doing so well.

Sarah smiled and thanked Carmen for her concern. Her meal was delicious, and it did warm her, but it didn't change the sick feeling she carried inside. She was going home but there was no joy in it. She could tell no one. She couldn't even tell them that she loved them all or say goodbye.

When she insisted, Carmen let her dry a few dishes. She knew how much this large well-maintained kitchen had become a part of her life, and how she would miss it and Carmen, Ramón, and María, and what might have been. She looked at the naked refrigerator as she left for her room and thought of their precious children's drawings it would never hold. She immediately went to the garden and sought the Lord in tears.

"Father, I am without peace and you are Jehovah-shalom, the Lord is Peace. I am frightened by the new face of Fillip I saw today. I have my ticket for home and it hasn't quieted my turmoil. I was only supposed to be gone for two weeks. Now months have passed, and I am saddened to leave what has become my new home."

"I feel like Ruth. I've left behind all I know and I'm a stranger in a new land. I have a husband who was kind, considerate, and generous, and now angry and frustrated at me and the situation I have caused. I have a new family here and friends. How can I leave any of them? I see that a vital ministry is needed here, and you have given me partners for praying again. But, I do not feel right about having children that would bind me *to Fillip."*

"I wanted to believe that Fillip would change, and we would be partnered in marriage and in service. He hasn't changed but certainly has made his position clear. I joined with him as one. I will forever feel his hands, his lips, his flesh pressed against mine. I want more of this intimacy—this life with him. Should I let my flesh and heart overrule my mind and training?"

Sarah stood quietly in the beautiful damp garden, and she revealed in its earthly beauty and the man who had ordered its creation carelessly because he could but made no time to enjoy it. She heard his angry words again. *"And, if you haven't conceived this month, then it will be the next month, or the month after that, and you'll still be my wife."* Sarah shuttered. *"No, Lord, it can't be right like that. Show me what to do. In Jesus blessed holy name. Amen."*

Darkness was quickly falling around her, and the air was cool, but she stood in the beautiful garden waiting to hear if she should go or stay.

"Señora Sarah you shouldn't be out here now. It is late and getting cold." Sarah turned and looked at María and slowly made her way to her. Sarah saw the glow on María's face and knew unquestionably that she had spent her afternoon off with Lupe. She grieved for each of them. Love was truly blind, but she took solace in knowing that God was all seeing.

Sarah didn't see Fillip until the next evening. He couldn't have had much rest before he went to his office, and then to the hospital again. Raúl was still stable, and the doctors had offered a chance that he might recover, but he would have to retire. Fillip had cajoled Elena into coming to share dinner with them and his family. Fillip and Sarah spoke distantly about her doctor's visit with Rubio, and Fillip was pleased that she would have no lingering effects from the fall. She didn't tell Fillip that she had brought home a copy of her medical records to take to America.

As she dressed in her finery for the evening, Sarah was grateful that Fillip was distracted by Raúl and his business. María did her hair up after she was dressed, and she proclaimed her to be truly lovely. Sarah admired her reflection in the mirror but didn't recognize herself.

It was not long after she joined Fillip in the formal living room that his family began to arrive. She first met Rosita and her husband Enrique, followed by the younger and more outgoing Isabel and her husband Esteban. Roberto and his wife Camila soon followed with the real Señora Castañola. Javier Mora came last and stepped aside with Fillip for a moment. She never saw the envelope he handed Fillip. Fillip disappeared, so she took the time to thank Javier once again for his part in saving her life.

"I believe it is I who should thank you. Fillip and I have been friends since college, and I thought he would remain a bachelor. My children are teens and Fillip has not found anyone who will put up with him and give him a family. I feel you have saved my friend and given him a life."

"You are kind, but our lives are far from settled." Sarah responded.

"Of course, but when you have recovered you will be blessed. Sí?"

"If it is God's will." She answered as expected without true hope.

They shared a cocktail hour together. Sarah had the sangria she favored. And Fillip kept his word and stayed near her as she engaged his family. Sarah found herself drawn to Isabel as she seemed satisfied with her own life, and tolerant of Sarah's new position in the family. Rosita treated her as with the distain of a poor relative that she had to tolerate. Roberto was charming and complimentary and reminded her of Fillip. Esteban flirted harmlessly with her and made her promise to dance with him, when she was through with what he called her training wheels.

Enrique welcomed her as another member of the outsiders and told her he'd help her fit in. Sarah felt sorry for him and pictured herself feeling like an outsider down the road if she stayed. She was especially grateful for Fillip's presence with mother Luisa as she questioned her. Sarah felt her cold appraisal and knew she was found unsuitable.

Just before dinner as Sarah came out of the guest bath she ran into Camila. Camila had been enjoying her family's consternation over meeting Sarah. As she passed Sarah on her way into the bathroom, she confided to Sarah that her becoming Fillip's wife had caused the biggest stir in the family since Fillip's affair with a prima-ballerina three years before. Camila had giggled with delight sharing the information with Sarah, and Sarah was grateful she had her walker to hold her up.

When she had sufficiently recovered from the information, she joined the family again, although she wanted to go to the garden. Fillip came to her immediately. Sarah was working hard to control her emotions. Then, Ramón came in with a framed portrait and Fillip presented her the framed painting she had selected for the first-floor suite and told his family. "You have to agree she has good taste, and she selected a painting we sent to her mother. This is only the first of many changes she will make in our home."

Sarah only smiled and looked at each of his family members, and immediately saw Luisa's frown. Fillip kissed her cheek to her chagrin and Carmen came and announced dinner. Sarah was relieved that they could go eat as she didn't want to talk to his family about her art selections or anything else. After acknowledging Carmen, Fillip handed the framed painting back to Ramón. They started to go into the dining room, but Enrique stopped them and toasted their marriage, and Sarah blushed when Fillip fully kissed her in front of them. Enrique had showed her his support, but it didn't seem to be a mutually held sentiment.

Shortly after they had started dinner, Elena arrived, and the conversation turned to Raúl. The wine flowed freely from the carafes in Ramón's hand and Carmen's meal was excellent. Sarah made a point of relishing her last dinner at El Alba Rosa even though she barely ate. She was grateful that her role as hostess would not be required again.

After dinner they retired to the living room again, but Fillip excused himself to go to his den with Roberto and their mother Luisa. Javier excused himself and insisted he could see himself out. He kissed Sarah on her cheek and said quietly. "Maybe you should only see them at church until you win them over. I don't believe they all attend at the same time." Sarah laughed, and Javier spoke for the family's benefit. "Tell Fillip I will look forward to finishing our business together."

Elena too decided to leave so she could go back to the hospital. In Fillip's absence Sarah walked her to the foyer and offered to get Fillip.

"Please don't interrupt him. Father and I have taken up a great deal of his time recently. He has been very good to us and Raphael, despite my protest to staying at the hospital tonight. Fillip deserves an evening with you and his family."

Sarah admired Elena. "I'm not sure Fillip has enjoyed this evening since his family has not greeted me with open arms. I know he hoped for more."

Elena laughed quietly. "I don't envy you having to meet them like this. Usually a family meets a girlfriend, who becomes a fiancé, before she becomes a bride, and they usually get to attend a wedding. Let them judge you harshly and prove them wrong. You really only need to make Fillip happy, and you seem to be doing just fine with him. My father is very taken with you. You remind him of my mother. Their love withstood a lot over the years."

"Thank you for understanding and your advice. Please tell Raúl I haven't forgotten to pray for him and you. I hope to see you tomorrow." She almost added before I leave.

Elena gave her a quick hug. "I will tell him. Good-night, Sarah."

Chapter 31

After saying good-night and closing the door, Sarah turned to go to the living room when she heard raised voices coming from the den. She was drawn there despite her upbringing. Luisa was talking and despite the speed of her diatribe Sarah understood enough.

"I never expected you to act so foolishly. You didn't need to save her life, by any act. How stupid to walk in front of a moving car! She is nothing, not here or in America. She admitted herself that she is a secretary and doesn't use her little degree. She can dress up in the finest things you can buy her, but she is not a suitable wife for you. I don't know why you never married Elena. Has it ever occurred to you that this woman is only after your money?"

Fillip laughed bitterly. "Of course, mother, she threw herself in front of my car when she didn't even know I would be there, nearly dying because she knew I would marry her, so she could be the wife of a wealthy man."

Roberto entered the conversation. "Fillip, please, mother only meant she has taken advantage of you since the accident."

"This conversation is ridiculous. If either of you knew Sarah, you would know that my money is more a deterrent than an incentive for her to be my wife."

"That doesn't explain the dress she is wearing." Luisa snorted.

"I bought the clothes, mother. Sarah is satisfied with the type of clothes María wears. And she's more than willing to go home." Sarah heard the weariness in his voice defending her, and her heart went out to him.

He shouldn't be in the position to defend her against his family. Frustration stirred her thinking. *Why hadn't she'd asked for the annulment when she still could and gone home? Why had she stayed and allowed him the rights of a husband?*

"It isn't wrong for me to give my wife nice things. I love her, and I want a full life with her. It can't be wrong for me to do what makes me happy."

Roberto answered although she heard Luisa grumbling in an undertone. "No, there's nothing wrong with that. But, why couldn't you find a woman of our country and faith, dear brother? Your marriage was only supposed to be a heroic effort, and then an annulment as quick as the marriage. Why have you continued this farce?"

Luisa interrupted. "With her dependency on a walker she can't be much in bed. And, the extent of her injuries means she has ugly scars."

Sarah didn't want to hear Fillip's answer. She had asked the same question. *How would he explain his unexplainable want of a tourist he ran into?* Not wanting to face the others she chose to go to the kitchen where there were kind faces and loving spirits. She heard Fillip lose his temper for the second time in little more twenty-four hours.

"Farce? This discussion is done. She is beautiful even with the scars *I created.* She's loving, vibrant, and she makes me feel alive. I don't owe you any explanation as—."

Carmen was startled to see Sarah in the kitchen. "Señora Sarah do you or the guests need something? You are deathly white. Whatever is the matter?"

Sarah shook her head as the words in her head couldn't be said with the effort needed to stop her tears. "I only needed to be some place where I am good enough, where I feel love." She looked at Fillip's servants dressed to serve a fancy dinner who were now staring at her in concern. "I never appreciated the way you accepted me and offered me friendship from the first afternoon. I never had to prove myself to any of you. I want to thank you for being so endearing and treating me so well."

Carmen came to console her and Ramón and María agreed with her comment. "I don't know what has been said or done to upset you like this but remember they'll all be going back to their homes soon and things will be the same here." She wanted to add the Fillip would choose her over his vindictive family, but she held her peace.

Sarah reached across her walker and hugged the older woman and whispered in her ear. "I love you Carmen, but things will never be the same here." Sarah didn't elaborate but spoke to them all. "I better get back."

Fillip was coming down the front hall when Sarah came though the kitchen door. Fillip raked his hand through his hair and was tense, but he spoke pleasantly. "There you are mi amor. I was just coming to look for you. The family business mother wanted to discuss is done and our guests are preparing to leave. Why were you in the kitchen?"

Sarah wanted to say hiding but smiled weakly and answered. "I went to check on things, after seeing Elena off. Forgive me. I just couldn't stay with your family."

Fillip nodded his head in understanding. "You don't need my forgiveness. They're leaving now, and I'll be with you as we say good-night. I expected them to act differently, so I am the one who is sorry. I expected them to give you the chance you deserve."

Their good-byes were mostly formal and cold, and Sarah was glad when the door closed behind them. Only Enrique had been kind and kissed her cheek and whispered, "Give them time. I envy Fillip's choice, little sister."

She was relieved now that his family was gone. He took her walker and set it aside and took her in his arms. Then, he picked her up and twirled them in a circle. "I know a place where we can get some fresh air."

He carried her to the garden. As he sat her on the bench he was breathing heavily and took of his jacket and placed it around her shoulders. They sat quietly for some time contemplating different things. Sarah loved the smell of him on his jacket and the warmth from his body that touched hers. "I am sorry that my family wasn't as receptive of you as I hoped. They don't know you. It is perhaps one of those things we will have to give more time."

Sarah took Fillip's hand in a gesture of compassion. "They love you and want only the best for you and I am a stranger that crashed into your life." Sarah laughed at her joke and he smiled ruefully. "Elena said that I should let them judge me harshly and then prove them wrong. She said a family usually meets a girlfriend and they have time to adjust to the two emerging as a couple. I was just dumped into their lives with an unattractive accessory."

Fillip kissed her hand. "You never cease to amaze me. From now on, when you are ready, we'll meet them as individual families with their children in tow. Then, they can't gang up on you with their attention divided over their unruly children."

Sarah laughed. Things were good like this. Fillip kissed her with uncertainly and brushed a strand of breeze blown hair back off her face. Sarah anticipated his follow-up kiss and met him in it. She knew what would follow from the passion and hunger that burned in his eyes. She knew he wanted to make up to her for their behavior, and maybe make her forget about them creating a bitter memory for the evening. And, she met his desire with her own as she had to remember it for a lifetime.

------------◆------------

Warning fairly danced into his audience with his master. He repeatedly flipped one of his reports excitedly in the air and offered it to Satan. "We won master! We won!"

Satan glared at him and grabbed the report. "Give me the short version. Are nuclear missiles being fired?"

"No master." Warning paused and regrouped. "The infectious Christian woman is leaving tomorrow. She is leaving her husband and he is still unsaved!"

"Really?" Satan didn't appear excited or relieved. "So, the huge squad of demons you sent against them have prevailed?"

Warning swallowed but knew the time had come to reveal the truth. "Deception couldn't win because the woman stood firm on her faith, and with the man slowing down Deception's plan he couldn't prevail quickly against them."

"So, Doubt and Frustration have won the battle for the man's soul?"

Warning didn't like it when his master was like this. "Frustration pushed the man hard and spoiled their day and Doubt used it against the woman."

"So, Frustration ruined a single day. Then our victory is due to Doubt?" Satan questioned pointedly.

"Doubt did his best, but the woman loves the man and is leaving him because she loves our enemy more." Warning almost added that their old enemy had handed them their victory, but he knew He didn't do such things in caring for his unsaved children.

"Hmm. Let me understand this the way you do. The woman loves God so much she is sacrificing her relationship with the man she loves?"

Warning bobbed up and down. "Yes master, she is deceitfully flying home tomorrow."

"Tell me." Satan picked up a dagger and twirled in his fingers. "Will his infectious Christian wife continue to pray for him?"

"Well, ah ..." Warning didn't want to answer "yes" and backed away with a non-answer. "She has made a habit of praying for the lost especially for those she loves."

"And, the praying servants will they stop praying for their employer?"

"I doubt they will change their habit now. The woman has strengthened their faith in Him and prayer." Warning took another step back.

"And, the praying American mother who taught her daughter to believe and pray will she stop praying for her son-in-law?"

"No, master. It isn't the habit of those who have walked with Him to give up praying."

"I see. Then, the waiter turned office manager after his salvation will stop praying for his new boss and for his dear American friend who introduced him to Christ?   Or, the nurse friend who has scouted buildings out for the woman to use as a mission has denounced God and prayer?"

"No, but the woman *is* leaving! The man will feel betrayed and when he discovers this he'll surely cut her out of his life." Warning added his last remark hopefully but took another step back.

Satan stood and bellowed. "You think we have won? We haven't won a single conflict, and the man's soul will not be mine!"

Warning argued. "But, you don't know the future master. Everything is in place for our success."

"After all these centuries do you not understand? I don't have to know the future when I can see the past." He bellowed, and all heard him. "When a man comes to the end of his own plans with praying people about him, he turns to Him."

Warning now stood at the door ready to turn and flee, but he offered one more hope. "He's only one man."

Satan screamed. "Get out! Get out now!" Warning barely turned before he heard the dagger splinter the wood beside his head.

Satan's anger boiled as he thought. *Only one man. She was only one woman—one infectious woman on vacation staying true to her faith, proving herself faithful, and proving she would give up all to serve God. She's already infected a waiter, bolstered the faith of all the faithful she touched, and now her therapist is hearing things of God from another innocent who the woman is mentoring.* Satan screamed so the angels and God could hear him. "You might win Toledo, but I still rule on earth."

———————◆———————

God didn't answer but smiled. He did see the future and knew when and where Fillip would surrender to the sweet call of His Only Son. He saw all of the believers at work not only in Toledo but all the cities of the world. He would end Satan's rule when time on earth was complete and the harvest was done. He'd take the deceiver, mankind's enemy, the roaring lion and chain him and all his demons in hell forever.

Chapter 32

Sarah stirred gently when Fillip kissed her good-bye but didn't awaken. He gave instructions that his sweet bride be allowed to sleep. When she awoke she only had a little time to spend with her friends before she closed the door on her life at El Alba Rosa.

She ate a quick breakfast to appease Carmen then asked Ramón to drive her to the hospital. When he agreed she retrieved her large shoulder bag where she had placed her medical records, journal, and Bible. She couldn't take any luggage with her. There were only a few of her American things remaining and she wore the best of those things. The costly things Fillip had given weren't needed in America. On the drive to the hospital, Sarah almost confided her plans to Ramón but couldn't bear to ask him to shoulder her secret plans.

Ramón retrieved Sarah's walker, and helped her out of the car.

"I will park the car quickly and wait for you in the CCU waiting room. "Sí?"

Sarah declined and impulsively kissed his cheek. "You can come in and visit with our friends, but don't wait for me. You have many things to do, and I want to stay as long as I can. Don't worry, I can manage." Then, she laughed sweetly. "I'll be safe in a hospital."

He was startled by her kiss and uncertain as what to do. He knew Fillip would want him to stay with her. "Call the house when you are ready, and I will come quickly and take you home."

Sarah nodded her head and another driver beeped his horn, so she turned to the hospital with one last look at Ramón. There were many words stuck in her throat, "sorry", "miss you all", and "love". But, her plans allowed no such conversation. Her progress through the hospital was slow but eventually she came to Raúl's CCU room. Elena saw her though the door and joined her in the hall. "It is good of you to come."

"I only wish I could stay with you. How is he today?" Sarah asked.

Elena looked back at the frail figure in the bed covered in the technology of the cardiac care unit. "The doctors are kindly still giving us a little hope, but he has resigned himself to go to God, and has refused any further medical intervention."

Sarah nodded sadly in understanding. "How do you feel about it?"

Elena pulled a handkerchief from her pocket and toyed with it. "The child in me wants her father no matter the cost. The adult daughter doesn't want to see him suffer more."

Elena's tears spilled over and Sarah leaned over and pulled her into her arms to comfort her. When she had them under control they went to a private sitting area to talk. "Forgive me, I am not being a very strong daughter."

"Not true...you are being remarkably strong. Raúl is your father and no one can tell you how to grieve his illness. We all face death in our own way, and for those like your father who are ready for heaven, the loss is hardest on the loved ones who stand nearby, feeling so helpless."

Sarah thought about the accident that had so quickly taken her father's life and felt a fresh pang of grief. "So many times, death comes unannounced, in grim circumstances, when the person is alone. To be with someone at the end of their life's journey, I think, is a gift not given to us all. It is not a weakness to mourn when death is so close to one you cherish. You are grieving your coming separation and the days you cannot still share."

Elena teared again, and Sarah drew her in. "I admire your father's peace. I wanted death for myself when I was in the SICU. He isn't complaining about his suffering or his wait to be received by his Loving Creator. I hope someday you'll find peace with God in this."

Fresh tears rolled down her cheeks and Sarah let her go until she was able to control them and had to find a tissue to wipe away her own tears. "He'll be with mother and I'll be alone."

"It's difficult to be an only child without siblings to share the memories or the grief. But remember, he isn't choosing to leave you. When my father, died a dear sweet older lady, Mrs. Link, from our church said to me, "There'll be joy in the morning equal to all the tears. Mourning is for only a season." I didn't understand her then. But I think she meant we mourn what we can't share now during our lifetime, but come the dawn of our first eternal day when we are with them again. Joy never ends."

"I didn't know you were an only child and lost your father?" Elena wiped her eyes and leaned back against the couch cushion.

Sarah patted her arm. "There's a lot we don't know about each other, and I'm afraid there won't be time for us to get to know each other better. But let me share one thing from my experience." Sarah rushed on to cover her slip. "When you get to a holiday like his birthday, celebrate them with joy not grief. Celebrate that he is still alive in eternal days just ahead of you. There's a day coming when we will all be together forever. I believe our fathers will be friends by the time we arrive."

Elena sat quietly for a time without new tears, and then asked. "Why won't we have time to get to know each other better?"

Sarah took a deep breath before she answered. "I—ah, hadn't meant to tell anyone. "I'm going home today. My plane leaves in just a few hours."

"Fillip is permitting you to go like this?" Elena asked surprised.

Sarah shook her head no. "This is not with his knowledge and certainly not with his permission. He has made it clear that I'm his wife, his wife, his wife."

"Do you not love him Sarah?" She asked momentarily distracted from her own life.

"Fillip committed himself to our marriage without love to save my life. I believe he is staying in it out of a sense of guilt over my injuries. We only knew each other a few hours before the accident. We were attracted to each other but that is not love."

Elena touched Sarah's hand. "Of course, he regrets your injuries, but you will make a full recovery. He is not the type of man that could be forced to do anything. The accident may have been the catalyst for your marriage, but since he has made you his wife he won't let you go easily. As for love, I see it in you both. You must know there have been other women in his life and words of love may have been exchanged, but they were shallow and meaningless. I believe he has found in you the type of love he has always wanted and despaired to ever find. He can't yet say the words that have proven empty before because he wants more with you then he had with them. Perhaps he needs to hear them from you first because you are the one who was injured, and his guilt keeps words of love unsaid until he knows they can be returned. Does he need to hear that you've forgiven him?"

"No. He doesn't need me to forgive him. He knows he is innocent in my eyes. The rest is too complicated, and I have a plane to catch. Since you know now please call the house after three and tell Ramón that I have left. Tell him I left letters for all my friends in my nightstand, and a letter for Fillip in his den. Please ask Ramón to deliver my letters to Jesús and Marguerite."

"I think you are wrong. Please talk to Fillip first?" Elena pleaded.

Sarah confessed. "I've sorry to involve you at a time like this. I was going to call from New York when I landed. But, if you help there will be less time for them to be concerned about me. Fillip needs a woman who is right for him. My shortcomings as his wife are too numerous to list, and I can't change how I live my faith, and Fillip is not pleased by it."

"I think you are the right woman for him. The women who have been in his life only loved his power and money. You love him and only want what is good for him. This is something only you have been willing to do for him." Elena rightly argued.

"I can't give him what he needs the most and that is a true relationship with God. He needs to be more than a good and successful man. Staying only strengthens a bond between us that can't be blessed or used by God." Sarah touched her arm. "My only regret, my sister, is those I leave behind especially because this is a difficult time in all your lives. Can we see your father now?"

Sarah's visit was brief, but she prayed over him with Elena and knew the Holy Spirit had joined them. Raúl indeed was comforted and at peace. Then Sarah left them and Spain.

The most difficult part of Sarah's trip home was reaching the clouds and seeing the coast of Spain slip away. Physically the trip was exhausting, and she ached to her bones even with the pain medicine. The airline staff was well trained, kind, and professional and pushed her around in a wheelchair. Her mother arrived at the airport to pick her up within an hour of her call.

El Alba Rosa went into total upheaval with Elena's phone call. Ramón retrieved the envelopes marked with each of their names. They read them together in the kitchen. Barely able to handle his own emotions, let alone those of his wife, and the hysterical María, Ramón called Lupe who was able to come and settle María. Once he had Carmen settled he faced the difficult task of calling Fillip.

Of all the letters Sarah wrote, Fillip's had been the most difficult to compose. After reading it Fillip crumbled it his palm and called the airlines for a ticket to retrieve his wife. He was so angry with Sarah that if she hadn't been so far away he wasn't sure how he would have dealt with her.

He questioned his servants closely to see how Sarah managed her plans without their help. In the end he had no one to blame because he hadn't anticipated her leaving either. She had given herself to him in the night without hesitation and then left him without a word. Her letter even spoke of loving him too much to let their relationship grow in its current state. He thought it was the worse type of betrayal. He set Ramón to pack for him and went to the hospital to see Raúl and Elena, and to talk to Raphael about their business interests.

On the drive to the hospital he tortured himself over his stupidity. *He had asked Sarah for the time to handle Raúl's illness and possible death. They needed the time to establish a relationship that would work for them both. How could she leave him now? After last night he knew it wasn't about their sexual compatibility.* Doubt whispered, "It's God's fault. She was so committed to Him that she wouldn't be the wife he deserved."

It reminded him of the time his father died. He had asked God to spare his father, and his father died anyway. He had asked God for Sarah's life, and, yes, she was still alive but not with him as he wanted. A part of him railed against God, but he remembered his conversation with Sarah about his anger. She had said, God was sovereign and could handle his anger.

He parked his car at the hospital and took a deep breath. He tried to pray. He asked for a bridge to spare his marriage but failed to accept the offer of salvation waiting for him. He felt no comfort, got out of the car slamming the door behind him. She was his wife, and he *would bring her home!*

He wanted to ask Elena about her conversation with Sarah. Sarah probably kept her plans to herself, but he had to know. Then, he could address business concerns with Raphael before he went to the U.S. He wished he could talk with Raúl who counseled him as a father, but his friend was too weak.

When Fillip gained Raúl's room, Raphael was standing alongside Elena steadily looking at Raúl. A look of peace had settled over his friend's face, the equipment in the room was silent, and Raúl chest no longer rose and fell. Fillip knew his dear friend was dead.

The next few weeks were dreadful for all who had loved Raúl. Death hadn't just claimed one prepared soul, but a parent, friend, and a business partner. Although Raúl had left his business and personal affairs in order, the legal system worked over them slowly. Fillip couldn't leave their business. Sarah sent a floral tribute and note to Elena. With effort she also sent a condolence note to Fillip. Javier at Fillip's direction saw to an income for Sarah. She had tried to refuse it but found she had no way to block or return it. She also learned from Javier that Fillip would not be sending divorce papers.

Fillip and Raphael helped Elena with the funeral arrangements and it was well attended. Fillip was a pallbearer for his friend and emotionally eulogized him during his service. He offered Elena any support she needed but Raphael would take care of Elena, so he could deal with his run-away bride.

Chapter 33

Six weeks later Fillip stood on the porch of the small two-story Kettering house nestled between similar houses. It was early evening when the taxi pulled to a stop in the driveway. Fillip settled his cab and climbed up the porch steps repeating the prayer he had said often over the last few weeks. He set his bag beside the door, rang the bell, and waited to be greeted. Mother Carol opened the door and looked at him puzzled.

"Mother Carol it's good to meet you at last." Fillip kissed her cheek and handed her a large bouquet of flowers.

"Fillip?" Mother Carol stood stunned in the doorway. "Come in. I can't believe you're here." Fillip set his bag inside.

"Thank you for the flowers, but I'm not sure you should have come. I don't believe you'll change her mind. She is firm about her decision."

The smile faded from Fillip's eyes. "Are you saying Sarah is happier here without me?"

Mother Carol shook her head as if still thinking over her answer. "No, she's not. You two have to work all that out. You've both been hurt and neither of you need to be hurt more."

Fillip nodded in agreement. "May I speak with her?"

Mother Carol nodded her head toward the rear of the house and stretched to her full height and planted her feet defensively before she spoke. "She's cleaning up the kitchen. Please don't hurt her anymore.'

Fillip kissed her cheek. "I won't. I promise she will like what I've come to say."

Mother Carol let out a long sigh of relief, just as Sarah came into the room to see what had caused her mother's delay. Sarah wasn't happy to see Fillip but wasn't surprised. She grabbed the back of a chair to steady herself as she said his name. "Fillip."

Fillip was beside her immediately and smiled happily. "Sarah, you can walk without your walker now?"

Sarah was grateful for a neutral question and was able to respond evenly. "I use a cane now, but I do quite well about the house with the furniture for support."

The room was silent for some moments as each person in the room searched for the next thing to say. Sarah found herself being drawn into the circle of Fillip's protective arms and she wanted to snuggle there, and Fillip wanted to never let her go.

Mother Carol broke the silence and excused herself from the room. "I'll go put these lovely flowers into water and make some coffee and I have Sarah's favorite pie for dessert."

Sarah nodded to her mother and started to move to assist her. Fillip stopped her by strengthening his hold on her. "Sarah, please, let's talk."

Sarah knew he was right, but she wasn't sure how she would be able to keep her control. Fillip's touch, his cologne, his voice, his nearness had already caused her to feel choked with tears. Fillip helped Sarah to the sofa, sat beside her, kissed her cheek quickly, and took her hands. Sarah stole some of his strength and looked into his face.

Fillip looked at her covetously and stroked her hair. "You are so beautiful, Sarah, so very beautiful. I have missed you more than I can say. I wanted to come sooner, but Raúl's death didn't allow it. I was very angry with you, and if I had been able to come, I wouldn't have handled myself well."

His words tore at her heart, but she was hurt that despite the pain of Raúl's death Fillip had never even phoned. Angry accusing words flooded her mind, but she couldn't say them to the tired face that looked at her so endearingly.

"I've missed you too and you don't look like you've taken care of yourself." Sarah touched his cheek. "Are there problems María hasn't told me about?"

"Only the one where I have to restore my bride." Fillip laughed and kissed her forehead. "I am tired Sarah. The weeks since Raúl's death have been difficult for me both personally and professionally. Raúl's death happened just after I learned that you had left me for America. I had booked a flight to come and get you, but I know I wouldn't have convinced you to come with me with things the same."

Sarah looked remorseful. "I saw Elena and Raúl before I left. How is she now?"

"She seems to have a certain peace. I believe in time, she will make a life for herself. She didn't marry before because she didn't want to leave Raúl on his own."

Fillip's words felt like a knife to her heart. She was slightly confused, he's said he wanted to restore his bride, but he knew she wouldn't have returned with him. *What was he trying to say?*

Fillip continued without noticing the strain on Sarah's face. "When the time is right she and Raphael will be married."

Sarah spoke in shock. "Elena is going to marry Raphael? Why?"

"With Raúl's death Raphael is a full vice-president of the company. He has worked hard to come up through the ranks and to earn his business degree, and Raúl left his business interest to Elena and Raphael knowing they would marry. His knowledge of the company and his rapport with the employees will assure our company's continued success and he and Elena will do well together."

Sarah was filled with relief that Fillip was not planning on marrying her, but she was still concerned for Elena. Would she marry just not to be alone? "Is this a business marriage?"

Fillip laughed and quickly kissed her lips. "There is a lot of love between our two friends, but a lot of pride too. Raphael was afraid of what people would think about him pursuing Elena without a degree or better position. They could have married a long time ago but there was his pride and her concern for Raúl' declining health."

Sarah sighed. She had thought of Elena as a rival and a more suitable wife for Fillip. But even then, she had prayed for the Lord to remove the jealousy that was trying to take root in her heart. Even if Fillip hadn't come to end their marriage, she still couldn't be the wife he wanted.

Fillips eyes glowed with his love for Sarah and he smiled. "Sarah there is an important event we have not yet discussed."

"Yes, Fillip."

"In the evening after Raúl's funeral Ramón brought me a cup of coffee. I don't know why Sarah, but I asked him to stay and talk with me." Fillip paused, "Ramón was startled by my request and he was very uneasy when he took a seat. I had never treated him like a confidant. I was angry with you and grieved by Raúl's death. But our servants were your friends, you treated them like family, and they felt the same about you. Every time they looked at me I knew they blamed me for your leaving."

Sarah smiled as she thought about them. "I do love them like family. They accepted me without judgement and I learned so much from them."

"Yes, they were better to you than my own family. María told me about your language lessons, and how well you were doing. I thought I'd need to get you a tutor when you were well, but you charged ahead and already had them. You not only loved them but taught them about your faith, Sarah. It made them grow in their own. You wisely never let your recovery hold you back from settling in, except where it came to your faith and settling for less from me."

Sarah blushed remembering how she used her language skills to listen to the private family discussion in the den, but that confession would have to wait for a later time. "What did I teach them?"

"You, mi amor, were the virtuous Christian woman. You were busy learning Spanish, helping were you could, sharing Bible studies, praying for all of us and our needs. You lived what you believed even when you were struggling with healing and struggling to be with me."

Fillip drew Sarah's clasped hands to his lips and pressed his warm lips against them. Tears glisten in his eyes and his voice trembled as he continued. "You brought a sense of life to my house that was never there before. Do you remember what you said about my painting, El Alba Rosa, at the art gallery? You said it was sterile."

Sarah pulled back from Fillip. "Oh, no Fillip, I never said such a thing."

Fillip laughed gently and drew her hands back into his. "No, you were not quite so harsh. You said Ramón's pristine lawns lacked color and needed to know the play of children."

Sarah remembered the feelings the house had stirred in her mind when she saw it in oil, and even more the feelings she had from living in it.

Fillip continued. "You were right about my house. There was a void there and in me. You filled much of the void and yet, I still couldn't be completely happy. You knew the void in my life could only be filled by God."

Fillip's words stirred a wonderful hope in her. "That evening in my den Ramón talked with me until the early hours of the morning. He shared with me the belief you all share." Tears formed in Fillip's eyes. "We knelt in my den and I prayed for forgiveness and gave my heart to God. The void was rightfully filled, and I became a new man."

Sarah drew her hands from his and threw her arms around him nearly tipping him over and hugged him tightly. Her heart sang words of thanksgiving, but she couldn't speak for the joy she felt, and her tears couldn't be held back. Fillip drew her back and kissed her tears and all. Eventually he drew a handkerchief from his pocket and wiped away her tears. Then he kissed her again with the passion that had become so familiar to her.

Sarah felt as if her real life had been given back to her and she was now whole. Fillip released her and kissed away an errant tear. "Now we need to heal our marriage, and plan for the future, Señora Castañola."

Mother Carol, almost forgotten, stuck her head though the door, and then came into the dining room. From the glow on their faces, Mother Carol knew the conversation had gone well. "Well, if things are settled, I can serve cherry pie and coffee."

"Mom . . ." Sarah blushed.

Fillip laughed as he stood up and went to kiss Mother's Carol's cheek. "It would be wrong to keep you imprisoned in your own kitchen. Let's get the coffee and dessert. It will be most delightful after airline food. Fillip smiled at Sarah. "We'll finish our conversation a little later."

Fillip put his arm around his mother-in-law's waist and walked her to the kitchen. "I was just telling Sarah how I came to know the Lord you so wisely lead her to love."

Within a few minutes Fillip carried in a tray laden with pie and coffee followed by a smiling Mother Carol. After dessert and conversation that included Mother Carol's move to Spain, Mother Carol cleared away the dishes and announced her plans to spend the night with a friend. Fillip protested politely but appreciated his mother-in-law's thoughtfulness.

When they were alone, Fillip renewed their conversation by pulling a chain out from under his shirt. The chain held Sarah's promise ring. "When you gave me this ring, you told me the importance of the gift it symbolized. It humbled me. You said it could only be replaced by the ring of the man God would choose to be your husband. "

Fillip pulled a jeweler's case from his jacket pocket. "I have much to learn about personal faith in Christ, but I believe He is the one who brought us together." He opened the box that held a large engagement ring and two matching wedding bands. He drew out the engagement ring and the smaller of two stunning gold diamond bands and held them between his fingers. "When I hadn't yet given God control of my life, He saw this day."

Sarah joyfully offered her left hand to Fillip and he gently pushed the rings onto her finger and kissed them in place. Tears filled Sarah's eyes as Fillip spoke. "Sarah, with these rings and in the presence of God and His angels, I declare my love for you. I will, with His guidance, be the Christian husband you desire until death separates us."

Fillip offered the jewelry case to her and collecting herself she took his wedding band from the box and placed it on his finger. "Fillip as God and His angels are my witnesses, I declare my love for you and I will with His guidance gladly accept you as my cherished husband and give you authority in my life until death claims one of us."

There was no need for a church, a minister, or legal documents because what God now ordained would be binding and *blessed*. Sarah thrived in the kiss of her groom. The power of demons had ultimately been thwarted and from the ashes of their attempts to destroy the potential of this couple, a new and stronger union was formed.

"We are proof of Romans 8:38-39 and God's love, husband. The scripture assures us that nothing, not even death can separate us from God." Sarah kissed Fillip and excitedly continued.

"Fillip we are all about love. We were made in God's image and He breathed eternal life in us through Adam. And, by surrendering our lives to Him we have not only fulfilled His love in us as individuals but as a couple. Fillip I couldn't love you more if I had known you for a year.

"Oh, Sarah, I couldn't love you more if you were what I thought I wanted, for I love you with all my heart just as you are."

Now with their exchanging of rings and vows and their confession of love, they knelt beside the sofa and prayed together as husband and wife. They prayed for their new life and their place of service to the Lord. After Fillip's amen, he got to his feet and pulled Sarah into his arms and held her tightly against his chest. Sarah now clearly saw the fields of the harvest and so did Fillip. They'd work in the fields together with their fellow harvesters until the beloved were all gather safely in.

———◆———

When they came together that night their lovemaking lacked the luxury of El Alba Rosa. Sarah slipped on the prettiest gown she owned. It was a soft red rose gown with white lace trim that accented her breast and fell just above her knees. She allowed herself a little makeup and perfume. She brushed her hair out and it reflected a soft glow that came from the love she had for God and her soul mate and husband Fillip.

She opened the door to her bedroom in great anticipation. This was the night she had dreamed of all her life. Fillip stood at the foot of her bed. The linens had been turned down and a few burning candles scented the room and gave it light.

Fillip had removed his jacket, footwear, and his shirt was pulled loose from his pants and the loosened buttons revealed his deep chest hair, and her promise ring. But, her gaze did not remain there, but went to the light of anticipation in his eyes and his extended hand of invitation. She willingly went into his arms and nestled against his chest. His strong arms held her, and she was home.

Fillip gently stroked her left cheek with the back of his fingers. "I didn't do anything to deserve you."

She answered from her nestling spot. "None of us deserve anything good, but God is a loving Creator and Good Father and plans only good for us. We can't be good enough or work hard enough to earn our restoration to God, but God saw to it through Jesus Christ." She looked up to his face and into his eyes that only reflected love. "We will have dark days and difficulties, but He will love us and keep us throughout them, just as He has already. We can trust Him through all of our days."

Fillip kissed her deeply and she returned his kiss with true love. He whispered against her lips. "I will always be grateful that He planned you for me."

Sarah's left hand moving in his hair caught and reflected the candlelight. "And, now we share these rings and I will look at mine and remember that God planned not just me for you, but you for me."

Although it was not their first time together, Sarah was now able to relish the demands of his more experienced body with an ardor of her own body that only grew over time. She would learn too that the *right of wedded intimacy as designed by God, and the knowledge and joy of its existing between them was as important as the completed act.* The way he'd look at her, touch her, bantered with her without actual intimacy would always please her —would always *make her feel loved.*

Epilogue

Before returning to Spain, Sarah and Fillip were united in marriage at her church by her pastor. Their quickly arranged service was lovely, and the bride wore a beautiful, simple, white gown and her groom a white rented tuxedo. They held the ceremony after the morning worship service and many of the congregants stayed to celebrate their vows. They had a lovely catered reception, a beautiful cake, and her maid of honor caught her flowers. Their wedding photographs were a part of her treasured possessions.

They live comfortably at El Alba Rosa, and it became a sanctuary of peace and acceptance for all who entered there. They opened a mission in the section of town where Marguerite and Jesús lived in one of the buildings Marguerite had scouted for them. Their households joined in friendship and in time Herman, Marina, and Lupe found the Lord. María never became a nun or a therapist but the beautiful bride of Lupe Serrano.

The Southern Baptist missionary board sent them a pastor and his family to serve there. The mission became a beacon of light and salt and a number of other churches were planted in Toledo over the years. The skills Sarah learned earning her degree was useful in the church and their home. The Molina family supported the mission too, along with their son, Jaime, who went into a medically unexplainable remission and fully recovered. He became one of the pastors called to serve in his city.

Fillip's family found his bride hard to accept. She totally disrupted their lives, but they eventually accepted their marriage. A few came to accept and support their work. Luisa hardened her heart against her and their mission. But, she softened a little more with the birth of each of their children. It was hard to deny the joy shared in her son's family.

The Castañola's did renew their wedding vows on their first

anniversary. Their Spanish family and friends celebrated with them. Mother Carol had come to live with them, but in time she found love again, remarried and left their home, but not their lives. They dedicated their four children to the Lord at the mission and many souls came to salvation and baptism there over the years, including each of their children.

Fillip asked her once which of their weddings meant the most to her, and she answered each of them. Her first wedding saved her life and gave her a life she never could have imagined, even though it wasn't rooted in love or legitimate law. Here he was her heroic groom proving his virtue. Their family weddings were traditional, but not gaudy or expensive, but being held on two different shores everyone they loved got to participate in religious ceremonies where her groom was all and more than she had ever prayed to have. Their best wedding was romantic, personal, and conducted by God and witnessed by angels alone. Their vows that night meant more because of Fillip's new commitment to Christ and their separation. Their union that night was the true consummation of their wedded love. On this night Sarah became Fillip's wife, not just his bride. It was the fulfillment of what God had ordained in Fillip's garden when Sarah heard the words, "What God has joined together let no man put asunder."

God had a plan for them and in His own time allowing Fillip free will, God had brought it all about. Their future brought life to a new generation, following generations, and eternal life to them and many others. God brought more than good from hardship; He brought life for the beloved. God was Big Enough, Bigger than the circumstance.

Fillip once thought that Sarah was a woman cut from cloth of angels in his garden. He learned she was that and more. She was a virtuous woman obedient to God and living under His grace.

"Strength and dignity are her clothing, and she smiles at the future. She opens her mouth in wisdom, and the teaching of kindness is on her tongue. She looks well to the ways of her household and does not eat the bread of idleness. Her children rise up and bless her: her husband also, and he praises her, saying: "Man daughters have done nobly, but you excel them all. Character is deceitful, and beauty is vain, but a woman who fears the Lord, she shall be praised." Proverbs 31:25-30. (NASB)

Introduction to Faith in Jesus

In the beginning God created the universe, and all His creation was good. In the midst of His great work, He created a garden, and in it He created a man, Adam, who He breathed life into, and from the man's rib, He created a woman, Eve. They were given dominion over of the garden and were satisfied.

God, their creator, visited with them in the garden and they walked together in the cool of the evening in pleasant fellowship and love. They could eat any of the fruits from the garden except the fruit from the Tree of the Knowledge of Good and Evil. Only this was withheld from them, as God knew it would overwhelm them.

The creator of the universe created messengers to serve Him. One of them, a beautiful angel named Lucifer (meaning bright and morning star) felt himself equal to God and a great war in heaven ended in his fall from service and one-third of the angels in heaven went with him. After their fall Lucifer became known as Satan (meaning astray and adversary—a malevolent entity who deceives mankind), and the fallen angels who served him were called demons.

One day in this beautiful garden of light, love, and satisfaction called _Eden_ the malevolent shadow of darkness came. The malevolent shadow entered a lovely creature, a serpent, to deceive Eve.

Now, Eve saw that the fruit of the Tree of the Knowledge of Good and Evil was pleasant to look at and knew that like all the other fruit in Eden that it would be good to taste. So, the Serpent lied to the woman saying that God was withholding the fruit from her and Adam, because God did not want them to become as powerful and all-knowing as God.

So, being deceived by the Serpent, she tasted the fruit and grew in the knowledge of good and evil. Then, she gave the fruit to Adam who ate the forbidden fruit of his own accord. But, they were not as powerful as God. And, both the man and the woman were ashamed, miserable, and no longer satisfied.

God came to walk with them in the cool of the evening after their disobedience, but now having the knowledge of good and evil, Adam and Eve hid from their loving creator. And, because of their disobedience sin and death entered the world.

Now God was not surprised by their disobedience, but it did sadden him. Still He loved His beautiful children, and so placed into action the plan that would give them a choice to be restored to fellowship with Him. Sadly though, they could no longer live in Eden for in the garden grew the Tree of Life, and they could not continue to eat from this tree and live in the beautiful garden with their corrupt spirits and bodies.

So, the plan of salvation and restoration was fulfilled when God's only Son left the throne room of heaven, and came to earth as the tiny infant, Jesus Christ. He walked the earth as God and Man for thirty-three years, and for three of those years he taught His disciples the plan of salvation by which man can be reconciled to God.

Then Jesus Christ became our sacrifice for the plan of salvation could not be free. Christ paid the cost to cover sin once and for all on the cross of Calvary, freely giving His life for ours. Oh, but death did not win for although He gave up His life, _He_ took it up again in just three days. Jesus Christ became our Redeemer removing the sting of death for any who would believe.

Then, Christ our Beloved Savior returned to the Father's throne from where God sent the Holy Spirit to not just live with us on earth as did Christ, but to live in us and so teach us to glory in the Creator day by day as we sojourn on this earthly plain.

We, beloved, have a God shaped void in us, put there by the Father so we would seek Him, the Christ, and the Holy Spirit. You may try to deny it. You may try to fill it with drugs, alcohol, sex, worldly games and distractions, but nothing can satisfy the God shape void in you, until you ask for the forgiveness paid by Jesus Christ crucified.

You can do nothing to earn this gift of salvation and restoration with God, for Christ already earned and shares it freely to all who ask. All you can bring to Christ is yourself and your sin, and Christ's blood will wash away your sin, and you then will live whole in Him.

Once asked, the gift comes. You are restored. Then, you will walk with Christ and your journey on earth will have meaning. You will be complete and never willingly disobey or sin again. Then one day the plan of restoration will be complete for you. You will leave this earth behind and take up your immortal glorified body and live forever with God.

There is a battle for your soul, beloved. A battle to where you will spend eternity. Christ would have you spend eternity in <u>His</u> light in heaven, the new garden, where sin may never again come. The Holy Spirit and angels will fight to give you this knowledge of forgiveness and life. Satan and his demons will fight to have you <u>spend</u> eternity in the eternal fires prepared just for them.

Do not be deceived beloved. Hell is a real place. It was not prepared for the beloved, but for Satan, demons, and those deceived by the lies of the malevolent spirits. Seek the truth. Seek light.

You are on your own journey and your life touches many others. I pray you will complete your journey to Christ. He died so you would not suffer the spiritual death of separation from the Eternal.

Prayer of Faith

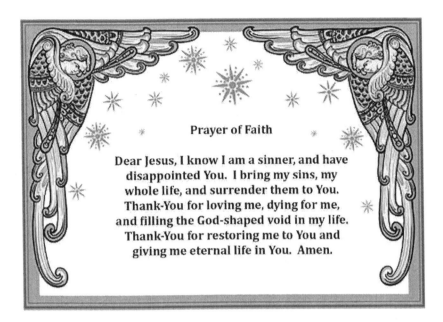

Prayer of Faith

Dear Jesus, I know I am a sinner, and have disappointed You. I bring my sins, my whole life, and surrender them to You. Thank-You for loving me, dying for me, and filling the God-shaped void in my life. Thank-You for restoring me to You and giving me eternal life in You. Amen.

What now?

If you prayed this prayer, take a minute and rest in the comfort of the Triune presence. There are over forty-two hundred religions, and you don't need to practice a religion, but worship and serve in a body of believers in Jesus. I would recommend a local Southern Baptist Church, but let the Holy Spirit lead you to a body of believers that will help you grow.

Your sister in Jesus Christ,
Rhoda Fegan

Our Daily Prayer

Father God, You are amazing, and we come to worship You
and invite You into our day. Forgive us our shortcomings and
cleanse our hearts so they are acceptable dwelling places for You.
We are not worthy to come to You but may because of
Your unconditional love, mercy, and grace for us.

Gracious Father continue to care for us, leading us through
wildernesses, over mountains, through shadowed valleys,
and the dry deserts of life and give us rest beside still waters.
Keep us on this journey to eternity giving us drink and food
for our bodies, minds, and souls.

Through Your mercy give us strength when we are weary.
When we lack might increase our power.
When our lives overwhelm us, when all we can do is struggle,
and when we can no longer walk gather us up gently
and carry us in Your loving arms.

Dwell in us and be our constant source.
Let Your Divine Animate Armor protect us against our enemy.
Let Your Holiness shine through us
and banish the darkness that threatens
so, we may stay focused on You.

Protect our peace and rebuke the enemy.
Do not let his lies penetrate our hearts and minds.
And grant that we always remember that
through Your grace and mercy,
we have all our sins forgiven and forgotten.

Let our lives be useful and full of service for Your kingdom.
Grant us healing when we are injured or fall ill,
and gather us to You when our time on earth is done.
Let our legacy of faith live on in those we love,
and let their lives and legacy touch others.

Give us Divine comfort when we mourn,
reminding us what all Christ suffered and lost for our sakes,
and that through His suffering and death we are all partakers
in His victory over hell and death, and that we Lord
will dwell in Your house forever. Amen.

Lean on God one day at a time and you will get safely through to your journey's end.

Rhoda Fegan

The Author

With a bit more than sixty-five years of experience, I am grateful for love and the gifts of love given without package, bow, or card. God's love provided for my salvation, family, marriage, children, grandchildren, and my friends. I am a disciple of Christ practicing my faith daily amongst other Southern Baptists. I have two very adult children and six addition blessings, my grandchildren. I am a retired widow with degrees in medical laboratory technology and communication. I have a developing interest in alternative medicine, essential oils, supplements, herbs, and cell salts. I believe in our Creator's designs for our bodies and spirits and their ability to heal given what they need. God's plans for us our good and eternal. Although I learned the mechanics of writing from teachers, the characters and their stories come from the Holy Spirit. My characters share the lessons of the Spirit I have been taught. Writing through the Holy Spirit is food for my soul, and the air I breath.

Rhoda Fegan

Badgley Publishing Company

For more great stories please visit our website:

www.BadgleyPublishingCompany.com

Thank you and have a great day.

Made in the USA
Lexington, KY
22 September 2018